A FAMILY SAGA
OF DEEP SPACE...
THE DAWN OF AN
EMPIRE BEYOND THE SUN

"Marta Randall has taken the popular family saga type of novel and turned it into a major piece of science fiction. *Journey* is the story of both a family, the Kennerins, and a frontier world. It covers 20 years in their lives—the characterizations are marvelous.

"Randall has created real frontier people and told their story, their triumphs and failures, both pleasures and emotions, with skill and understanding.

"The book is extremely long but never dull. I made the mistake of starting it late one night. . . .

"The best original novel I've read so far this year. Highly recommended."
—N. Brown,
Isaac Asimov's Science Fiction Magazine

JOURNEY

MARTA RANDALL

A KANGAROO BOOK
PUBLISHED BY POCKET BOOKS NEW YORK

Another *Original* publication of POCKET BOOKS

POCKET BOOKS, a Simon & Schuster division of
GULF & WESTERN CORPORATION
1230 Avenue of the Americas, New York, N.Y. 10020

ISBN: 0-671-81207-6

First Pocket Books printing May, 1978

Trademarks registered in the United States and other countries.

Interior design by Sofia Grunfeld

Printed in the U.S.A.

For Richard Curtis and Adele Leone Hull,
without whom

CONTENTS

There are only two or three human stories, and they go on repeating themselves as fiercely as if they had never happened before.

—Willa Cather

Part One

1216
New Time

A WORLD
OF
SUDDEN
STRANGERS

"Oh, what a troublesome thing it is to go
and discover new lands."
—Bernal Diaz del Castillo, 1576

THE BARN SAT AT THE EDGE OF A LEVEL
meadow, facing the broad, rich fields, its back to the hill,
house, and landing pad. It was a long, wide building with
huge doors at either end and a roof pitched and curved
at seeming random; during the day its roof and walls of
flexible solar panels darkened as they soaked in the light,
and throughout the night it glowed gently in the reflection
of a million stars. Within, a series of lofts and balconies
rose above the cavernous main floor, connected by swaying rope ladders over which, on other days, the three Kennerin children scampered and swung in pursuit of their
intricate, carefully plotted games. Mish Kennerin had
seen them as tiny, luminous figures darting through the
dim reaches of the barn, so far from her that the sound of
their voices and the padding of their feet muted with distance, becoming small, almost subliminal whisperings in
the still air. At those times Mish paused, almost breathless, her usual resentment of the excessively large building
replaced by a confusion of loss, a sense that the structure
breathed a dark magic which was slowly and certainly
taking her children from her. Uneasy and baffled, she
would blink in the dimness before turning away, often
forgetting why and for what she had come, and stand
leaning at the monstrous doors, caught halfway between
the darkness and the light.

Even now the barn seemed to absorb the crowd of refugees, accepting them into a segregated corner and re-
serving its distances for darkness and quiet. Mish stood at
the edge of a third-level balcony, her arms full of blankets, and looked down at the bright corner of light. What
seemed chaos was in reality an almost shapeless order.

2

The refugees lined up for the stew and bread which Quilla and Jes ladled from the steaming caldron or popped from large, cloth-covered baskets; the few bowls and plates were quickly emptied and handed to those still in line. Children ran shouting through the crowd, adults called out over their bobbing heads, babies wailed. It seemed to Mish that the barn floor below her boiled with an excess of emotion, a tide of relief. She remembered her own landing on Terra so many years and lightyears before, stumbling from the crowded belly of the ship into a winter of inspectors and hard-faced guards, herded silently through examinations and searches, separated without explanation into the group of workers allotted to the Altacostas, the group to the Karlovs, the group to the Kennerins. But the contrast did not lighten her mood, nor quell her foreboding. There were too many of them, too many arms and legs and mouths and feet—so many fresh and unknown souls that she shivered unwillingly before moving down the swaying rope ladder, blankets piled on her shoulders, a small frown between her brows.

They had reeled from the shuttles onto alien ground, more than two hundred of them, plucked by Jason Kennerin from a world gone suddenly sour, a world soon to die. Carrying their paltry, miscellaneous belongings clutched to their bodies, bringing memories of persecution and snow. Their world was dying, their leaders had abdicated to the realms of insanity; this much Mish knew, had known when Jason left on Captain Hetch's silver shuttle, gone to rescue those he could, gone to make one family's paltry gesture of help. They had expected no more than fifty people, sixty at the very most; one shuttle's worth of refugees, one winter's surplus of food and clothing, no more—most importantly, only fifty new faces, new bodies, new minds. Enough to handle, enough to understand. After twelve years alone on Aerie, just Mish and Jason, Laur and the three children, and the calm, marsupial native kasirene, Mish's memories of other humans had blurred, until the crowds of her childhood took on Kennerin faces, and although she fought against the impression as false, as dangerous, she had not been able to shake it. The refugees would not be uniformly brown, Mongol-eyed, thin people. They would be—what? Strangers. Immigrants. Aliens. And so they were, more than four times as many as she had expected, short and fat and thin and dark and light, hair of many shades, faces in all

3

shapes and sizes, eyes of colors she had forgotten existed. For twelve years, Jason had been the only tall one in the universe; now these strangers towered over her, tired, dirty, broken, gaunt. Yet she remembered where they had come from, could guess at what they had been through, and she forced herself to retreat from fear, to remember their humanity despite their numbers, or colors, or scents. The rope ladder shifted beneath her feet; she waited until it steadied, then continued down.

She dropped the blankets into a corner where some few of the refugees were already curled in the dense, sweet hay, and she nodded to them in strained friendliness before hurrying along the edge of the crowd toward the head of the food line. The voices melted into a continuous, painful cacophony against which she had little defense. She hunched her shoulders, slipped through standing and sitting groups, and stopped as she saw the front of the line. Jes and Quilla stood stiffly, ladling stew and passing bread, their heads down and their eyes fastened on the work of their hands. They seemed to Mish completely rooted automatons—the luminous, enchanted creatures of the lofts transformed by the pull and press of the mob. A fierce, protective tenderness rose in her, and she pushed her way to them, her own uneasiness for the moment forgotten.

"Jes? Quilla?"

Jes looked up and tried to smile. His blue eyes were rimmed with darkness and looked unnaturally large in his weary face.

"I don't think there's going to be enough," Quilla muttered without glancing at her mother. "We're almost out of stew, and the bread's about gone." She lifted her head, her face expressionless and damp.

"We'll manage," Mish said. "There aren't too many left in line. Where's Laur?"

"She said the stench was too much for her, and their accents are barbarous," Jes said. "She went back to the house."

"Damn," Mish said. This was no time for the fierce old woman to haul out her genteel upbringing and delicate sensibilities, but there was no help for it. Mish scanned the barn, looking for her youngest child. "We'll set up showers tomorrow; she really shouldn't have left. Where's Hart?"

"Probably home with Laur," Jes said. Mish put her arm around him as he swayed.

4

"You go on home, Jessie. I'll take care of this."

Jes looked at her with gratitude and ran, not through the crowd to the nearest door, but into the darkness of the unused portion of the barn. Mish watched him, wishing that she, too, were taking the long, quiet way home. Quilla continued to ladle stew, her face once again turned away from the people. Quilla had been two when Jason and Mish left Terra. Jes and Hart were born on Aerie, and had never seen humans other than the family and Laur; Quilla probably could not remember the crowds of her birthworld.

And I forgot to worry about that, Mish thought wearily. No help for this, either. She touched her daughter's cheek, in love and apology.

"Can you last it out a bit more?"

"I guess so. I'm tired."

"I know. I'll take care of this. Can you go up to the storage loft and see if there are any more blankets, anything we can use down here?"

Quilla managed a smile. "Sure. The third loft? Is anyone up there?"

"No. Bring the stuff down by the door. People should be able to find it there."

Quilla gave her mother the ladle and slipped away, going as her brother had into the far emptiness of the barn, and Mish knew that her daughter would follow a maze of ropes and balconies, finding solace in the quiet darkness. Mish ladled stew until the caldron was empty, then raised her head. A gaunt, determined man stood before her and thrust a bowl at her face.

"I want some more," he said harshly. "That crap you gave me wasn't enough."

"There'll be more food tomorrow. The stew's gone."

"I want more now. I'm still hungry."

A hand appeared on the man's shoulder. "We're all still hungry, Gren, but we'll last. Calm down."

Mish looked at the speaker: a gray-eyed young man with a flute tucked under his belt, pale yellow hair matted and dirty around his face, torn clothing, bare feet. As alien as possible, yet he smiled wearily at her and took Gren by the arm, and Mish felt a tide of amity and of relief.

"Come on, kiter," the young man said. "You've had a bowl."

5

"He's had two," a child said importantly. "I saw him. He's already had two."

Gren jerked away, flung his bowl on the ground, and stalked into the crowd. The man picked up the bowl.

"I'm sorry Gren was nasty. He lost his family on New-Home, and it's made him worse than usual."

"It's all right." She took the bowl and held it, then dropped it into the empty caldron. "I'm Mish Kennerin," she said, not knowing what else to say.

"I know. I'm Tabor Grif." He smiled at her until she smiled back and her shoulders relaxed.

"I guess we're all a bit tense. We weren't expecting quite so many of you."

Tabor shrugged. His smooth, pale face darkened momentarily, and he touched his flute. "Your husband's a remarkable man. We were going to die there, in the camps. Many of us already had." He gestured at the barn, the people, the caldron, at Mish. "It's hard to believe we're here. That we're alive. That we've eaten. That they won't come after us again tomorrow, and the day after, and the day after that."

Mish touched his arm. "It was very bad?"

"Ask Jason." He smiled again. "But here we are. Can I collect the empty bowls and put them in the pot? Would that help?"

"Yes." Mish realized that her hand was still on his arm. She stepped back quickly, smiled, watched him turn and begin searching through the crowd. She moved away from the caldron. Fewer people were about and the noise had abated considerably as the refugees crept into the piles of hay, settled themselves and their belongings, and slept. Mish walked slowly, looking for Jason.

Eventually she found him directing the placement of more hay in the sleeping areas, and she stood silent, watching the shift of his muscles under his light suit. Save for the brief embrace at the landing field, they had barely seen or spoken to each other during the long evening. He reached forward to grab a bale from the pile, turned with it, put it down, raised an arm, called something; the barn blurred until he moved in her vision against a backdrop of running darks and lights, and when he glanced at her she gave him a look of such intensity that he turned from the work and walked to the barn door. Together and in silence they crossed the fields, until the sounds from the

6

barn were muted with distance. Mish lay in the unmown grasses, suddenly urgent, and pulled him to her.

In the warmth after lovemaking, Mish's unease returned. She collected their scattered clothing and pulled it around them, and Jason settled his head on her breast and sighed. His eyes closed, but before she could collect her thoughts into rationality, he moved still closer and touched her cheek with his fingers.

"I couldn't leave them," he murmured. "They were in a camp, near the port, so many of them, and bodies thrown outside the fence like garbage. We had to fight our way out. I thought the Council would be glad to let me take them, but . . . Captain Hetch let them all on; he didn't turn anyone back. Oh, Mish, there were so many bodies on NewHome."

His voice carried pain and fatigue, and she held him tightly. "It's all right, Jase. They're safe now."

"I don't even know who they are. I just grabbed people, behind me, running, grabbing people, pushing, and people falling down in the snow, sick or killed or old, I tried, Mish, but there were so many bodies." He shivered against her.

"Don't they know about their primary?"

"Maybe. Certainly. They're all crazy there. They don't care. Trying to make a killing before the killing." He laughed bleakly. "Too busy persecuting people, killing people until their sun kills them. Soon, Hetch said. Maybe not soon enough. Their souls are rotted." Jason put his hand over his eyes, and Mish kissed his fingers. "So many bodies, Mish. So many bodies, and so much snow."

He fell asleep, curled as close to her as possible. She held him and listened to the remote noises from the barn. Two crescent moons floated overhead, and behind them the innumerable stars of The Spiral glowed against a backdrop of black velvet. She wondered what the stars looked like from NewHome, seen through the cold air of a winter camp. So many bodies on NewHome: dark, like hers; light, like Tabor Grif's. Old men. Children. What Hetch had told her of the purges made no sense—politics, parties, religious convictions, philosophies. The sun moving toward nova and the climate of NewHome entering chaos—those were the real villains. Five years of drought and three of famine, and if the government of NewHome had any sense, they would have evacuated in the third year, when the primary shift became certain. But there was no vengeance to be had on a star, on an atmosphere, on meteorological conditions, on blight. And no profit, either. Scapegoats were needed, instant symbols of The Enemy, symbols which could be broken and killed—unlike the long dryness, unlike the dying sun. Symbols which could be looted, could be sacked. Old women. Children. Snow. The National Confederation of Great Barrier reaching across boundaries to smite the foe. No wonder the Council had not wanted Jason to take the people. The Council wanted revenge, and there is no satisfaction in revenge enacted on absent parties.

A small, six-legged lizard ran up Mish's arm, stopped, chattered at her indignantly, and sprang into the grass. One moon slipped below the horizon, and the other sat directly overhead, so that the stars of The Spiral seemed to radiate from it. Mish turned her head, nestling her cheek in Jason's hair, and he moved in her arms. She closed her eyes. Tomorrow they could talk about Gren, and Laur, and the food, and they would make plans to deal with so many people, so many needs, so much uncertainty. Tomorrow. She deliberately relaxed and tried to push the worry from her mind, but it pursued her into sleep and colored her fitful dreams.

HART KNELT IN THE SOFT HAY OF AN UPPER balcony, his hands gripping the slim railing, and he stared through the darkness at the patch of light below. The shapes of the refugees seemed to melt and run together; they reminded him of the way maggots looked under the translucent skins of dead fourbirds. Mish moved through the crowd to Jes and Quilla, and Jason stood near the main doors, talking, pausing, pointing, walking. Hart tried to watch all four of them at the same time and trembled, terrified that they would be absorbed forever into the mass below.

They said it would be different. It was going to be different. He had expected more Kennerins, more kasirene; people like the people he loved, aliens like the aliens he had known for all his seven years, who were as familiar as the shadows in his room, or the heavy-leaved kaedos on the hills. Not these almost-Kennerins, odd of speech, dirty, evil smelling, the colors of the dead. A white man, there, with pale hair; a maggot-man holding a slim silver rod in his hand. Smile, point, kill—What did that rod do? Jason carrying a maggot-woman to the straw; she held a lapful of holocubes, which tumbled out of her dress and scattered on the barn's floor. Jason put her down, and she scrabbled weakly at the cubes, started crying. Jason picked them up carefully and piled them around her, and she clutched them with pale hands, arms, fingers. Damp. Sticky. Slimy. How could he touch her? How could they all be down there, accepting them, talking to them, feeding them? Hart trembled more violently and his hands tightened on the railing. Let them go, then. Let them be

9

eaten up. They hate me. They made it all happen and they hate me.

Heavy, unnatural noises boomed amid the quiet of Hart's barn; alien boots trod his floors and alien bodies curled into his hay. The stench of unwashed bodies nauseated him. His knuckles whitened against the dark wood of the railing and he shook violently. These maggot-people would steal his island as they had stolen his barn; they would fill his planet and cover his meadows, poison his seas and darken his skies, and come for him, reach their white hands to him, suffocate him, *touch* him. *Touch him.* His muscles locked and he screamed, helpless to stop himself. The loft rocked under his feet.

Then hands gripped his shoulders and shook him, and through his screams he saw the face of his sister. Her mouth moved silently, words drowned in noise. He hungered for the warmth and protection of her arms, for the comfort of her voice, but could not stop the high keening, could not unfreeze his limbs. She stopped shaking him, bit her lip, and slapped his face, breaking his hold on the railing and breaking the terror's hold on him. He collapsed onto her, and she gathered him to her body as he sobbed.

"What's wrong?" she said urgently. "Hart, baby, what's wrong?"

He had no words, and he sobbed more loudly and shook his head against her shoulder.

"Hart? Are you hurt?"

He pointed a shaky finger downward. She craned her neck to look over the railing and saw only the crowd of tired, hungry refugees.

"The people, baby? Is that it?"

He nodded, his sobs lessening. Now Quilla would understand, as she had understood scraped knees and cut fingers and nightmares. She would perform a magic equivalent to that of antiseptic, bandages, and kisses, and make the world right again.

Instead, she said, with calm practicality, "It's only people, baby. They won't hurt you. Here, come down with me and you'll see."

Hart stared at her in shock. Her face seemed to shift, to become briefly maggot-like. Before the features of his sister reestablished themselves, he pushed violently from her arms, swayed for a moment, then kicked her thigh viciously and fled down the length of the balcony.

10

"Hart!" Quilla cried, but his single-minded flight did not change. He leaped at a rope ladder and barely caught it, swayed precariously for a moment, then swarmed down the ladder out of sight. Quilla stood gingerly and rubbed her thigh. She picked up the glow lamp and glanced down the length of the balcony before turning toward the storage bins.

She did not stop at the outer bins, knowing that Mish would have already emptied them. Instead, she moved toward the wall of the barn, skirting bailing ropes and castaway lumber, until she stood before a large bin almost hidden amid the barn's detritus. She reached up without looking and hung the glow lamp on a nail, pushed aside the lid of the box, and stared within at the stuff of fantasy. A spare piece of solar sheeting made a spacer's cloak; a tattered red blanket had dignified the banquets and judgments of monarchs and friends. The jaunty green hat of a space merchant, the peaked cap of a Contestor, the epaulets of the Warlord of Saturn V, all made of twisted and braided grass. Laur's old gowns, now the vestments of emperors and courtesans, pirates and fools. Crowns, swords, blasters, shrouds, tents, rugs, all the years of Quilla's childhood thrown together in a heap of rags and glory. The muted noise of the refugees and the soft, dark smells of the barn faded, and Quilla saw magic in the box before her, the simple sorceries which allowed the figures of her books and of her dreams to come to life and, briefly inhabiting her body, and Jes', and Hart's, stalk the narrow passageways of the barn, living their stories again. Then the noises from below pressed in on her, and for a moment she could almost find her way into Hart's pain and terror. She lingered briefly on a ledge of comprehension and loss before the magic within the box paled into a jumble of tawdry, stained, and ragged cloth. She lifted out the canopies of kings, the shroud of a dead warlock, the rugs from far, imaginary cities, the tents of nomads, the spacer's cloak, carefully folding the cloth and piling it on the floor beside her, until all that remained in the box were a few bits of wood, some shards of plastic, and the caps of grass. She lowered the lid of the box and slung the cloth over her shoulder. Picking up the lamp, she hesitated again, then trudged toward the rope ladder, her weariness suddenly hard upon her.

She stepped from the swaying ladder and turned to face the crowd, searching for her father amid the moving shapes. Eventually she saw him standing near the far wall wielding a pitchfork, while others collected the hay he tossed to them and spread it deeply over the hard-packed dirt floor. Already people curled into the hay, their coats tucked under their heads and arms over their eyes. One woman lay with an infant held to her breast; the woman with the holocubes had spread them around her and activated them, and she slept surrounded by the pale light of beloved faces. Quilla turned again to search for her mother, but as she did so, people came to her and looked at the cloths. She offered them mutely to the waiting hands, then dumped the remainder by the door and wandered through the barn, trying to find a familiar face. Jason climbed from the loft and, leaning against his pitchfork, watched the spreading of the hay. She took a step toward him, then he bent to arrange hay and she could not see him. Her eyes felt dry and her feet hurt. People jostled against her and, unused to moving in a crowd, she lost her balance again and again, clinging to the struts and beams of the barn to keep from falling. She moved without purpose, forgetting why she was here but knowing that she could not leave, and the sights and sounds became meaningless. Then a hand grabbed her forearm briefly and swung her around. She staggered and held to a beam.

"Girl, give me a blanket."

Quilla faced a young woman, whose age she could not judge, save that she seemed older than Quilla but younger than Mish, and it took her a moment to push enough of the fog from her mind to understand that the woman was talking to her.

"I'm sorry. What did you say?"

The woman looked exasperated. "I said, fetch me a blanket. Can't you hear?"

Quilla shook her head to clear it. "They're over in the corner," she said, trying not to let weariness slur the words. She pivoted slightly and pointed toward the barn door.

"I didn't ask where they are, stupid!" People gathered around, faces blank, and the woman flipped red-brown hair from her face and tilted her chin imperiously. "I want a blanket and I want it now, so get it! I'm not going to wait all night."

Always remember that you are a Kennerin, Laur's voice said with calm assurance, and under that Quilla

12

heard Hart's thin screams of terror, saw Jes' tired eyes, remembered Mish's stories of a different life on a different planet, saw her father bow with equal respect to the kasirene in the fields. It seemed to her that she stepped from her own skin and watched with amazement as some other Quilla straightened smoothly, set her hands on her hips, and stared at the woman. When the words came, they came from someplace Quilla did not know, and she heard her voice say them calmly and clearly.

"My name is Quilla Kennerin. My family owns this planet. We fetch and carry for no one. Do you understand?"

"Well," the woman said, the beginnings of uncertainty in her voice. She suddenly looked much younger than before.

"Do you understand?" Quilla demanded. The girl nodded reluctantly. "Good. The blankets are in the corner. You may have one, and not more than one, and you'll get it for yourself."

The girl's hands fluttered as though in protest, then she turned abruptly and walked toward the blankets. Quilla watched, still baffled by this wonderful stranger who had taken over her body and her mouth, and had done the right and proper thing. The girl selected a blanket. Quilla turned and moved toward the door, conscious now of the many eyes on her, still too amazed to glory in her own performance and her own dignity. Then a tall, pale man with gray eyes touched her arm lightly and saluted her with his flute.

"Good for you," he said in a low voice. His smile barely creased the corners of his mouth. "Taine's had that coming for a long time."

She looked at him as though he had just told her that her jeans were split behind. Her composure vanished. She nodded, desperately holding on to her dignity, stared at his eyes, turned, and stumbled and flailed awkwardly as she lost her balance. He reached for her shoulders and steadied her.

"You must be as tired as I am," he said pleasantly. She gaped at him, still off balance, and grabbed his flute. Her dignity shattered totally. She thrust the flute at him and fled through the door. He caught the flute before it hit the floor and stood, head cocked, watching her ungainly exit. She glanced back as she rounded the door, moaned slightly, and rushed into the night.

He shook his head, amused, and picked up the last

empty bowl. He carried it to the caldron and stacked it atop the others, thinking about Quilla's eyes. She rides her soul on her face, he thought, brown and terrified and soft. He slipped the flute under his belt, then went to find a blanket and a place to sleep. As he neared the door, he saw Mish Kennerin and her husband slip into the darkness; sexual tension sang between them. Brown and soft, and not at all terrified. Lost in thought, he found a place in the hay, ignored the lack of a blanket, and stretched thoroughly before turning on his side to sleep. Despite his weariness, though, sleep escaped him, no matter how he turned and twisted. He sat and leaned against the wall of the barn. Lights dimmed around him until the barn was filled only with its natural luminescence, and in the semidarkness he slipped his flute from his belt and blew softly, letting melodies shape themselves in the stillness. The sounds of people sleeping rose gently through the clear tones, and Tabor felt for the first time an almost palpable homesickness. The tall mountains of Great Barrier rose before him, blackened, majestic, and beloved, and the flat green rivers of Kilnvale; the high, white streets of Mestican, with their tinkling fountains and sparkling shops, the cries of birds he would never see again, resting in the boughs of trees now lost to him forever. Tabor breathed into the flute and its music painted the beauty of his homeworld. Hatred, persecution, camps, and death were forgotten; only loveliness remained. The flute sang in the alien night.

He felt a gentle rustle in the hay beside him, and when he let the last note linger and die, he put aside his flute and saw a young boy sitting nearby, staring with fascination at the instrument. Even in the dimness his features were instantly recognizable, and Tabor wondered again at the strong resemblance each Kennerin had to the others.

"Would you like to see it?" he whispered, holding out the flute to the boy. The child nodded and with great care took the flute into his hand.

"It's a flute, isn't it?"

Tabor nodded.

"I've never seen one before. Do you blow here?"

"Yes. I'll teach you how, if you like."

"Could you?" the child said with wonderment, then grinned. "I'm Jes Kennerin."

"I'm Tabor Grif." Tabor offered his hand, and Jes

14

stared at it without comprehension. "Don't you shake hands on Aerie?"

"There's never anyone to shake hands with." Jes offered his own hand hesitantly, and Tabor showed him how to lock thumbs, palm against palm, and press briefly.

"That's all there is to it. I can give you a flute lesson tomorrow, if you like."

"Why not now?"

"Because in the beginning you'll make terrible noises, and people are sleeping now."

"Oh. Okay," Jes said easily. He gave back the flute, rapidly made a nest of hay, and slid into it. "Good night."

"Are you supposed to sleep here?" Tabor said.

"Oh, I sleep wherever I want to. I sleep in the barn lots of nights. You'll get used to it."

"Probably."

"Put a lump of straw under your head," Jes advised. "It's more comfortable that way."

Tabor did so, and within seconds he was asleep, his flute clutched loosely in his hand. Jes raised himself on an elbow, reached over, and touched the flute, then slid it next to Tabor's chest. He touched the man's pale hair and, content, slid into his own nest of straw. Laur's wrong, he thought sleepily. They're not barbarians, not if they can play the flute, and they'll take baths tomorrow after Jason sets up the showers, and I'm glad they've come, all of them. Aerie is not the only planet, Eagle not the only sun. There's so much to learn now, he thought with satisfaction. There's so much new to know.

JASON WOKE GROGGILY AND WONDERED WHY the snow felt so warm. The sky through the window was blue and cloudless and the lace of the halaea's slim branches and feathery leaves overlaid the blue like a delicate shadow. He stared at it blankly, then felt a stirring and weight on his chest and glanced down to see Mish's head cradled on his shoulder, her arm thrown across his waist, and the tumbled blankets of their bed piled haphazardly on the floor. Home, he thought with gratitude and benediction, and let the sunlight flood his soul. Great Barrier is four lightyears and four weeks in the past. He brought his arm up to cradle Mish and gently nuzzled her hair. She stirred against him.

"You're not asleep," he whispered.

He felt her lips curve in a smile against his chest, and he held her more closely. It was hours past dawn, the morning furor of the birds had quieted now, the air was still sweet with the freshness of dew—his world, his fertile black loam, the upward bending of his halaea tree, the warm body of his wife nestled against him in the pleasant disarray of his own bed. Jason was well content. Jason the scholar, Jason the dreamer, had necessarily slipped into the background years ago, giving way to Jason the practical, Jason the farmer. But in the quiet mornings and evenings of his land, a deep, peaceful joy pervaded him and he looked on the world about him with a poet's and a lover's eyes, filled with a voiceless singing of thankfulness and praise. This morning, as every morning for the past month, the land seemed an especial gift to him, a personal grace from the universe which took his care and toil and returned them a thousandfold, returned not only the

16

bounty of the land, but the land's beauty, something he could never hope to earn but could only accept with a deep and endless gratitude.

He sometimes wondered whether Mish, so small and soft beside him, stopped in the midst of the fields to look with wonderment on their world, and although he would have liked it to be so, he doubted it. Mish, twice an outcast, loved the land with a passion which he knew to be both deeper than and different from his, loved it with a fierce protectiveness which had as its genesis pride rather than wonderment, determination rather than gratitude, and he could understand although not share her feelings.

Jason had been born to a world of luxury and un-questioned superiority, a member of an aristocratic family which had never left Terra to colonize, and which, along with only four hundred other families, owned all of the mother world and ruled it completely. In Jason's world, the lower orders were those who did not own land; below them were those who had lost land, colonists returned from failed or failing worlds. From this scorned and abused class came Mish, born on a world whose poisonous atmo-sphere eventually defeated humanity's efforts to conquer it, daughter of a mining engineer and a doctor, nei-ther of whom had made it off their doomed planet. Under the complex, inescapable class structure of Terra, an affair between Jason and Mish could be tolerated, an infatuation noted with disapproval, and a marriage considered almost against the laws of nature. But married they had, too much in love to consider the consequences, too much in love to consider their subsequent banishment from Terra as a tragedy. They took the payoff money from Jason's fam-ily and bought Aerie sight unseen; shipped out with a bare minimum of necessities, their infant daughter, and Laur na-Kennerin, Jason's old nurse, who had insisted on coming with them. And they had set about building a world, an Eden, of their own, safe from those who would separate them.

Kennerins had lived and worked their lands on Terra since before the Expansion, with a basic, unquestioned, and portable security; possession was so natural to them that they never paused to consider the possibility of loss. Even exiled from Terra and Kennerin Manor, Jason had taken the security of ownership with him, and because Aerie was his and his only, he loved it all the more. But Mish, who had had nothing, seemed almost to distrust the

17

land, seemed forever ready to battle those who would take it from her. Had her possessiveness been any less intense, Jason would have viewed it with amusement. But he knew that while he would work and fight for his world, Mish might kill for it, despite her moral reservations. When they had originally discussed bringing the refugees to Aerie, Mish insisted that the land remain theirs, that no title to any speck of it pass to people not in the family, and Jason had accepted her demand. She had also insisted that the refugees be treated as equals, that they not be forced into the same tight, miserable life Mish had lived on Terra; she feared being either oppressed or oppressor with as much intensity as she feared loss of her land, and Jason wondered uneasily which desire was the deeper. But she ran her fingers down the length of his body, teasingly, and he bent to cover her mouth with his own. Soon the sheets followed the blankets to the floor.

"How late is it?" he murmured afterward.

"Almost ai'l," she said, and sat. Her long black hair tumbled down her back, and the strands of early gray caught and glistened in the sunlight, bright against her copper skin. She pushed her locks from her face with slender fingers and reached for the brush. "You worked until well past v'al last night again, and I thought you could use the rest."

Jason stretched slowly and thoroughly. "I should have been out hours ago," he said with no real urgency. "There are logs to be brought in today, and we can finish the doctor's house once we have the lumber. And I promised the kassies I'd come down and check on the sands."

"Tabor's already gone," Mish said. "And Hirem left for the forest last night, while you were busy with the forge."

"A musician and a lawyer." Jason grimaced and swung his legs to the floor. "What good will they do?"

"You can't treat them like children, Jase. They'll learn by doing, just like a poet I know learned by doing."

"Perhaps. But I didn't expect to cart home a bunch of soft-handed professionals, that's for sure."

Mish glanced down at her own work-roughened hands, and Jason grinned. "Always been fond of hard-handed women," he said. Mish smiled and twisted her hair into a knot at the back of her head, so that two wings of dark hair framed her Oriental face. Jason stopped dressing to watch her.

"Why the knot? You used to let it hang loose."

18

To his surprise, Mish flushed and turned away from him.

"Someone told me it looks nicer this way," she said. "And it does keep it out of my face."

"I like it." He pulled his shirt over his shoulders, gave Mish a swift kiss, and move down the stairs to the kitchen at the back of the house. Laur gave him a cup of tea and an indignant look and the two kasirene cooks tittered.

"Well, I'm glad to see you're finally up," Laur said sharply. "It's past ai'l already, and the people are waiting for you." She inspected his pants critically. "You've got a stain on your seat," she said. "You're as hard to keep presentable as the children."

Jason grinned and plucked a fresh roll from her hand. She slapped at his wrist and missed. "Jason Kennerin, I don't know how I manage. You stop bothering me. I'm not getting any younger."

"Nonsense," Jason said comfortably as he put down the empty cup and slipped the roll into his pocket. "You'll outlast all of us, Laur na-Kennerin. Just see if you don't."

Laur sniffed and turned to yell at the cooks, and Jason strode down the hill toward the city the refugees called Haven.

"City" was, perhaps, too fine a word for the place. Village, Jason thought, would be more apt, although even that was stretching the truth a little. Two streets had been laid out, crossing each other, and land for public buildings and shops had been set aside at this intersection. Plots of land for houses lay beyond, mapped out in string and sticks. There had been wrangling over whose house to build first, and where. Jason had decreed that the houses of those whose skills were the most important would be the first built and the most centrally located. This, in turn, led to acrimony over who was most valued, and to a certain extent this argument continued, although considerably abated. The refugees had set to work eagerly. Doctor Hoku was important, on this everyone agreed, and the Doctor's house was almost finished, lacking only some interior work. The Doctor had already taken possession and set up her surgery, and a stream of wounded fingers, abraded knees, and sore backs passed under her skillful fingers as the clumsy professionals of Great Barrier learned the basics of carpentry, metalwork, milling, and casting. The old woman treated them all with quick com-

19

petence and sarcastic words, and Jason smiled at her as he approached the village. She stood at the door of her surgery, arms folded and wiry gray hair plastered with water to her head.

"Dr. Hoku, good morning to you," Jason called. "Idle hands on a bright day?"

"Waiting for the walking wounded," she said. "And better idle hands than an idle body." She surveyed him thoroughly and nodded. "Good for you. Procreation's a necessary evil on a new world."

Jason laughed. "Don't tell me how you do it," he said. "I'd hate to know."

"Probably," she replied calmly, and Jason waved as he rounded the house. Before him, people swarmed over the skeleton of a building. Under the direction of the carpenters, who had been considered lower class on NewHome, lawyer and accountant and judge and engineer and contestor and fisherman swung hammers and pulled saws, meekly accepting orders that issued from the lanky young woman who sat atop the rooftree with a level in her hand. The intersection had been turned into a temporary foundry, and here sands from the beaches and spare metals of almost every description were dumped into the processor, which then spewed out nails and nuts and screws and bolts, supplementing the wooden joints which were carved in the evenings by the glowing light of the barn. The kasirene had undertaken to keep the processor supplied with sand, and a constant line of them trudged into Haven, staring at the construction and the busy humans. The refugees were distrustful of the tall, four-armed, marsupial sentients. NewHome had killed its last native sentients centuries before, and these six-limbed creatures looked dangerous, they thought. The kasirene, however, accepted the new humans with their usual combination of taciturnity and curiosity. Their local population seemed to have undergone one of its mysterious, random increases, and Jason was pleased. The kassies worked steadily and for little in the way of goods, and he needed all the help he could get. He finished his roll, shook crumbs from his hands, and grabbed a hammer before swinging himself up through the beams of the unfinished house.

At jev'al the work broke for lunch. Jason climbed from the rooftree and accepted a cup of soup from one of the refugees. As he finished he heard a buzzing in the distance, and Jes rushed over the brow of the hill.

20

"It's a shuttle!" he shouted. "A shuttle, coming toward the pad! Jason! A shuttle's coming!"

A quick silence descended as the news spread, and the refugees put down their cups and stood uneasily, staring toward the east. Jason quietly picked up his hammer and glanced around.

"Jes, you get the children together and take them to the barn. Take them up to the lofts and play with them, don't let any of them leave."

"But why, Jason? What's wrong?"

Jason glanced at his son. "We don't know who's in that shuttle, Jes. I want the children to be safe."

"But . . ."

"It might be from NewHome," Jason said. "Go on. I'll let you know when it's safe to come out."

Jes, wide-eyed, nodded and hurried through Haven to the meadow where the children played. Jason shifted the hammer from hand to hand.

"I'll go meet them," he said to the refugees. "You get into the woods until we know what's happening. If it's bad, head south to the mountains and . . ."

"No." Medi Lount, the sculptor, stepped forward, a wrench clutched in her pale hand. Behind her, Tabor Grif lifted a length of pipe and rested it on his shoulder.

"This is our home now," Medi said. "We're not leaving."

"Don't be foolish," Jason said, then Dr. Hoku marched to them. She held a scalpel in one hand and a splint in the other.

"Quit chattering," she said sharply. "It's coming in fast."

"All right," Jason said. "Stake out the pad, get behind the trees or boulders, out of sight. If the shuttle's from New-Home, wait until they come to you; don't go charging them. They'll have weapons better than awls and hammers." He listened intently for a moment. "Okay, let's get going."

Within seconds Haven was deserted. As Jason reached the pad, Mish ran in from the fields, a heavy sickle in her hands. She looked at Jason's hammer and gestured derisively. Together they slipped behind the dirt barrier, and the roar of the shuttle filled the small valley.

Jason stared at the piled dirt, trying not to see the snowfields of Great Barrier. He listened to the increasing roar, the sudden, heart-stopping silence as the shuttle reversed thrust, and the solid, final thunk as it settled to the ground. He peered carefully around the edge of the barrier. The shuttle's nose pointed toward him, and he could not see the Federation registry numbers on its side. Mish slipped between the bank and his body and looked out over the crook of his arm.

The shuttle's hatch swung out and down, and a figure appeared at the opening. It stopped abruptly and looked around the deserted pad, then moved cautiously down the ramp. Jason squinted against the light, his hands suddenly clammy, then shouted and threw his hammer to the dirt.

"It's Hetch!" he yelled as he ran down the slope to the shuttle. "Captain Hetch!"

The small, rotund captain stopped at the bottom of the ramp and looked at Jason, then stared as the refugees appeared from behind trees and rocks, their rude weapons clutched in their hands. When he saw the sickle that Mish carried, he sat slowly on the ramp and put his head in his hands, and when Jason touched his shoulder, he saw that Hetch was laughing.

MANUEL HETCH BURPED CONTENTEDLY AND patted his round belly.

"Best table in West Wing," he said with appreciation, and Mish smiled as she handed him a glass of wine. The sounds of dishwashing floated in from the kitchen. Laur had chased Hart and Jes to bed; they could still be heard complaining in the rooms overhead. A small fire filled the room with yellow light, and Quilla sprawled on the couch, her determination to stay awake with the adults conflicting with her sleepiness. With Jason busy in Haven, Quilla had taken over his share of work in the fields. Her clothes were stained and dirty, and bits of leaves clung to her hair. Jason touched her hair as he passed behind her couch, and she smiled at him. He sat beside Mish and looked around the room at the comfortable, makeshift furniture and the clean floors of kaedo wood, the curtains of homespun river willows and the crackling fire, and felt his unvoiced evening benediction fill his mind.

"However," Manny Hetch said, "this isn't a purely social visit."

Jason spread his hands. "There are no orders now," he said. "I could fill your ship twice over with the things we need, but I can't make payments. We've barely got enough to last us through the winter."

"I wasn't expecting orders, not this trip. But you're going to need things, things you can't make here, and you'll need more of them than you think. Thought about how you're going to get them?"

Jason glanced at Mish, and she shrugged.

"No," she said. "Some of the people were talking

about getting property or fremarks from NewHome, but now . . ." She shook her head.

Hetch had been besieged by refugees as soon as they found out who he was, people who wanted to thank him for their lives, people desperate for news of home and relatives. Hetch stood in the clear sunlight of the port and told them. Confiscation, disappearances, martial law, curfews, rationing of what little food was available, unseasonable storms, and the purges continuing. Great Barrier had not connected Hetch with the people's escape; Hetch had been discreet in his inquiries. The refugees owned only what they had taken with them. Nothing more. They listened in silence, and in silence turned away. Hetch left the pad growling bitterly, but a good dinner and good wine had restored his usual high spirits. Jason lifted his own glass and looked at the captain through the yellow wine.

"Forget about NewHome," Hetch said with a trace of his earlier bitterness. "Nothing's coming in from there."

"We'll manage," Jason said.

Hetch snorted. "Not this way, you won't. You need something to export, Jase—something that will bring in money from the outside."

"What?" Mish said. "We're not set up for mining, and even if we were, you know that metals don't pay. There's nothing here exotic enough to create a market . . . no valuable crafts. We've been through this before, Manny. All we've got is the foodstuffs you buy from us, and that's barely enough to provision your ship. This year we can hardly provision ourselves."

"You've got land, haven't you?" Hetch demanded. "Good fertile land and the climate to grow things."

"Come on, Manny, we can't export dirt."

Hetch grinned. "Nope. But you can export this." He reached into his belt pouch and removed a small box, which he handed to Jason. Jason glanced at him curiously, then opened the box while Mish leaned over his shoulder and stared down. Quilla opened her eyes and watched from across the room.

Jason reached into the box and removed a fine wire, almost white, which felt cool and metallic to his fingers. He handed it to Mish and picked up an amber-colored rectangle. It shimmered in the light of the fire as Jason held it up. Next was a gray lump, slightly resilient. Jason's fingers molded it gently and Mish put her fingertips in the indentations he had left. Four fuzzy brown seeds. Mish set them carefully at the end of the row she had made on the small table beside Jason's chair, and together the Kennerins looked at Captain Hetch with silent curiosity. Quilla's eyes closed again and she stirred gently on the couch.

Hetch pulled his moustache and leaned forward to tap the wire. "Best and cheapest electrical conductor I've found. Won't rust, won't break, almost no resistance at all. Sells for maybe seven fremarks the kilo on Althing Green." He tapped the amber rectangle. "Comes from this. Second stage processing. Orbiting factories, needs the freefall to come out right. Crystallize the things, I think. Looks like this"—he tapped the gray lump—"before processing starts. Raw material."

Mish folded her hands in her lap. Hetch lifted the seeds and spread them in the calloused palm of his hand. *"Zimania rubiflora,"* he said. "Native to Marquez's Landing. Grows about one hundred fifty centimeters tall, about one twenty round. Bright red flowers, inedible fruit. Yellow. Trunk's about forty centimeters around, scaly brown bark. You cut the trunk halfway up and collect the sap. Harden it to this." He tossed the gray lump into the air and caught it deftly. "Send it to the orbiting factory and, hey presto, the best conductor in the Federation."

Jason frowned. "Electrical wire from sap? You're pulling me, Hetch."

"Truth and light," Hetch swore solemnly. "They crystallize it and polarize the crystals. Something like that. I've been using it for the past ten, eleven runs, and it works beautifully. Cheaper than metal, easier to store, won't freeze, won't rust, damn near won't melt, either. And you don't need a lot of equipment to produce the raw stuff, just good, arable land and a little work."

"But the factories—" Mish said, and Hetch waved his hand.

"Albion-Drake, over by Shipwright, has a dozen factories begging for the stuff, they can't get it fast enough. All you have to do is grow the plants, collect the sap, harden it, and ship it off."

"Ship it off?" Jason said.

"You ship with me." Hetch reached for his wineglass, and Mish refilled it. "That's my end of the deal. You sell to me, I sell to Albion-Drake. We both make a good profit. And I'll advance you credit until the first load's ready."

"How long?" Mish said.

"About four years, I'd guess. The plants flower and fruit after two years, and you'll want to take seeds from the first batch to plant out the rest. By the fourth year, you would have enough mature plants to produce a good harvest, and we start shipping then. What do you think?"

Jason leaned back and crossed his arms. "Manny, did you steal these seeds?"

Hetch looked honestly surprised. "Steal them? Of course not. What makes you think I stole them?"

"Anything this valuable isn't going to be floating around for anyone to pick up. And Marquez's Landing—"

"Can't even keep up with the demand," Hetch said. "No, it's a question of where it'll grow. Aerie shows up on my scopes almost identical to Marquez—the seasons are pretty much the same, climate's about equal, sunlight, trace minerals. Not a usual pattern, water-worlds with this sort of primary, this far from it. My bet's that Marquez and Aerie are the only places it'll grow. Seller's market. Well?"

"You didn't answer my question," Jason said. Hetch grinned and waved his arm. Mish took the seeds from Hetch and spread them over her palm. Jason recognized the look in her eyes. The back of his neck felt suddenly tight.

"When's your next trip through?" she said to Hetch, without looking up.

"Four, five swings. That's, what, five months Aerie? Next spring?"

Mish nodded. "If they germinate, if I have growing plants by that time. Jason?"

She glanced at him, and Jason nodded slowly.

"Yes," he said. "You'll have your answer in the spring."

"Good enough." Hetch stood and stretched, his belly thrusting out before him. "I've got more seeds in the shuttle, and a manual for you. I'll bring them in the morning."

He waited until Mish awakened Quilla and sent her up to bed, then said his good nights and followed her upstairs. Mish stood by the fire, cradling the seeds. Jason cupped her extended hand in his own, his dark fingers

26

curving over her amber palm. The four brown seeds seemed like the heads of nails, binding the hands together. Mish smiled, and Jason brushed her hair with his cheek as he turned to bank the fire.

"Jase? I smell something burning."

"The fireplace," he said without turning.

"No, different. Can you—Sweet Mother!"

Jason turned abruptly. Mish had thrust the curtains aside and a sullen red glow pervaded the room. She opened the window and acrid smoke billowed past her head.

"The kitchen or Haven," she said. "Get the children!"

The door crashed open as she ran out of the house. Jason stood for a moment, staring at the seeds she had dropped on the floor, then turned and pounded up the stairs.

"GET OUT OF THE HOUSE!" JASON'S VOICE shouted. "Fire!"

Quilla leaped from the bed and grabbed at her clothes. Jason shouted at her brothers' doors, and she rushed from the room, still struggling with the fasteners on her shirt. Someone brushed by her in the dark, and she cried out before recognizing the musty, ship's air smell of Manny Hetch. She followed him down the stairs, grabbing at the banister to keep her balance, and ran out the front door. A red, smoky light filled the sky, reflected from the bellies of clouds. She stared at the house, trying to find the origin of the glow. Her eyes hurt. Then she turned in place and felt cold relief. The house was standing and untouched. Haven was burning.

"Quilla!' Mish grabbed her arm and shouted over the sounds of burning wood and yelling voices. "Find Hart and Jes and keep them here. Don't leave the hill."

Mish was gone before Quilla could speak. She fumbled with the last clasp on her shirt, then gave up and turned to find her brothers. Jes stumbled from the house and stood close to her, staring at the flames.

"Mish says to stay here," Quilla told him. "You're not supposed to go down to Haven. Jes! Listen to me!"

"All right," Jes said impatiently, and shook her hand from his arm. "Look, Quil, the whole town's going up!"

Quilla stared down the hill. "No, it's just the doctor's house. Stay here. I've got to find Hart."

Jes' answer was lost as the roof of Hoku's house caught fire with a hollow roar. Quilla looked about in the sullen light but could not see Hart. She ran toward the house.

28

Laur stood at the door, whimpering, wrapped in a blanket. A corner of the blanket slipped from her shoulder as she grabbed at Quilla.

"I can't find Hart!" the old woman cried.

"Did you look in his room?"

"I looked, he's not there!" Laur wailed. "I can't find him! He'll be hurt, he'll—"

"Stay here," Quilla commanded. Laur stared at her, then nodded and clung to the doorframe, her face turned toward the burning. Quilla slid past her and ran up the stairs.

"Hart?"

The room was empty. She opened the closet door, but he was not hiding beneath the toys and clothes. Nor was he beneath the bed, and the small alcove by his window was empty. Quilla gnawed at her lip, then ran into Laur's room. When badly frightened, Hart often crawled into the narrow bed and clung to Laur until she quieted his fears and sent him back to his own room. But this room, too, was empty. Quilla checked the entire top floor before running down the steps again. From the window at the landing, she saw forms passing buckets of water from the stream; they seemed barely human, outlined against the dancing light of the fire. At the far side of the stream, kasirene gathered to stare at the burning house.

Hart was nowhere on the main floor, either. She paused at the kitchen door, frowning, then grabbed a light and ran down the hillside toward the barn. People milled around the barn's wide doors. She stumbled over a small shape, which cried out in fear, and she stopped and lowered the light. A child crouched in the grass, staring at her with wide eyes. Quilla picked the child up, set it on her hip, and hurried toward the barn.

The holocube lady sat in hay, pinched with fear, surrounded by her lighted ghosts. Quilla thrust the child at her. "Here. Make sure the children stay in the barn."

"What's happening? Is it the Guardians? Are the Guardians coming? Are they killing—"

"No, the doctor's house is burning. That's all. Stay here, and keep the children with you."

The woman nodded and turned off her holocubes, and the child huddled beside her. Quilla scrambled up the ropes, the lantern's grip clenched between her teeth, and sped through the lofts and balconies. Lamplight swung wildly amid the crates and timbers. No Hart.

29

The sky flared and wavered through the smoke. Her eyes watered. She stared at the far outlines of the kaedo trees, then turned decisively and ran toward Haven. Finding Hart was more important than staying away from town.

She circled the bucket brigade and ran toward the stream. The smoke hurt her throat. Hart maintained a secret place that she was not supposed to know about, and she splashed through the shallows and waterplants until she breached the cane cover of the hut and found Hart kneeling in the water. He backed away rapidly, but she cried his name and clutched him to her, almost babbling with relief. His body loosened and he held to her, weeping.

"Why did you come here," she demanded. His body tightened in her arms. "I've been looking everywhere for you. Why didn't you stay at home?"

"I heard a noise," he said. His voice strengthened away from tears. "I came down to see what it was, and I saw the fire and got scared. So I came here and I hid. I saw the whole thing."

Quilla glanced at him sharply, but could not make out his features in the dim light. "All of it?"

He pushed away from her. "I heard a noise and I came down to see what it was," he repeated stubbornly.

Quilla took his hand and stood. He tried to tug away, but she held him tightly. "Come on. Laur's probably half crazy, wondering where you are." Hart staggered as he stood, and she stooped to lift him.

"I can walk by myself," he announced, and led the way across the stream. The sky paled toward dawn, and the light of the flames slackened. They stood for a moment halfway up the hill, watching the fire die under buckets of water. Burned planks and charred beams littered Haven's one intersection, and ashes floated solemnly in the air. The doctor's house was a total ruin.

"Quilla?" Hart slipped his hand into hers.

"It's all right now," she said absently. "The fire's almost out."

"Do you . . ." He paused, and she glanced at him. "Do you think they'll go home now?"

Quilla squeezed his hand, remembering his terror in the barn the night the refugees had arrived.

"No, Hart. This is their home now, baby. They'll build the house again."

Hart pulled his hand away and raced up the hill, and Quilla trudged after him. As the boy reached the house, Laur grabbed him and held him tightly, berating him and sobbing with relief. He stood quietly in her arms, his face turned from Haven. Quilla sighed and sat with her back against the halaea. Smoke dissipated in the morning wind and Quilla saw the kasirene gathered around the ruins of the doctor's house, staring at the burned wood. The refugees avoided them as they splashed water over the house, and small clouds of white steam billowed into the pale blue sky. Quilla closed her eyes.

"Quilla, Jason says we're supposed to go to the barn, and Laur's supposed to get some breakfast down, and you're to bring the medkit. I think someone was hurt." Jes stood before her, almost dancing with impatience, and Quilla nodded and stood. Jes vanished down the hillside while Quilla told Laur what was needed.

"If those damned cooks are around," Laur muttered. "Undependable, lazy kassies—they'll probably not appear all day." She walked through the hall, still grumbling. Hart followed, his hand holding a trailing edge of Laur's blanket. Quilla lugged the heavy medkit from its niche in the wall, shouldered it, and carried it awkwardly down the hill.

Dr. Hoku had set aside a corner of the barn as an infirmary. Quilla staggered through groups of talking people and dumped the medkit on a pile of hay beside the doctor. Two people lay gasping, their faces dark with smoke. Manny Hetch wrestled open the clasp of the medkit and pulled out the air pumps and masks. He settled one over each of the smudged faces. The air pump hissed softly, and Hoku nodded before bending again over a third form. Quilla craned her neck and saw Tabor Grif, his face more pale than usual, and his lips clenched tightly together. Hoku ripped his pants open, exposing a blistered, oozing area on his left thigh.

"Hurts, right?" the doctor demanded, and Tabor nodded.

"Good." Hoku turned her head and saw Quilla.

"Open my bag, girl." Hoku gestured, and Quilla touched the bag's hasp. It opened into a surprising number of layers. "Top, to the left. I want the red ampule and the hypogun beside it."

Quilla lifted them out and handed them to the doctor, who fitted ampule into hypo with a practiced flick of her fingers and pressed the gun against Tabor's side. He grimaced and his face relaxed slightly.

"That's better," he said. "Still hurts."

"Takes time. You," Hoku said to Hetch, "bring me that medkit. You ever worked with burns before?"

Hetch nodded. "On shipboard."

"Good enough. I need someone else. You, girl. No vomiting, understand?"

Quilla nodded, took a deep breath, and knelt in the straw beside Tabor. He tried to smile at her, and she touched his neck briefly before turning her attention to the doctor. Hetch handed instruments and drugs from the two kits, Hoku worked swiftly with them, and Quilla took the used instruments and dropped them into the holding sac. Hoku muttered as she probed and sliced and cleansed, and occasionally Tabor winced. Quilla rested her left hand on his shoulder and he covered it with his right, squeezing hard whenever the doctor probed deeply. Quilla tried not to look at the layers of flesh that Hoku manipulated, but she could not close out the smell of burned meat. Her stomach churned, and she pushed the sensation aside. Tabor fainted.

"He's unconscious," Quilla said.

Hoku put a hand on Tabor's wrist, then nodded. "He's all right," she said, and her fingers flew again.

Finally she poured healant over Tabor's thigh and layered dressings into place. She moistened electrodes and pasted them to his skin, checked the readings, sighed, and rocked back on her heels. Her wrinkled face was damp with sweat.

"Girl, you stay and watch him. If anything looks funny, any of these dials goes into red, you yell for me until I come. Understand?" Hoku glanced at Quilla, then gave her a brief, hard smile. "Good work, girl." She stood slowly, ignoring Hetch's offered hand, and stretched.

"You ever want a place on shipboard . . ." Hetch began, and Hoku snorted.

"I've been on ship twice in my life," the doctor said. "Hated it. No, thanks. You retire here, I'll take you on as my nurse."

Hetch shrugged. "I've got three years of nursing. Hated it."

They packed the instruments into the sterilizer. Laur and the kasirene cooks brought tea and bread into the

32

barn, and a quick silence descended while the refugees stared at the kassies with distrust.

"They started it," someone said. A murmur of assent moved through the barn.

"I saw them . . . "

". . . standing around staring . . ."

". . . got in during the night . . ."

". . . started it . . ."

". . . fire . . ."

"No," Jason said loudly, and the voices paused. "It's impossible. Fire's sacred to them."

"So what's to stop them from building a big one?"

"We don't even know if it was arson," Mish said. "We don't know how it started. It might have been a lantern that someone forgot to put out. It could have been anything."

Hoku shook her head, but remained silent.

"Could have been deliberate, too," someone said.

"It almost took out the place next to the doctor's."

"They'll burn us right off the planet."

Voices rose in anger, and Quilla glanced at Tabor's face. He remained unconscious, but the dials were steady.

"Listen to me!" Jason shouted. "We'll investigate. If it was set, I'll talk to the kasirene."

"They'll lie . . ."

"I've worked with them for twelve years!" Jason bellowed. "Do you think you know more about them than I do? You couldn't even cope with your own natives; you killed them all off. Does this give you a right to tell me about mine?"

In the ensuing silence, a voice said, "We didn't do it, not us. That happened a century ago."

"Are you going to tell me how to run my planet?"

Tabor moaned, and Quilla looked at him. He moved his hand under hers but did not waken.

"All right," Jason said finally, "we'll do it my way. Understood?"

They assented grudgingly, and Quilla let her breath out. She slipped her hand away from Tabor's, drew up her knees, and cradled her head in her arms.

HART SAT IN A CORNER OF THE KITCHEN, HIS arms tight around his knees, and watched the kasirene cooks pummeling bread dough at the large tables. They chattered to each other, but Hart ignored their light voices. A kassie pup lay by his feet, near the warmth of the ovens, and Hart idly played with its small hands. It kicked its feet at his wrist, snaked its lower arms through his fingers, and used its upper arms to stuff his thumb into its mouth. Hart shook his hand away. The pup wailed, and one of the cooks came over, picked up the pup, and dropped it into her pouch. The pouch jiggled as the pup squirmed toward the hidden nipple. The cook popped a piece of bread dough into Hart's mouth with one hand and tweaked his ear with another.

"Thanks," he said shortly in kasiri. The cook laughed as she returned to the table. Hart rose casually, pulled at his short jacket to straighten it, and stole a fritter on his way out of the kitchen. The second cook saw him and said something quickly, then laughed as Hart slipped out the door.

Autumn had come to To'an Cault, the equatorial island on Aerie where the Kennerins had made their home. On the far hills the leaves of the kaedos and halaeas browned and fluttered, exposing stark white branches, and the wind cooled the air. Jason and Mish had talked about the weather last night; the kasirene predicted that this year would bring snow to the summits of the hills, and certainly would frost the flanks of the mountains to the south. Shaggies had been seen far north of their usual territory. Mish talked about insulating her new greenhouse, and Quilla offered to fetch the leftover solar sheet-

34

ing from the barn. Hart could see Quilla now, helping Mish stretch the sheets tautly over the greenhouse, while Tabor leaned on his crutches and offered verbal help. Hart scooted behind some bushes, then parted the leaves and glared at Tabor, willing the pale man to disappear. Tabor gave Jes flute lessons in the evenings, during the times that Jes and Hart would otherwise have been playing in the attic of the house. He sat after dinner with Mish and Jason and talked about politics and farming. Every time he entered a room, Quilla would stammer nervously and bump into things. Worse, Tabor spent much of the afternoon in the kitchen, talking with Laur, and to Hart's disgust Laur seemed to like it. Jason and Mish had taken Tabor in after the fire, Quilla had nursed him, Jes had amused him, and Laur had fed him. Hart could not have put it into words, but he felt that Tabor symbolized all that Hart hated in the refugees—their disruption of his life, their changing of his schedules, their usurpation of his world. Hart moved behind the rows of bushes and down the hill, looking for Laur. This afternoon she, at least, would be alone.

He found her in the barn, a building Laur shunned unless she was forced to enter. She stood in the hay, a length of material in her hands, and together she and the holocube lady smoothed and folded the cloth.

"Well, I don't say I entirely approve, either," Laur said. Her stiff black gown creaked as she bent to catch a corner of the cloth. Hart remembered Mish saying that Laur was so respectable it made one's teeth ache, and the words had lodged in his head, associated with the creak of Laur's stiff clothing. He touched his jaw and moved through the door.

"The children should work in the fields," Laur continued. "But they need their schooling, too."

"Hold classes at night," the other woman said. She folded the cloth with abrupt movements of her arms. "For the older ones, I mean. Younger ones can be in school daytimes, keep them from underfoot."

"But there's only one teacher." Laur sighed. "It would probably just make trouble, classes day and nights, too."

"Enough trouble already," the other woman agreed. "I never expected to see such trouble."

"Well, with the fire and all that—"

"I don't mean just that. After everything else, that's almost minor."

35

"It just about burned the entire town." Laur sniffed. "That doesn't sound minor to me."

"No, of course not," the other woman said soothingly. They walked together, flipping the cloth into neat folds, until they met in the middle and Laur took the folded material and laid it to one side. They picked up another length and began the folding again.

"I still think the kassies did it," the holocube lady whispered, but Laur shook her head emphatically.

"They're like children," Laur said, "superstitious, and you can't count on them. Sometimes they show up to work, sometimes they don't, but there's always enough of them around, one way or another. Just certain ones come and go, you know. Teach some of them to do one thing, and the next thing you know they're gone and you have to teach others all over again. But they wouldn't hurt a thing. Why, when Jes was just little, he disappeared one day and I almost lost my mind looking for him, and that evening . . . "

"Laur, I'm hungry," Hart said loudly. "I want something to eat."

"Oh, go ask the cooks, Hart. Go on, I'm busy."

"But I want you to feed me," he insisted. Laur freed a hand from the cloth and pinched his shoulder.

"Go on, child. You drive me to distraction. Go find something to eat in the kitchen and get back to school, hear? You're going to be late. You never give me a chance to do anything. These children . . ."

Hart retreated, but did not leave the barn. Instead, he circled around the working women and slid into the hay nearby, where he could still hear them.

" . . . he'd just spent the entire day in the village, and they brought him home that night. Taken good care of him, for kassies, but just didn't understand that he was supposed to be at home. They can't think straight, but they wouldn't harm anyone. Not deliberately."

"Well, I don't know. Back on Great Barrier, they're still telling stories about the natives. You wouldn't believe some of the things they did to the early colonists."

"Really?" Laur's voice was breathless with curiosity.

"Well, they were humanoid, you know. I mean, more than your kassies are. Only two arms. And big— you wouldn't believe how big. I heard that in some of the outlying towns, or on some of the farms, if they caught a

36

woman by herself . . . " The woman's voice dropped. She and Laur stood leaning together, their voices a small, unintelligible buzzing. Hart lay back and ate the fritter, watching dust motes float from the distant lofts through the sun-speckled air. He knew that he should be in the newly built schoolhouse, listening to the droning of Simit, the teacher, and the hum of his classmates, but he did not rise to leave. He hated the classroom, his teacher, the other students, and resented having to waste his time sitting on the uncomfortable benches learning historic nonsense. Quilla didn't have to go to school. She was only fourteen, and there were students older than that in the school. But, Jason had told him, Quilla had absorbed the tapes and lessons well before the refugees arrived. Hart didn't see why he couldn't do the same thing in the privacy of his room. Besides, the school was next door to where Gren had built his shack, and Hart was afraid of the taciturn, violent old man.

Even without Gren's unwelcome presence, Hart would have resisted going to school. He already knew how to read and write and cipher, and the lessons on the poisonous plants of Aerie left him cold. He had known them for years, and if all his schoolmates killed themselves eating the roots of airflowers, or the leaves of crepeberries, it would be to the good. As for the other subjects, he saw no use for them whatsoever. He knew what he needed to know; besides, he was a Kennerin. He shouldn't have to go to school. Even if the others were against him, even if Jason and Mish insisted and Quilla tried to explain and Jes teased, he knew that Laur would take his side. He turned in the hay, moved a stalk out of his way, and closed his eyes. Laur's voice and that of the holocube lady continued to buzz comfortably, and he slept.

He woke some hours later as the refugees came into the barn at the end of their day's work. Although much of Haven was finished and many of them now had houses of their own, they still gathered in the barn in the late afternoon, and Hart could not understand what good it did them. He glanced around, did not see Laur, and stole out of the barn and up to Tor Kennerin.

The cooks were gone, leaving the family's dinner simmering on the stoves. Laur put a pile of dishes on the kneading table and the holocube woman picked them up and took them into the dining room.

"What's she doing here?" Hart demanded. Laur made a surprised noise as she turned to him.

"Well! It's about time you came back. I've been looking for you all afternoon. Go wash up and tell everyone that dinner's ready. And get yourself clean this time, hear me?"

"I want to know what that woman's doing here," Hart repeated stubbornly.

Laur grimaced. "Her name is Mim, and she's going to be helping me from now on. You don't think I can run this entire circus by myself, do you? Now, get going!"

"Is she going to live with us?"

"She has a room here, I helped her move in today. Now, *move*, child, I can't spend all night answering your questions." She pushed him toward the door. "And wash your neck this time, understand?" she shouted after him.

He splashed water over his face and hands, rubbed them dry on a towel, and left the bathroom after making sure that the ends of his hair were wet. Laur always checked them to make sure he had washed properly, and the dampness always convinced her that he had. He entered his room, made sure no one had come in during his absence, and pulled on a clean shirt, tossing the dirty one under the bed. He could hear Jes' voice from the room beside his, singing some dumb song they had learned in school yesterday. Hart listened and felt vastly superior to his brother. Jes was a trefik, a stupe, and had forfeited Hart's regard forever by accepting school, accepting Tabor, accepting the entire invasion as though it were a wonderful adventure. Hart slammed his bedroom door behind him and went to the living room.

"Laur says dinner is ready," he said loudly as he came in, and the adults stopped their conversation. Tabor smiled at him, but Hart turned away and said to his father, "Do you know that there's someone else here? That lady named Mim, she's going to live here."

"Yep," Jason said easily. "About time Laur had some help, too, other than from the kassies. You'll get used to her, Hart." He pulled Hart onto his lap and kissed his son's cheek. Hart wriggled away and stood stiffly by the fireplace until the adults left the room. He went to the base of the stairwell and howled until Quilla and Jes clattered downstairs. Jes held him back from the dining room door.

"You're going to get in big trouble," Jes whispered. "You weren't in school today, and Simit asked where you were."

"You shut up about that," Hart said vehemently. "You tell anyone and you'll be sorry."

Jes shrugged maddeningly and went into the dining room. Hart took a deep breath before following him.

During dinner, Hart spilled a glass of juice over Mim's gown. Mish said, "You must learn to be more careful, baby." Mim, though, caught the look Hart sent in her direction, and she frowned as she left the room to change her dress. The adults continued discussing Mish's greenhouse and the progress of her silly plants. Jes caught Hart's eye and winked, and Hart spent the remainder of the meal stubbornly staring at his plate.

After dinner Hart sat by the fireplace idly poking branches into the flames while the adults sipped wine and talked. Jes had taken Tabor's flute to his room, and Hart could hear the whistles and slides as Jes practiced the scale.

Jason said "Hart? Don't you have any studying to do?"

"No, I don't need to," Hart said glibly. "I already know all that stuff."

He saw his parents glance at each other. Then Mish shrugged and Hart turned his attention to the fire again. He wondered if he could talk Quilla into playing with him in the barn, then remembered the refugees there. Besides, Quilla was too busy making big eyes at Tabor and falling over her own feet.

Just before sebet'al, as Mish was beginning her bedtime prodding, someone knocked at the door. Jason went to answer it. Hart glanced up as his father, and Simit, the teacher, entered, and he quickly thrust the remains of the twig into the fire and stood to leave.

"No, Hart, wait," Jason said. "Mish, Simit wants to talk to us."

"Maybe I should go," Tabor said, but Jason waved him to his seat again.

"I want Laur," Hart said sullenly.

His mother glanced at him, then nodded to the teacher. "Go on, Simit. What is it?"

"I want Laur!" Hart shouted. "I won't stay here unless Laur comes! I want Laur!"

"Oh, Sweet Mother," Mish swore. Jes clattered down

the stairs, attracted by the noise, and Mish sent him to fetch Laur. Hart quieted, but when Laur entered he went to her swiftly and held her hand.

"Simit?" Jason said.

"It's Hart," the teacher said uneasily. "I know he's not used to school, it's something new to him, and maybe he just forgets, so I don't want to make a big issue of it."

"But?" Mish prompted. Jes, leaning against the doorframe, winked at Hart again.

"Well, we've had school for four days now, and he was there all day the first day, just the morning the second day, part of the morning yesterday, and he wasn't there at all today. I thought maybe you could remind him to come?" Simit looked uncomfortable.

Mish and Jason turned to look at Hart. He tried to slide behind Laur, but she pushed him into the center of the room. Quilla reached for his hand, but he jumped away from her.

"Hart, I remind you every morning," Mish said.

"He comes in to get lunch," Laur reported. "I always tell him to hurry back to school."

"And you lied to me about your studying this evening." Jason frowned. Hart looked at them with growing defiance.

"I don't have to go," he said. "I know all that stuff, I don't need to learn any more. I can do other things, like Quilla, she doesn't have to go to school. I hate the other kids. I hate all of them. I'm a Kennerin. I don't have to go to that dumb school!"

His parents glanced at each other, and Jason grew as angry as Hart had ever seen him. With no warning, he grabbed Hart, flipped the boy across his knees, and spanked him as hard as he could. Hart howled and shouted, hurt and embarrassed. When his father finally set him on his feet, he backed away. His eyes felt hot and his throat hurt. Mish said his name and held her arms out, but he ignored her.

"I hate all of you!" he said, his voice unsteady. "All of you! I hope you all die!" He spat on the rug.

Laur grabbed him, spun him around, and slapped him so violently that he almost lost his balance.

"You pay attention to your father!" she shouted. "I never, never want to hear words like that out of you again! You tell your parents you're sorry, and you apologize to your teacher and to Tabor, too, for the way you acted! And you're never going to miss another day of school in your life! Hear me? Do you hear me?"

Hart stared at her, his eyes wide with shock, then bolted from the room. No one followed him.

HART CROUCHED BY THE WINDOW, HOLDING the sash with one hand, and listened to the footsteps coming down the hallway. They paused outside his locked door, and the knob rattled gently.

"Hart?"

Quilla's voice.

"Hart? Let me in."

"Go away," he said.

"I've brought you some fritters. They're still hot."

"I don't want any."

"Come on, baby. Let me in. Please?"

"No! I'm not a baby! I don't want to see any of you!"

He held his breath as the footsteps moved away down the hall, then leaned his forehead against the glass. Quilla always meddled; Quilla didn't really care about him. If she did, she would understand, she would stay away from the refugees, she would take his side. She was no better than the rest of them.

By listening carefully he could hear voices from the living room, rising and falling, talking about him, and he flung a shaft of silent hatred down to them. It was all right to hate them, he told himself, because they hated him. If they didn't, they would do what he wanted them to do; they would know how he felt. But he'd take care of it. He'd get rid of the maggots, and then his family would understand him and forgive him and know that he had always been right.

Thus bolstered, he raised the sash carefully and slid his leg over the sill. The roof of the kitchen curved away from his window, its flexible solar panels bright in the starlight as they rose in serrated ridges over the support beams. On other nights they had looked to Hart like frozen waves on a choppy sea, gleaming with a life of their own, but tonight his interest lay only with the thick branch of the halaea reaching over the roof toward his window. He dangled by his fingers from the sill, his toes barely touching the roof, then dropped softly on a beam and crouched for a moment to make sure of his balance before crossing to the tree. He swung hand over hand along the cool limbs, slid down the trunk, and scuttled behind the hedge of creeper vines. Their cascades of night-blooming flowers smelled sweet and tangled in his hair as he peered through the vines at the living room window. Framed in light, the adults talked and gestured. They had not heard him leave.

The night wind was cold, and he pulled his jacket closed as he ran down the hillside toward the stream. He crossed the water on a series of small rocks, disturbing the night peepers and a few tiny, six-legged lizards. He left the stream east of Haven and moved through the meadow, coming up on the schoolhouse away from town. The teacher's window was dark, and Hart expected that Simit was probably back at Tor Kennerin, talking with Mish and Jason. In the distance Hoku's surgery glowed faintly. Hart hid in the shadows and listened intently, then fumbled the lightsticks from his pocket and held them loosely in his hand. Dead leaves from the kaedo were piled under the porch of the school. He could start the fire there.

The leaves rustled gently underfoot as he knelt by the porch and felt for the catch on one of the lightsticks. His hand shook slightly, and he caught his lip between his teeth and concentrated, his thumb searching for the small node of the catch. Finally he touched it, flicked it, and a yellow flame appeared in his hand. He extended his arm toward the pile of leaves, staring at the flame to make sure it did not die. As the flame licked the topmost leaf, a hand reached from the darkness, grabbed his forearm, and almost lifted him from the ground. Hart cried out and a hand clamped over his mouth. His chest ached with fear, and he dropped the lightstick. A thick voice cursed, and Hart was jerked back and forth as his captor stamped out the small fire. A smell of singed leaves floated on the air. Still cursing, Hart's captor dragged him from the school. The ache of terror rose from his chest and clenched in his throat, almost paralyzing him, but when

Hart realized where they were going, he doubled his efforts to get free, kicking and squirming and trying to bite the hand over his mouth. A door banged open, and Hart was flung headlong into Gren's shack.

Hart lay on the floor and heard himself whimper; the sound shocked him. Kennerins don't cry, he thought fiercely, and the terror lessened slightly. He rose and stood unsteadily while Gren bolted the door and moved toward the fireplace. Gren stood warming his hands, silent, and Hart moved quietly toward the door.

"You stay where you are," Gren said without turning, and Hart froze in place. Gren shrugged out of his jacket and tossed it onto a rickety cot against the far wall, then turned and reached over the fireplace for a jar. He lifted the jar to his lips and drank, shuddered, set the jar back with a bang, then bent to stir a pot which hung suspended over the flames. He lifted a spoon and tasted the pot's contents, then reached for a loaf of kasirene bread.

The knot in Hart's throat loosened, and he looked around the shack, at the beaten-earth floor, the chinked walls, the pitched roof overhead, the stone fireplace which belched thin smoke into the room. Lengths of unfinished lumber balanced on stumps served as a table, and two stumps rested by the wall. Gren dragged one of them to the table and sat on it, within easy reach of the cooking pot. A few articles of clothing hung from nails on the walls, and a large wooden box occupied one corner, its top firmly closed and locked with a great metal clasp. The only light came from the fireplace at the far end of the cabin. Closer, a length of thick material covered the one window, and cold seeped in through it. Hart's legs felt stiff, and he flexed his knees.

"Stay put," Gren said, again without looking, and began to eat.

"You'd better let me go," Hart said, his defiance marred by the shake of fear in his voice. "I'll tell my parents that you stole me, and——"

"And I'll tell your parents that you tried to burn the school, and that you're the one who set fire to the doctor's house."

"They won't believe you."

"They will. Stay put." Gren continued eating.

Hart stayed put and considered Gren's statement. If Mish and Jason had been angry at his refusal to go to school, how would they react to what he had tried to do

44

tonight, or what he had done four weeks ago to the doctor's house? The more Hart thought about it, the more unhappy he became. His nose felt warm and stuffy, and his eyes prickled.

"I want to sit down," he said finally, and Gren waved toward the other stump. Hart sat, his feet barely touching the floor, and tried not to cry.

Gren finished his meal and pushed the pot and plate aside, then turned to face the boy. He crossed his legs, and his pale eyes looked impenetrable in the flickering light.

"Rich kid," Gren said with disgust, and Hart looked up, surprised. "Spoiled rich kid. Think you own the universe, don't you? I know your type. Think you can get away with anything and crap on anyone else. Think everything's a game made to amuse you, and everyone else is a toy, an animal. You don't have to worry for anything and don't have to give a damn." Gren spat into the fire. "Just take whatever you want, come in and take everything you've got, everything you've worked all your life for, and throw it away. Robbing me of my life, damn it!"

"I haven't robbed you!" Hart shouted, his tears forgotten. "You came here and stole my planet! You stole my house and my barn and my—"

Gren reached over and hit the boy's head, knocking Hart to the floor, but Hart had been hit so much that day that the blow did not shock him. He lay as he had fallen, feeling pain at his temple, and refused to stand. Gren cursed, picked him up, and dropped him onto the cot.

"You're not hurt," Gren said, but Hart turned away from him.

"I am so," he muttered. The sheets smelled acrid.

"And I didn't steal anything of yours. You stole my entire world, and my family, and all the work I'd done."

"I didn't. I wasn't even there."

"Your type of people did it—just the type of person you're going to grow into."

Hart sat abruptly and glared at Gren, his fear gone. "If you don't like my type of people, you can go away. You can leave Aerie and take all of those other people with you. I don't want you here; I didn't ask you to come. I wish you would all die and leave me alone."

Gren stared at him for a moment, then his mouth opened and made a harsh, breaking sound. Hart realized that Gren was laughing, and his fear returned. He cowered back on the cot as Gren reached for his jar on the mantelpiece and drank again. The man sat at the edge of the cot, almost tipping it over, and smiled at Hart with cold amiability.

"I'll break you," Gren said without anger. "I'll change your song soon enough, rich kid. I'm not going to leave you alone."

"If you don't, I'll tell my parents," Hart said with more bravery than he felt.

"And I'll tell them about your fires, shall I? It's called arson, rich kid. You're an arsonist. Back on NewHome, when they catch an arsonist, they burn him alive. Have you ever seen anyone burned alive?"

Hart stared at Gren and his mind made flickering, painful visions. He began shivering uncontrollably, unceasingly, and Gren cursed and wrapped a blanket around Hart's shoulders. The fire hissed and Gren tossed another log into it. Hart started and cried out, and Gren smiled again.

"Don't tell them," Hart whispered finally. "Don't tell them."

"Maybe," Gren said, and sat, abruptly businesslike. "I'll not tell them provided you do something for me, too."

Hart stared silently, and after a moment Gren continued.

"You come here every day after school, understand? Every single day, and I don't want you telling anyone where you go. All right?"

"Why?"

"Don't ask questions!" Gren shouted. "Are you going to do what I say, or shall we go talk to your parents?"

"I'll come," Hart promised quickly. "Every day, I promise—I'll always come."

"Good." Gren stood and crossed to the chest in the corner, beckoning to Hart. Hart held the dirty blanket around his shoulders and followed.

Gren opened the lock and prized up the lid of the trunk, and Hart looked down at gleaming metal and shining glass. Gren lifted beakers and scalpels and plates and tubes, his fingers gentle and assured, and he waved them before Hart's eyes.

"I had an assistant back home," he said. His expression relaxed while he played with his implements. "Gone, like everything else, except this. I killed three people to keep

46

my lab, and I'd do it again. But I have it now, and I'm not too old to start once more." He replaced a scalpel carefully and stared into the trunk. "I'm a biologist, rich kid. You know what a biologist is?"

Hart shook his head. Gren stared at him, then shut the trunk abruptly, his cold humor gone.

"You will, before long." He grabbed the blanket from the boy's fingers and pushed him toward the door.

"Go home!" Gren shouted. "Go on, get out! And if you tell anyone, I'll burn you alive myself! Go!"

Hart stumbled from the door, gasped, and ran blindly, demons at his heels. Skittering night birds rose from the grasses, cawing wildly, water from the stream splashed his legs and filled his shoes, and the bark of the halaea tree was cold and harsh against the palms of his hands. He scrambled into his room, closed and bolted the window behind him, and hid in the depths of his closet, cold, sobbing, and bereft in a world full of sudden strangers.

MISH

IIIIIIIIIIIC3IIIIIIIIIIIC3IIIIIIIIIIIC3IIIIIIIIIIIC3IIIIIIIIIIIC3IIIIIIIIIIIC3IIIIIIIIIIIC3IIIIIIIIIIIC

IT WAS A LONG, UNHAPPY TIME, THAT FIRST
Aerite winter after the refugees came. We didn't have
enough food, of course, despite the provisions which
Hetch had left with us in late autumn. The grain gave out
first, then the dried vegetables and fruits, and the meat we
had salted and preserved. Toward winter the last of
Hetch's ship provisions were gone, and there was some
talk of eating the livestock. The refugees were sullen,
pinched, blue, and would trudge through the mud to Tor
Kennerin to make long, angry speeches of complaint, as
though they did not realize that we, too, were hungry.
They seemed to me, then, a plague, a rapacious horde
consisting solely of gaping mouths and a constant, buzzing
noise of dissatisfaction.

Winds swept from the northern icecaps and frozen islands, bringing us the coldest winter we could remember.
Snow piled high on the flanks of the southern mountains
and eddied through the hills near Haven, while a constant, bitter rain fell on the fields and village, mixed with
hail, driven by a screaming wind. Eagle, our sun, completely disappeared behind skies of unrelenting gray. Tor
Kennerin was always cold that winter, and I kept low
fires burning in the greenhouse as I watched the sickly
Zimania seedlings. Of the five hundred seeds Hetch had
given me, only one hundred fifty germinated, and of these
I lost twelve to the cold. A sorry beginning for a plantation.

A sorrier beginning for the refugees, though. Often, as
I paused at a window or in the soggy yard before the
house, I could see the huddled figure of Hoku amid the
storm, moving from house to cabin to shack as she tended

the many sick. We lost four people to the cold and to hunger before the kasirene came to our midwinter rescue with gifts of fish, and more fish, and more fish yet, until Tor Kennerin and everyone in it reeked of the sea, and I swore that I would starve rather than eat another bite. Hoku came, poked at my swollen belly, and snappishly ordered me to eat whether I liked it or not, since she didn't give a damn if I starved, but she wouldn't let me starve the baby. I gave in with muttered complaints, which were ignored. I complained much that season.

I had entered pregnancy joyfully, seeing it as a reaffirmation, a promise that the basics of my life would remain the same despite Aerie's changing face. Quilla had marked the beginning of our marriage, Jes the beginning of our life on Aerie, and Hart was conceived the spring we realized that we had established ourselves, that we would not fail on this new world. And this winter child would mark the change, would tie it to the past and link it to the future. There would always be Kennerins on Aerie. Yet when I told Jason, he said, "Good Lord, woman, isn't there enough to do already?" before smiling and kissing me, and it seemed from that time that a coolness grew between us, that Jason lacked the concern and pleasure that my other pregnancies had brought him. The winter seemed to pass in his absence, and when we were together he chattered constantly of his plans for Haven, the progress of the building, and, most of all, the lives of his new friends, their sayings, thoughts, quirks, desires, tempers. I came to realize that Jason was far less solitary a person than I, and that he viewed the Aerites with the same insatiable glee with which a child views a pile of presents on GiftDay. It annoyed me, but I told myself to be patient, that the wonder would wear itself into a commonplace acceptance, with time. That Jason would bring his energy back to me. I was sick in the mornings, and vomited at the smell of fish.

Then, toward the end of winter, Jason came home one evening full of new plans and new adventures. They had started building a boat that day, and when spring came he and his friends planned to sail to To'an Betes, our sister island, to explore. He bubbled and crowed and drew plans on the dining table with a wet fork.

"What about the spring planting?" I asked mildly.

"Oh, you can look after that," he said. He dipped his

finger in his glass and drew a wet hull around his dinner plate.

"The baby will be due then."

But he was busy with his fork, tracing beams and planks on the moist tabletop. I broke a small branch from the halaea and kept it by my bed.

A month later, when his plans showed no signs of changing, I made my slow and awkward way to the barn and stood by him as he crouched in the hay, tinkering with the hull of the boat.

"I don't see why you have to go," I said.

"I want to see if there's farmland over there," he replied through a mouthful of nails. "Our population's going to grow, you know, and we'll need more space." He gave my belly a fond pat as he reached for a hammer.

"There's plenty of space here. You can go exploring next year, or this summer, after the fields are planted." After my baby's born, I thought, but he seemed to have forgotten how to touch my mind. He shrugged and positioned a nail.

"Better in the spring," he said, and drove the nail into the wood. "Weather's better then."

"Go next spring . . . or the spring after. I need you here."

"There're plenty of people [bang] to do the plowing and planting [bang]. You'll get along just fine. [Bang.] And Hoku will be here [bang], so you won't have to worry."

Bang.

I don't want Hoku, I thought bitterly. I want you.

Jason continued his pounding and planning, and I left the barn, walked to the halaea, and stood holding its trunk.

Jason left on the first day of Pel ke'Biant, taking with him Ved Hirem the lawyer, Ped Kohl the brewer, Medi Lount the sculptor, and a miscellaneous assortment of younger people, all of them stuffed to the brim with expectations and the sense of adventure. I stood by the shore, holding my belly where the baby kicked, while provisions were dumped into the makeshift boat. I was sure that the broad-beamed, awkward tub would sink as soon as it touched the water of the strait, burdened as it was with ten idiots and their gear, but it remained afloat and Jason waved happily as the oars flailed the light spring air and eventually bit into the waves in something approaching unison. I waved back angrily and left before the boat was out of sight. He had promised to be back within two weeks, well before the baby was due. I didn't know whether to believe him.

One week later three of the younger people returned with the boat to tell us that the expedition was going well and that they would be back later than expected. Four more people left for To'an Betes with them. Twelve days after that another messenger returned, picked up provisions, told me that the explorers were still busy and everyone was well, and departed, again with new recruits. I made bitter pictures in my mind of Jason and his argonauts busy looking for harpies to slay and fleece to steal, and my initial worry festered into a bickering, nagging, unpleasant anger, which I lavished indiscriminately on the world around me. The children avoided me, Laur left me alone, and Mim stared at me from corners and nooks, undoubtedly wondering what type of maniac had employed her. I woke each morning expecting the slow pulse of contractions in my abdomen, rose wearily to eat the huge breakfast of fish and early fruits on which Hoku insisted, and which I invariably vomited up during the morning. My back hurt. I dragged myself to fields or barn or town, listening to disputes, quelling tempers, trying to turn two hundred-odd city dwellers into farmers before the planting season ended and we faced another lean winter.

The Aerites distrusted the kasirene, despite the winter's kindnesses, and would not let them work the fields. The drayclones which Hetch had sold us on credit were not yet fully grown, and the Aerites complained about pulling their own plows. Everyone, it seemed, felt slighted by the apportioning of the fields. They complained about their neighbors, their houses, their work, their children, the weather, the kasirene, the seeds, the land, the plowing, the food, until it seemed that the very air I breathed was a lamentation. I grew snappish, out of temper, grim, and they in turn grew ever more sullen and dissatisfied. I knew the cycle, saw its progression, yet could not break free of it. The world lacked solace, and I had lost my childhood knack of comforting myself.

Tabor had declined the offer to go a-roving and remained at Tor Kennerin, taking care of the children, helping Laur, doing as much as he could of the myriad small things that I could no longer handle and that Jason was not there to do. During the spring he graduated from

51

crutches to cane, and I listened for the triple tapping of his progress around the house or barn. In the evening he sat before the fire, teaching Jes to play the flute, while I lay sprawled and tired in the only comfortable chair and considered with bewilderment the person I felt myself becoming. After Jes went up to bed, Tabor would play complicated, delicate melodies while I listened and hovered at the edge of sleep. Eventually he would put his hand on my shoulder to wake me, to start me up the stairs to bed, and I believe these were the only times during that spring that I smiled.

Four weeks after Jason left, Hoku grabbed me as I finished a bitter argument with one of the Aerites, marched me to Tor Kennerin, examined me in her usual brusque manner, and forbade me the farmlands or Haven.

"But exercise," she dictated as she snapped her case closed, "upstairs, downstairs. Take a walk. Do some cooking. Jump fences. But no going into Haven, understand? You're turning into a raving lunatic, and I won't have it."

"But who's to watch the planting, who'll make sure it gets done?"

"Laur," said Hoku with immense practicality. I considered the awesome spectacle of Laur na-Kennerin, beetle-browed and creaking with dignity, descending on the unsuspecting Aerites, and I laughed.

"That's better," Hoku said, and granted me one of her rare, tight smiles.

So I stayed home. Quilla helped with the housework, Mim supervised the cooks, and Laur browbeat the Aerites. Despite my initial misgivings, it seemed to work well. I moved about the house, swollen and awkward, trying to do this or that and generally getting in the way. Tabor took me on long walks, his limp and my slowness keeping us at the same pace. He moved about the house setting things to rights, rubbed my back when it hurt, mediated the children's quarrels. He prepared food for me that stayed in my stomach, and made sure that I took the medicines Hoku prescribed. And he spent the evenings with me, letting the music of his flute create a shell of peace and comfort.

The week of rest did much to restore me to my right mind. The day the baby was born, I woke early and easily, smiling at the residue of a silly, spirited dream.

The halaea outside my window etched itself against a pale sky puffed with clouds, and as I watched the sun rose entirely and the blue overhead deepened. A vermilion fourbird perched in the tree, hopping on one foot and stopping every so often to warble out of key, or to fluff and straighten its assortment of feathers and wings. I performed the ungainly contortions that got me and my belly out of bed and upright, pulled on a robe, and stood before my mirror, brushing my hair into order again, clucking at the increasing strands of gray, peering at the lines around my eyes, counting the creases on my forehead, and generally enjoying myself. The pinched look had gone from me, and I felt as full and fresh as the spring.

The doorknob rattled, and when I called an entrance Quilla came in, carefully balancing a tray in her hands.

"I absolutely can't," I said. "Also, I categorically refuse, and I won't do it."

Generally Quilla loved to scold and nag me into eating, and would stand proudly vigilant over me until I had finished every bite. But this morning she did not reply, and I glanced at her face. Her eyes were dark with misery, and her mouth pinched down at the corners.

"Is something wrong, Quilla?" But my daughter was silent. She set the tray on a table by the window and turned to leave. I caught her arm.

"Quilla, what is it, love? What's wrong?"

"I wish I was dead!" Quilla wailed. "Leave me alone!" She broke free and ran from the room. I stared after her with amazement. The door of her room slammed shut. I contemplated going after her, then shrugged it aside. Quilla had been behaving oddly all winter, though not so oddly as I, and I thought it was merely growing pains, or the advent of the Aerites. She would get over it.

The house seemed unusually silent. I tied my robe around me, ignored breakfast, and crept down the stairs. As I reached the landing I felt the first gentle contraction building within me, and I stopped and waited until it was over. If this labor was like the others, there would be plenty of time yet. I continued toward the kitchen.

The kassie cooks were conferring in the far corner, and they looked up at me with their saucer-sized, violet eyes. Mim mixed something in a bowl with abrupt, violent movements of her arms. When I asked for Laur, she pointed her chin at the far door, and I went into the

53

kitchen garden. Laur sat amid the rows of seedlings, her hands in her lap and her head bowed.

"Laur?"

The old woman looked at me, then scrambled to her feet and plastered a false smile across her face.

"You shouldn't be outside," she said, "not dressed like that. Go indoors."

"What's wrong?" I demanded.

She looked surprised. "Nothing's wrong. Whatever gave you that idea? You get inside now, before the whole village sees you wandering around in your nightdress. Go on, get yourself inside."

I waited motionless as another contraction came and went, while Laur tugged at my arm. She looked miserable, and a dread built up inside me.

"It's Jason, isn't it?" I said. "You'd better tell me, Laur. Has something happened to Jason?"

"Jason?" she repeated. "Bless your heart, of course not. Oh, did I scare you? No, no, Quia Jason's fine, wherever he is. Of course it's not Jason. Come on, let's go inside."

"Yes, it is," I said. My knees felt weak. "You're trying to hide it from me. Tell me what's happened to Jason!"

"Hush now, hush. Jason's fine. It's not Jason." Laur bit on her lip a moment as I stared at her with disbelief. "It's Tabor," she said finally. "He's going away."

The immediate relief was quickly followed by dismay. "Oh, Laur, he can't be, not now. Where is he? I'll talk to him. He can't leave now."

"He's in his room. I don't know what I'll do without him. There's so much to get done."

I turned toward the house. Laur caught up with me in the kitchen and grabbed my arm. I stopped, but only to let another contraction build and fade. They seemed to be increasing in strength very rapidly.

"You can't go up to his room," Laur was babbling. "Even to think of such a thing! What would Jason say? You wait right by the stairs, Quia Mish, until he comes down. His room! That wouldn't do at all!"

I shrugged her off and climbed the stairs while Laur stood wringing her hands and calling on Mim for aid. I pushed open Tabor's door without knocking. He stood by the bed, folding his clothes into his pack. His flute was tucked firmly under his belt. I leaned against the doorframe and stared silently at him. He looked at me, then pressed the pack closed and sat on the bed, sighing.

54

"I told them not to tell you," he said wearily, "not until I had left." I didn't reply. "You've been very kind to let me stay on as long as I have." This with great formality. "But I'm well enough to travel now, and I think it's time to be going."

"That's absurd," I said. "You know you've been welcome, and you've helped us when we needed all the help we could get. You worked for your welcome, so don't give me this crap about leaving. Besides, where would you go?"

"Cault Tereth," he said immediately.

"The mountains? They're still covered with snow. There're no fields there. That's no place to live."

"Still, that's where I'm going."

I shook my head and sat in the room's one chair.

"Please, Tabor, be reasonable. Jason won't be back until the Mother only knows when, and I'm going to be out of commission for a while. We need you here. I don't think we could have made it without you."

I stopped for another contraction. It was considerably stronger than the others, but I was silent, and Tabor, staring out the window, did not notice.

"I'm sorry," he said finally, "but I'm not going to change my mind."

I lost my temper. "No, I'd imagine that you're not," I said sarcastically. "We took you in and helped you when you needed it, and now that you're well enough you'll just go running out when we need some help in return. You and your damned flute! You're exactly like the rest of them, always taking and never willing to give anything at all!"

"Mish," he pleaded.

"Well, go, then, and to hell with you. We can get along without you very well. We did before you came, and we can do it again." By now I was crying, and my back ached from sitting in the chair. He squatted beside me and held my hand, and I clenched his. Another pain. I turned my head away and fought the contraction, and, of course, it only hurt worse.

"Mish, listen," Tabor was saying, "it's not fair, not to you and not to Jason. Listen to me. If I could think of a way to stay with you, I'd do it, I swear I'd do it. But I can't. I don't want to leave you, ever, but I have to go. Mish? I love you."

"Me?" I said stupidly.

He bent his head to my belly and kissed it lightly.

55

"Can you see that it's not fair for me to stay? It would only make trouble, make me unhappy and you unhappy, and it's a terrible thing to do to Jason. I've got to go now, before I can't go at all. Do you understand?"

I didn't. All I understood was that he said he loved me, yet he was leaving me just when I needed him most, as Jason had left me, and that I was to be completely alone again. I stared at him with silent misery, and he rose abruptly, grabbed his pack, clutched his cane, and stumped toward the door. The flute gleamed from his waist. I had to hurt him; the need rose in me swiftly and fiercely, and I called his name. He stopped at the door, his back to me, and waited. He seemed to me, suddenly, as vulnerable as one of the children, and the urge to hurt him disappeared.

"When you reach Haven, send Hoku up." The words seemed very clear and distant to me. "The baby's coming."

He made a small, helpless gesture and almost turned around. Then he was gone down the stairs, and I listened to the sound of his cane in the yard until another contraction took me. This time I screamed.

The labor was short and comparatively easy. By early evening Hoku handed me my child and pressed on my stomach to empty out the afterbirth. I looked at this new daughter and saw in her a winter of misery and a spring of pain. I handed her to Laur and turned my head away.

When they asked, I told them to call her Meya and to find a nurse from the village for her. Jason came home two days later, apologetic for his tardiness and pleased with his daughter. She lay quietly in his arms, staring at him with enormous dark eyes set in a tiny, oval face, while he dandled her and cooed and made a cheerful fool of himself. I sat apart from them, looking through the window toward the south. The mountains were barely visible as a smudge of purple against a light spring sky, and the wind in the kaedos made a noise like that of flutes.

Part Two

1219

New Time

THE
DEATH
OF
DELTA-THREE

"Prepare the zappers, Contestor. There are some things which have to be done."
— Tri-Captain Delta-Three

JES CREPT CLOSER TO THE DOOR AND LIS-
tened, holding his breath. The hallway was warm and
dark, illuminated only by the thread of light which slid
beneath the closed doors of the living room.

"Hell, Manny, you said they were too busy killing
themselves to bother with us." Jason's voice was rough
with worry.

"I was wrong. They're crazier than I thought. Some of
them are talking about evacuating, finally, but they're not
planning to take everyone, just the uppers. And they want
to come here. Take the place over. They've got maps,
scans—they figure if you're all here on To'an Cault; well,
there're plenty of other islands. They'd just slag Cault and
colonize elsewhere on Aerie." Hetch coughed nervously.
"You know I don't scare easy. I wouldn't have brought
the news if I didn't think they were serious."

"I believe you," Mish said. Her voice was calm. Jes
shivered and put his hands in his armpits. "The question
remains: How are we going to stop them? We haven't got
a ship of our own, no armaments, nothing. And the Federation—"

"The Federation's not going to do shit," Hetch said.
"Glorified regulatory agency, that's what it is, and as
long as NewHome doesn't touch Federal communications
or transport, they're not going to lift a finger. Even if they
were willing to help, we couldn't bring them in. No, let
me finish. You tell them you're being invaded from New-
Home, and NewHome tells them that it's a retaliatory
strike, that you raided them three years ago. We did
make the first move, you know."

"But they were killing people!" Jason yelled.

"And still are. That's not Federation business. You can run your own planet any damned way you want, all the Federation's concerned with is what you do off-planet. You raided NewHome, ran off with a bunch of citizens, killed some government employees, violated their system, made all kinds of trouble, without any provocation on their part. How's that going to look in a report to Althing Green? Besides, if you bring the Federation in on this, they're going to find out that you used my ship for the raid, and I'll lose my license. Hell, I'll lose everything I've got; you'll lose your contacts with Albion-Drake, might as well burn down your plantations, and NewHome'll take you over, anyway." Hetch snorted.

Jes heard the sounds of glass on glass, and the gurgle of liquid. He moved a bit closer to the doors and closed his eyes. The kaedo wood smelled warm and spicy, and made his nose itch.

"So if there's anything to be done, we do it ourselves," Mish said, "with no ships, no weapons, no army, and no help."

Jes wondered what his mother looked like as she said that. Small, calm, and golden, he thought. Her eyes would be steady, her face without expression—as still as a figure in an old Oriental print. But his father's dark face would be darker with fury, and Captain Hetch would be rubbing his bald head as though trying to pull on the absent hair. The hallway felt colder.

"In about ten days?" Jason said.

"NewHome time. That's about seven days Aerie. I'm sorry, Jase. I came as soon as I knew, but—"

"Forget it, Manny. Mish, we could evacuate Cault, hide out for the duration."

"What duration? They'd come in anyway, just take over the entire planet while we're hiding our heads. No."

"Maybe you've got a better idea?" Jason's voice was sarcastic.

"I don't know, Jase. But we can't let them walk in and take it over. We can't let it go."

"I can't even think anymore," Hetch said.

"Let's sleep on it. We're not going to get anything done tonight. Mish? All right?"

Jes heard mumbled agreements as he ran silently up the stairs. When Mish came into his room for her usual check, he was bundled under the blankets, feigning sleep. She brushed his hair from his forehead, then closed the door behind her. He lay still, listening to doors closing and the padding of feet. When the house was silent, he rose quietly and lit a lamp.

The news both frightened and excited him. He had been nine when Jason brought the refugees to Aerie, and in the excitement of their arrival had paid little attention to the stories of their trials and deaths. NewHome's star was pre-nova; that much he knew. NewHome's government, instead of sensibly evacuating the planet, had turned instead to bloodshed and plunder, raping their dying world in an orgy of greed and fear. That, at least, was how Simit, the teacher, put it, standing at the head of the class with his hands clenched and his scar white with tension. Hetch had come to Aerie with his news of NewHome's troubles, and Jason had gone back with the tubby captain to NewHome, had freed the entire population of one of Great Barrier's winter death camps, had brought two hundred fifty starving, distraught, terrified refugees back to Aerie, and given them a new and peaceful life. Jes remembered that the refugees had feared retaliation for their escape, but it had never materialized, and the fear was buried under all the incessant, important trivia of living. Now, though, NewHome had remembered them with malice. Now they would come.

Jes sat at the edge of his bed and let his fingers play silently over his flute. He knew that Hetch had brought bad news when the captain had refused Jes the usual tour of his shuttle, but Jes forgave this now. He prowled his room for a while, then turned off the lamp, tucked the flute under his pillow, and lay back in his bed. If Aerie could not be defended on planet, it would have to be defended in space. Of course. Having reached that conclusion, Jes could not take the problem further. His eyes narrowed as he thought.

What would Tri-Captain Delta-Three do in a case like this? He closed his eyes.

The Tri-Captain spun her ship from the grab, zappers blazing as the NewHome fleet rushed toward her. She bent over the console, her fingers moving so fast that they blurred. The *Tiger* rocked.

"Near miss, Captain," said Contestor Alta-Nine.

The Tri-Captain grinned and slagged the fleet's flagship. The rest of the fleet turned tail and ran toward New-Home.

"Shall we follow them, Captain?"

The Tri-Captain frowned. "I think so, Contestor. I don't like slagging entire planets, but this one is a danger to the Federation and everyone in it." The Tri-Captain squared her shoulders. "Prepare the zappers, Contestor. There are some things which have to be done."

The Contestor saluted and ran from the bridge, while Tri-Captain Delta-Three raced her ship toward the enemy planet.

And if the Tri-Captain didn't have her ship? Or the zappers? Then what? Well, she could fuse sand to make a huge mirror, and as the enemy ships came through the grab she'd focus Eagle's rays on them and . . .

Jes was still considering the problem when he fell asleep.

Breakfast the next morning was an uncomfortable affair. The adults made a great effort to be calm and casual, but to Jes every movement they made or sound they uttered was fraught with meaning. His young brother, Hart, ignored everyone, as usual, stuffing himself with cakes and milk and leaving the table as soon as he finished. Quilla, his older sister, bounced Meya on her lap and talked with Mish about the irrigation systems, her gaunt figure hunched in the chair, mop of frizzy hair framing her lean face. She looked tall and gangly beside their tiny, compact mother. Jes had heard the older children in Haven talk about Quilla as ugly, and although he slugged anyone he heard saying that, he suspected that they were right. Still, Quilla was Quilla. It didn't matter what she looked like. Jes thought that the Contestor Alta-Nine would look like Quilla, all brains and angles. That made him think of the Tri-Captain and NewHome again. What *would* she do?

"Jes, you're going to be late for school," Mish said. Jes looked up, startled. "Come on, you've daydreamed long enough."

"I wasn't daydreaming," he said indignantly.

"I don't have time to argue. Now, get your pack and go on, and don't forget your lunch."

Jes pulled his shoulders back and stalked out of the room. He tucked the flute more firmly under his belt. Laur stood at the main door, holding his pack in one hand and a comb in the other.

"My hair's all right," he said, alarmed.

Laur looked skeptical and grabbed his shoulder. "Looks like a hayloft," she said. "Hold still. I'm not going to let

61

people think that all Kennerins are wasters. There. And you remember to bring me some bread on your way home, hear? Go on, scoot!"

Jes ran down the hill, his scalp smarting. The roofs of Haven stretched below him, white and red and blue, each one supporting a tightly spinning kite over its chimney. Airflowers popped in the grass, filling the warm sunlight with traces of sweetness. Jes checked to make sure Laur had gone inside, then slowed his pace. The kites twisted swiftly in the morning breeze, their lines turning gears turning axles turning rods turning generators, and the air above Haven remained clear and bright. Jason had invented the kites one summer when he'd noticed the smudge of burning woodsmoke lying in the valley like a sleepy bird, and he had railed and ranted about the purity of his island until the Aerites avoided him on the streets and whispered behind his back, shaking their heads. What did Kennerin expect, if he said they didn't have the fremarks to buy a nuclear plant? Perhaps he wanted them to freeze in the winter, or depend solely on the inadequate solar sheeting. There were more than enough trees on To'an Cault for building and burning; besides, To'an Betes, across the strait, was almost entirely forest, a free warehouse just next door.

When Jason heard these mutterings, his face grew darker and his blue eyes glared. He locked himself in the barn for a week with Dene Beletes, the engineer, and when they emerged Dene carried a bright red kite, four meters wide, in her stubby hands. Within a month each house in Haven was equipped with its own kite, supplying enough power to supplement the solar sheeting. Jes found the sight enchanting, and watched the brightly colored shapes dancing above the village. One of these days a big wind would come up, he thought, and all the kites would go spinning into the clouds, carrying Haven along with them. A city in the air.

Simit, at the door of the schoolhouse, raised his horn to his lips and blew three shrill blasts. Jes cursed silently and ran through the village, arriving at the school just before Simit closed the doors.

"Walk faster and dream less."

"Yes, Quia Simit," Jes muttered and found his seat.

He couldn't concentrate. The room smelled of berry ink and, faintly, of sour milk, and light made patches of

62

yellow on the scuffed wooden floors. Simit droned through Languages, Structures, and Recitations. Jes glanced around the room at the small, age-graded groups. Except for the youngest, except for the two kasirene students who sat apart from the humans in the far end of the room, all the children could remember NewHome. What would they do if Jes told them Hetch's news? He imagined a shadow at the window, the Tri-Captain beckoning him out of the room and whispering, "I'm going to take NewHome. I need your help." Jes nodded gravely and within seconds they were in the Tri-Captain's ship, rushing through Aerie grab into tau space, plunging from NewHome grab with zappers blazing into a confusion of black ships and deadly invisible rays.

"That's enough!" Simit shouted. "I've just about lost patience with you, Jes Kennerin. I expect to be listened to when I talk. March!"

The students tittered as Simit marched Jes to the hard-stool and left him there.

Simit had a long, red welt crossing his face diagonally, from forehead to nose to cheek and around the side of his neck into his hair. It had been given to him on NewHome. Jes watched the scar pucker and stretch as Simit talked. This time, his fantasy was far darker.

At lunch, Hart sat beside him under the schoolyard's kaedo and grabbed at his lunch.

"You eat your own," Jes said angrily. "You always take half of mine and I never get enough."

"Come on, Jes, I'm hungry."

"Where's your lunch?"

"I forgot it." Hart looked at his brother innocently.

"You didn't. I saw you leaving with it this morning."

"I lost it. Come on, give me some. You've got too much, anyway. Laur always gives you more than me."

"Oh, all right. But don't eat all the cake this time, okay?"

Hart grabbed half his brother's cheese and stuffed it into his mouth, then took all of the cake and ran across the schoolyard.

"I'll get you for that!" Jes yelled, but his heart wasn't in it. Hart stuck out his tongue and went around the side of the schoolhouse. The two kassies squatted by the far gate, taking their lunches from their marsupial pouches. Jes could hear them talking to each other in kasiri. Jason had insisted that Aerie's native sentients be admitted to the school and treated exactly like the human children, but Jes doubted whether the kassies liked this any more than did the Aerites. The older kassie stretched her first arms over her head and fiddled in her pouch with her second arms. Jes looked away and stood up. Simit had gone inside, and his two helpers stood in the building's shade, holding hands and oblivious to the children. Jes strolled to the edge of the yard and lounged against the fence, idly inspecting his boots. He glanced around again, then vaulted over the fence and ran into the bushes. No one cried out after him. Crazy old Gren appeared at his window, mouthed silent insults, and withdrew. He didn't leave his house, though, and after a moment Jes crossed the stream and made his way back to the Tor.

Laur was in the garden behind the house, pulling weeds from the ground with sharp movements of her hands and elbows. Meya played in the mud nearby, her chubby face streaked with dirt. Jes crept around the house until he heard voices coming from the study windows.

" . . . nothing else we can do," Mish said.

"I still don't like it," Jason muttered.

"That's too bad. It may not be much of a chance, but it's the only one we've got—unless you've got some miracle up your sleeve."

"If I did, I'd have said so!" Jason yelled.

"Neither of you is rational," Hetch said with disgust. "Jase, Mish is right. We went over all of this last night. We don't have to do it again. I'll leave for NewHome and come back as soon as I have definite news—a date, a time. You evacuate Haven, talk with the kasirene, prepare for some sort of guerrilla action here."

"I still think the Federation—"

"Forget it, Jase. They're not going to get involved unless they have to."

"All right! So it's our only hope! I accept! But, damn it, Mish—"

"No, Jason, I'm going with Hetch. I can't just sit here and wait. Besides, you can handle the Aerites better than I can."

Jes caught his breath and stared at the blank wall of the house. The sunlight felt hot on his back.

"Mish," Hetch said, placatingly.

"Don't you Mish me, Manny Hetch. I'm going. Why can't you both accept that?"

"Because if I have to die, I'd rather die beside you than alone," Jason said.

Jes made a face.

"I'm sorry," Mish said finally. "I'm going to get some stuff together. We should leave soon. You'll remember to take the caster with you, so you'll hear us when we're back?"

Jason didn't reply. Footsteps sounded, and Jes crept into the bushes. He crouched there for a moment, touching his flute, then ran down the hill to the pad. Hetch had, as usual, left the shuttle unlocked. Jes swung himself up through the hatchway and glanced around the corridor. He went quickly to the cargo hold and hid in a nest of webbing. It was cold and smelled sharply of metal and oil. He pulled a web firmly around him, then froze as he heard Captain Hetch and his mother enter the ship. They didn't come into the hold. Within moments the shuttle's engines kicked to life, and their pounding moved in counterpoint to the pounding of his own heart.

There were no ports or screens in the hold, of course, but Jes knew what the *Folly* looked like. She'd be a Class 5b/14 merchant ship, shaped like a layer cake. Her top layer housed bridge, crew quarters, passenger quarters, galley, and all the human places on a ship. Her bottom layer would be engine room, reactors, and, spaced evenly around the bottom of the layer, the huge thrusters which propelled her through space. It didn't matter that her broadest surface faced forward; she never entered an atmosphere where resistance would be any problem. On short hops, like the four-lightyear jump between Aerie and NewHome, *Folly* would be accelerating almost constantly, and the acceleration pull would serve as a pseudo-gravity.

The Tri-Captain's main ship never entered an atmosphere, either, Jes remembered, but the illustrations showed the *Tiger* as sleek, pointed, finned, and shiny—a far more exciting shape than *Folly*'s flatness.

The shuttle docked with the *Folly* amid a clanging of metal on metal and a shriek of hinges. Jes remained very still as Mish and the captain climbed out of the hatch. He could hear voices in the bay, Hetch giving orders, others responding, his mother explaining something in a firm, even tone. The voices moved away, and after listening to the silence for a while, Jes undid his webbing and ventured into the corridor. The hatch was still open; beyond it he could see the dim reaches of the bay, and the shapes of the other shuttles lined one after another in the darkness. The pressure in his ears shifted, an almost subliminal hum ran through the hold, and *Folly* slid out of orbit toward the grab. Excited, Jes peered around until he found the corridor and ran toward it silently, his shoes in his hands.

The corridor was empty and brightly lit, punctuated by closed doors down its length. Jes could not tell what direction he faced, and he walked quickly and cautiously, his eyes and ears alert. The pressure shifted again, and the *Folly* veered abruptly. He lost his balance and fell hard against the corridor's curved wall.

"Holy light!" A thin, fair spacer stuck his head out of a door and saw Jes. "Creeping Jesus! What the hell—" The spacer grabbed Jes and hauled him into the room. "You dumb brat, don't you know we're about to—"

The room seemed to shrink, expand, turn inside out, flutter, and before Jes could cry out it stabilized again.

"—go through grab? Who the hell are you? Bakar, what's this?"

"My name is Jes Kennerin," Jes said loudly. "My mother and I are going to spy on NewHome."

The one named Bakar rose and glared at Jes. "Wait'll Hetch hears about this," he said gloomily. "Come on, snuff. March."

"Where?" Jes demanded.

"Bridge first. Maybe the brig after. Stowaways aren't welcome."

"The bridge?" Jes repeated. "Okay, let's go."

Bakar grimaced, wrapped a large, scarred hand around Jes' smaller one, and dragged him out of the room and up the corridor.

One bulkhead in the bridge was covered with clocks, handed and digital, one-, two-, and three-dimensioned, lit and dark, large and small. Jes slumped lower in his seat and stared at them while Mish and Hetch argued over his head.

"Damn it, Manny, I'm not a mind-reader. I didn't know he had stowed away."

"I can't run this ship with a kid aboard. I didn't want to go to NewHome to begin with; it's dangerous. Bad enough that you're aboard, but a kid—"

"Will you pay atten——"

"Comes from letting them run wild. Why in hell don't you keep a watch on—"

"Shut up," Bakar said. "Not going to change things by yelling. Kid's aboard. Now what?"

Jes risked a glance at the adults. Mish stood with her arms folded, back to Hetch, while the short, rotund captain glared at his first mate.

"You, Bakar." Hetch's face turned purple. "I've about had it with you."

Bakar gestured negligently. "You want me to flip around?"

"No," Mish said. She turned back to Hetch and put her hand on the stargrid. Darkness and pricks of light outlined her fingers. "We haven't got time. If we go back to Aerie now, we might as well not leave again."

Hetch glanced at the chronometers, then raised his hands, palms up. "All right, the kid stays."

Jes cheered and bounded from his chair. Bakar swiped at him and knocked him back down.

"The brig, Captain?"

"It's an idea." Hetch tugged at his beard and looked at Jes. "It would keep him out of the way."

"Oh, come on," Jes protested. "Mish, you tell him not to lock me up."

"It's his ship." Mish rapped her fingers against the stargrid. "I have no say in the matter."

"How am I going to help save Aerie if you keep me locked up?"

His mother and the captain looked startled. Under their prodding, Jes reluctantly explained how he had overheard their discussions.

"Stowaway, and a spy, too. I *should* put you in the brig, but I haven't got the crew to watch you." Behind Hetch, the screens showed the dizzying lights of tau space. They gleamed, reflected off the captain's bald head. Hetch smiled suddenly and looked at Bakar.

"You watch him," Hetch said.

"I'm mate, not a nursemaid." Bakar sounded alarmed.

"Too bad. Next time watch your mouth around me. Make sure he doesn't break anything or get hurt."

"Give him to Tham. Or Merkit."

"Merkit's pulled engine room. Go on, get him out of here."

Glowering, Bakar grabbed Jes' arm and dragged him from the bridge. Jes looked eagerly down the smooth, curved corridor, twisting his head to look at the passing doors.

"How long are we in tau? How fast are we going? Are they going to shoot at us? Will you teach me how to fly the ship? Why did you—"

"Shut up," Bakar said. He pushed Jes through a door and entered after him. The spacer who'd spotted Jes originally looked up from a mess of wires and black panels. He grinned at Bakar.

"Hello, nanny," he said. Bakar swung at him and he ducked. "Hetch left the coms on."

Bakar said something under his breath and pushed Jes into a seat.

"Stay put." He went into an adjoining room.

"Are you Merkit?" Jes said to the spacer.

"Me? Hell, no, I'm not that ugly. I'm Tham Hecate." Tham stuck out his hand, and Jes shook it.

"Are you a mate, too?"

"Nope. I'm your all-around spacejock. Anything needs doing, I'm it. Hump it, fix it, run it, find it, make it—that's me."

Bakar came in with two strips of brown stuff and a tube. He thrust a strip and the tube at Jes.

"Eat."

Jes looked at the tube and strip doubtfully. "I'm not hungry."

"Will be. Don't eat now, won't until next watch. Ship, not a suckin' restaurant."

Jes put the strip to his mouth and licked it. It was tough and blandly flavored.

"Go on. Eat it."

Bakar chomped down his strip and went into the next room. Jes leaned toward Tham.

"Is he always this mean?" Jes whispered.

Tham laughed loudly. "Bakar's the meanest bastard in West Wing."

Bakar came in again. "You're the stupidest. Come on, snuff."

"I'm not through."

Bakar swore. "You watch him, Tham. That's an order." The mate stepped into the corridor and slammed the door behind him.

Jes took another bite and looked around the cabin. The metal walls and floor were clean but scuffed and stained. Someone had scratched words over the doorframe. Jes puzzled out the sounds, but although the script was Standard, the language was one he didn't know. Battered seats lined the room, many taped together where supports had broken or cushions ripped. A rack of tapes hung on one wall, surrounded by photographs and prints stuck up haphazardly, one over the other. Pictures of heaps of fruit, pastries, meats roasted and dripping with juice, glasses of pale liquids, pots of stew. A sensum device lay on the floor, its stage littered with wires and screens. The Tri-Captain's ship certainly didn't look like this.

"Next project," Tham said, nodding at the sensum. "Work first, pleasure later. You finished yet?"

Jes crammed the last of the strip into his mouth and nodded.

"Okay, tube in the galley. Here, I'll show you."

The galley was the size of a closet. Every available space was covered with storage racks, heaters, dispensers, or keepers. Tham showed Jes how to squeeze the water from his tube, and put the empty tube in a mouth by the heater. The mouth sucked the tube out of sight.

"Where are we going?" Jes had to skip to keep pace with Tham's long legs.

"Engine room. Hold onto this." Tham tucked the box in his shirt, grabbed a pole in a recess, and plummeted out of sight. Jes gaped after him.

"Come on," Tham's voice called through the floor. "It won't bite you."

Jes gripped his flute and put his hand on the pole. Immediately the floor disappeared. He gasped, feeling the cool smoothness of the pole slipping through his clenched hand. Tham caught him at the bottom of the drop.

"Like that?" Tham put him on the floor.

"What is it?"

"Free drop. If you're down, it takes you up; up, it takes you down. Come on."

Tham strode along an elevated catwalk. Metal hulks lined the room, each one a different color. Meters on their sides flashed numbers quickly, endlessly. A robot stopped below them, chittered, and scurried into an alley out of sight.

"Where are we?"

"Engine room. Watch yourself."

The walk descended, then bent sharply and opened into a large platform. Jes stopped and gaped.

A semicircular console ran along one side of the platform, its top littered with dials, switches, screens, and other devices so mysterious that Jes could not name them, let alone determine their function. A series of mechanical arms perched along the top of the console; one or two or ten would swoop down, blurring with speed, and punch and poke and pry before springing rigidly to attention again. Small 'bots ran on tracks along the platform deck like a congregation of manic, mechanical dwarves, while overhead huge conduits pulsed with fluorescent colors. The air tingled with the smell of ozone. And the entire show was silent, save for the whish of air or the quiet tapping of plastic on plastic. Jes boggled, completely unprepared. The Tri-Captain never went to or spoke about her engine rooms—for all that was shown or said on the tapes, the *Tiger* might have run on wishes.

"Where?" Jes whispered.

"Controls," Tham said at normal volume. Jes started and glanced around, but the silent show continued without a break.

"That's Merkit over there." Tham pointed at a figure almost lost amid the regiments of 'bots and hands. Jes saw a vaguely human form within a semi-opaque suit. Wires stretched in every direction, holding the suit rigidly upright a meter from the platform. Nearby, another suit dangled limp and empty. "She's got another hour of watch. And I get to bring us out of tau, damn the luck. I always pull the hard shifts. You coming?"

Jes carefully followed Tham though the maze of tracks. He held his breath until they had reached the far side, then glanced back. Merkit seemed to be looking at him through the muddled clarity of her suit. Jes shifted the flute from hand to hand and hurried after Tham.

"Life bays," Tham said, slapping a bulkhead.

"What?"

"Lifers—lifeships. Every ship's got 'em, and all in the same place. Regulations. For emergencies, see? That's what this is for." Tham pulled the box out of his shirt. The bulkhead accordioned back, exposing a long, narrow bay. A slim, battered needle of a ship rested on tracks, its sharp nose pointed toward the outer bulkhead. Tham motioned Jes into the bay.

"Okay, cadet. This is important. Don't touch anything, hear me? You want to know what something is, you ask me. You got pockets?"

"Yes." Jes slapped at his hips.

"Put your hands in 'em."

Jes slid the flute under his belt and obediently put his hands in his pockets, then followed Tham into the lifeship.

One narrow cabin stretched the length of the ship, with a control panel at one end and three-tiered rows of webs along the sides. Tham motioned Jes to one of the control seats, warned him again not to touch anything, and checked over the banks of meters before unlocking the panel and swinging it up and over. The multicolored guts of the control board lay exposed. Tham wedged himself under the board and began tinkering.

"What are you doing?"

"Box is a seeker. If the ship's in tau, it plucks the grab position from the main computers and heads the lifer to it. Regulation."

"Regulation?"

"Yeah. Every lifer's got to have one. Not that anyone sane ditches in tau—'cept Hetch."

"Captain Hetch?"

Tham grunted. "Crazy spiker. Made a bet with his captain once, way back, that he could reach grab before the ship did. Hand me that breaker, the green one. Right. Pockets. Anyway, Hetch jumps a lifer and takes off. Opens the emergency on top of the thrusters, beats it through in about four even. Burned hell out of the lifer, of course." Tham laughed.

"How do you fly it?"

Tham squirmed around and looked at Jes. "Your hands in your pockets?"

Jes nodded.

"Keep 'em there. See those four red spots, top of the panel? Sequence, they close the lifer, open the bay, push out, and activate the thrusters."

"Is that all?"

"That's all for tau. Outside tau, you scan for destination, punch the coordinates over there, on the port side, and let the automatics take over."

"Oh." Jes peered at the panel. It was tilted against the left bulkhead and he had to twist his head to see it properly. "What's that big screen for, on the right side?"

"Sta'board."

"Sta'board? What's it do?"

"It doesn't do—it is. Sta'board's right, port's left."

71

"Okay. What's it do?"

"Stargrid, viewer, readout—all-purpose. You key it underneath, that slab of colors."

"I see them. What's the green switch for?"

"Emergency power. Like if you're running away from flotsam. Here, take these."

Jes took his hands from his pockets and held the assortment of tools that Tham gave him. Tham wriggled from under the console, ran a few quick checks, then locked the panel into place again.

The speaker above the panel squawked. "Where's that kid?" Hetch's voice demanded.

Tham touched a switch on the seat's armrest. "Got him with me, Captain. Lifer bay one."

Hetch swore. "Get him to hold four. We've got trouble."

"Yes, sir." Tham closed the switch and grabbed Jes' arm. "Come on, cadet, let's hump it."

"What's going on?"

"Hell should I know?" They raced through the control room. Merkit hung motionless amid flashing colors. Tham let go of Jes' arm as they reached the narrow catwalk. Jes ran ahead and stopped at the pole.

"How—" he said.

Tham picked him up and grabbed the pole. Jes' stomach tightened as they rushed upward.

Mish and the captain stood at the far end of the hold. Hetch, kneeling, was fumbling around the floor panels.

"Oh," Tham said. He released Jes and pushed him forward. "Go on. See you later."

"Why?" Jes said, frightened. "Don't go."

"Go on." Tham pushed him roughly. "Big secret." The spacer ran out of the hold. Jes stared after him, then trudged toward his mother.

"There." Hetch grunted and lifted a panel from the floor. "It's shielded; you'll be safe."

Jes looked into the small, dark space below.

"Manny Hetch," Mish said. Her grin was strained. "I do believe you've been smuggling."

Hetch glowered and threw some cloth into the hole. "It'll be cold in there. Get in. No talking; it's not soundproof. I'll let you know when it's safe."

"Okay. Jes, you first."

"Why?"

Mish touched his shoulder. "Hetch got a beam from

72

NewHome grab. They want to search the *Folly*. We can't let them know we're aboard."

Jes glanced at Hetch, then climbed into the hole. Mish followed. Hetch dropped the panel back in place. In the sudden blackness, Jes reached out and took his mother's hand.

Jes closed his eyes and opened them again. It made no difference; the darkness was as dense as the silence. He could hear his own heartbeat. He wriggled impatiently. Mish put her hand on his shoulder and he stopped. He wondered how much time had passed since Hetch had closed the panel on them. Mish would know, but he couldn't ask her. He wriggled again, and her fingers tightened. The Tri-Captain wouldn't hide, he thought grimly. She'd be out there cutting down the enemy in hand-to-hand combat, not cowering in a smuggler's hole. Come to think of it, she probably wouldn't hang out with smugglers to begin with. Even if she didn't know about them at the time?

She'd know, Jes decided. The Tri-Captain knew everything.

He wondered how.

The pounding in his ears grew irregular, and Mish's fingers dug into his shoulder. He raised his face. Footsteps sounded, coming closer. More than one. More than two. Someone stamped directly overhead. Voices buzzed unpleasantly, just beyond comprehension. The footsteps moved away.

Jes let his breath out slowly. Mish flexed her fingers and raised her hand to touch his cheek. The sound of her fingers on his skin was startlingly loud.

The *Folly* lurched suddenly and steadied, and Jes heard the main hatches thunk open. He grabbed Mish's hand. He knew what to expect if vacuum flooded the hold. It was one of the Tri-Captain's greatest and most constant dangers. Noises filled the hold, and Mish pulled him closer.

"Probably coupled with another ship," she whispered under the noise.

"Why?"

He felt her hair brush his cheek as she shook her head. He heard the peculiar, high-pitched hum of 'bots moving overhead. Mish put her fingers over his lips.

"I don't think there's anyone out there but 'bots," she said. "Loading something." She paused. "If they put something on top of us, we may not be able to breathe."

"Hetch said to stay put. We don't know what's happening."

"That was before." Mish knelt. Her fingers rasped against the panel. Jes reached up.

"Here," Mish whispered. He touched her upraised hand and felt the edge-line near her fingers.

"Get ready."

He braced himself. The 'bots whined away.

"Now."

They pushed at the panel. It shifted sideways.

"Harder."

Another shove raised the panel a few centimeters. They pushed it aside a little. Pale light slid into the hole, and Jes blinked. Mish sucked in her breath and moved her head to the opening. She ducked back in again.

"Go on," she said urgently in kasiri. Jes pushed at the panel and scrambled out. Mish followed him.

'Bots moved at the main hatch, shifting large crates into the hold. One crate tipped and broke, and rich fabrics spilled over the metal deck. Mish ducked into a narrow alley between crates and Jes followed her. She peered around a corner and jumped back. Jes squinted around her and saw a guard by the hatchway. The man wore a uniform of red and black, with the NewHome crest sewn onto the sleeve. He cradled a rifle in his arms.

Jes fisted his hands. One dumb guard.

Tri-Captain Delta-Three put her slim fingers to her lips, tensed, then vaulted over the crates.

"Wha?" the guard said. Then the Tri-Captain had her hands on his neck. He slumped to the deck, lifeless. She spun around, taking in the entire hold, then gestured quickly.

"Come on," she said. She drew her blaster from her belt and moved into the corridor. Jes and Mish followed her quietly.

"We've got to get to the bridge," the Tri-Captain said. "Jes, you take the vanguard. Don't shoot unless you have to."

She put a blaster in Jes' hands. He nodded and ran quickly ahead of them.

But the Tri-Captain wasn't here, and neither was her blaster. Besides, Jes thought, her blaster could punch

74

through anything. Why didn't it ever punch through the ship's bulkhead and let the vacuum in? He'd have to think about that later. For now the guard could have been a mountain, for all the chance they had of getting by him.

Mish peered between the slats of a nearby crate, then stuck her hand inside. Jes watched her tease a box toward the slats, carefully working it through layers of cloth. She urged the box around until she reached the catch. It clicked under her fingers. Jes risked a glance at the guard, who looked around the hold, then returned his attention to the 'bots. When Jes turned back to Mish, she held a large, flashing jewel in her palm. He opened his mouth to tell her indignantly that this was no time for filching things.

"How's it going?"

Jes froze.

"All right. Another load and they're done."

"Good. Avila wants the hold sealed and purged once they're finished."

"Not taking any chances, huh? Is he afraid the 'bots will rob him blind?"

"You watch it, soldier. You're not indispensable."

"Yes'm."

Footsteps clicked away. Jes heard the guard swear softly. He leaned against the crate and took a deep breath. The air smelled of fruit, and he poked his fingers into the crate. Berries. They'd looted fields and storehouses, too, he thought.

"Closing this end," a distant voice called. Mish touched Jes' shoulder and gestured that he was to be ready to run. He crouched and nodded. A hatch clanged shut at the far end of the hold. Mish stood and threw the jewel away from the guard. It made a startling, clacking sound as it landed.

"Hold it!" the guard shouted, and ran toward the noise. Mish and Jes bolted toward the door. As they reached the gate, another guard appeared suddenly and ran into Jes. Jes sprawled hard in the corridor, his wind gone. The guard made a surprised noise and staggered. Mish wheeled and kicked her into the hold, then slapped the control board. The doorway disappeared and Jes heard a soft "whump."

Vacuum. He thought of imploded berries, then of the two guards. He struggled to take a breath. His stomach felt queasy. Mish hauled him to his feet.

75

"We have to hide," she whispered fiercely.

Jes gasped for air. "The lifers," he said, choking.

"Too far. The storage holds. Can you run?"

Jes nodded and ran after her, holding his side. They skidded around a corner and he banged his ankle, but kept running. Voices sounded behind them. Mish jerked open a door and waved at him. The *Folly* lurched again. Jes slipped. Mish fell into the doorway. The door snapped closed behind her.

"Halt! Don't move!"

Jes lay still, his heart pounding. The deck felt cold against his nose. Someone jerked him to his feet.

"It's a kid," one of the soldiers said. "Look."

He spun Jes around to face another soldier. Jes saw the corridor beyond the man's side. All the doors were closed. He began to sniffle.

"I want to go home," he bawled.

The soldiers laughed.

"Sure you'll go home, snuff. But you're taking a little walk first. Kalet, take him to the bridge. Avila ought to be interested."

Hands clamped around Jes' wrists. He tilted his head back and howled.

"I want my mommy!" he cried. Then, in kasiri, he said, "I'm all right."

"Come on, infant," the soldier said, and hauled him away.

Hetch was staring at the stargrid. He looked sick. Beside him, a short, thin man in a red-and-black uniform poked the grid with his fingers and talked in a quick, low voice. The NewHome crest on his sleeve was picked in silver and ebony, and glittered in the light of the grid. The soldier held Jes by the neck and shoved him deeper into the room.

"General, we found something."

The thin man turned around and raised his eyebrows. "Since when, Hetch, do you run a flying nursery?"

Hetch spun around. The relief on his face disappeared into surprise and fury.

"You said you were shipping goods, Avila. Not children."

"I am. I'm not. Where are you from, child?"

Jes sniffled again. "I want to go home."

"Not a NewHome accent. Let him go."

76

Kalet released him. Jes put his hands to his neck.

"Where's he from, Hetch?"

"How should I know? I service fourteen worlds. I can't keep track of every child on all of them."

"I snuck in," Jes said. "I want to be a spacer."

Avila smiled. "So did I," he said.

Tham came in, under guard. He saw Jes and opened his mouth, but Hetch said quickly, "You're supposed to relieve Merkit. She's taken us through two grabs. She can't do another set."

"Yes, sir. I—"

"And next time we're on planet, if I tell you to guard ship, you guard it. Look what sneaked aboard."

Tham looked at Jes innocently. "*I* didn't see him, Captain."

"Get going," Avila said. "We leave in twenty."

Tham was herded off the bridge. Avila looked at Jes closely, frowning, then snapped his fingers.

"Fletcher."

"Sir?"

"You were at Barrier Two?"

"No, sir. Kleim was."

"Get him." Avila turned to Hetch. "All right, Captain, you follow us to Aerie, orbit until we clear you, and shuttle down the goods. Understand?"

Hetch crossed his arms and glared. "It's a Federation offense to hijack a registered transport."

Avila gestured and smiled. "This is West Wing, Captain, not Central. By the time Althing Green gets your complaint, we'll be well established on Aerie and you'll be crying for our trade. Think of it as advertising."

The captain snorted. "Then get your men the hell off my ship. I'll run your goods, but not your damned army."

"Oh, no. The hold's much too full, Hetch. I don't trust you. I'm leaving four guards, one for each of you. They can all pilot, so don't think they won't kill."

"And I don't want to run tail, either," Hetch said. "This crate'll bust up in your wake. Put me first."

"No way, Captain. Second, perhaps."

Hetch made a disgusted gesture and turned away. Jes stared at him, baffled. Could Hetch have betrayed them so easily? Certainly he had pretended not to know Jes, had not said anything about Mish, but it might have been just to save his own skin. Jes touched his flute unhappily.

"General, you wanted to see me?"

"Kleim. You were at Barrier Two during the raid."

"Yes, sir."

Jes stiffened.

"Look at this child."

A hand took Jes' chin and turned his head. Jes looked into black eyes set in a dark, scarred face. The eyes narrowed.

"Well?"

Jes' head was jerked from side to side. Kleim's fingers hurt his chin.

"Kennerin, sir? Could be. Eyes and coloring are right. The man didn't have slanty eyelids, though."

"His wife's supposed to have slant eyes."

"Then yes, sir. Almost definitely."

The hand let go. Jes stared at Avila defiantly.

"Now, then, child, you are a Kennerin, aren't you?"

"I want to be a spacer," Jes muttered.

"And so you shall be." Avila's voice was full of good humor. "Give your spacejock a commendation, Hetch. Hc's done me a good turn."

"Yeah?"

"If Jason Kennerin risked his life to save a handful of strangers, what's he going to risk to save his son? A nice, bloodless conquest, Hetch. I thank you. Fletcher!"

"Sir?"

"Post Kleim and the other three here, and move out. Come along, young Kennerin." Avila took Jes by the upper arm and lifted him from his seat. "I'm going to show you what a *real* ship looks like.

Jes looked over his shoulder as Avila led him from the bridge. Hetch's face was stony.

The two ships had uncoupled after *Folly*'s hold was loaded, and now moving between them was a cumbersome process, involving suits, guy lines, and fear. Jes hung midway across the line, with the suit ballooned out around him, and looked "up." The *Folly*'s side loomed over him, curving away at the top into a field punctured by the steady lights of real space. To his left Avila's ship hunkered close, identical to the *Folly*, save that her sides were decked with weapons mounts. Jes could see the bolts and welds which held them in place. Each ship carried the symbols of a merchant's registry. The soldier behind prodded Jes in the back, and Jes scrambled along the line. The ships looked as though they would rub together and crush him. Hands pulled him into the entry and shoved him in the airlock. His ears hurt.

The Tri-Captain flitted from ship to ship in a sleek, needle-like pod, slipped in and out of docking locks like water, and her ears never hurt. Jes was beginning, however, to doubt her evidence.

Avila's ship was new and shiny. The bulkheads reflected Jes' shape as he was stripped of the suit. He had watched them put it on him, remembering each move and maneuver. He watched now with equal care. A soldier took him by the shoulder, and he marched along a corridor behind the general. He passed closed doors, lounging soldiers, and a free-drop pole. The corridor looked like one on *Folly*, but cleaner. And more frightening. One doorway opened and a young girl looked out. She wrinkled her nose at the soldiers and withdrew. Her cheeks were full, her arms rounded. Jes remembered the gaunt, terrified refugees his father had brought to Aerie three years ago. She's been eating other people's food, Jes thought. She might as well have been eating their bodies. The thought startled him.

The bridge was larger than *Folly*'s, with more seats and more controls. Jes was put in a seat to the side and webbed firmly. A guard stood over him. Avila sat beside the console and tapped the plates before him.

"*Grafit One* to all ships. *Grafit One* to all ships. We enter grab in four, repeat, four. Order *Grafit One, Folly, Helmsholm, Grafit Two, Equinox, Grafit Three, Frene's Best, Grafit Five*. Confirm and repeat. Over."

The com hummed, and Hetch's voice repeated the sequence. Avila acknowledged him, then acknowledged the other six ships.

"*Grafit One* counting to grab. Seven, six, five, four, three, two, one, go!"

Jes looked at the screens. The ship slid into the grab's coils, rested a moment, and the coil began shimmering, shifting, winking. As the now-familiar sickness touched Jes' stomach, the grab spat them out into tau.

"Move it on," Avila said.

"Sir." The pilot's hands danced over the panel.

"Six, five," Avila muttered. The screen over his head showed the grab. "Three, two—where's—Alt'Emiri!"

The *Folly* popped into tau and rushed toward them,

by them, beyond them, before Avila had finished his curse. The general pounded on the panel.

"If that bastard's broken the coil—"

"Two, one—no sir, here's *Helmsholm.*"

"Can we catch him?"

The pilot shrugged. "We'd have to build up, sir. I think he must have started acceleration before he hit the grab." The pilot glanced at the screen. "It's tricky. He's a damned good pilot, sir."

"Idiot." Avila tore his web away and stalked around the bridge. He glared at Jes. Jes stopped bouncing in the seat and stopped grinning.

"Don't look so happy, brat. Pilot, what's your estimate of *Folly*'s time to grab?"

"Two, two and a half, sir. She's pushing it."

"And ours?"

"Three. Two and a half if we open up."

Avila stared at Jes, then smiled suddenly and returned to his seat. "Don't bother. Hetch'll get to Aerie ahead of us and tell them we have the kid. They're more likely to believe him than us." Avila stretched and put his hands behind his head. "Easy as sin," he said confidently. "The kid'll do it all for us."

Jes sat back, his stomach cold. Avila was right; Avila was absolutely right. There had to be something he could do. His fingers touched the lock of the safety webbing.

If only Hetch had blown NewHome grab, there would be only one ship to worry about. But all the fleet was in tau, and Hetch's ship plunged toward Aerie. Racing.

Jes caught his breath. Racing. If only he could get to the lifeships.

The Tri-Captain leaped to her feet. Her right arm caught the guard squarely on the chin and laid him out cold on the deck, but before he hit it she had turned with awesome speed to the control panel. One flick of her hand sent the pilot slumping in his seat, and before the general could turn around she had him by the throat, turned him in front of her to face the milling guards, and pointed a blaster at his middle.

"One move and he gets it," she said. "Take us to the lifeships."

Shit, Jes thought. It just doesn't work that way. I'm a twelve-year-old kid from a backwash planet and I'm in trouble and I've got to get myself out. Racing. He fideted in his seat, then stopped and looked at the back of Avila's head.

"General," he said, whining.

"What?" Avila didn't turn around.

"I've got to go."

"Go where? Oh. You, take him to the head. And keep an eye on him, hear?"

"Sir."

Jes made a show of unlocking his webbing and followed the soldier out of the bridge.

"Can't you walk faster?"

"My leg hurts." The drop pole was just ahead. Jes looked down the corridor, praying for something to distract the soldier.

"Sir? What's that?"

"What?"

"Over there—the red light. It's flashing."

The soldier glanced behind him. Jes wrenched his arm free and leaped for the drop pole. The soldier shouted.

The drop end jolted him. He glanced up the shaft, then ran along the catwalk. The engine room resembled *Folly*'s, as did the control platform. His breath sobbed through his teeth as he ran through the maze of midget 'bots and up the final walk.

The bulkhead was blank, unbroken by doors. Footsteps pounded behind him. He slapped frantically along the wall, then spotted the red emergency symbol a few meters down. He rushed to it and palmed it, and the wall opened before him. Inside the bay lay the sleek ship, its hatch open and gleaming.

Jes slid into the control seat and pulled the webbing tight. The panel was slightly different from that of the ship on *Folly*, but he easily found the four red spots. He pushed them in sequence, holding his breath, and when the lifer's hatch clanged shut and the main bay opened, he was torn between elation and terror. The lifer dropped from *Grafit One*'s belly, drifted, then its thrusters kicked on. Jes was pushed back in the seat. He struggled forward and ran through the screen modes until tau space opened before him, smeared with shattered stars. The dim flicker of the *Folly* rode the screen ahead.

"Who's in there?" the speaker roared. "Identify or we'll open fire!"

Jes' diaphragm contracted. He tore the web loose,

reached up, and stabbed the emergency switch. The acceleration slammed him into his seat.

"What happens in tau space," Simit's voice said, "is that the entire times of the universe converge in one place, simultaneously. Each and every millimeter of tau holds each and every piece of matter that has ever existed in that location. Do you understand? Everything from all times all at once. Think of it as a mountain, or a stone wall, except that it's much denser, of course. Now, then, how do you think a ship can move through tau, remembering that two solid objects can not occupy the same space at the same time? Does anyone know? Well, it's very simple, really. The ship simply picks times in tau when a particular space was unoccupied and travels through those times. So, if the ship is coming to a place where there's a planet, say, it simply jumps to a time when that planet wasn't in that space. The computers do it, of course."

Jes had thought about that until it gave him a headache, and he still didn't understand it. But he knew now what it looked like. The screen flickered, showing the lifer about to crash into a sun, a moon, a meteor storm, another ship, each of which flickered by him so fast he could barely grasp one catastrophe before another loomed ahead. He closed his eyes, sick, and punched the screen controls. When he looked again, a display grid lay before him. The *Folly*'s bright red dot ran before, his own location seemed to be a blue circle, and behind were the five blue lines of the NewHome fleet. The blue line closest to him pulled away from the others.

"Kid, this is Avila." Jes glanced at the speaker and pressed his lips together. "Listen, I'm sure you're having a wonderful time out there, but it's a lot more dangerous than you think. We're coming up to you. I want you to slow down and let us reel you in, all right? Do it now and you won't get into trouble."

Jes opened his mouth, then thought better of the insult and remained silent. He felt as though large hands were pushing his body into the seat, deeper and deeper, and he wondered whether he would pop through the cushions and metal and out the other side. The speed indicator wobbled higher on the face of the dial.

"Kid, I'm giving you one more chance. Cut speed now, or we'll open fire."

"Jes? Are you in there? Jessie, answer me."

Jes dragged his hand toward the comswitch on the seat's armrest. He dropped his hand, and the switch dug into his palm.

"Mommy? I'm all right. Mish. I got away."

"Hetch, have you got all the suckin' Kennerins in that tub of yours? Cut speed, you bastard, or I'll . . . "

"Won't work, big man," Hetch's voice said.

Jes stared at the speaker, bewildered.

"Jes," Mish said, "speak kasiri."

"I got away. They caught me. Tham told me how to make the lifer go faster."

"Good, Jes, very good. Hold in."

"Hetch, you slow or I'll blast the kid."

"It won't work in tau, Avila. Think about times. Now, shut up."

"All right, Jessie," Mish said, "listen carefully. I want you to get out of the seat and find the lifesuit. Can you get into it? Do you know how?"

"I watched them. On the other ship."

"Good. Get into the suit and wait by the emergency hatch at the front of the lifer. Can you see it?"

"Yes. But—"

"Listen! We're going to slow a bit when we get to the grab. When you hear Hetch yell, you jettison. You'll be pushed forward into the grab, and you should come out in our wake, before the grab clears. Hetch will have a net spread for you. Do you understand?"

"I can't . . . move."

"I know, Jessie. Try. You've got one and a half. That's plenty of time."

Jes glanced at the grid. *Grafit One* was closing, but still far behind him, while *Folly* seemed closer. He pulled himself from the chair, hand over hand, and fell to the floor. He fought against throwing up, terrified that if he did the heavy vomit would stick in his throat and suffocate him.

It seemed to take forever. He had to pull himself up the wall to release the suit, then fell beside it and worked it over his legs and torso. The acceleration pull increased. He seamed the front of the suit crooked and had to do it again. He'd forgotten the helmet, which hung high on the wall.

A siren at the panel began to wail. Jes pulled himself up the wall and looked at the panel. The speed indicator was pinned in the red. He slid down the wall with the helmet

83

in his arms. It took almost all of his strength to fit it over his head, and when the self-seals clicked shut he didn't have the energy to feel relief. He crawled to the forward emergency hatch. As he passed the console, he saw *Grafit One*'s blue line far too close, and the *Folly* about to hit the grab. He put his hand over the hatch's release plate. The speaker in his helmet crackled and hummed.

"Now!" Hetch's voice screamed in the helmet. Jes pushed against the release bar and was flung from the lifer. He cartwheeled through the density of tau, suddenly light and free. The still-shimmering bands of the coils closed around him, and in another second the shattered stars disappeared and he fell through an infinity of black.

"Mish!" he screamed.

"It's all right! You made it! It's all right!"

He saw the tail of the *Folly* slide by him rapidly, and Eagle danced crazily past his faceplate. The stars seemed to whirl. A huge, tightly woven net spread suddenly around him, tangling him. Then the sky bloomed with light and his suit was shaken and battered. His head knocked against the helmet, and he screamed again.

The suit steadied. A figure clambered down the net toward him, upside down, right side up, sideways, like a giant space-going spider. The figure reached him and took hold of his sleeve. Through the helmet's visor, he saw a strange woman grinning at him.

"Hi, spacer," she said. "I'm Merkit. Reel us in, Hetch."

Jes turned to look at the grab. The light had fled, and he saw nothing but an expanse of black sky and the sweeping stars of The Spiral. The grab was gone.

"I was hoping the grab would just jam," Hetch said. "Trying to deal with two objects and two different times at the same time. But the lifer's reactors must have blown when it reached the grab and took the entire thing out with it."

Jes nodded sleepily. Mish tightened her arms around him, and he snuggled closer.

Merkit appeared and lifted a body from the bridge deck. "Last one," she said, then grinned at Jes with black teeth and dragged the body out. Jes closed his eyes. Mish had told him how she had been knocked cold when the lurch threw her into the storage hold, how she had come to and sneaked out to find a guard over Bakar. She had killed the guard, then she and Bakar had freed Hetch and the two spacejocks. Bakar and Tham had harnessed together in the control room, pushing *Folly* as fast as she would go through tau. *Folly* had come through NewHome grab so fast she'd lost a beam on her tail, and come through Aerie grab so quickly she'd lost a piece of her nose. But Jes' lifer had snapped in half as the grab closed after *Folly*. And probably taken *Grafit One* with it.

"Tham told me about racing the lifer," Jess muttered. "It worked, didn't it?"

"Shouldn't have," Hetch said. "That should teach you to leave space alone."

Jes opened his eyes and looked at the captain.

"I'm still going to be a spacer," he said and yawned. "Besides, I bet I beat your time."

Hetch sighed, and Mish laughed. "You'd better take us on home, Captain," she said.

Jes looked at the screen. Aerie turned blue and white and brown and green against the void. He closed his eyes. He'd be seeing his home again this way, he thought. He'd come through grab more times than he could count. He put his head on Mish's shoulder and fell asleep.

JASON

‚

||||||||||⊂‖||||||||||⊂‖||||||||||⊂‖||||||||||⊂‖||||||||||⊂‖||||||||||⊂‖||||||||||⊂‖||||||||||⊂‖||||||||⊂

WE WERE HIDING IN THE BRANCHES, SILENT
as fear itself, when Hetch called. At first it was hard to
make out what he was saying—something about ships and
grabs and disaster. I shouted into the mike, he shouted out
of the speaker, the Aerites heard me and began shouting
themselves, and it was a good ten minutes before I realized that we were safe and Hetch was bringing the shuttle
in. I could hear the news spreading through the trees in
concentric rings of silence. We had been so prepared for
doom, so wordlessly convinced that we were to die,
that it took a moment to understand our deliverance, to
comprehend safety again. Then the cheering began, and
weapons rained from the trees. Pitchforks, brooms, hand-
made spears, clubs, slingshots, all the paltry defenses of
Aerie—it was a wonder we didn't kill ourselves. People
leaped from the branches and ran toward the pad, and
I ran with them, as loud and silly as everyone else. I
passed Dr. Hoku, who almost capered, all eyes and grin.
Laur stumped along beside her, announcing loudly that
she'd never doubted the outcome, that Kennerins always
took care of their own. If anyone took offense, it wasn't
mentioned. The doctor grabbed my arm.

"Another yearly celebration," she shouted over the
noise. I looked at her without comprehension, and she
jabbed my chest with one long, brown finger. "This nonsense, another reason to get drunk. Does us good,
Kennerin. We need ritual and ceremony. You run an interesting planet."

I picked her up, kissed her, put her down, and ran.

The shuttle angled in over To'an Betes, and before it
had completely settled the Aerites mobbed it, cheering

and flinging things. The hatch creaked open and our saviors appeared, and I thought the people would rupture their throats with yelling.

Hetch, Merkit, Tham. Bakar carrying Jes. Injured? My throat tightened, and I pushed forward, but Bakar shook my son and put him down. Jes rubbed his eyes, then saw the people and looked at first surprised, then sheepish. Mish came from the shuttle and put her hand on his shoulder, and my throat tightened again. I knew that set of face, that absence of expression, and I batted people out of my way, trying to reach her. Jes said something to her and she smiled, a flat, terrible rictus. Jes laughed, and the people surged up the ramp and down again, carrying my wife, my son, my friend, and the crew on their shoulders. Mish's lips were pale around her grimace. I saw Hoku standing on the packed dirt barrier, looking at Mish. The doctor began shouting, but couldn't be heard. I bulled my way through the crowd, ignoring the shouts.

"Hey!" I yelled. "Gimme my wife!"

The people laughed. Mish stretched her arms toward me and fell, and I caught her to my chest. She grabbed me and hid her face against my neck. Her body shook. I carried her from the pad amid cheers and ribaldry, then ran through the meadow to the nearest shelter, the trees along the stream. Water splashed into my boots, and when I found a small clearing I sat, still holding her. She held tight, shaking. She wasn't crying.

"Mish, are you hurt? Are you all right?"

Her nod was a jab of chin against my neck. After a time the shaking lessened. She pulled away and put her hands to her face, breathing deeply, unevenly. I waited.

"Jes and I were in the hold, and we had to get out. I pushed two guards into the hold and I emptied it." Her voice was without inflection, and she didn't look at me. "Jes and I ran away, and I fell into a storage bin and hit my head. When I came to, Jessie was gone. I looked all over for him. Bakar was in the crew room. There was a guard. The guard told Bakar that they'd taken Jessie to another ship. He didn't see me."

She stopped. I put my hand on her arm, but she twitched away from me, and I put my hand back in my lap.

"I picked up a pipe and I killed the guard. I hit him on the back of his neck and I killed him. Bakar and I went to the bridge and we killed Hetch's guard. Bakar strangled her. Hetch and Bakar went to the control room and killed the other two guards. I don't know how. I think Merkit killed one of them. Then we went through the grab, then Jessie came back."

She stopped again. She still hadn't looked up at me. I didn't speak.

"Before we came down, we opened the hold to see what was there. If we could bring it down. Some of it. I pushed two soldiers into the hold. I emptied it." She began shaking again. "There were, there, pieces of them, Jason? They were alive when I, but, pieces of uniforms. Gray stuff. Red. All over. I killed them, Jase. And the one in the crew room." She looked up at me now, her face pale and still.

"I killed three people," she said. "Three. And I'd do it again."

And there she sat, as though awaiting judgment. I stared back at her. I knew how Mish felt about killing. She had once come before the Family Council on Terra, come to argue for the life of one of her coworkers. The hearing had been held, the man judged guilty, the sentence passed, yet she walked into the Council room small and intense and furious, and delivered herself of a lecture on morality such as I doubted the Council had heard in years. To kill, she said, is to commit an act of murder. To kill in self-defense is still to commit an act of murder. To kill as punishment is to commit an act of murder. To murder is a foul and evil thing. Did the Council wish themselves to be seen as a pack of murderers? As no better than those whom they judged? If the punishment for death was death, they would all, by their own laws, have to commit suicide the moment the sentence was executed on the prisoner, and she doubted whether they had the courage or conscience to do so. Therefore, their only rational course of action was to commute the sentence. Tiny, logical, furious Mish. They paid no more attention to her than they had paid to similar arguments over the years. We confirmed the sentence. And I descended from the dais to argue further with this irritating gnat of a woman, and fell in love.

To kill is to murder. No exceptions. No excuses.

That she had done it, and said that she would do it again if necessary, did not mean that she stood ready to disregard her own moral imperatives. She had killed in the defense of her son and of herself; self-defense is no excuse. It could be argued that her killing of the soldiers had saved our entire planet, but the murder nevertheless remained.

I had killed people myself, during that first raid on NewHome. No more clean then she, yet she looked to me for judgment, and I could find no way around the morals to the comfort, no logical argument to clear her mind.

She sat and looked at me as though prepared to spend the remainder of her life in that small clearing. Giving me her guilt. And she had changed again, from the warm, strong woman of our solitary years, from the cool, distant woman she had become since Meya's birth. She had been lost to me, and now that it seemed I could reach through, touch her, bring back the warmth and strength, I sat silent, terrified of saying the wrong thing and losing her forever.

We need ritual and ceremony, Hoku had said to me. *Does us good.*

I rose and waited while Mish struggled to her feet, then turned and walked back to the stream, hearing the brush crackle and snap as she stumbled behind me. A few meters downstream the water made a deep pool, surrounded by stones and forest. I waited until she stood beside me, then nodded toward the water. Without hesitation, she walked right off the bank and disappeared.

She didn't come up again. Her fall had stirred the murk, and I squinted, unable to see her. The water settled again. She didn't come up.

I took three running steps and dove in. Mish sat cross-legged on the soft floor of the pool. Bubbles were caught in her fine, dark hair, and one hand grasped the root of a tree. She looked at me and opened her mouth, loosing a stream of bubbles, and I grabbed her and hauled her out of the pool.

She was shaking again, but this time with cold. I held her in my lap, rubbed her arms and shoulders, and babbled incoherently. She put her finger on my lips.

"You came for me."

"Of course I did! Sweet Mother, did you think I wanted you to drown?"

"I didn't know," she said simply.

I put my face in her wet hair, held her tightly, and cursed her wearily and at length. Then I cursed myself. Mish put her arms around my neck and cried. A little bit for lost innocence, perhaps; a little bit for finding in herself the same sins and darkness as the rest of us. Whatever. After a while she fell asleep. Her face looked older.

When I picked her up to carry her home, she woke and insisted on walking. And when we walked through Haven, she smiled at the people, and nodded, and held my hand.

I didn't know the Mish I brought home that afternoon. Knew very little, save that she had changed again, and the change was, this time, to warmth.

A delegation of bloody-minded Aerites went up to the *Folly* and cleaned imploded soldiers off the crates. Much of the red stuff, they reported, was the remains of a crate of berries, but Mish still avoided the goods they brought to Haven.

Gaudy fabrics, flashing jewels, tins of exotic foods, crates of artwork, enough small weaponry to outfit a regiment. The weapons, by common consent, were placed under lock and key in Haven's new Town Hall. Fabrics and food were apportioned evenly, and the jewelry, after some bickering, went to Hetch to pay off some of what we owed him. He needn't have given us the goods at all; Mish and Ved and Hoku and I all told him so, but he shrugged and blustered and ignored us. And bargained the price of the jewelry to a minimum.

Hetch and his crew were effectively stranded on Aerie until the grab was fixed, but it seemed a small problem. The Aerites took Hetch out regularly and got him roaring drunk, and he would stumble back to the Tor five days later, violently hung over and kilograms fatter. The crew we saw even less frequently. They were passed from family to family in Haven, from board to bed and back again, and by late winter Haven seemed populated exclusively by women walking around belly forward. Hoku grumbled and yelled and trained a midwife. But the spring crop turned up only three children with Tham's fair hair, and two with Bakar's disposition. Hoku lectured on the biological reaction to warfare and advised against diapers. Merkit found the kasirene after the second week on planet, and spent most of her time in the native village. I'd see her tall, broad shape stalking out of Haven with a case of beer on her shoulder, and if she saw me she'd give me her black-toothed grin and wave as she swung on down the valley.

Mish would reach a hand to touch me as I walked by her, or spend afternoons in the barn with me as I tinkered in the shop. Coming toward me rather than away from me; when we argued about the farm or plantation or village, the intensity remained, but the bitterness was gone. I dreamed about another child, but remembered Meya and did not want to ask. Rough and careful edges, avoidances and small silences, but the warmth was there. Something to grow. I can't remember that I was always happy, but I can remember that I was content. It seemed enough.

Meya learned to read that winter, and Jes put his heroism aside and went back to school. Hoku put Hetch on a diet, and to my amazement he kept to it. He claimed to be more terrified of Hoku than of any three NewHome warships, and I believed him. Hart spent most of his time in Haven, intent on his own business. And Quilla worked and retreated more deeply into silence, insisting that she preferred to be alone. She was seventeen that winter, old enough to know her own mind. I let her be. Tham married one of his big-bellied ladies and two weeks after Year'sEnd went from house to house with his new daughter bundled in his arms. Hoku chased him home before he was too drunk to walk. Mish told me about Tabor. Nothing changed.

The winter was a mild one, one of those seasons for which every farmer prays—a minimum of frost, a sufficiency of rain, a number of days of sunlight breaking through the usual gray overcast. We had gathered enough seed from the first sickly seedlings to plant out about four or five thousand Zimania bushes, in neat, contoured rows, well drained, and in full sunlight, when the sunlight came. Looking at the plantation from the Tor, I could see the oldest plants already at their full growth, and the two-year plants next to them. At the edge of the field were the small green bundles of the one-year seedlings, and beyond them the empty fields stretched, cleared, and waiting for the newest seedlings to be planted in the spring. We would gather our first harvest during the year —a small harvest, more a token of what would come later than any real return for our efforts and time. Hetch estimated that we would produce barely enough to meet our first repayment to him, but he offered extended credit, and in gratitude for his help and optimism, we accepted. How sweet the future looked, that winter after the New-

Home scare. I felt my land seeding and fruiting, felt my people moving and growing, becoming ever more firmly Aerites, slowly erasing the scars of their past. The air smelled clean and fresh and hopeful, and I sang as I worked my world.

Ten months Aerie after what Hoku termed "The Great Salvation," the Federation repair crew appeared and cluttered up the sky with hunks of orbiting machinery. They brought with them a Galactic Federation Security Inspector, Division of Transport, Department of Cohen/Albrecht Effect Devices, Malfunction Investigation Desk. We all trooped down to the pad to meet her. She was a brisk, sharp-faced woman in a uniform, and she marched down the ramp and glared at Captain Hetch.

"You, I take it, are the owner and captain of that orbiting scrap heap up there," she said.

"Bet your ass," Hetch said genially. "Bet I can beat your time, too."

Jes grinned.

The Inspector clamped her lips as tight as a cold winter and marched up the hill to the Tor.

She had a questionnaire fourteen sheets long. She sat behind the dining table, shooting questions at Mish and myself as Aerie's owners, Hetch as what she termed the "Transport Factor," and Ved Hirem and Hoku as Haven's community leaders. She did the most effective squash of Ved's long-windedness I had ever seen. When she'd filled all fourteen sheets with information on Aerie and its population, location, planet pattern, native-to-human ratio, climate, crops, imports, and exports, and on *Folly,* its captain, crew, and most minute specifications, she pulled out another questionnaire and set to it with grim satisfaction. She interrogated Mish, Jes, Hetch, and the crew about the grab's destruction. Merkit offered her a beer. Laur insisted on a dinner break. The Inspector maintained a disapproving silence throughout the meal, then set to her questions again. No one left. Meya fell asleep in my arms.

Finally the inspector snapped her case and rose.

"The grab repairs will come to two hundred forty-nine thousand, seven hundred eighty-two fremarks," she said. "You'll be tariffed accordingly."

In the ensuing chaos, Hetch leaped to his feet and pounded on the table. His face turned purple.

"What in suckin' hell do you mean, tariffed accordingly? Who do you—"

"Not you, Captain—Aerie."

"That's what I meant! We didn't break your suckin' grab; it was a NewHome ship. Tariff NewHome, damn it!"

"The Federation is not a charity, Captain. If we let people destroy Federation property without penalty, we'd be bankrupt."

"That's not the point!" Hetch roared. "Penalties assessed against the damaging party or the party owning the damaging property: section four-oh-nine, sub-fifteen, sub-nineteen. Regulations! Tariff NewHome!"

People muttered agreement. Mish stood, fists clenched, ready to leap to the attack the moment Hetch faltered. I took her hand, and she shook me away.

The Inspector glared at Hetch and banged on the table herself. "We can't!" she said, shouting to be heard. "New-Home's primary went nova three weeks ago standard. There's nothing there to tariff."

The room silenced instantly, and heads turned slowly toward the window.

The Inspector sniffed. "You won't see it for four years standard. Even backwashers ought to know that."

Hoku touched her arm. "We're most of us from New-Home," she said. "You'd better leave."

The people moved aside to let her pass. In a few minutes the lights of her shuttle winked through the sky and disappeared, and one by one the people left the house and went down the hill to Haven. Mish and I and the children stood in the yard and watched their quiet, terrible progress.

"They're really Aerites now," Mish said. She put her head against my chest. I watched the lights of Haven go out, one by one, and bent to rest my cheek against her hair.

Two months after the tariff was imposed, Simit appeared at the Tor for his annual State of the School address, and this time his normal praises of progress and requests for more funds included an interesting piece of information.

"Hart has been doing quite well," Simit told us conversationally after the main business of the school had been discussed. "He shows an aptitude for the sciences, which I find quite pleasing. Due to Gren's influence, no doubt."

Mish and I looked at each other with surprise.

"Gren?" Mish said.

"Kalor Gren, who lives next door to the school. Surely you know about that," the teacher said. "He and Hart have been quite close friends for, oh, quite a while now. Since the beginning, almost."

"Are you sure?" I said, astounded. "Hart doesn't like any of . . . anyone outside this family. He's a very withdrawn boy. If he were to make friends with anyone, it wouldn't be Gren."

Simit managed to look both distressed and disapproving, and his scar darkened. "I had no idea that you would disapprove, or I would have mentioned it earlier. I had assumed that you would, of course, know what Hart was doing."

I suspect that Mish and I both looked distinctly uncomfortable.

"We've been very busy," I said. "All this tariff stuff, you know. Paperwork."

Mish took the initiative, covering her uneasiness with an air of earnest inquiry. "How does Gren tie in with the sciences?" she said, leaning forward.

"He was a biochemist on NewHome," Simit said, "quite a famous one, at least on planet. He studied with Harmon, you know, on Kroeber." Simit laughed quickly, his disapproval fading. "At least Gren didn't pick up any of Harmon's habits. The combination would have been impossible."

"Habits?" I said, eager to keep Simit off the subject of our lack of knowledge of our son's ways.

"Oh, didn't you know about that? Harmon spent a year teaching on NewHome, and I had the opportunity to study under him. Brilliant man, but somewhat eccentric. Kept his clothing in his carry-case, and every time he needed some papers, he'd open the case and out would pop socks and shirts and old crusts of bread. Kept dyeing his beard, too. A regular demon when it came to research, I'm told."

"Fascinating," I murmured. "More tea?"

Simit shook his head. "Gren did research, too, back home." Simit paused, then said carefully, "Back on New-Home. In any event, he's taken quite a liking to Hart. I believe they spend every afternoon together. I had assumed that Hart had your approval." He cleared his throat. "If you would like me to see that Hart remains busy after school . . ."

"No, that's all right," Mish said. "Everything's fine."

Simit smiled his relief, and I felt briefly sorry for the man. He obviously felt that as a, teacher his duty was to scold us for our inattention, but as a citizen of Aerie he had to look up to us as the owners of the planet—an uneasy dilemma. We chatted briefly about this and that, and as I walked him to the door he said suddenly, "Oh, Gren was working in genetic chemistry, that was it." Simit sighed. "No way to use that here, I suspect. Oh, well, in time. In time."

When I came back to the living room, Mish was staring into the fire, her hands folded in her lap. I stood behind her and put my hand on her shoulder, and she bent her head to rest her cheek against my arm.

"You didn't know?" she said.

"Not a thing. And you?"

She shook her head. "Should we do anything about it?"

I came around beside her and sat on the footstool. "I don't know. It's probably harmless. I'm most ashamed of not knowing about it, of not paying sufficient attention."

"Neither of us did. We're all so damned busy, Jase. We end up paying attention only when something goes wrong. I don't like that."

"I don't like it, either. I guess I've just assumed that if the children were doing something new, they'd let us know."

"Jes does. Quilla does. But Hart's a quiet one; he never seems to say much at all."

"Thinks a lot, though. Watches things."

Mish nodded, frowning.

"Mim doesn't like him," I said.

She looked at me. "You noticed that?"

"I'm not totally insensitive," I said defensively. Mish smiled. "Anyway, it's pretty obvious."

"Yes, and he doesn't like her, either."

Mish put her elbow on the arm of the chair and propped her chin on her fist. She looked weary.

"I suppose we should talk to Hart," I said.

She nodded. "At least find out what's going on. Make sure he's safe."

"He's probably safe enough." I went upstairs to Hart's

95

room. He was lying on his bed reading, and he came readily enough when I asked him to.

Hart had turned ten that year. He would not, I thought, be as tall as either Jes or myself, but he was a slender, well-built child, perhaps the most handsome of us all— save for a hint of sullenness about the mouth, a faint gleam of disbelief in the eyes. Jes at his age had been a being of endless, enthusiastic curiosity, as open as a clean window; a bright child. But Hart, although perhaps equally curious about the world around him, was dark, despite the gleaming of his blue eyes, the shine of his skin. Now that I looked at him closely, I found it extraordinary that he should be my son. But, then, I found all my children extraordinary, when I looked at them.

"Hi," Mish said as we came into the room. Hart still held his bookreel, his finger on the switch to mark his place. "What are you reading?"

He showed us the title—some elementary biophysics test. I was surprised. I didn't know he had advanced that far.

"Did Gren suggest it?"

Hart glanced at me and nodded his head warily. "I already know most of this stuff," he said. "This is just brush-up work."

"Oh." I looked over his head at Mish, at a loss for what to say next.

"He's rather unpleasant, isn't he?" she said.

Hart frowned. "He used to be, at first. But he's become a lot better recently." My son smiled, a captivating grin which, vaguely, disturbed me. "He's quite nice, now. And I do learn a lot from him."

"I wish you'd told us about seeing him," I said. "We like to know what you're doing."

"I didn't think it was that important," Hart said casually. "You're always so busy; I didn't want to disturb you. And it's better than hanging around the schoolyard playing dumb games with the other kids. I like learning, and sometimes the school is boring. It's too slow." He turned earnestly to Mish. "And it's perfectly safe. We don't do anything dangerous, just cutting up plants and dissecting dead animals. It's not like we're mixing up explosives. I like it. I'd like to be a biochemist, eventually."

He couldn't, I thought, have rehearsed that. He said it easily, extemporaneously, with exactly the proper amount of sincerity. But it was so damned smooth!

"I don't want to stop the studies," Hart said. "It's the most interesting thing I'm doing."

"Well, fine," Mish said helplessly. "Only, please let us know what you're up to, okay? We don't want to pry, but we do think we should know where you are. In case something happens, and we have to find you. In case of an emergency," she finished lamely.

"I understand. Of course I'll let you know. For now, I'm at Gren's during the afternoons. If we're out collecting, I'll leave a note. Will that be all right?"

I nodded and Hart gave us another brilliant smile and went back upstairs. I sat, trying to assess the sarcasm-quotient of his last statement.

"Are you sure he's only ten?" I said to Mish.

She nodded without smiling. "It probably is a good thing for him. Maybe a good thing for Gren, too. He's been less obviously nasty lately. That may be because of Hart." She knelt and banked the fire. "I suppose we just leave him be."

"I don't see what else we can do. There seems to be nothing to object to."

She shrugged, and we went upstairs to bed. Mish fell asleep quickly, but I spent a good deal of the night staring out the window at the halaea, and trying to banish the image of my son carefully and diligently rehearsing speeches for our benefit. Finally, exasperated, I told myself that even if he had, it was nothing to worry about. I curled my body around Mish, put my face near her scented hair, and fell asleep.

Part Three

1223

New Time

MAKING LIFE

"Men have died from time to time and worms have eaten them, but not for love."
—William Shakespeare, 1598

"DON'T GO YET."

Quilla turned and Tabor put his arm over her waist. The room was still dark; she couldn't tell whether his eyes were open or closed.

"It's almost dawn," she replied.

"Not yet. Another half hour."

"I'll be late." The cool autumn night had left the room chilly, and she pulled the blankets up to her chin. Tabor's body felt warm and comfortable beside her. She put her face against his shoulder and closed her eyes.

They had been awake until early morning, loving, resting, loving again; now desire was a small, sleepy warmth between them, easily satisfied by their lazy embrace. She thought fuzzily about the long day ahead: the barn to be cleaned in the morning, the town meeting in the afternoon, tonight's Harvest and Rescue celebration, Mish and Jason due back. She burrowed deeper under the covers. Tabor's cheek rested on her forehead. His breath warmed her ear.

"I'm glad you ran away from home," he whispered. "I wish I'd thought it up myself."

"That was three years ago," she said. "Don't talk about it."

"Why not?" He pulled away from her. The darkness had lifted slightly; she could make out the shape of his head above hers. She touched his lips with her fingertip.

"It's not important," she said, and pulled his head down against hers again. "But I'm glad that you're glad."

He kissed her shoulder. She wondered if he was going to talk about it again. The subject embarrassed her, reminded her of how young she had been, how young she still was. Yet Aerie had seemed such a dreary world three years ago, a world of people working and growing and loving and changing, while tall, gawky Quilla Kennerin peered in and watched, envious. Her childhood ended when the refugees arrived, and she helped on the farm while her parents took care of Aerie's new people. When Meya was born, Quilla took over her care and raising. The start of the plantations had pulled Jason and Mish completely away from the farm, and Quilla at seventeen held responsibility for the vegetables and fruits which kept the family alive, the livestock and their care, and the twenty to thirty kasirene who worked the farm and tended the animals. She didn't attend school with the refugee children. She knew enough already, her parents had said, and they needed her at home; there wasn't the time for school. She missed the outings and trips and parties; something always needed doing, and she was always there to do it. Hart kept to himself, moving deeper into his studies and further from the family. Jes stowed away to adventure and heroism aboard Hetch's starship. Meya ran free, from family to Aerites to kasirene, a quick, lovely doll of a child, reaping love, while her gaunt, ugly sister watched and wondered if there would be any love left over for her. There never seemed to be.

Tabor fell asleep again. She moved away slowly, but his arm tightened around her waist. She turned so that her back nestled against his stomach. He mumbled and quieted.

She had been promised Kroeber. It had seemed a normal part of the universe, that she would grow, that the sun would rise, that the crops would ripen, that on her eighteenth birthday she would be sent through grabs and tau to the university. The promise was not kept. The family lacked the money. There wasn't time. Had the refugees not come, she would have gone, of course, naturally, because children grow into women and men who need men and women, and on Aerie there had been only family and the tall, alien kasirene. But now Aerie was populated—now there was an entire village of other people barely a kilometer away. No reason for Quilla to leave. And there was work to do.

The memory of her lost adventure still made her angry. She had raged and stormed with un-Quilla-like ferocity, locked herself in her room for days. When Aerites and kasirene were busy with the harvest, she had packed provisions, taken the orbital map of To'an Cault, and marched southward. No one followed her, or so it seemed. She walked the broad back of the island, amid the silence of birds and grasslands, and the silence settled into her and calmed her rage. The anger and regret passed, as did the awkwardness. She moved through a realm without words, through a different time, and arrived at Cault Tereth, the southern mountains, entirely at peace.

Tabor waited for her at the mountain pass, took her to his valley, his home, and his bed, and destroyed her serenity by telling her that her freedom had been carefully observed and constantly monitored, that the kasirene had watched and reported to the Kennerins in the north and to Tabor in the south. Her new-found confidence fled, leaving her caught between the unhappy adolescent of Tor Kennerin and the adult of the broad, empty plains. The calm silence was harder to reach now, the words overwhelmed the quiet, and in its place she put the closest thing to hand. Tabor. Love.

But love, it seemed, was never quite enough. She went south to the Cault, or Tabor came north to the Tor; when he wasn't with her she missed him fiercely, and when they were together she felt an emptiness, a distance which she tried to fill with words and caresses. The emptiness remained.

This time, when she moved away he let her go. She swung her legs from warmth to the chill air and dressed quickly. Already she heard the kasirene gathering in the barn at the foot of the hill, and pale light filtered through the curtains. She sat on the edge of the bed to lace her boots, and Tabor turned and grabbed her arm.

"Quilla, marry me."

She looked at him, surprised.

"I mean it. This doesn't make sense. I see you for a month in the winter and a month in the summer, and it's not enough. Quilla? We live well together, our bodies like each other."

"Did you come all the way from the Cault to ask me that?" She smiled nervously. Her skin suddenly felt damp.

"You weren't happy to see me?"

"Of course I was." She stared down at her boots.

"Your parents would be pleased if we married. I don't like being apart from you. We could live here if you want. I don't have to live in the south."

"You sound like a court paper."

"I've thought it out." He ran his finger down the line of her arm. "I do love you."

"Quilla!" Laur shouted from the kitchen. Quilla jumped away from the bed, hitting her shin on the chair.

"Later," she said to Tabor. "I'm late."

She almost ran from the room. Her shin hurt.

Meya made a puddle of her milk and ran her finger through it, tracing the outlines of ungainly birds with four wings, and pregnant airflowers. Quilla stared at the outlines somberly.

"Looks good," she said. "Maybe a little more lift to this wing here."

"Quilla, you stop that," Laur said. The old woman waved her spoon threateningly. "Meya's not supposed to do that, you just stop encouraging her, hear? Jes, finish your breakfast."

"Yes'm, Captain," Jes said. Laur frowned and turned back to the stove. Jes winked at Quilla, and she grinned.

"What are you doing today?" she said.

"Usual. I promised Dene that I'd help her with the new comsystem. Ved keeps complaining that it buzzes, but we're damned if we can figure out why." He put the last bite of sausage into his mouth. "Laur, can I have some more of this? Thanks."

"Close your mouth when you chew," Laur said.

"Then I thought I'd practice a bit. Now that harvest's over, and Tabor's here, maybe we can play some duets. Is he up yet?"

"Soon, I'd guess. Meya, finish your breakfast, okay?" She filled her teacup and Jes'. "Did Ved ask you to give a speech tonight?"

"Yeah, since Hetch won't be here. Ved's the only person I know who gives a speech to ask you to give one. I don't know what to say."

"Simple." Quilla waved her teacup grandly. "You tell them how humble and grateful you feel at being the object of their adulation, and it wasn't anything, really, but it sure took a lot of guts and smarts, anyway, all for the greater glory of Aerie, now how about some dancing and would someone please bring you a beer."

Jes laughed, then shook his head. "I did the equations a couple of months ago, Quil, and they scared hell out of me. I was this close to being cindered." He finished his second helping of sausages. "I wish Hetch was here."

"Another three days, Jes. Are you coming to the meeting this afternoon? Meya, finish your milk."

"Only if Dene needs me there. I thought I'd head on down to the Glents' house and see the new baby. I haven't seen her yet. She's supposed to be pretty."

"So I hear. Meya, if you don't finish your milk and get going, you'll be late for school."

Jes leaned toward his young sister. "And then Simit will beat you. I know; I've been through it."

Meya snorted. "You're a damned liar, Jes Kennerin. Besides, you only want to see the new baby because Taine's watching it, and you've got lizards in your pants."

"Meya Kennerin!" Laur said. Meya gulped her milk and fled the kitchen while her brother and sister ducked their heads, grinning.

"It's your fault, talking that way around the child." Laur glared at them. "If your parents were here—"

"Jason and Mish talk exactly the same way," Jes said, but Quilla waved at him to be quiet.

"It's all right, Laur. I'm sorry. Sometimes I forget that she's around. We'll watch it, won't we, Jes?"

He winced as she kicked him under the table, and nodded.

"Sure, promise," he said. "Any sausages left?"

Quilla heard the uneven, three-tapping sound of Tabor descending the stairs, the click of his cane against the railing. She drank her tea quickly and stood.

"Late today," she said. She kissed Laur quickly on the forehead and touched Jes' shoulder as she passed. "Mish and Jason ought to be back by this afternoon. I'll be in town at the meeting. Send someone to tell me, all right?"

Laur shouted a grumpy agreement as Quilla walked rapidly down the hill toward the barn. The kasirene stood lounging in the sunny doorway, their equipment piled beside them. Someone had already taken the livestock to the pens, she could hear the lowing of the cloned cows competing with the morning chatter of the fourbirds. She knotted a cloth over her unruly hair as she walked, and Palen shouted a greeting in kasiri. Quilla shouted back, and walked into the welcoming maw of the barn.

Late morning sunlight fell into the barn through the high windows; the air in the loft was warm and close, heavy with the sweet smell of curing *Zimania* sap and the scent of fresh-mown hay. The pitchfork felt easy and

104

comfortable in her hands, and the hay swished and landed with a deep, satisfying whump on the barn floor below. Palen worked at the other side of the hay pile, manipulating her fork with an efficient swing which, Quilla suspected, it took four arms even to think about.

"Enough," someone called in kasiri. Quilla leaned on her fork and wiped her face with her sleeve, then reached for the jug Palen offered. The kaea was warm but refreshing. Quilla handed the jug back and looked over the edge of the loft. Below, kasirene workers pitched the hay over the newly cleaned floors.

"Leave more along the walls," Quilla called.

"Then give us more."

She dumped a load over the edge onto the kasir's head. He sputtered curses and Palen laughed. Quilla sat with her feet dangling over the drop, and Palen came around the stack and sat beside her.

"Tonight you celebrate the time the grab blew up," she said.

Quilla nodded and lay back in the hay. "That and the harvest. Big rocker. Food and speeches and beer and dancing. Are you coming?"

Palen executed the kasirene shrug, using her lower shoulders to move her upper set. "We always come. We stand and watch your new people, and they make polite noises and impolite thoughts. Then we go away. It grows monotonous."

Quilla grinned. "You're easily bored, Palen."

"One doesn't grow bored with dislike—uneasy, wary, distrustful, but not bored. We can't afford that."

"They won't hurt you."

Palen tucked her foot into her lap and inspected the sole. "Are you sure?"

"I don't know. They're as alien to me as to you."

"They're your people."

"For whatever that's worth." Quilla rolled on her side and touched Palen's foot. "Cut yourself?"

"No, stepped on something. I can't see it."

"Here, sit still." Quilla pulled the kasir's foot onto her lap, and Palen lay back in the hay and put some of her arms behind her head.

"Noontime, Quilla," one of the kasirene called.

"Fine. Break for an hour, then do the last two fields before dinner. Irrigation channels need clearing, and it's time to weed. I'll be out during the afternoon if I can make it."

The kasirene trooped out of the barn, and Quilla bent over Paen's foot. Dust motes floated through the shafts of sunlight.

"You're half distant," Palen said.

Quilla glanced at her. Palen's large violet eyes were closed; her slightly snouted face was smooth and untroubled.

"Yes." Quilla poked at Palen's foot again. There was something wedged between the first and second pads, and she picked at it with her fingernail.

"Do you want to walk again?"

"I don't know." Quilla pulled a small knife from her pocket and opened it. She laughed. "Remember that first walk back, when we tried to drown each other?"

"You have a funny sense of humor, albiana," Palen said grouchily. "Don't cut off the entire foot."

Palen had appeared two days into Quilla's journey back to Haven from the Cault, and Quilla had been sure that the tall, young kasir was sent to spy on her, to guide her back, to take care of her. She had deeply resented it, and Palen, who had been walking from her own troubles, resented Quilla's resentment. They journeyed together, hating each other's company, yet unable to part, arguing bitterly in kasiri over the slightest matters, engaging in a pitched battle in one of To'an Cault's many lakes, grudgingly lending each other assistance and refusing to give or accept thanks. When they reached Haven they swore the bloodfriendship. Palen claimed that Quilla was the only person she'd met with less sense than a fourbird. Quilla claimed that Palen's silence made more sense than her speech. When troubled, they walked together, covering the island with their restlessness. They'd not been seriously apart in three years.

"Do you want to walk?" Palen asked again.

"I don't know. Not yet." Quilla urged the tip of her knife under the stone. "Tabor wants to marry me."

"That's this albiana thing, you tie yourselves to each other?"

"You make it sound terrible. Here, I got the stone out."

Palen sat and looked at her foot. "Thank you. It is terrible. None of you makes any sense. Am I bleeding?"

"With feet like yours? Come on, I'm hungry."

106

Quilla took the pitchforks and put them in their bin, then swung down the rope ladders to the barn floor. Palen followed more slowly, using all of her hands to grab at the ropes, and muttering as she came. The night's chill had fled; the day was hot and still.

"Are you going to do it?" Palen said as they sat against the barn's side. The orderly rows of the farm stretched before them, backed by the dark, green-black of the *Zimania* orchards. Palen took their lunch from her pouch and handed some to Quilla.

"I don't know. People expect to get married, you know. My parents are."

"Doesn't answer the question."

"I can't answer now." Quilla leaned against the warm wood and closed her eyes. The world turned red beneath her lids. "I don't know. Maybe we should walk again . . . soon."

Palen shifted beside her, and they ate their meal in silence.

Simit closed school early so that he could attend the afternoon town meeting, and the streets of Haven teemed with children. In a corner of the marketplace, a miscellaneous group of humans and kasirene played a long, complicated game. Meya ran among them, shouting orders as a Commander of the Galactic Imperium. She ordered soldiers into battle positions and deployed her spies in strategic locations; plotted long campaigns against the Freestar Confederation; choreographed swift, bloody battles among the empty vegetable and fish stalls; and argued with her commanders in chief. She was about to launch a flying attack on an enemy stronghold when she saw her sister cross the far corner of the marketplace on her way to the Town Hall. Meya immediately grabbed her chest and fell dramatically to the street.

"I've been hit!" she yelled. "Carry on, troops! Remember that right is on our side!" She dropped her head against the rough pavement and spreadeagled her arms.

"No one shot at you! That's not fair!"

"Commanders aren't supposed to die until the big battle, not now!"

"You can't change the rules!"

"Sorry," Meya said, rising and brushing off the seat of her pants, "I'm dead. See you later."

She ran quickly through the stalls and up Market Street.

Quilla stood on the steps of the meeting hall, talking with Ved Hirem, Haven's new, only, and self-appointed judge. Meya frowned and hid in a doorway. Ved smelled funny and talked in long sentences. Jason said the smell was from an ointment that Ved used on his joints, and he talked that way because he was a lawyer and that's the way lawyers talked. He was Jason's friend. Meya wondered at her father's taste and kept away from the long-winded old man.

"But we have to codify the laws," Ved was saying. "The mainstay of any civilization is in its structure of legalistic and moral overviews of its society, and without this structure it would be impossible, perhaps even dangerous, to continue in an expansion which would only lead, eventually and inevitably, to an increasingly chaotic state insofar as the citizen and the state are concerned. Do you get my meaning?"

"What you're really saying," Quilla said, "is that you can't be a judge unless you have laws and lawyers to argue them before you. We've gone over this before, Ved. There are three hundred sixty people in Haven, we all know each other, all of the adults participate in the meetings, there are no major disputes. We don't need a system of laws yet; they'd only complicate things. Don't do unto others as you wouldn't have them do unto you, isn't that the way Hoku put it?"

Ved grimaced. "No person shall harm or defraud, or cause to be harmed or defrauded, any other person."

"Exactly, and disputes and breaches heard by the community. We don't need anything more than that."

Ved jerked at the lapels on his jacket. "I'll talk to your parents," he said, and went into the hall. Quilla looked angry. Meya came out of her doorway and climbed the stairs.

"What are you doing here?" Quilla said. The lines on her forehead smoothed.

"Coming to the meeting." Meya stuck her hand into her sister's.

"You'll be bored."

"I won't! I promise, I won't get bored, I won't say anything, I just want to listen."

"Well, all right. But sit in the back near the door, okay? Then if you want to leave early, you can go without disturbing anyone."

Meya nodded and walked into the crowded room.

Voices rose and fell; Aerites stood talking in groups, shouting their opinions. The representatives from the kasirene village lounged against a wall, arms crossed or hanging or around each other's shoulders. A pup stuck its head out of a pouch, looked around, chattered, and dove for the hidden nipple again. Meya found an empty chair near the door, and Quilla walked to the head of the room and mounted the platform. Ved had already taken his seat; he turned his back to Quilla. Old Dr. Hoku, seated at Quilla's other side, grinned and said something. Quilla laughed briefly and picked up the gavel. To the sound of wood pounding on wood, the people found seats and quieted.

"Order of business," Quilla said. "Dene Beletes on the coms and the kites, Hoku on the hospital, Simit on the school, Ved on the court, report from the kasirene, open discussion. Report and response. Dene?"

"Where're Jason and Mish?" someone called from the audience.

"They're not back yet. I'm expecting them later this afternoon. Dene?"

"Let's wait for them."

Quilla crossed her arms. Some of her frizzy hair escaped from her kerchief and stuck out around her face. Meya pulled on her own smooth black hair and stuck some of it in her mouth.

"Town meeting's regularly scheduled," Quilla said. "We have a celebration tonight, and I'm sure we all want to attend it. If the feel of this meeting is that you'd like to wait for Jason and Mish, despite the fact that they'll be damned tired when they get in, and that you'd like to cancel tonight's party, then let's hear a motion. If not, perhaps we can get on with things."

No one made a motion, and Dene Beletes dragged her usual charts and graphs to the dais.

"Snippy bitch," said a woman seated in front of Meya. Meya kicked her chair hard, and when the woman turned around Meya stuck her tongue out. The woman glared and faced front. Jes slid into the seat beside Meya.

"Where's Tabor?" Meya said.

"Hush. I want to hear Dene."

Dene talked about the need for more kites, hitched directly to generators. She had a scheme for putting windmills around the perimeter of Haven, and gestured at charts full of lines and figures. Jes looked fascinated.

Maya thought about brightly colored windmills standing in fields of airflowers and decided that she liked the idea. Dene talked about the comsystem. Ved objected vehemently to her assurances that the lines were clear and static-free, and Quilla terminated the discussion after Ved shouted the same objection for the fourth time. The kasirene wanted to know more about the windmills, and Quilla spoke to them rapidly in kasiri, repeating Dene's statements. They seemed satisfied. Dene collected her charts and stood down, and Dr. Hoku hauled her chair forward, pressed her wiry gray hair flat over her ears, and harangued the people on the benefits of the hospital she wanted. She painted grim pictures of Haven stricken with epidemic sicknesses, of the dire consequences of not having adequate diagnostic equipment, of the personal importance of life-support equipment, and generally scared everyone in the room.

"And you, I suppose, would run the entire thing," Ved said.

Hoku nailed him with a cold glance. "You got any other doctors on this mudball, Judge? Maybe you'd best leave medicine to people who can tell arthritis from senility."

People laughed, and Ved tightened his lips and crossed his arms. Someone moved that Hoku's hospital be included in the next budget. Quilla amended the motion to shape it as a recommendation to the director of Kennerin Plantations, and the vote carried. Hoku pushed her chair into place and fell asleep.

"Where's Tabor?" Meya whispered again. "You were supposed to practice with him, weren't you?"

"Couldn't find him," Jes whispered back. "Got anything to eat?"

Meya dug into her beltpouch and pulled out a grubby sweet. Jes looked at it suspiciously and put it in his mouth.

"I'll bet Taine's getting awful lonely, with only that baby around," Meya said. "Do babies like flute music?"

"I don't care about Taine," Jes said.

"Ha. Ha. Ha."

"Shut up," the woman in front of them said. Meya stuck her tongue out again and slouched in her chair. Simit droned on about the progress of the students and reminded the parents present that at least half a child's education took place in the home. He made Quilla trans-

110

late that for the benefit of the kasirene. He concluded with a plea for more books and tapes. That, too, went on the recommended budget. Quilla called a break, and Meya slipped out of the hall and went back to the marketplace. The children had left. Sunlight bleached the wooden frames of the vendors' booths. It was as hot as summer, and no breeze yet. She looked down Market Street, then ran over to Schoolhouse Road and went toward the stream. The children would most likely be there, playing in the water.

The schoolhouse looked dim and slightly frightening, empty of children's voices. Meya let her fingers run along the smooth wooden boards of the fence. A splinter lodged in her finger. She looked around quickly, said "shit" with emphasis, and pulled the splinter out, then put her finger in her mouth. She rounded the corner of the fence and saw Hart perched atop old man Gren's roof, nails in his mouth.

"Hey, what are you doing up there?" Meya called.

Hart turned, startled, and dropped the shingle in his hand. "None of your business. Look what you made me do."

"I didn't make you do anything." Meya shaded her eyes to look up at him. Hart had grown rapidly in the last year. He had cut the legs from all of his pants, but the seats were still tight for him. His dark hair shone in the sunlight. "What are you helping crazy old Gren for, anyway?"

"Go away. Go study something. I'm busy."

Meya shrugged and considered the likelihood of Hart's falling from the roof. He looked well seated, though; besides, the drop to the ground wasn't very far.

"Can I help you?"

"Last thing I need is some nosy kid getting into things. Go away, will you?" He drove a nail into the roof with hard, loud smacks of the hammer.

Meya made a face and ran toward the stream. She hoped that Hart would fall down. He was like Mish was sometimes, abrupt and distant, and she wondered why her mother and Hart didn't like each other more. Maybe neither of them could like anyone. No, that wasn't fair. Mish loved Jason, of that Meya was quite sure. Mish loved Quilla, and Jes, and she probably loved Hart, and maybe even Meya. But on this count Meya was never quite sure. Her mother called her "winter child" when they got along. Meya didn't like the name; it didn't feel right. But Hart didn't get along with anyone except old Gren, although they often fought. Meya shrugged and jumped into the shallow stream, remembering too late that Laur got mad when Meya muddied her shoes. Adults were impenetrable.

Downstream, she heard the whisper of voices and moved closer. The children were playing Swamp Raider, with the kasirene, as usual, playing the Rats. The kasirene never got to play Raiders; they were too good at tracking, and the game was always over too fast. Meya untied her shoes and shoved them into the crotch of a tree, pulled her straight black hair behind her ears, and crept toward the voices. Zeonea the MasterRat was about to strike!

"Jes."

He turned, not sure whether he'd heard the call in the tumult of the room. Quilla lounged against the podium, sipping from a cup of water and listening to the arguments of a mixed group of kasirene and terrans. Hoku said something to Ved Hirem, who frowned and marched away from her. Hoku grinned. People pressed toward the door, eager for fresh air. Jes stepped out of their way.

"Jes!"

Dene Beletes touched his arm and nodded her head toward a free corner. Jes followed her through the disorderly rows of chairs.

"It went well, didn't it?" she said. "Do you think it did? Did they seem interested?"

Jes nodded. "It's a good plan," he said.

"The plan's nothing. Windmills are old. Do you think your father will like the idea? The plan's nothing, it's how things will be put together, that's the new stuff. How to apply it here. With the sea breezes. Did they listen when I talked about the wind patterns?"

"Yes."

Dene put down her drawings and ran her stubby, scarred fingers through her red hair, then shrugged. "It's your father's decision. You'll tell him about it?"

"I think it would be better if you came up the Tor and told him yourself. Besides, Quilla will mention it when she tells them about the meeting."

"Perhaps. Perhaps." Dene grinned suddenly. "Hoku spiked Ved again, didn't she? Wish I had her guts."

Jes nodded. Dene abruptly gathered her drawings and

headed toward the podium. "Leave these with Quilla," she said over her shoulder. "She can take them up the Tor. Show your father before the party tomorrow. We can talk about it."

Jes watched her elbow her way through the crowd, then turned toward the door. As he walked down the steps he heard Quilla banging the gavel to start the meeting again. He hesitated, then continued down Market Street.

The Glents' place was one of the newer houses in Haven, built a year ago when the young couple declared that they refused to live with either set of parents any longer and applied for the lot. Jes had helped with the construction, laying in solar paneling under Dene's directions, learning the rudiments of framing, brick-laying, and cabinet work. It had been his idea to build the porch around the halaea that stood on the land, and the sight of the smooth, pale trunk rising through the porch flooring and the roof pleased him. When he built a house for himself, he would weave trees through it. Roots for foundations and leaves for a ceiling. He pictured the house in his mind, and saw himself coming home, spaceport behind him, dress greens neat and fresh; saw Taine waiting by the door, smiling. The image wavered, not entirely acceptable. He shook his head and crossed the flat, sundrenched lawn to the porch.

Taine opened the door before he could knock, and put her fingers to her lips. "The baby's asleep," she said, and came out onto the porch.

Jes flushed. "That's why I came," he said. "To see the baby. I haven't seen it yet—"

"Her. It's a girl."

"Oh. Yes, of course." Jes stared at the planks of the porch floor and fingered his flute uncertainly. "Well, I thought I'd see her. I guess I can come back later—when she's awake, I mean."

He glanced up quickly and saw Taine's lips quirk in a smile. He turned to leave.

"No, it's all right," she said and touched his arm. "You can look at her now." She moved toward the door. "Well, come on."

Jes stuck his hands under his belt and followed her into the cool dimness of the house.

The baby was chubby, bald, and tan-colored. She lay naked in the crib, her bottom thrust toward the ceiling. Jes

113

stared at her, then touched her shoulder with his fingertip.

"She's tiny," he whispered.

"No tinier than most," Taine replied. "She'll be as big as her mother, in time."

Jes thought of that, but it seemed impossible that this small sleeping baby could grow to the size of Kala Glent. He shook his head and followed Taine from the room.

"Want something to drink?" Taine said before he could think of an excuse for staying. He nodded gratefully, and she led him into the kitchen. She opened the thick-walled stone cooler and brought out a pitcher of juice.

"The meeting's still going on," Jes said as she poured juice from pitcher to cup.

"Talk," Taine said scornfully. She poured herself a cup of juice and sat at the table across from Jes. "You'd think no one here has anything better to do with his time."

"It is important," Jes said earnestly. "It's how we run things properly. Otherwise . . ."

"I know." Taine shook her hair. It slid around her face, a red-brown wing shining in the light. Jes bit his lip, then sipped his juice. Taine stared out the window.

"Are you living here now?" Jes said to break the silence.

"Yes. Then Medi wants me for a month, and after that I'll spend some time with Hoku."

"Hoku?" Jes looked surprised.

"Not for herself. She said she'd need someone for the ward then; there are two or three babies due, including Tham's new one."

"That makes three," Jes said. He thought about Tham doing extra runs to support his family. "He sure keeps busy, doesn't he?"

Taine laughed and Jes blushed, realizing how that must have sounded to her. He drank quickly from his cup. She looked at him, amused.

"Why can I talk to everyone except you?" he said, staring into his cup.

She stood and took the pitcher away. When she bent to the cooler, her hair slid forward and hid her face.

"Maybe you try too hard," she said.

The baby whimpered and she went out of the kitchen. Jes stood at the door until she appeared with the baby over her shoulder. She put the baby on a couch in the living room and bent to diaper it.

114

"How does it feel, always living in other people's houses?" Jes said.

Taine shrugged, her mouth full of pins. She folded the white cloth around the baby's bottom and pinnned it quickly and expertly.

"Different," she said, then picked up the baby. "Better than not living in any house at all."

"That's not the choice, is it?"

She looked at him, and they went onto the porch. Jes held the baby in his lap. It wriggled around, cooing, and dribbled on his shirt. Taine sat on the porch rail and brushed her hair from her face.

"My folks were pretty rich," she said finally, as though talking only to herself. "You know that sort of thing—private tutors, clothes, having servants for everything. I guess I thought it would always be that way: doing only what I wanted to, getting everything I asked for, having people obey me. Then the—the trouble came. My dad disappeared. Mom and I were taken to Great Barrier after that, just a little while before your father came. Maybe two weeks." She twisted a strand of hair around her finger, still not looking at him. "Mom was pretty good-looking. They took her away the second day. No one would tell me where she was, but I could guess. There weren't too many pretty women, not there. Either they were taken away, or they got ugly very fast. So I guess maybe Mom was lucky. At least they made sure that the pro—that the pretty women ate."

The baby grabbed for Jes' hand. He tickled her stomach and looked from the baby to Taine, puzzled at her sudden confidences. Taine set her shoulders back suddenly and put her hands on her hips.

"There was an old woman in the camp. She made me cover my face with mud, and she put something on my teeth to make them ugly. She told me not to wash and she tied knots in my hair. I guess I looked pretty awful, and smelled worse. Anyway, they left me alone. I don't remember much of it. I guess I wasn't thinking much. I know I wasn't. Jason says he had to shout at me, and when I didn't move he picked me up and carried me until I started running by myself. I didn't know why I was running, either. I just followed everyone else."

Her face looked tight and without expression, like a mask. Jes said her name, and she turned her head more sharply away from him.

115

"Someone in the ship gave me a washcloth, and someone else brought me a blanket, and I decided that the nightmare was over, that things were going to be exactly as they were before. That I was Princess Taine again, and I owned the world. That wasn't true, either."

The baby started crying. Jes automatically put her against his shoulder and rubbed her back, murmuring. She quieted.

"You do that very well," Taine said, then took the baby from him. "So do I. That's how I live, on your planet. I can't do anything else."

"Don't you like it?"

"I suppose. I like children." She said it wistfully, and her face softened.

Jes wet his lips, wondering how much talk she would allow. "You're different with children," he said tentatively. "You're not so . . . so . . . "

She looked at him, her eyebrows cocked sarcastically, and he pressed his lips together.

"Ved wants to marry me," she said.

"Ved Hirem?" Jes stood, upset. "But you can't—he's too old."

Taine looked at him.

"Are you going to do it?"

She shrugged and took the baby into the house. Jes sat back on the porch and pulled his flute from his belt. He played a few notes unhappily.

Taine came to the door. "No," she said, then went inside again.

Jes continued playing aimlessly. He felt like crying.

Ved was expostulating about the beauties of the law when the kasirene pup bounded onto the dais and whispered in Quilla's ear. She whispered back and, as the pup left, awoke Hoku.

"Mish and Jason are home. Can you take over the meeting?"

Hoku nodded, and Quilla left the hall. Any character assassination that Ved tried after she left would be dealt with by Hoku; there was no love lost between the abrasive doctor and the windbag lawyer. The heat had increased. Quilla pulled her damp shirt away from her breasts and wished for a breeze, but none came. Down Market Street, she heard the plaintive notes of her brother's flute and saw Jes sitting alone on the Glents' front porch. Taine, bouncing a baby on her hip, stood at the window. She looked impassive. Quilla sighed and shook her head. She'd hoped that Jes would outgrow his infatuation, but it seemed only to increase. Snippy, pretty, self-sufficient Taine treated the entire thing as a joke.

We don't seem to do love very well, Quilla thought. She passed the last house and started up the hill to the Tor. Jes and Taine, Tabor and me. Even Mish and Jason have their rough times, lasting years. They cope by going away together in the summer, walking the island, learning about each other again. It seems to work, for them. Maybe all of us carry our emotions in our feet.

Mish and Jason were already in the hot tub behind the house. Quilla took some beer from the kitchen and went up to the enclosed tubhouse.

"Got room for some beer?" she asked.

"Quilla? Come on in."

Jason and Mish lay in the hot water, sweat beading their foreheads. Quilla handed Mish a beer and kissed her forehead, and Jason grabbed for his kiss and beer simultaneously.

"You're both crazy," Quilla said, retreating to the door. "A hot bath, in weather like this?"

"I'm trying to boil my muscles loose," Jason said. "Your mother thinks a leisurely hike means covering eighty kilometers a day. Uphill."

"Liar," Mish said comfortably.

"How was it?" Quilla said.

"Good. Long. Hot. Pretty."

"That about covers everything," Jason said.

Quilla laughed.

"And here?"

Quilla drank her beer and brought them up to date on the farm, orchard, and village.

"Ved's been giving me a hard time, but that's not surprising," she said, concluding. "He's on the rub about his laws again, and every time I try to reason with him he pinches his nose and tells me he'll talk it over with you. I get a little tired of being treated like a child."

"I'll take care of him," Jason said. "Anything else?"

"No. Tabor's here."

Jason moved his legs in the water. He took up half the length of the tub; beside him, Mish looked as tiny as a child.

"He's here in the summer?" Mish said. "Why?"

117

Quilla shrugged and finished her beer. "Got tired of mountains, I guess. Are you up to the celebration tonight?"

"Sure," Jason said. "How can I miss hearing about how my wife and son defeated an entire armada of bloodthirsty maniacs? Is Ved doing the oration this year?"

"Who else? Oh, and Jes will be talking. Hetch commed to say he'd be a few days late."

"Too bad, he'll miss a great performance."

"Sure." Quilla grinned. "Last year Ved upped the fleet to twelve ships and a battle cruiser. You want to bet that this year it's twenty ships and four chargers?"

Jason pulled on his moustache. "No, that's not enough: thirty-two ships, three chargers, and a Federation crusier, at least."

Mish laughed. "And this year, maybe he'll give me a blaster. I could have used one. How about another beer?"

"Coming up."

As she approached the tubhouse again, Quilla heard Jason say, "Think he's asked her yet?"

"I don't know. She'd have mentioned it."

"Maybe not. Quilla's a still one, Mish."

Quilla wet her lips. The beer steins felt cold in her hands.

"Think she'll say yes?" Mish said.

"You didn't," Jason said. "Is she any less stubborn than you are?"

"Not funny, Jase. That was an entirely different thing. She's twenty-one already."

"Give her time."

Quilla walked back a few meters and leaned her forehead against a tree. She put one of the steins to her cheek, then took a few deep breaths and went back to the tubhouse, letting her feet scuffle in the dirt. She handed her parents the beer, invented work at the house, and left. The barn was full of people putting up decorations; the Tor echoed with Laur's shouts and Mim's answering yells. Palen was in the distant fields. Quilla walked to the front of the house, glanced around, and scrambled into the halaea tree. The many feathery leaves screened her from the house and valley. She sat on a high branch, rested her cheek against the bark, and looked at the dappled light. The serenity wouldn't come.

118

The barn doors stood open, and lamplight gleamed on the clean floors. Quilla wanted to swing up the ropes and along the lofts to the quietness near the barn's rooftree, but instead stood with her family at the opened door, welcoming Aerites and kasirene as they rounded the hill. Crowds made her uncomfortable. Tabor took her hand and squeezed it reassuringly. She nodded without looking at him and moved away.

"Meya, don't get so dirty so fast," she said. Meya put her hands behind her back and smiled. Jes was dressed in his finest, conscious of his status as official Aerie Hero. Hart stood beside his mother, his expression unreadable. Quilla watched him, wondering why he had come. Hart had refused to participate in any celebrations before, not even attending the BeginningDay festivals, or the Year's-End parties. Yet here he was, distant and cool but present nonetheless. Quilla decided that he simply wished, finally, to be part of Aerie, part of its rituals and mythologies.

"Hetch isn't here," Ved said as he came in.

Jason shook his head. "Quilla got a com about three days ago. He said he'd be late."

"I know. I've amended the recitation to include Jes, although, frankly, I'd have preferred the captain's presence this evening. However, it is obvious that he will not participate by making a few short remarks if he fails to appear in order to do so, is it not? Have you any advice?"

"You're on your own, Judge," Jason said. "I'm sure you'll do a great job."

Ved pulled at his lower lip and went into the barn. Meya stuck her tongue out at him while he wasn't looking, and Laur threatened her with an upraised hand. Aerites poured through the barn doors, talking and carrying pots of food and jugs of homemade wine. Jes and Tabor climbed to one of the lower lofts and played duets. Their legs dangled over the loft's edge, and a number of Meya's friends pitched fruit at their feet, until Mim descended on them like a mute, vengeful Figure of Authority, and they fled to the ends of the barn, laughing. Jason sat beside Ved near the wine table, and they bent their heads over Ved's speech. The kasirene came last. Quilla, her hands full of cakes, nodded to Palen and put the cakes on the long table. The band arrived and tuned up. Jes and Tabor came down from the loft. Quilla stepped back into shadows and watched Tabor look around, then move toward Mish. Her mother and her lover stood talking beside the doors. Tabor touched Mish's shoulder. Mish put her hand over his and smiled. Quilla turned away.

Ved always wanted to speechify before the dancing, but was always voted down on the assumption that by the time he finished, the band would be asleep. Hoku settled in a seat where she could observe the proceedings, and collared children as they passed; she soon had a steady flow of young ones moving between her seat and the wine and food tables. Jes lounged against a pillar among several other young men. Quilla could see the gleam of Taine's red hair over their shoulders. Mish danced with Jason, and Tabor watched her solemnly. Mish is forty-four this year, Quilla thought. And I'm twenty-one already. It doesn't seem to make much difference.

Hart came in from the night, took a jug of wine, and went to the door again. He stood drinking and watching the sky. For Hetch? Quilla doubted it. She walked around the walls of the barn and stood beside him.

"Give me some," she said.

Hart looked at her and gave her the jug. She drank.

"Ugh. Why don't you drink kaea instead? It's better than this swill."

"I don't like kasirene shit," Hart said amiably. Quilla started to reply, then saw his smile and closed her mouth, confused. She'd had increasingly little to do with her brother over the past five years, and could no longer balance his statements, abstract the humor from the serious. She looked up. Two moons rode the sky, one at its zenith and the other rising above the eastern horizon. Stars lay thick along the arms of The Spiral.

Hart touched her arm. "Look at that." He nodded into the barn.

Quilla turned and saw Tabor sitting with Mish; they laughed, then Tabor bent his head as he talked and gestured. Telling some story. His cane lay beside him in the hay; his bad leg was stretched out comfortably. Mish's hand rested on his knee. Quilla looked at Hart and shrugged, and he smiled and turned his attention to the stars again.

"They were lovers," Hart said.

"No. I know that story. Tabor left because he felt

120

uncomfortable. He didn't want to come between Jason and Mish. He couldn't. But they were never lovers."

"That's the story." Hart said and smiled.

"You don't change, do you? If there's ever anything to be twisted, you're ready to twist it."

Hart shrugged. "Even if they weren't lovers, even if they didn't fuck, he certainly loved her enough to leave her. Think he still does?"

"Don't be an idiot," Quilla said sharply and turned to go inside.

Hart grabbed her shoulder. "Look! It's starting, look at that!"

As Quilla turned, Hart ran into the barn, shouting. She looked up. The sky to the north of The Spiral lightened rapidly. The music stopped, and she heard Hart's voice. People began to crowd through the barn door, looking up. Quilla turned angrily and suddenly the sky filled with light. The people gasped. The light intensified, flooding the valley with color and a sudden feel of warmth. After the initial gasp a deep silence fell, and Hart's voice was loud and clear.

"You forgot the time, didn't you?" His voice was good-humored. "You all forgot how to count. That's New-Home's primary, ladies and gentlemen. That's your birthworld, going up in flames. Four standard years ago, friends and neighbors. And you all of you forgot."

"No," Mim said harshly.

Someone moaned. Someone wept. NewHome had driven them out, tried to kill them, murdered family and friends, yet it was their homeworld, and this was the light of its death. Hart sauntered past Quilla, winked, and disappeared around the corner of the barn. The people drew closer together, as though seeking warmth.

The Aerites went home. Quilla stood at the barn door and listened to the sound of their footsteps in the grass. Hoku, muttering about tranquilizers, patted Quilla's arm as she left. Ved was, for once, completely silent. Jason and Mish looked at the empty barn, the pile of food and drink, the cleared dance area, and went up the hill to the Tor. Quilla closed the barn doors. Tabor leaned against the outer wall, his face turned to the light. Quilla went to him and took his hand.

"There were mountains," Tabor said quietly, "all white and green and brown, with streams running down their sides. And Mestican all made of white walls and gardens,

121

and fountains, and singing birds. Valleys. The sea." He touched his flute. "I knew this four years ago. But somehow it didn't seem real until tonight."

Quilla waited, silent. After a long time his shoulders shook and he pressed his face against the wall. Later they went home.

Jason was up early, sitting in the kitchen having a cup of steaming tea while Laur complained of the kassies, the townspeople, the supplies, and Jes' effect on Meya's language. Mim brought him a plate of hot meat pies. Jason tilted his chin toward Laur and raised an eyebrow. Mim rolled her eyes, shrugged, and smiled quickly. Laur was all right then, just practicing her complaints. He wondered what she'd do if she had nothing to complain of, and remembered the one time when, to her intense embarrassment, he had taken her grievances seriously and called a town meeting to discuss her comments about the merchants. Laur had refused to appear. Hoku claimed that as long as Laur had something to complain about, she'd live forever. Jason was inclined to agree.

The unseasonably hot weather had not broken, although the dawn light was spare and cool. Quilla came down, dressed in shorts and halter, and smiled sleepily as she poured herself a cup of tea and waved away Mim's offer of pies.

"If you don't eat, you'll fall over for sure," Laur predicted.

"Not hungry, Laur. Really. I'll take some along for lunch, though."

"You'll take more than pies," Laur said, and began listing the things Mim was to pack in Quilla's lunch. Mim, as usual, halved everything. Jason stood up.

"If you're not going to eat, how about showing me the farm?" he said. "I've lost track of progress these past three weeks."

"Sure." Quilla finished her tea and stood.

"Quilla Kennerin, you're not leaving this house dressed like that," Laur said. "You've barely got any clothes on at all. You go on upstairs and put something on before everyone sees you like that."

"Laur. I love you dearly, but it's hot as sin out there during the day, and I'm not going to die of heat just because you don't like the way I'm dressed. It's for my health."

"And what about decency? What about my peace of mind? And you, Jason, you're no better, letting your children run around half naked. Savages, that's what you are. What would your grandmother say?"

"Nothing," Jason said. "She's been dead for fifty years, remember? Tell Mish that I'll be on the farm."

"Nothing but a walking message board," Laur said and turned back to the stove.

Daylight had faded the light of NewHome's dying, although two day-bright nights had thoroughly confused the fourbirds. They gathered suspiciously in the boughs of the trees. They looked hung over. Jason looked at them and shook his head.

"Is Tabor taking it badly?"

Quilla stiffened and shrugged. "Not too much. Bad enough. He remembers more than most, I guess. Nightmares."

"Light keeps him awake?"

Quilla nodded.

"Ved says it's responsible for this hot weather," Jason said.

"The weather was hot for a week before this. Ved's a fool. Come on, I want to show you the winter fields we're putting in. The new seeds Hetch brought last time are supposed to do well in our winters. I'm eager to try them."

The rich black soil was turned and tilled, waiting for the seeding. Quilla talked about the contours of the land, compost, mulch, irrigation systems, and politicked for a pump to run the sprinklers that she wanted to put in. Jason took his shoes off and walked barefoot through the soft dirt. The land seemed alive under his feet. Quilla talked about alkalinity and acidity. The sun rose higher. They walked through unharvested fields, where kasirene hoed and weeded. The land smelled dark and fertile and welcoming. Jason wanted to sing.

"Do I get my pump?" Quilla said finally. They stopped under a stand of kaedos and sat, leaning against the trunks.

"Sure. I think it's a good idea. Can Dene make you one?"

"No. I've asked her. She says they've developed something over on Hogarth's Dump, something solid this and cross that and intersecting the other. The wiring's all from our sap. She says it should last forever. I want to ask

123

Hetch to pick one up for me, he should be able to get it before next summer."

"If it's the right one, and not too expensive. Talk it over with Mish."

"All right."

He closed his eyes and wondered how he could bring up the subject of Tabor. He hadn't been pleased when he'd first discovered that she'd been sleeping with Tabor. She was his daughter, his firstborn, and he reserved the right to feel a loss at her gain. Yet Tabor seemed to make her happier, less discontent. Jason still felt guilty for what he considered to be his own neglect of Quilla, his assumption that everything in her life was rosy while he was busy with his own pursuits. Her flight had awakened him to a time of rough and miserable reappraisal of himself; his most serious weakness, he thought, was in not paying sufficient attention, in not taking care. If Tabor made some of it up to his daughter, he was content. But Mish wanted grandchildren, wanted Kennerins springing from the land like airflowers, covering Aerie. He didn't think that Mish had pushed Tabor into asking Quilla to marry him, but he wasn't entirely sure. And there was always that old business, back during the first year. No jealousy there; what rough times he and Mish had lived through had bound them more closely together. But he wondered uncomfortably whether Mish wasn't pushing Quilla and Tabor together in order, in some complicated way, to recompense Tabor for his loss of Mish herself.

On the other hand, he often wondered whether he didn't invent complications just to keep his mind occupied. He opened his eyes again. Quilla held a dried kaedo leaf in her hand.

"Almost winter," she said. "Things changing again."

"Always do, Quil." He laughed. "That was a dumb thing I said."

"At least with kaedos, I know what they're changing into. I know that they'll be back again. Other things . . ." She shrugged. "I sometimes feel as though I'm standing on a floor that might disappear at any second, leaving me without anything to hold onto." She looked at him. "Does that make any sense?"

"Yes. I haven't felt that way for years, though. I guess, you get older, you don't feel some of the changes as much. No, what I mean is, maybe you see the changes coming, or you're a bit more confident about what they mean and where they're leading."

"Seeing deeper into things?"

"No. Sometimes you've already looked deep into something, and you don't have to worry about it anymore. It makes life easier. Then it turns around and changes on you anyway. Mysterious stuff."

Quilla crushed the leaf in her hand, then brushed the fragments from her palm. "I think I want to go walking again with Palen. After the winter planting you won't need me for a while."

"If you want." Jason stared over the plowed fields. "Something bothering you, Quil? Something specific?"

"You know damned well what it is."

Jason tried to look innocent, but made a mess of it.

"Okay. Mish told me that Tabor said he was going to ask you to marry him. We met him on the way down. Did he tell you?"

Quilla shook her head.

"I'm sorry. He should have. We should have." Jason looked at his feet.

"Treating me like a child again," Quilla said. "Taking care of my life behind my back."

"It wasn't that way. I know it looks that way, but I really thought Tabor would tell you, and that you would tell us. I'm sorry, Quilla. I should have thought it out."

She touched his wrist lightly. "Okay, Jase. Forgiven."

Jason wet his lips. "Are you going to marry him?"

"I don't know." Quilla rolled onto her stomach and poked at the dirt. "People change. Things change. I don't know if I love him. Or maybe I do, but not enough to marry him. I don't know. Things change."

"Some things don't change," Jason said. He scooped a handful of dirt from around the kaedo's roots. "This—the land—that doesn't change. You put work and love into it, and it gives you food and fruit and flowers and beauty. The things you do with your hands and your mind and your body don't change. Making things grow—the importance of that doesn't change. I mean, things change, sure, but their importance—what they mean—that doesn't change much. Sunlight, the earth, water, children. Making life."

"Making life," Quilla said. She smiled. "I guess that's stability enough, for now. Come on, if I don't get you back in time for lunch, Laur will have my head."

125

"That's one thing that doesn't change, either," Jason said, and they walked back to the Tor.

After she left, though, he realized that he still didn't know her answer. He ate his lunch unhappily and thought about weddings. Cault Tereth was a long way away.

"Unplug me," Quilla said. Hoku looked at her and frowned.

"You sure?"

"Yes."

"Marrying Tabor?"

"I don't know."

Hoku thought about that for a moment. "Want to talk about it?"

"No. Unplug me."

"Well, you're going to listen about it." Hoku stood and walked to her window. She pushed aside the curtains and glanced around, then let them fall in place again. "Tabor's after you to marry him, and Mish and Jason are pushing you to do it."

"Not Jason. So what?"

"So maybe you shouldn't." Hoku came back to her desk and perched on its side, staring at Quilla. "There's nothing wrong with being alone."

"Except being lonely."

"Got nothing to do with marriage. You don't need to be alone to be lonely."

"You don't like Tabor."

"I like him. I like you. I like Hetch, too, but that doesn't mean I'm about to marry him, or marry you to him. Some people come in pairs, some don't."

Quilla felt her nose turn red, and she glared at Hoku. "And I'm one of the ones who's supposed to come alone, is that it? I'm not allowed not to be lonely, I don't even get a chance to try it, do I?"

Hoku snorted. "Get off. I thought you gave up melodrama years ago."

"Damn it, Hoku!"

"You want to marry Tabor, go ahead. He's a good man, he'll do his best."

"You make him sound like a biostat."

"I'd trust a biostat more than a marriage."

Quilla jumped up. "Besides, I didn't say I was going to do it."

"You're thinking about it."

126

"I can think about any damned thing I please!"

"Thinking with your cunt?"

Quilla folded her arms and glared down at the doctor. "I'm not exactly Taine Alendreu, am I? Men don't go chasing me down the streets with their tongues hanging out of their mouths. Maybe when I find one man blind enough to think I'm attractive, I should grab onto him. He may be unique, you know."

"It's that important?"

"I don't know." Quilla slumped into the chair, put her feet on Hoku's desk, and shoved her hands in her pockets. "I don't want to fight with you, Hoku. I don't want to fight with anyone. Even myself. Why shouldn't I marry Tabor, if I want to?"

"Do you want to?"

"Don't start that argument again. Why shouldn't Tabor marry me?"

"Don't know."

"Then what are you arguing about?"

Hoku sat in her own chair and put her feet on the desk. She and Quilla looked at each other over their toes.

"I don't think you'd be marrying Tabor, and he wouldn't be marrying you," Hoku said. "I think you've got this picture in your mind that's maybe one-fourth Tabor Grif and three-quarters what you want him to be, what you think he is. Has little to do with what Tabor thinks he is or wants to be. If you're going to tie your life up with someone else, you should at least know what you're doing."

"I know his faults."

"Not a question of faults. Question of expectations."

"We've all got expectations."

"Some more realistic than others. And Tabor wouldn't be marrying you, either."

Quilla put her feet down. "Hart says that Mish and Tabor were lovers. Maybe they still are."

"Hart's got a malicious computer for a brain. They were never lovers."

"How do you know?"

"I'm a doctor. I'm not going to tell you that."

Quilla twisted in her chair. "I thought that maybe Tabor wants to marry me because it's the nearest he can get to Mish."

Hoku pursed her lips. "Close, but not close enough. He's not in love with Mish, not anymore. Not that much.

Tabor's in love with all of you, every Kennerin around. Except Hart, but I'm willing to concede even that."

Quilla caught her breath. She walked to the sink and poured herself a cup of water, and brought it back to the desk.

"In other words, Tabor only loves me because I'm a Kennerin. He doesn't find me attractive either, then, not all by myself."

"Is it that important? To be attractive? To be beautiful? I'm not."

"I'm twenty-one, Hoku! I don't like being ugly."

"You're not ugly. Stupid sometimes, but not ugly."

"Don't feed me that. I know what I look like."

"You don't. You look in the mirror and want to see Taine, and you're upset when you don't. You're not beautiful. But you're not ugly, either. You're Quilla, that's all. Besides, that's not the point."

"And the point is?"

"Hell should I know?" Hoku grinned. "I just want you to think about what you're doing, is all."

"Will you unplug me?"

"You getting married?"

"I don't know!"

"Back where we started from. That's what I hate about you Kennerins—when you're stubborn, you do it in circles."

Hoku went to the cabinet and opened drawers, and when she turned around she held a scalpel.

"Come on, I haven't got all day," she said.

Quilla pushed her chair to the exam table, sat down, and stretched her arm along the table's surface, palm up. Hoku poked at the tan flesh of her forearm, frowning, then splashed some anesthetic on the arm and made a small incision. She pulled out a capsule, put it on the table, and closed the incision with two stitches. Quilla flexed her arm.

"Give it a week for the last of it to get through your system, and you'll be fecund," Hoku said.

Quilla pulled her sleeve down and fastened it at her wrist. "What do I owe you?"

"Your tanberries are ripe now, aren't they? I could use a kilo or two."

"I'll send Meya down with them this afternoon. Anything else?"

"A promise."

Quilla looked at the doctor silently.

128

"You've only got yourself, Quilla. Everything else is external, out of you. Just your body, just your mind. You can lend yourself around, try to give pieces of yourself to people or things. Just remember that all you've got is you, and be careful what you do with it."

"All right."

"Promise."

"Hoku, I'm not a child anymore."

"Promise."

"Sweet Mother, you're a stubborn old bird. I promise, all right? Cross my heart and make this vow, it will last forever, I will always keep to it, I will break it never. There, satisfied?"

"Satisfied. Is Hetch coming in today?"

"Sometime tonight, I think."

"Tell him I want to see him. He's probably off his diet."

Quilla grinned and closed the door behind her. Heatwaves rose from the streetstones. Her arm began to sting.

Hetch came in at sunset. Tham's pregnant wife was already at the port, two children clinging to her pants and another in her arms. They swooped around Tham as he came out of the shuttle. Bakar swore at them and held out his hand. Jes put a stein of beer into it. Merkit called a greeting in kasiri and swung off toward the native village. But Hetch stared gloomily around the pad, his face uncharacteristically downcast. Jes touched his arm.

"Something wrong, Captain?"

"Jason and Mish around? I've got to talk to the directors."

"We're all here, and supper's waiting."

The mention of food didn't dispel the captain's gloominess, which persisted through greetings, supper, and into the evening. Jes had grown, he noticed. Hart wasn't home. Good. Hart made him feel nervous. Meya was growing up beautiful. It didn't make him any happier. After dinner they trooped into the living room. Jason closed the doors and opened the brandy Hetch had brought. Hetch emptied his glass with one gulp and Jason refilled it.

"Manny?" Jason said.

"I'm busted," Hetch said bitterly. Quilla and Jes looked at him, their faces serious. On the couch Meya slept, her head on Quilla's lap.

"Busted?" Jason said. "Bankrupt? I don't see how. The *Zimania* sap is pulling a huge profit, and you must make

129

a fair profit yourself. You added three new ships last year, and you've still got the monopoly in West Wing, don't you?"

Hetch shook his head. "You're six months behind, Jase. I've got one ship now, the *Folly*, and it's the oldest of the bunch. Parallax, over on Mi Patria, moved into the third and fourth sub-sectors, and they're big enough to undercut my rates. Matter of loyalty to an old shipper over profit with a new one. You know how that always ends. And they're warring over in sub-seven, too."

"So?"

"So *Balclutha* and *Obregon* were docked at Grey's Landing, unloading spices, when Monde Nuveau came through the grab and cindered the entire southern continent. Lost both ships, two damned fine captains, both crews, and cargo. The *Peri* was lost last quarter going through tau to East Wing. I'm left with *Folly* and she's due for scrapping three runs from now, I've got contracts that I can't handle with one ship and Parallax is scooping them up. The insurance companies on Althing Green are refusing to pick up on the loss of *Balclutha* and *Obregon*. Claim that losses in war are no province of theirs, and I don't have the capital to take it before the Tribunal." Hetch reached for his brandy. "And that, Kennerin, is why I'm late and don't have your new bailers. *Peri* was going to pick them up. The other two are gone, and *Folly* can barely make it through tau in West Wing. If I tried to put her through inter-tau, she'd shatter." He stared into the glass. "Luck," he said, and drained the brandy.

"We're left with a barn full of sap and no way to get it to market," Jason said.

Mish picked up her glass. "Is Parallax planning runs out this way?"

"No. They've got sub-three and -four, and they'll probably move into two and five next, then one and eight. Seven they can ignore; there's nothing there, anyway. Nine'll be last on their list. They probably won't get here for another ten, maybe eleven years standard."

"And we're to be completely cut off for that long?" Jason demanded. "That's impossible."

Hetch shrugged unhappily. "I can't afford to keep *Folly* running. Don't have the capital for repairs, licenses, dock fees, salaries. Hell, I can't even afford crew gains. They know damned well there won't be any."

"But Tham's got family here," Jes said. "Merkit and

Bakar, it's like another home to them. They won't desert us."

Hetch looked at Jes sadly. "We're spacers, Jes. Without a job, how's Tham going to feed that brood of his? He doesn't know shit about farming. Besides, he's a spacer. He'd hate it. None of us can stay planetbound. We'd flip."

Quilla touched Jes' hand and looked at Hetch. "We won't be cut off for ten years. Parallax isn't going to let us slip by. The sap's worth too much to them. They'll send in a line by next year's harvest, or they're too stupid to stay in business."

"Sorry, Quilla. They'll do to Aerie what they did to Griffin, or Costa Azul. They'll wait until you're starving, then come in with an offer to buy you out entirely. And you'll be so damned hungry you'll jump at the chance."

A brief silence descended.

"We made it through before," Jason said. "That first year, when the refugees came and Haven burned."

"We made it because of the kasirene first," Mish said, "then because of Hetch. By now we're too dependent on the trade to break it on our own. We need too many things we can't make here."

"It's insane!" Jason jumped up. "To have a million fremarks' worth of sap sitting in the barn, and the orchards going full speed, and then sit here and talk about starving!"

"Hetch?"

The captain turned reluctantly to Quilla again. Long legs and long, cold glances, and a cold, quick mind. She made him feel stiff, wary, confused. But now she was looking past him, her eyes unfocused, and her fingers tapped on her arm as though she were counting rapidly. Meya turned her head, and Quilla put her hand on her sister's hair.

"What's your price for the sap?" she said.

"Last year, one ninety-three the kilo. Year before that, one ninety-two. The stuff's getting popular; the supply is scarce. If I could make it to market this year, it would fetch maybe two even, maybe a bit more."

"We've gotten tons of sap sitting in the barn," she said slowly. "That's about two million fremarks, price at Ship-wright. Yes?"

"About," Hetch said. "But—"

She waved him to be quiet. "How much do you need to get *Folly* back in shape?"

131

"Quarter of a million. Crew gains about fifty thou total for a run, dock fees and licenses another twenty-five or thirty, grab fees maybe ten, payments and taxes another hundred. Incidentals, provisions, about fifteen. Fuel, seventy. And some for backup."

"That's still only about four hundred thousand. Barely cuts into the profit."

"Damn it, I don't have the money to buy the sap! I don't have the damned million capital to take it off Aerie."

"Can you make one more haul, present conditions?" she said quietly.

"Probably. But don't you see—"

"Run the sap on consignment. We'll pay the repairs and fees out of the gross profits, take care of your other expenses, and buy *Folly* from you. You'll get a salary for the first run, and if you want to stay on as captain you'll either get salary or gains, whichever you prefer. And take Jes along as an apprentice."

Jes gasped.

Hetch started to reply, then saw the look that Quilla and Mish exchanged. Quilla's face was calm, and Mish nodded once, unsmiling. For a moment it seemed to the captain that the room had shifted, that some subtle interchange had occurred and the currents in the room stabilized into a new pattern. Baffled, he turned to Jason and spread his hands.

"Sell the *Folly?*" he said.

"Buy the *Folly?*" Jason said. "Mish, I don't think Quilla understands . . . "

Mish glanced at Jason, then back to Quilla and nodded.

"I understand perfectly," Quilla said. "Either we buy the *Folly* and have a chance to make it, or we don't, we're out of the Federation for a couple of years, and we sell out to Parallax whenever they snap their fingers. And if Hetch doesn't sell us the ship, he loses her to scrap in two runs."

"But we're farmers," Jason said, "not shippers."

"Not now. If Hetch stays on, he takes care of the shipping for us. Jes learns the trade and can direct the company. The market's bound to increase. It did for Hetch until he had a run of bum luck, and it will for us. Only we're going to be damned careful who we haul for, and where. If Parallax doesn't move in for a decade or so, we

132

can have sub-five through -nine tight, and when they try to undercut us we'll have the sap to carry us through."

Meya woke sleepily and reached for Quilla's shoulders. Quilla pulled her onto her lap and kissed her hair.

"Seems obvious to me," Quilla said easily. She rose and carried Meya to the door while the others watched in silence.

"It's almost ai'l," she said over her shoulder. "I suggest we all get some sleep."

"She's crazy," Jason murmured as Quilla closed the door.

Mish shook her head. "I think she's right, Jase. I think she's come up with the only possible answer."

"But sell *Folly?*" Hetch demanded. "I'd sooner sell my soul."

Two weeks later the last of the *Zimania* sap was loaded onto the shuttle. Merkit and Bakar had gone up to the *Folly* with the first load, and now Hetch, Tham, and Jes stood by the shuttle's ramp. The entire population of Haven had come to see them off.

Jes was almost bouncing with eagerness, striving at the same time to look as dignified as possible. Quilla grinned, then saw Taine watching her brother. She stood apart from the crowd and looked both sad and troubled. Quilla felt an urge to go to her, say something of comfort. Then Jason touched her arm and said something about the cargo, and she forgot Taine in the excitement. Tham stood holding his latest child, making loud promises to return as soon as his slave-driver of a captain pointed the ship toward Aerie again, and Hetch went the rounds of the people, shaking hands solemnly. He would transport the sap to Shipwright, have the *Folly* made completely spaceworthy again, and stop at Althing Green to record the change of ownership and register the new planetary company of Aerie-Kennerin, growers and shippers, fairshared by every Aerite over the age of sixteen and directed by the family Kennerin, with Captain Manuel Hetch as sole head of the shipping division. He rather liked the ring of that, Director of Shipping Division; it sounded better than Freewaster, he claimed.

Quilla thought that he was trying to make it easier to give up ownership of the *Folly*, and when he shook her hand she pulled him close and kissed his cheek. He blushed furiously, grinned, and patted her hand pater-

133

nally. Quilla laughed. Tham's wife gathered her children and marched them away. Jes almost pulled Manny Hetch up the ramp, and within moments the shuttle slanted into the clouded sky.

Quilla pulled the straps of her pack over her shoulders. Mish and Jason kissed her, Laur handed her a heavy sack of provisions and admonished her to be careful, and Palen stood at the edge of the clearing, impatiently crossing and uncrossing her arms. The Aerites straggled back toward Haven, and soon the Kennerins followed them. Quilla watched them go, and turned to Tabor.

"You could have waited until the spring," he said. "We could have walked south together."

Quilla shook her head. "This I want to do alone."

"You won't change your mind? About us?"

"No. I'm sorry." She touched his arm. "I don't want to change the way we are together, I told you that. But I don't want to get married. I don't think it's necessary."

"To me it is."

She looked at him silently. Tabor walked away wordlessly and climbed out of sight. Quilla watched him for a moment, then walked to Palen.

"All finished?" Palen said. "Said good-bye to everyone on the damned island? Forgotten anyone?"

Quilla laughed. "It's all go, kassie. Come on."

That night, eighteen kilometers south of Haven, Palen heaved the cloak over her shoulders, cursed the small, light rain, and peered at Quilla over the rapidly dying fire.

"You've been grinning all day," Palen said. "What's on your mind? Making trouble?"

"No." Quilla pulled her hood over her head and patted her flat stomach. "Just making life, Palen. Changing."

Palen snorted. "That I know about. Are you coming?"

Quilla came around the fire. They wrapped their cloaks together and lay down. Quilla put her head on Palen's shoulder, and the kasir wrapped four arms around the human. In a few moments they were both asleep.

134

HART

I SIT AND WATCH THEM ALL DURING DINNER, as they eat and talk and giggle at each other's jokes. As usual, they don't seem to notice my silence; as usual, I don't care. Meya has discovered puns, and is busy punning in Standard. Stupid, infantile twisting of words, over which Jes would chortle were he not off hopping through the Wing, playing at being a spacer. Frivolous people, both of them.

Mish talks about kasiri. You can't make a pun in kasiri, she says. She leans back and pats her stomach, exaggerating the amount she has eaten. Flat stomach, flat woman. My mother. Mish. My father serves himself again and again, putting heaps of food into his own flat body, pushing hair from his forehead, eyeing my mother over his cups of wine. Lechery. Lechery! Quilla, my older sister, my beloved Quilla, dear Quilla, with a belly like an inflated bladder pressed against the table's edge; Quilla with her unborn get, sipping at her wine and smiling. Secretive. Quiet. As though she carries the answer to the mystery of the universe tucked in her belly. She talks with Jason about this and that, the farm, the shipping company, the people. She reaches for the jug of wine. She nibbles cheese. Pregnancy has made her sensuous, slow, filled the planes and angles of her face, softened her eyes. Self-sufficient bitch. She'd taken maggot seed and brewed it into maggot life, parroted about love and meaning and change and death, and spat Tabor from her life, having emptied him of what she wanted. She won't marry him. My sister the bitch is brewing a bastard. And Tabor doesn't realize how thoroughly he's been used. He comes back, of course; he'll always come back, and she'll al-

135

ways take from him and give nothing in return. (She used to give. She used to give to me. Love and bandages. Quilla?) They're all like that, my dear family. Takers. Eaters. Self-sufficient, self-contained people. The maggots have turned them into vampires, and they're too blind to know it. Too blind to know how well I know them.

And I do know them, very well do I know them, completely do I know them. How could I not know them? I know myself, and I am like them. Seed and spawn. Blood of my blood, frivolity of my frivolity. Lust of my lust.

Mim comes in from the kitchen behind me, walks along the side of the room, puts a plate before my father, walks back. Avoiding my chair. Mim doesn't like me and I don't like her. Mim the maggot. Alien. Short-spoken woman. She's trying to turn Laur against me, but it won't work. Laur hasn't the brains to turn against me, and for this I love her.

I'm fifteen years old. I keep my head. I balance my life. I go my way. Tonight I will go my way again, pack my bags and move from them, tonight I can afford to look at them calmly, dispassionately, coldly, thoroughly.

"Dessert, Hart?"

That's Quilla, leaning awkwardly toward me, smiling, holding a bowl of cream and sweets.

Quilla.

Sweet, brackish Laur, black stick, old woman, supervises while Mim clears the table. Laur brings her cup of tea and sits near me, eyes my plate, shakes her head. Mim sits beside my distant, pregnant sister, they bend their heads and speak, I presume, of the repulsive. What else does one discuss with a pregnant woman? Placentas. Contractions. Lactation. Baby shit. Vomit. I could tell her more about any of these subjects than she could guess or want to know. Shall I tell you how life is made, fecund Quilla? Not the grunting of body against body and a spurt of slime, not a shiver in the loins and emotional masturbation. Chemicals and atoms, Quilla. Cells and changes. Purity, biological cleanliness, surrounded by so much corruption, so unhappily embedded in so much human flesh. Secrets of the flesh. Flesh of my flesh. Quilla. Does your baby have two heads?

I push away from the table and leave the room. They notice, of course, but say nothing. My head hurts.

My room is small and cramped and heavy with stale

air and stale objects. The window through which I used to crawl to meet with Gren. Terrifying Gren. How could that broken, scared old man have terrified me?

A child, that's all. A small child. I grew. I learned. Am learning still, while the rest of them sit at the table and exchange information as old and battered and worthless as their lives.

My family.

My bags are already packed; there is little here I wish to take. Clothing. Some journals. A few tools. I've moved most of my books and tapes out already. What remains?

A blanket Mish made for me, long ago. All the knotted, colored yarn, pattern on pattern. Made it with her hands, her fingers, sitting one winter before the fire. Before the maggots.

Drums my father made me. Jason. Hollowed wood and kelva pods, painted with the figures of birds.

Jes' old whistle, battered and shrill.

A puppet made from one of Quilla's shirts.

A wooden ship.

The windowsill comes to my thighs; I remember when it came to my shoulders. I lean against the glass, looking out over the kitchen roof, over the tall, bending tree. My eyes sting.

"Hart?"

I turn suddenly and things spill from my arms. Blanket, drums, whistle, toys. Muffle and clatter on the floor—I thought they had said my name.

Quilla stands leaning at the doorway, puzzled. She should have moved more loudly, this double-personed person, and here she has come silently to startle me. When she says my name, she plays with the "r," drawing it out, softening it.

"What do you want?"

Has she noticed my eyes? I don't dare lift my hand to wipe at my cheeks. The light is behind me on the bedside table; she won't notice my eyes. No.

"Nothing," she says. She walks into the room and sits. Her belly fills her lap. "I saw you leaving the dining room and thought you might be upset."

"No."

"What are you doing?"

"Leaving." I stuff more things into my bag, kick the toys and blanket and whistles and memories under the bed. She makes me feel uneasy.

137

"Where?"

"Haven. Gren and I have a house."

"Gren," she says. "Have you asked Mish or Jason?"

"I don't need to. In three months I'll be a voting adult. I don't need their permission."

She folds her hands over the bulk of her middle. The child kicks within her; I can see her hands bounce up and down. Flesh.

"Have you at least told them?"

"They'll find out soon enough."

"They won't like it."

"Too bad."

Her forehead creases, her lips thin. I know what's coming, I know that look.

"Has someone hurt you, Hart?"

Oh, that's a nasty one, that's an underhanded one. Echoes back, years back, before the maggots, before I lost them all. Her question makes my throat tight, and that makes me angry. I seam the bag closed and throw it over my shoulder. I think of all the bitter, biting things I could say, but my throat is stiff and I won't risk spoiling my exit. Dignified silence. I turn. I step toward the door. Yes. Icy. Cold.

But Quilla stands and blocks my way, puts her hand on my shoulder, puts her hand on my chin, tries to tilt my head up to look at her. I jerk away.

"Hart. Please."

"Leave me alone!"

"I'm only trying—"

"Leave me alone!" Oh, God. Oh shit. I'm crying. "Just get away from me. Go maggot with your friends. Let me go."

"Hart—"

"Why did you have to do that?" I jab at her belly with my finger. She steps back and puts her arm across her belly protectively. "Why weren't we good enough for you? Why did you have to go with, with him, with that man? Why couldn't you let things be?"

She reaches for me again. I push her and run from the room, down the stairs. I hear her falling. Jason sticks his head into the hallway and says something, but I don't stop. Let Quilla explain it. She'll think of something good.

I have to stop at the bottom of the hill, lay in the grasses, catch my breath. Better. Better.

Gren stands in the doorway of the house on Schoolhouse Road; peers suspiciously at the few houses around this one, afraid that his new neighbors will come steal all his precious secrets. Precious, indeed. I have mastered all of them, elementary biology, elementary biomedicine, chemistry. Gren hasn't been able to teach me anything for a year or more, save how to frighten him more thoroughly. Sick old man. He has his uses.

He knows, for example, how to shut up. In silence he carries my bags to my room, in silence retreats to his own niche, in silence does whatever it is that he does to prepare for bed. I walk about the house, lighting lamps, inspecting things. A good enough place. Private, despite the neighbors. And when the basement is finished, it will be a perfect place. There are people to the right and left and across the street, but behind stretch scrubby bushes and then the stream. I can walk from house to stream and no one will see. Gren doesn't yet understand how important this is.

I take my shirt off, and my skin prickles in the cool air. Draw water from the kitchen pump and heat it, gather buckets and brushes, and scrub. Start with the front room. The original maggots, maggot-like, left a mess. It needs fixing. And Mish and Jason and Laur will exclaim over the neatness of the house that Gren and I keep, how clean things are, how nice things are. Surely nothing can be wrong with letting a young boy help an old man through his final years, not in a house as neat as this.

The kitchen. The hallway. Slosh and scrub and dust and clean. A charitable deed, this, which will reflect well on all Kennerins. Yes. Sweep.

I'll let anyone in except Quilla. Except Quilla.

I finish. I put things away. I check things over. I go to bed.

My head hurts.

I didn't mean to cry.

Part Four

1226

New Time

DECADE

"Rock meeting rock can know love better
Than eyes that stare or lips that touch.
All that we know in love is bitter
And it is not much."

—Conrad Aiken

LAUR STRODE DOWN THE HILL TO HAVEN, HER
market basket slung over one arm. The midsummer
sun floated overhead, bathing the landscape in warmth.
The village had grown in the past ten years, from a
sorry collection of makeshift houses and shops to a
respectable town, complete with marketplace, school,
hospital, meeting hall, and the actions and ceremonies
necessary for a sense of community. Everything, she
thought approvingly, had changed, and generally for
the better. The plantation produced punctually and
fully; the farms and gardens kept the market supplied
with a steady line of fruits and vegetables. The kasirene
brought in fresh fish every other day, and the ranches in
the hills kept Haven supplied with fresh meat. She even
approved, albeit grudgingly, of the brewery on the out-
skirts of the town. At least now they were no longer
dependent on kaea, that vile kasirene concoction; their
own native wines improved year by year. And tomorrow was nem'mai Biant Meir, BeginningDay. This year
the celebration would be long and joyous, as the Aerites
remembered the day they had arrived on planet, rescued
by Jason Kennerin from the political horrors of their native planet, nurtured by Mish Kennerin through a harsh
winter and unhappy spring, given a home. Laur did not
have to doubt the gratitude of the Aerites. It was taken
for granted, and of this, also, she approved.

The marketplace teemed with householders bickering
for goods and food. Laur straightened her shoulders and
marched through, nodding to her acquaintances, stopping
to gossip with her friends, pretending not to notice when
the line before the butcher's, the baker's, the potter's, the

142

grocer's mysteriously melted before her. She hired her favorite urchins to run her purchases up the hill to Tor Kennerin, knowing that they accepted her dictates not simply through respect, but because, their errands finished in the warm kitchens of the Tor, the kassie cooks would be waiting with hot, sweet rolls and cool glasses of juice. Largesse from Aerie's lords, Laur thought. And approved.

The fishmonger's shop was the most crowded. Here Laur stood in line, for the kasirene behind the counters lacked a sense of proportion, and made her wait just as the other householders waited. She stood patiently, letting the sunlight soak through her black gown and warm her bones. Medi Lount, the sculptor, stood ahead of her and they gossiped about the offices for Aerie-Kennerin that Medi had designed, and for which she would create the statues and friezes. Haven's latest debate concerned the inclusion of kasirene figures amid the large statues, rather than merely in the smaller, less imposing friezes. Laur, as a Kennerin, felt that she should express no opinion, for her thoughts would carry too much weight and might tip the balance in favor of the minority. She therefore listened to Medi's harangue in silence, nodding at appropriate moments, but not paying too much attention to the sculptor's words.

The smiling, bowing kasir behind the counter sold her two large kavets and a smaller tele-tele. They packed the fish in ice and wrapped the entire bundle in grass mats. Laur looked around for a trustworthy urchin. No children seemed available. She stepped toward the edge of the crowd, hoping for a better view, and saw Hart moving rapidly through the main square. He held a large bundle in his arms.

"Hart!" she called. He did not stop. She elbowed her way through the crowd, calling his name again. Since moving away from the Tor over two years ago, he had been home only to demand money from his parents. The last time he and Jason had argued violently, and Hart had sworn never to return. Laur could not bear the thought of never seeing her favorite again, but he had kept his oath, and the few times she had been to his home he had not been there. Now she followed, scurrying along with complete disregard of the creaking of her muscles. Once away from the market she shouted his name again, and it seemed to her that he hesitated, then moved more quickly through the streets, dodging carts and drayclones. She set her lips firmly, then returned to the fish vendor's and tucked the package of fish into her basket before marching resolutely down Schoolhouse Road to Hart's house. Hart might be a young man now, seventeen and out of school, but that did not give him leave to treat her badly.

She climbed the steps to his front door, caught her breath, and knocked loudly. The house was quiet. She huffed with annoyance and banged harder, knowing that he was in, and as she waited she grew more annoyed.

"Hart, you open this door right now!" she shouted. "Hear me. You open up or I'll, I'll—" She paused, trying to find an effective threat, and as she hesitated the door opened a crack and Hart slid out. He closed the door firmly behind him.

"Hello, Laur," he said easily. His smile was, as always, both charming and mocking, but Laur refused to give up her anger. She glared up at him.

"And why do you keep me waiting?" she demanded. "Why did I have to follow you through the streets just like a dog? I suppose you want everyone in Haven to laugh at me. I'm completely winded and my heart hurts, and it's all your fault. At least you can offer me a cup of tea."

Hart shook his head, his expression regretful. "I'm sorry, Laur. I'm busy right now."

"Have you got a young woman in there?" She cocked her head and looked archly at him. "It's all right. I'd like to meet her. After all, I'm sure old Laur has a right to know who you've been seeing, don't I? Not everyone in Haven is suitable."

"No one in Haven is suitable," Hart said, his humor briefly gone. "No, I don't have a woman in there, Laur. But I am busy. Why don't you come back tomorrow afternoon? We can have tea and cakes and a nice long talk. All right?" He started to open the door.

"Tomorrow's BeginningDay," Laur said. "You know very well there'll be no time for tea tomorrow. Come on, baby, my feet hurt."

"I'm sorry. I don't have the time now. Maybe next week." He slipped into the house and closed the door, and she heard the sound of locks snapping into place.

Up to no good, she thought. Something he shouldn't be doing, and not enough sense to know when he's getting himself into trouble. She pondered this a moment, then glanced around the street. The square, unpainted houses were still; no one in sight. She crept around the side of Hart's house. Hart had to be protected, especially from himself. She was sure he had some unsuitable woman in there, and unless she did something immediately he would find himself saddled with an unacceptable alliance. One scandal was enough for a family. She set the basket of fish under a bush and moved quietly toward the first window. The sill was a good hundred centimeters from the ground; she stretched as high as she could and peeped within.

The front room was sparsely furnished and completely messy. Hart's books and clothing lay piled in the corners, his boots sitting atop a stack of shirts; dirty cups and plates littered the table. Wall shelves held hundreds of tapes, piled haphazardly. Through an open door she could see the kitchen, in an equal state of chaos, and she pursed her lips. Hart was usually so clean. It must be that terrible, filthy old man he lived with. He would have to let her in, if only to clean things up. She inspected the corners of the room with increasing boldness, but Hart was not to be seen.

She found the bedroom window, looked in, and saw equal filth and an equal absence of Hart. Gren's door stood open, and that room, too, was empty. Puzzled, she relaxed against the wall and opened the top button of her gown. The house had only one door; he could not have left while she was there. Then she saw the low window set at ground level—a basement, of course. If Hart was up to something, he would be sure to do it where he could not be seen. She repressed a groan as she lowered herself to the ground, lay on her belly, and peered in the window.

The window was curtained, but one edge of the cloth had caught on something and revealed a portion of the room. She squirmed closer and could hear sounds in the basement. Something moved rapidly back and forth, and she saw Gren's head for a moment. Naturally, Gren would be there. Anything involving Gren was sure to be no good, and Laur didn't like the way the old man led Hart about, teaching him evil, satiric ways. She lifted her hand to rap sharply on the glass, but at that moment heard a muffled scream which prickled at her skin. Gren's expression was one of disapproval, and he moved

145

out of sight. The scream ceased abruptly. Muted voices argued. Laur craned her neck, trying to see more, but she could only make out the corner of the cellar directly before her. Hart came into view, talking and waving one arm emphatically. Laur squinted. He seemed to be carrying something in his other arm. Almost as if to oblige her, Hart turned and Laur saw that he held a tiny, unweaned kassie pup in his palm. As he talked, his free hand grasped a knife and casually beheaded the pup. Its body shivered and was still, and Hart held up the tiny head, gesturing at it with the point of his knife, discoursing. He tossed the head and body out of sight, moved away, and returned, carrying a young kassie female in his arms. She was bound, her snout gagged, and she stared at him dully. He smiled at her and said something, then carried her out of sight.

Laur pushed herself upright, leaned against the side of the house, and vomited. The sun felt hot and fierce against her bare head. The stream twinkled distantly through the bushes. She stood shakily and moved toward it, stumbling over the uneven ground.

She should tell Jason. She should tell Mish. She should tell someone, should not let this go on. It was Gren's doing, Gren who led Hart astray, Gren in back of the entire terrible thing. She would clean her dress and go right home—yes, go home and tell Jason. Jason would know what to do. Jason would take care of it. Jason would punish Gren for what he had done to Hart. Jason would . . .

She reached the stream and sat beside it, and her stomach heaved again. The earth below her spun and lurched. She clung to a tree and closed her eyes, and Hart found her that way—dirty, tired, terrified. She looked at him, beyond screams, and he smiled and knelt beside her. He held her basket in his hand.

"You forgot your fish," he said gently. "It's the sun, you know. It's so hot it bubbles your brain sometimes. Here, let me help you clean yourself up."

She watched as he dipped his handkerchief in the stream and cleaned her face, then passed the wet cloth over her dress.

"You've really got to be more careful," he said as he worked. "At your age, just a little sun can hurt you. You forget things, and sometimes you see things that didn't really happen. You must have stood in the marketplace for too long. You ought to make Mim do the marketing, you shouldn't have to do it yourself. Here, move your chin a little. Good. I'll bet that Mim refuses to do the work, right? She made you come down and do it all yourself, and she knows how hot it is. It's simply not fair the way she takes advantage of you. There, that's a bit better. Are you feeling all right now?"

Laur nodded weakly. Hart smiled at her again, then picked her up. She stared at him, her mind blank.

"I'll help you get home," he said. "What you need is a glass of cold water and some rest. You have to take care of yourself, Laur. I don't want to lose you."

She felt tiny in his arms, and saw a picture in her mind of Hart carrying a kassie through the cellar. But that was an illusion, she thought in confusion. Too much sun. Hart wouldn't do a thing like that.

"Remember the time I stole your fish?" he said. He carried her through the trees and up the hill. "I was about ten, wasn't I? And you were so mad at me. Remember that, Laur?"

She nodded.

"You made me eat fish for an entire week—breakfast, lunch, and dinner. Oh, how I hated that." He laughed and she smiled. A long time ago. Hart. It's all Mim's fault.

He stopped a few meters from the kitchen door and set her on her feet.

"There," he said. "You don't want to let anyone see that you're weak, do you? It wouldn't do for them to think that you're getting too old. Mim might want to take over everything, and that would not be right."

Laur nodded and straightened her shoulders, and Hart patted her back.

"That's right. You go in and take a long rest, and I won't say a word about your sunstroke. After all, it can happen to anyone when they're made to stand in the heat. Right? Sure. I'll come up tomorrow during the feast, and you can come down next week and have tea and cakes with me. I've got a good cook; you'll like it. All right, Laur? Is that all right?"

She nodded uncertainly and he kissed her cheek, smiled, and walked quickly down the hill toward Haven. She clutched her basket and moved slowly toward the house, feeling the sun beating on her head. She'd make Mim do the marketing from now on. It wasn't fair that she should have to do it, not at all. Imagine, forcing her

147

to go into the sun, with her health so delicate. Mim was up to something, surely, but she'd catch it for this, sure enough. Mim would really catch it.

Jes stood before the glass in his room and surveyed himself with dissatisfaction. The soft blue shirt was fine and gave him an air of poetic distraction of which he approved. But the pants were definitely wrong, the blue neither mixing nor melding with the blue of the shirt. Besides, they were too baggy around the ass. Hard work on the *Folly* had slimmed and tautened his body, and none of his clothes fit pleasingly. He stripped the pants off impatiently and threw them on the pile of clothes which covered the bed. The white pants, perhaps? But they were dirty, stained with engine grease on both knees, and there wasn't time to wash them. The yellow? No, he'd look like some stupid knocker just off the dirt. Yellow pants and yellow shirt? Too much like a uniform. He wondered if Jason had any pants he could borrow, then remembered that he'd outgrown his father's pants two years ago. He stood uncertainly, naked from the waist down, and glared at his clothes niche.

Someone knocked on the door. "Just a minute," he called and scrambled into the first pair of pants he could reach. The door opened as he seamed them together, and Meya came in.

"Jes? Can I come in?"

"You are." He pushed clothing from a corner of the bed. Meya closed the door and sat. She held a package in her hands.

"Getting dressed for tomorrow already?" Her eyes twinkled mischievously. "You'll get yourself all wrinkled, and then nobody will make eyes at you."

"Of course I'm not, lumpkin. I'm just trying to decide what to wear is all."

"Huh," she said skeptically, surveying the piled bed. "You're making more of a mess than anyone else. I've been all around, and even Quilla's playing with her clothes. She's got the prettiest clothes for the twins, just wait until you see them. Tabor's coming. Why don't you just wear your spacer's suit? It looks good."

"Because tomorrow's a party, lump. When you go to a party, you get all dressed up." He sat beside her on the bed. "But I can't decide what to wear. Everything's either

148

dirty or it doesn't fit or the colors aren't right. Maybe I won't go to the damned party at all."

"Taine'll be mad at you," Meya said wisely. "And she'll spend the whole night dancing with someone else, while you sit at home all angry because you don't have anything to wear."

"You shut it, you little wise-ass!" Jes said. He tickled her and she rolled about on the clothes, chortling and gasping. "I'll teach you to make fun of your elders. There!"

Meya wiped tears from her eyes and cuddled next to him.

"Quilla's going to wear a dress," she said importantly. "It's sort of orangy-browny, and it comes all the way to here." She pointed to her knees. "Mim told her that she should take it up, but she said she didn't want to."

"It's her own choice."

Meya plucked her package from the bed, grinned at Jes, and pulled at the string. "Anyway, since she wasn't going to be wearing them, I asked her if you could wear these. I washed them all by myself."

Meya pulled a pair of pants from the package and held them out. They were a soft spring green, of a fine material that draped over Jes' hands.

"Oh, Meya. They'll never fit."

"Sure they will. Go ahead and put them on. Quilla said you both wear the same size. Go on, don't just sit there."

Jes grinned suddenly and stripped off his pants, then put on the green ones. They molded to his thighs and hips, and fit snugly over buttocks and crotch.

"They're perfect," he said. "But I don't have a shirt to go with them."

"So don't wear a shirt at all. Taine'll love that."

"Will you cut out this Taine stuff? She doesn't care about me one way or another, and that's that." He looked down at himself regretfully. "It's a pity about the shirt."

"Oh, close your eyes," Meya said.

"Why?"

"Just close them, or I'll make Quilla take the pants back."

Jes sighed and closed his eyes tightly. He heard a rustle of paper and string, then felt Meya's small fingers at the seams of his blue shirt.

"What are you doing?"

"Don't open your eyes! You just be still. I'll be done in

a minute." She slid the shirt away and grabbed at his arm, pulling something over it. He obligingly extended the other arm and stood still, repressing a smile, as she fumbled at the seam. Finally she sighed and said, "Okay, you can open your eyes now."

Jes stared at himself in the mirror. The shirt was cut tightly about the torso and loose in the arms, made of the same fine material as the pants. Its intricate print echoed the green of the pants amid swirling colors. Jes smiled, then grinned, then laughed aloud.

"It's wonderful! Where in the world did you get it?"

"I made it," she said offhandedly. "Well, Mim helped me a lot, but mostly I made it myself. I did the basting, and I told Haive what colors to put in the cloth, too. That's a lot."

"It certainly is, lumpkin." Jes picked his sister up and swung her around the room, then kissed her forehead and dumped her back on the bed. She collected the remains of her package and went to the door.

"Taine'll go wild when she sees you," she predicted confidently. Jes swore happily and threw a shirt at her retreating form.

Tabor picked up his naked daughter and held her on his hip. She reached for his silky, pale beard and yanked on it. He yelped. His son laughed and slapped the water with his hands, spattering Quilla as she knelt on the wooden platform beside the small tub.

"Jared, cut that out," she said. "Decca, leave your father's beard alone."

"No," the children said simultaneously.

Quilla sighed. "It's their favorite word this month. I think they don't know any others."

"Do so," Jared said, insulted. He grabbed at the bar of soap. Quilla took it from him, rinsed him, and put him on a towel. He wriggled enthusiastically and gripped the towel with his teeth. Tabor put Decca in the tub.

"When does the party begin?" he said.

"Another hour or two. Mim said she'd watch them while we dressed."

"You're filthy," Tabor said to Decca. She ignored him, intent on popping a bubble with her toes. He put a towel over her eyes and held it there while he poured water over her head.

"No!" she howled. "Don't like it!"

"Got to wash your hair, pretty. Come on, don't do that. Damn it, Decca, I don't want a bath."

"Bath," she repeated and giggled. Her light hair darkened with water and lay flat along her cheeks and neck. Tabor rubbed the soap into her hair and worked up a lather.

Jared escaped from Quilla's grasp and made a dash for the tub. Quilla grabbed him and took him to the pile of clothes against the half-wall. Steam beaded along the kaedo leaves overhead and fell down as Jared hammered on the wall with his fists.

"Remember to wash her bottom," Quilla called over her shoulder. She pulled Jared away from the wall and reached for his shirt. "She likes to sit in the dirt."

"I've noticed. Here, stand up, Decca. Come on. Hold onto my shoulder. There, that's a girl."

"Mim!" Quilla yelled.

"Want to stay with Keka," Jared announced. He sat abruptly and held onto the bench.

Decca tried to climb out of the tub. "Be with Aded!" she yelled.

"Okay, okay," Tabor said. He wrestled her into the tub again and rinsed her off. "There. Now hold still for a moment."

Eventually, overalled and damp, the children were collected by Mim and taken back to the house. Quilla sighed and tilted the tub over the platform's edge, splashing water into the drain trough below, then pulled the cover from the hot tub while Tabor collected the damp towels and piled them in a corner. By the time he finished, Quilla was already soaping herself in the shower, and when he entered she kissed him quickly and slid into the tub. She gasped as the hot water lapped up her shoulders.

He turned off the water and stood for a moment by the entrance, listening to the distant sounds from the barn. He could hear Meya's high, ringing shout, and an answering yell from some adult. Kasirene moved between Tor and barn and village, carrying plates and pots of food. The last of the morning mist had burned away, leaving the day fair and warm. A child's sandal lay abandoned on the platform. Tabor picked it up and looked at it, then put it atop the pile of clothing and stepped into the tub beside Quilla.

"This isn't working," he said after a while. She turned her head to look at him.

"What isn't working?"

"Being a distant father. I've only seen them twelve times in the past two years. It's not enough, Quilla."

"So move here. You know you can live with me if you want, and if you don't you can find a place in Haven. The children can live with both of us—sometimes in Haven and sometimes at the Tor—if you don't want to live here."

"What kind of life is that?" Tabor slid down until the water reached his chin. "Living in Haven. Dividing them up like muffins. They're my children, Quilla. I want them."

"Tabor, be realistic. How would a lame man, living alone, cope with a pair of two-year-old twins? Even I can't manage them alone. But there's Mim, and Laur, and Jason, and Mish to help out. Even Meya."

"Children need a father."

"They have a father. They also have an entire house full of family to care for them and love them. They're fine right here."

"They're not with me right here."

"So move to Haven."

"Move them to the Cault."

"Tabor, you know very well that won't work. The Cault's completely snowbound in the winter. What if something should happen to them? Even in the summer the mountains are more dangerous than the Tor. They could get hurt, and you wouldn't be able to get them to help." She looked at him evenly. "I don't understand you. You want the children, but you don't want to move here and you can't take care of them alone up there."

"I don't want them alone up there."

"Then what in the Mother's name do you want?" she said, exasperated.

"Marry me."

She turned angrily to leave the tub, but he caught her wrist and held her tightly.

"Quilla, listen to me. I've wanted to marry you for years. I didn't get in your way when you got pregnant, even though you didn't see fit to tell me about it. I haven't made any trouble for you since. I just want to be with my children. I want to be with you."

"What does that have to do with marriage?"

"Everything, damn it!" He breathed deeply and released her wrist. She sat again, not looking at him.

152

"You say you don't want to tie me down, that if we married things would be just the way they are now. Except that we'd live together all the time. I don't see why we can't live together all the time without being married."

"Maybe I'm a traditionalist. Perhaps I'm afraid."

"Of what?"

"You might leave me."

"I don't think you've a right to say that. I don't think I belong to you. I go my own way. If I wanted to leave you, and I don't see why I would, it wouldn't make any difference whether we were married or not."

"I'm thirty-three, Quilla. You're twenty-four. That's nine years."

"So?"

"I'm lame."

"And you worry about it more than I do."

"I love you. You know that. I wish you could feel the same way about me."

She looked away and remained silent. He wanted to reach for her, touch her, but instead climbed out of the tub, wrapped himself in a towel, and walked back to the Tor.

She came into the room as he finished dressing, and still had nothing to say.

Jason strode down the hill, a grandchild under each arm.

"Hey, Manny!" he shouted. "How much to ship these out? Price at Shipwright?"

The children howled with glee.

"About four each," Hetch said, frowning. He poked Jared in the belly. "Maybe a little more for this dumpling. What good are they?"

"Exercise machines." Jason set the children on the floor of the barn. They immediately joined hands and ran toward the haystacks. Jason watched until they disappeared into a group of kasirene.

"Beer?" Hetch said. Jason nodded and the captain handed him a cold stein. Jason sat in the hay and took a long drink. The barn was almost ready. Bright flags and banners floated from the lofts and beams, blankets covered piles of hay to make comfortable couches, and the tables were loaded with food and drink. An area had been cleared for dancing, and the musicians were present, tuning their instruments and making jokes. Jason

153

waved to them and tugged at the leg of Hetch's dress uniform.

"Sit down, Manny. We won't have another chance to talk until tomorrow."

"What's to talk about? Beer and dancing, that's enough for one evening." But Hetch sat and held his stein.

"How's Jes doing?"

The captain shrugged. "He's still in love with being a spacer, and until he gets over that he's not going to be much good. Oh, he's fine crew, does what he's told, learns fast, takes orders. He can even figure things out on his own. He's bright, and that's good. But until he gets over this romantic nonsense, he's going to be a lousy officer, and that's that."

"What romantic nonsense? Don't tell me he's fallen for Merkit."

"Don't mean romance that way, Jase. But he's wild about space, got visions of commanding ship in dire emergencies. That sort of stuff. Won't believe me when I tell him the whole idea of space travel is to get from A to B in the most boring way. Excitement's no good up there. Emergencies can kill you."

Jason frowned and drank. "Think he'll get over it?"

"Yeah. Once he gets laid."

"Manny, you've got to be kidding. Jes is a virgin? After two years in space? Don't you give him planet leave?"

"Sure. He spends it hanging around the port talking with spacers."

"Just talking? Not doing anything?"

"It's not for want of wanting," Hetch said. He rubbed his palm over his bald head. "He's as randy as they come, or talks that way. I think he's saving it for something special. Tied in with that Jes-on-the-bridge crap."

Jason shook his head. "All my children are crazy," he said sadly.

Palen appeared in the distance. The twins rode in her capacious pouch, and they giggled as she admonished them not to kick her nipples. Jason watched her. She'd pupped soon after the twins were born, but the child had disappeared a few months ago. Palen wouldn't talk about it, and neither would the local kasirene. Jason remembered that the kasirene exchanged pups as casually as humans exchanged clothing, and that any one kasir pup might move in comfort from mother to father to aunt to stranger, suckling indiscriminately, traveling the length

154

and breadth of Aerie before leaving the pouch permanently. Palen's pup was, more than likely, summering in the mountains, or with some distant tribe by the shores of Mother Sea. She had, it seemed to him, adopted Quilla's children with the same lack of ceremony as kasirene traded their own offspring back and forth; the twins spent entire days and nights in the kasirene village, to Laur's flustered disapproval.

If Palen was the twins' adoptive mother, did that make the kasir Jason's adoptive daughter? She was as crazy as any of his blood-children; she might as well be family.

Hetch stood, finished his beer, and put the stein on a table.

"Promised Hoku I'd bring some stuff up for her," he said glumly. "Think she wants to weigh me again."

Jason laughed and finished his own beer. Palen told him that she'd be willing to watch the children until the party began, and he walked up the hill again. Mish would be ready by now, he thought. Warm and perfumed from bathing; tiny. Sweet. His loins tingled as he grinned, and his pace quickened. There would be plenty of time before the party.

Dr. Hoku sat in a place of honor, convenient to the punchbowl, and observed her patients with a quick, exacting eye. She considered everyone in Haven her patient, including the kasirene from the neighboring village, and she watched them all intently. Old Ved Hirem stumped by and nodded shortly to her; Ved was still convinced that he suffered from arthritis, although if he had arthritis, she had wings. She dosed him with analgesics and harsh words, both of which he took with ill humor. She nodded back to him and grabbed a passing child.

"You're Kridee, aren't you?" The child nodded. "Right. Go fetch me more punch."

The child took the cup and scampered toward the table. Born on a cold winter's night, Hoku remembered. Rain on the roof and his father moaning and gnawing at his fingers. Healthy baby. Kridee brought her punch, and she ruffled his hair and sent him on his way.

Hart and Gren entered, and Hoku watched them, her face calm and her mind suspicious. Gren was negligible, had been for the past five years, and she suspected that Hart had something to do with the old man's incessant drinking and cringing demeanor. She'd have given a lot

155

to discover what the two of them were up to, there in Hart's basement, but suspected that she'd just as soon not know. Gren's mind was so befuddled by alcohol and what tasted like fright that she could not read him, and Hart projected a cold sarcasm that kept her at bay, as his earlier, total hatred had blocked her. Gren and Hart walked to the table and took plates of food, then faded into the crowd. If this BeginningDay was like others, they would eat together, sit making unpleasant comments about the celebrants, and leave well before the dancing started. Hoku grunted and turned her attention elsewhere.

Hetch getting fat again, and fatter before the night was out. Second helping piled on his plate, third or fourth stein of beer, and the party barely started. She considered summoning him, then decided against it. He could fast next week; let him enjoy himself tonight. Cagy, space-bound old bastard. She liked him.

Jes glided by, dressed in finery, and Hoku nodded. Expectations confirmed. He would be out to impress Taine. And where was Taine? There, by the tables. She, too, had seen Jes enter, and, to Hoku's surprise, she left her circle of admirers and crossed the barn to Jes, touched his arm, and smiled at him. Hoku frowned thoughtfully. Something had changed in Taine recently. The young woman had become increasingly unhappy beneath her layer of frosty reserve; then within the past day the unhappiness had changed to something with the flavor of intense resolution —something to do only peripherally with Jes, Hoku guessed. She wished that she could talk with Taine, but Taine avoided Hoku whenever possible and icily refused even the smallest attempt at intimacy. Hoku wondered whether Taine remembered those two weeks at the Great Barrier camp, remembered Hoku's forcible besmirching of her face and hair. She suspected that while Taine remembered the events, she had repressed the identities. The doctor sighed and hoped that Taine was not aiming herself for even more unhappiness. In the distance, Taine held Jes' arm and laughed.

Quilla and Tabor, looking prickly. Typical.

Sweet Mother, what's happened to Laur? The old woman creaked into the barn, her usually straight back bent, shoulders hunched, as though age had finally caught up with her and now sat full weight on her neck. Laur was close to seventy-eight or so, but still, not this sudden a change. Hoku watched with surprise as Laur made her

slow way toward the table, then saw Hart and stopped.
She's afraid, Hoku thought. Of Hart? Of her favorite?
The barn was too crowded for the doctor to pick out
Laur's emotions. Hart immediately came to Laur and
guided the old woman to a seat in the hay, then sent Gren
to bring her a plate. He bent his head and talked, smiling,
touching. Eventually the old woman smiled uncertainly.
She accepted the plate from Gren and bent her head to it.
I'll have to talk with her, Hoku decided. As soon as pos-
sible. Something's gravely wrong.

Ho. Pita made it after all. She's going to have that baby
any moment now. Where's Jed? What good's a trained
midwife if he's never around when you need him?

She snapped up another child. "You're Haley, Tham's
child, yes? Find Jed and tell him that I want to see him.
Now. Go on."

Haley tore off through the crowd, and Hoku returned
to her people-watching. The kasirene contingent entered
in one group, led by Palen tor-Altemet, Quilla's friend.
Palen carried Decca and Jared in her pouch. She hauled
them out and sent them scampering toward their parents.
The kasirene bowed and chattered, and Hoku was
pleased to see the Aerites accept them, with tolerance if
not with warmth. The kasirene brought their roasted fishes
to the table and spread them out, and soon another rush
toward the tables began. Hoku decided to wait for the
fish. There would be plenty to go around.

Meya, standing by her sister, saw Palen and gave a
squeal of delight as she launched herself toward the kasir.
Palen picked her up, hugged her, and set her on the
ground before turning to embrace Quilla. Quilla's back relaxed and she stood talking with Palen while Meya danced
around them demanding attention. Quilla gave Meya and
the twins sticks of bread and sent them off. Tabor
watched Quilla and Palen in silence. Meya capered
around the room, the recipient of caresses and smiles
from Aerites and kasirene both. Hoku watched the child
fondly, half expecting her to take to the air. Such a light,
bright child to come from such a winter, Hoku thought.
From such a spring. I'm glad she's here.

"Doctor?"

She glanced up at her assistant. "Good. Where's Pita?
There, you see her? You keep your eye on her, she'll go
into labor within the next three hours. I want you nearby.
I don't think she'll have an easy time of it. Best alert some-

157

one to help you get her to the hospital. There's no use trying to convince her to leave early."

"I really don't think she will," Jed said. "She's not due for two weeks, and—"

"And I know what I'm thinking about," Hoku said. "You stick with her and don't give me any nonsense. Go on, get."

She watched him move through the crowd toward Pita and nodded. That one was going to be a real fight.

When Meya capered by, Hoku sent her for food. By the time she finished eating, the center of the barn had been cleared and Ved Hirem's Recitation was beginning. Hoku frowned and yawned. Various Aerites, dressed in rags, stumbled through the barn, their well-fed bodies striving to mime exhaustion and hunger. Jason made his traditional speech of welcome. Hetch was glorified. The burning of Haven was narrated, and the kasirene appeared with their gifts of fish. The To'an Betes expedition was given its due. Generally Mish left the barn at this point, but tonight she sat quietly, her hands in her lap. Jason put his arm around her shoulders and whispered something to her, and she smiled.

Hetch presented *Zimania* seeds, making the same speech he had made before. Hoku, traditionally, fell asleep. Music woke her. The sun was setting beyond the strand of kaedos, and the dancing began.

A small commotion drew her attention. Jed and a woman were carrying Pita from the room, and Hoku nodded, worried. Jed would send for her if he needed her, and the hospital was, thank the Mother, well stocked. She'd have to remember to make Jed apologize in the morning for doubting her diagnosis, but it was minor. Jed would do as well as he could, which wasn't at all bad. Hoku had trained him well.

Taine and Jes slipped from the barn, and didn't return. Hoku felt surprised, then shrugged. Maybe Jes would finally get laid. About time, too. As long as he didn't take it too seriously.

Quilla and Tabor were talking, their gestures growing more and more pronounced. Eventually they turned away from each other simultaneously and stalked in opposite directions. Mish and Jason continued to dance, bodies close, Mish's head resting against Jason's chest, oblivious. Aerites nudged each other and pointed at them, smiling. Meya was asleep in the hay, with a twin cuddled on either side. Mim was trying to help Laur out of the barn. The old woman jerked away and said something, her face wrinkled with fury. Mim marched off. Quilla and Palen stood talking against a wall, shoulder to shoulder.

Hoku looked at them all again, sighed, and leaned back in her chair. Kennerins, she thought. Silly fools, every one of them. She turned off her mind, relaxed, and fell asleep.

Once away from the barn's light, Taine's hair darkened; red to auburn to brown to a deep loam color, rich and soft. But the highlights in her hair remained, catching and reflecting the gleaming of stars and moon. Her gait emphasized the movement of her hips, and Jes' gaze flickered from swaying bottom to swaying hair. His breath felt tight and full in his chest. She seemed perfect now, silent, moving through the warmly scented night.

She paused at the crest of the hill and Jes stopped behind her and to the side, not yet willing to see her face. The Tor reared dark against the starlit sky, all angles and slopes; the feathery leaves of the halaea shone in the pale light. Beyond, the lamps of Haven glowed. Taine stared toward house and village, then shivered quickly and crossed her arms, putting her hands on her shoulders.

"Are you cold?"

She shook her head and walked on, more slowly now, as though deep in thought. Jes walked behind her, content to accept her mood without questioning it. Nightgoddess, he thought. She walks in beauty, like the night —and like the day, too, all that fine, pale skin and firehair, and the way she turns tawny at sunset. How does she look at dawn? How would she look in spaceflight, weightless in the diffused amber lights of the observation bubble, her hair floating around her? Spacegoddess, nightwalker, daybringer, starsinger. Wrap her in thick white pelts from Stroshine, crown her with blue gems from Tozun, a diadem of nebulae, a tiara of worlds. Barely enough for her, for this grace, this loveliness.

He was drunk and he knew it, although he had not taken a drop of alcohol that day. Drunk with Taine. From the moment she had seen him in the barn she had not left his side, had reserved the warmest of her laughter and the gentlest of her teasing for him. Had danced with him only, pressing the supple length of her body against him, and smiling slyly at his body's strong response. And had led him from the barn with mysterious smiles and promising eyes. His thighs ached with tension, but he ignored them, content simply to be with her, alone on the dark hillside. Nor did her shift from flirtatiousness to solemn thought disturb him. Nothing she did this evening could be wrong.

She led him around the tubhouse and into the grove of kaedos, stopping well within the line of trees. When he reached her, she turned to him swiftly, put her arms around his neck, and pulled his face down to hers. Startled, he lost his balance and they tumbled into the soft duff of the grove. She wriggled until she lay half atop him.

"Taine," he whispered.

"Hush," she said urgently and kissed him again. Her fingers moved down the seam of his shirt and it fell open. He tried to push her hands away, confused by the speed of it all, striving for the room to understand what she wanted of him and why. Then her tongue slid into his mouth and her hand cupped the crotch of his pants, and his objections were lost in a flood of warmth. Her fingers burned down the length of his body, and he fumbled clumsily for the seam of her shirt. Her nipples stiffened against the palm of his hand; her belly was smooth and warm. Her clothing slid quickly from her body; he arched his hips to help her strip him of his pants. He stroked her hips, and when he touched her gently between her legs, afraid of hurting her, she gasped and moved sharply against his hand. Then she swung her legs over him and slid onto his prick before he knew what she was doing. The universe became a sheath of tightness and warmth. He moaned, arched his back, and came immediately.

When he tried to speak, she muffled his words with kisses, caressed him, and he stiffened again. This time she slid below him and let him set the pace, guiding him with sweet, gentle motions of her hands and hips, until her body tautened and she cried his name. He held himself back desperately as she arched beneath him, then rushed helplessly into orgasm, and from orgasm to night.

It passed quickly. He breathed deeply; great, delighted gasps; gathered her to him and rocked their bodies amid the fallen kaedo leaves.

"I love you," he whispered finally. "I love you, I love you."

"Hush."

"I love you. We'll be married tomorrow, tonight, as

160

soon as we can. I love you. Come to the stars with me. I love you. . . ."

She was shaking her head against his chest. He drew back and looked down at her, barely able to see her face in the dim light.

"No," she said.

"But . . . "

"No." She pulled away from him, sat, drew her legs up, and clasped her arms around her knees. "I'm sorry, Jes. No."

"But you love me. . . ."

"Did I ever say that?"

He stared at her, more puzzled than angry. "I don't understand."

She sighed. "Ever since NewHome, I've never had a place of my own. I want one. I want a house, I want a home. I want a place to be. Do you think I could be happy, not even having a planet?"

"You could stay here," Jes said. "You could live at the Tor."

"I want a house of my own."

"Then we'll build one, in Haven—with trees and gardens and windows and anything you want. I swear we will. We can start tomorrow."

"No, Jes. I want someone to stay with me. All the time."

"I'm never gone long, Taine."

"All the time. Please listen to me, Jes. I don't want to marry you. I couldn't take it."

Jes struggled briefly. "Okay," he said. "I don't need to go with Hetch. There's plenty for me to do here."

"Jessie, don't be a fool." She moved as though to touch his face, but stopped midway and clasped her knees again. "Do you think you'd be happy, staying on Aerie when you really wanted to be in space? How soon before you started resenting me for keeping you here? How soon before I started resenting you? I don't want a spacer for a husband. I want someone solid and steady, I want someone who won't surprise me, who won't change on me. Who won't disappear. I want my own home, and my own children to raise. I want someone who will go off every morning and come back every night, day in and day out."

"But I could . . . "

"No. I want a dull, boring, safe, and steady life, Jes. You could never give me that, no matter how much you tried."

161

"But why?" he demanded, sitting up. "You don't have to live that way. You'd go crazy living that way."

"No, I wouldn't. I've had enough excitement; I don't want any more. I don't want to be a Kennerin, moving things and changing things and doing things. I want to be Taine Somebody Alendreu, who lives in Haven and has children and pets and mends clothing and does the wash and cooks meals and gossips with the neighbors." She was almost shouting.

"But, Taine . . . "

"Don't argue with me! It won't help!" She groped for her clothing, found her shirt, and wiped her face with it. "This afternoon I told Kayman Olet that I'd marry him."

"The preacher?" Jes said with disbelief. Kayman Olet was a pleasant, bland man in his thirties, a blank of a man, an absolute void of a man. Taine began pulling on her clothing.

"You can't do that!" Jes said.

Taine seamed her shirt closed and began pulling on her shoes. She didn't answer him.

"Taine, please, listen to me. You're making a mistake. I can make you happy, I swear I can. I promise. Please marry me. Taine, listen to me. Please."

She stood and brushed leaves from her clothes. Jes leaped to his feet and reached for her, but she eluded his fingers. He put his hands at his sides and stared at her.

"Then, why this?" he whispered.

She touched his cheek briefly. "Because I do love you," she said quietly, then ran through the trees.

Jes knelt slowly and gathered his clothes, then sat, put his hands over his face, and wept.

Laur held up the burned loaf of bread and glowered around the kitchen. The kasirene cooks stood to one side, looking uncomfortable.

"Biara," Laur said. A cook shuffled forward, her head bent.

"This is completely unacceptable, and you know it. This loaf isn't even worth salvaging. How could you expect us to eat this cinder?"

"I'm sorry," the kasir said.

"Sorry is not adequate. You'll have to stay until you've done it all again—and done it right. Mind you, I shouldn't be giving you another chance, but I am. I trust you'll keep that in mind."

"In mind?" The kasir lifted her head suddenly. "I can't stay here. I have to go home. I can't bake your bread."

"Biara!" Laur was genuinely shocked.

The kasir tore the apron from her torso and threw it to the floor.

"I won't do it!" she cried. "I hate your bread, and your kitchen, and you, and I won't stay!" She rushed from the kitchen, slamming the door. Laur gaped.

The second cook bent to the apron. He smoothed it slowly, folded it, and set it on the table.

"Please understand," he said quietly. "Don't be angry with her."

"Not angry? After what she did? What she said? Not be angry?" Laur was so furious that she forgot to raise her voice.

"She has problems. She's worried about her child."

"Kalen? The baby? Is he ill? Why didn't she say so, she could have stayed home today. I'm not a monster."

"The child isn't ill." The cook folded all of his arms and looked at Laur, unblinking. "Three months ago Biara's suckle-mate disappeared, with her womb-child. Now Kalen is gone. She's very worried."

Laur put her hand on the table and lowered herself into a chair. "Surely they've just wandered off," she said without conviction, "gone visiting. They'll be back."

The kasir shook his head. "We've searched. Kalen was only five weeks out of pouch. He couldn't have wandered off by himself. And no one took him."

Laur's hands clenched. She put them in her pockets. The kasir sat, balanced on his thick tail, and watched her.

"How many?" she said finally.

"Eight. Biara's suckle-mate and child, Kalen, Palen's pup, Alanet who came visiting, two borrow-pups, and Altemet's latest."

"Where are they?" Laur whispered. The kasir did not reply. Laur sighed and put her hands on the table, then put her head against them. "Go home, Pao. I'll take care of the baking. And tell Biara that I'm sorry. Please."

Pao folded his apron and put it on the table, then touched Laur's hair gently and left.

Laur closed her eyes. The image of Hart rose unbidden, and she stood and moved about the kitchen quickly. The image refused to leave, appearing between herself and stove, pantry, table, window.

I was sick that day, she thought. Too much sun, too

163

much standing. I imagined things. I didn't see that. I was ill. And Hart helped me, Hart took care of me. Hart said that . . . Hart said that I was ill.

Was I?

She grabbed a pad and scoured the triple sinks. The pad made a grating, unpleasant noise, and scratched at her fingers. Her chest felt tight.

It can't be Hart. Surely not my Hart, my little boy. He's been led astray. By Gren. He's just a child, still a child. It's all Gren's doing.

Hart cut the pup's head and smiled. Laur dropped the pad in the sink, turned jerkily, and put her hand to her breast.

It's Mish and Jason. They should never have let him leave home, they should have known what Gren would do. I told them so, I told them and they didn't listen to me. And now he's in trouble, and I have to help him. Before it gets worse. Before he's found out. I'll go to him and . . .

I can't. He won't pay attention, he'll tell me that I'm sick and old and tired. He won't listen to me.

Kalen, Biara's pup. Palen's child. Eight heads in the basement? Eight bodies? Hart?

Laur ran outside and vomited into the bushes. She returned to the kitchen, washed her face and hands and, taking her hat and coat from the peg by the door, moved resolutely down the hill toward Haven.

Hoku waved Laur toward a chair. The child on the exam table squirmed and stared while Hoku bandaged the injured knee.

"There you go," Hoku said, applying the last length of bandage. The thin material flowed over the knee and molded itself to the flesh. "Out with you."

The child hesitated. "My mother said you would tell me something."

"What?"

"She said you would tell me not to climb trees." The child looked miserable.

"Nonsense. Climb all the trees you want. But don't land on your head next time, stick to your knees. Go on, get."

The patient grinned and scampered from the room. Hoku washed her hands.

"You're not due for your medicines yet," she said over her shoulder. "Back still bothering you?"

"That's not why I came," Laur said. "Where's Quilla?"

"How should I know? In the fields, most likely. Why?"

"I want to talk to her. To both of you."

"Something wrong with the twins?" Hoku said quickly.

"No, of course not. I just want to talk."

"All right. Talk."

"To both of you—together."

The doctor shrugged. "I'll come up to the Tor this evening, if you want. I can't leave the clinic now."

"After dark, then. And come round the back way. Don't tell anyone but Quilla."

Hoku frowned. "You want to tell me what this is all about?"

Laur shook her head emphatically and rose. "No. This evening. And be careful, hear?"

"Laur, are you feeling all right?"

Laur looked at the doctor. "No. But you can't help me."

Hoku reached toward her, and Laur went quickly out of the room. The street was warm and filled with the sounds of kasirene and humans. Farmers and houseworkers mingled in the streets, talking with the tired cheerfulness of after-work hours. The smell of cooking filled the air. Laur straightened, remembering that dinner was not yet cooked; tonight she and Mim would have to do it themselves. Much to be done, she thought with distraction. Much to do yet. She started up Schoolhouse Road toward the Tor.

Then Hart walked up to her and took her arm. She stared at him. Her chest hurt. He slid his arm through hers.

"You're out in the sun again," he said with gentle surprise. "I thought you were going to take it easy, Laur. I saw you coming out of the clinic, are you sick?"

"It's my back," she whispered. She wet her lips and tried again. "My back. And my chest. They bother me. I had to see the doctor. I'm all right, Hart, Really."

"I'm sure Hoku will take good care of you." He pulled at her arm, guiding her away from the Tor.

"I have to go home! I have to cook dinner, there's too much to do. Let me be, Hart, let me get my work done!"

She tugged her arm, but he held her firmly.

"You have time for a cup of tea, don't you? The kassies will take care of dinner, as usual."

Kassies. Laur closed her lips, afraid of saying anything suspicious, and let him urge her down the street. But when they reached his house she jerked her arm away.

"I must go home!" she said frantically. "There's too much to do. Let me go, Hart, be a good boy. You let me go, hear?"

He grinned and took her arm again, hurting her, and almost dragged her to the door. "Come on, Laur, I make great tea. And I've cakes that my cook made this morning. They're still fresh." He unlocked the door and pulled her inside. The sharp sound of the door locking behind her made her jump. Her skin suddenly felt cold.

"Look, Laur," Hart said. He turned her around to face the room. It was sparsely furnished but clean and neat. The shelves of tapes were orderly and dusted, and the rug on the floor was pale with washing.

"It's very neat," she said, surprised.

"I'm an adult, Laur, and you were a good teacher. Here, come with me while I make the tea."

The tiny kitchen sparkled, countertops scrubbed, windows crystalline, floor shining. Hart filled a kettle and put it on the stove, then opened the firebox and blew until flames appeared. He put some wood into the fire and closed the door again.

"I'm hoping to get a generator in here soon, next year, perhaps." He measured dried leaves into the pot. "The methane tank doesn't generate enough to run the stove, not with just the two of us using it. But it's a cozy place. Do you like it?"

"It's nice," Laur said. The tightness in her chest loosened. Surely nothing terrible could go on in such a neat, clean little house. Then she thought of Biara's pup and the basement window. She looked at the floor carefully. It seemed solid; nothing on it even remotely resembled a door.

"The cook cleans the floor," Hart said.

Laur, startled, looked at him and flushed. "It's very clean," she said. "It's a very good job."

"Do you want to look around?" Hart smiled. "It will take a while for the tea to brew. Go right ahead. My bedroom's to the left, and Gren's is to the right. He's not in now. The bath's on the other side of the hall." He turned toward the cupboards and began making a great clatter with the cups. Laur stared at him uncertainly, then turned and walked into his bedroom.

A large bed almost filled the room. She glanced under it quickly, but saw nothing. The clothes niche was neatly curtained, and within it Hart's clothes were stacked or

166

hung along the walls. Gren's room was no more than a closet, and completely filled with clothes, reels, and curious glass objects. If there was a hatch leading down, Laur thought, they'd never be able to find it in the mess. She pressed her lips together tightly and closed the door behind her. The bathroom was even tinier than she expected. When she opened the door it banged against the toilet, and she had to squeeze between the shower and sink to reach the window. Nothing here, either. She closed her eyes and leaned her head against the glass. Her head felt oddly light.

"Do you like my view?" Hart said.

She turned and held onto the shower's wall.

"I was looking for a garden. You don't have one? You should have one. I'll bring you some plants, some vegetables. Seeds. You really should have a garden."

Hart laughed. "I suppose you'll be telling me what to do for the rest of my life, won't you?" he said fondly. "The tea's ready. When we're done, you can have a look at the outside before you go."

Laur sat in the neat living room and sipped at her tea while Hart smiled and chatted. Surely she had been hallucinating that day before the feast. Certainly Hart, who made tea and conversation, who cheerfully and openly showed her his house, who worried about her health, could not have done what she saw him do. Thought she saw him do. Not her little Hart.

Her cup was empty. She stared at it, confused, then stood and put her hat over her gray hair.

"Late," she said. "I have to get home before supper. The tea was very nice, and the cakes, but I have to go, Hart. I have to go now."

"Look at my garden first," he said, taking her arm again. "Or look at where my garden will be. I've tried to do a little work on it, but haven't really had the time. Come see what I've done."

He guided her around the yard, pointing out future flowerbeds and vegetable patches. They passed the bush where she had left the fish basket that hot day before the feast, and her heart beat faster. But Hart seemed not to notice as he directed her to look here, or there, and eventually brought her to a halt facing the wall of the house.

"I want some flowers here," he said, forcing her to

167

look down, "right along this side so that they can climb up the house. I think that will look very nice, won't it?"

Laur glanced down fearfully, and almost gasped. The window through which she had seen horrors, the curtained window close to the ground, had completely disappeared. The painted wood of the house wall extended without a break from eaves to earth.

"Do you think it will be a good place?" Hart said.

Laur nodded feebly, holding onto his arm, and turned away.

"I have to go home. I'm an old woman, I'm tired. Let me go, Hart."

"Shall I walk you home?"

"No! No, thank you. I'll be fine. Please. I must hurry, see how late it is?" She moved toward the street.

"Aren't you going to give me a kiss, Laur?" he said, surprised.

She hesitated, then tiptoed. She kissed his cheek quickly and ran from the garden.

Instead of entering Tor Kennerin through the kitchen, as she normally did, she slipped in through the front door and immediately went upstairs to her room. She could hear a commotion in the kitchen, Mim's voice raised in complaint and Mish being both placating and exasperating. Tabor kept yelling for more vegetables for the soup. Laur locked her door, then took off her hat and jacket, put them away, and lay on the bed, holding her side. She could not decide whether she was more frightened of what she had seen or what she had not seen, whether Hart was deliberately misleading her or whether she was misleading herself. She bunched the coverlet in her fists. Old woman. How old am I? Eighty standard? More? Less? Surely Hart isn't doing that. Surely I've not lost my mind. The window. Neat little house. Tea. Hart. She moaned and pulled at the coverlet.

Someone rapped lightly at the door. She bolted upright and stared.

"Laur?" Meya. Laur gulped air.

"I've got a headache," Laur said. "Leave me alone. My head hurts."

"Oh. Do you want any dinner?"

"No. I'm going to sleep."

"Okay."

Meya is afraid of Hart. But Hart is gentle and kind.

168

Biara's pup. Palen. Eight of them. But not, surely not Hart. Not my baby Hart. She closed her eyes.

A quiet rapping on the door woke her. The room was dark, the house silent.

"Who is it?" she called as she fumbled with the lamp.

"Quilla. And Hoku."

Hart. Laur froze, then panicked.

"Go away," she demanded. "I have a headache. I don't want to see you."

"You asked me to come," Hoku said.

"I was wrong. I don't need to see you. Please go away."

"At least let me help your headache." Hoku's voice sounded oddly gentle. Laur reluctantly opened the door. Hoku and Quilla stepped inside, and Quilla locked the door. Laur retreated to the bed and sat on it, staring at the other women.

Quilla sat beside Laur and took her hand. "What is it, Laur? You look sick."

"No," Hoku said, "she looks terrified."

Laur looked from Hoku's calm, wrinkled face to Quilla's concerned, smooth one. Such strong people. So much stronger than her. Strong enough to carry the doubt, strong enough to make sense of it. They would help, and Quilla would take care of everything. Of her. Of Hart.

She held tightly to Quilla's hand and told them the entire story, commencing with the meeting with Hart before BeginningDay, including Biara's rebellion, concluding with the missing basement window. She emphasized Hart's kindness and concern, she talked about the heat and her own increasing confusion. Quilla and Hoku listened quietly, and she felt her fear lessen.

Hoku sat back and frowned. "Only one way of telling," she muttered.

"By going to Hart's?" Quilla said. It wasn't really a question. Hoku nodded and opened her bag.

"Laur, I'll give you something to let you sleep. By morning we should know."

"No," Laur said firmly. "If you're going, I'm going. I won't let you knock me out."

"Damn it, Laur, you're an old woman."

"I'm no older than you are, or not much. Someone has to take care of Hart."

"He's not a child, Laur!" Hoku snapped her case closed and glared. "He's an adult, and he's dangerous."

"Hoku, please." Quilla put her hand on the doctor's arm. "We don't know that yet. It may not be his fault."

"You think not?" Hoku said sarcastically.

Quilla pulled her hand back. "He's my brother," she said.

Hoku snorted. "Listen, both of you. If Hart's not up to anything, fine. But if he is, and either one of you think to cover up for him, then you'd better say so right now. I'll find someone else to go with me. But I am going, and you're not going to stop me. Eight kasirene—eight any-one—is too damned many."

"I'll go," Quilla said slowly. "Palen lost her pup. But don't forget that he's my brother, Hoku. You'd have to prove he's at fault, I won't just accept it without evidence."

Laur nodded vehemently. Hoku shrugged. "All right, then. Laur, you have to get out of that gown. Got any dark pants? Put them on. Quilla, we'll need a wrench, crowbar, anything like that. Solid and heavy. Good. I'll meet you by the halaea out front in five minutes. And don't wake anyone."

"What if something happens?" Laur whispered.

Hoku reached into her medical bag. "I've got this," she said calmly. Laur recognized one of the small, square stunners that had been salvaged years before from the NewHome ships.

"Don't kill him," Laur said. Hoku put the stunner into her bag and left the room.

Hoku led them along the stream. Water soaked into Laur's shoes, and the night seemed dense and terribly quiet. Ahead of her, Hoku moved with surprising agility along the bank of the stream. She could hear Quilla walking carefully in the rear. Both moons were out of the sky, one set and one not yet risen. She felt as though she walked in a dream, moving through a fantastical place on a fantastical mission. Her own lack of fear was also fantastical. She wondered if the walk would ever end.

Suddenly Hoku stopped and ducked into some bushes. Laur and Quilla crouched beside her, and Quilla carefully raised her head. She touched the others on their shoulders and motioned them to look.

Hart and Gren, dressed darkly, crossed the stream a scant meter ahead. Gren stumbled and cursed under his

170

breath. Hart carried something on his back. The women watched in silence as the men moved out of sight; once they were gone Laur realized that she'd been holding her breath. Reality and fear returned, and the ground felt solid beneath her wet feet. Quilla and Hoku were already moving rapidly away, cutting away from the stream toward the row of houses. Laur followed as quickly as she could.

They approached Hart's house from the rear. Hoku asked in a whisper where the window had been, and when Laur showed her, the doctor shook her head. Quilla walked quickly around the entire house, returned, shrugged, and Hoku pointed toward the front door, gesturing that they had no choice.

Quilla took the crowbar from the loop of her belt and quietly climbed the two steps to the door. She tried the knob, then slid the crowbar between the door and the sill beside the knob, braced herself, and jerked. The sound of splintering wood was loud in the darkness, but before the sound faded Hoku pushed Laur into the house and closed the door firmly. There were no cries or noises from outside.

"We need a light," Hoku whispered.

"I've got lightsticks," Quilla said. Her clothing rustled.

"Wait until I check the windows," Laur said, and Quilla waited while she moved through the rooms, making sure that the heavy curtains were tightly closed. She bumped into the couch, then into the table, which hurt her hip.

"All right," she said.

Quilla struck the light. It flickered. Hoku found an oil lamp and lit it, and in its glow they searched the house for the hidden door.

Fifteen minutes later they looked at each other with bafflement. Hoku opened her mouth, but Quilla waved a hand at her.

"Wait," she said, frowning. She paced the length, then the breadth, of the house, her lips moving slightly. Laur leaned against a table and watched, her mind blank. Quilla's footsteps stopped beside the wall where the living room and bedroom met.

"There are about sixty centimeters missing somewhere," Quilla said finally. "I think it's in the clothes niche."

It was. The shelves of neatly folded clothing were

171

hinged at the side, and as Hoku jiggled them they moved, revealing a gap in the flooring through which a ladder poked its top.

"I'll go first," Hoku said. All the lines in her face seemed turned down.

Quilla gestured, then turned away, and Hoku put her foot on the top rung of the ladder. Laur took a breath and stepped to the hole in the floor.

"You don't have to go," Quilla said. The doctor was out of sight. Laur put her other foot on the ladder and descended.

The ladder shook under her feet and hands, and the light from Hoku's lamp made the darkness seem to shiver. Laur looked down at ranks of jars and bottles shelved against the nearest wall. Wine jugs, oil jars, miscellaneous bottles. Some empty, some filled, all neatly labeled. As she moved lower, she saw a long, wide bench littered with bewildering equipment, things with knobs and slides and dials and gauges. Parts of toys. Pieces of tubing. Sheets of solar paneling. Patched-together raggedy machinery, homemade wonders. She shivered and put her feet on the floor, then turned to face the rest of the cellar.

The window still existed on the inside of the cellar. Laur felt quickly weak with relief, then looked below the window to the large wooden table. Lengths of heavy material hung from its sides in long strips, and it had a crank at either end for raising or lowering it. A lamp on a hook hung directly over it. The table was scrubbed clean, the dirt floor packed hard and obviously dampened to keep the dust down. The walls were sealed against moisture. Even the large, transparent vat at the far end of the room glistened, and the shape within it swayed rhythmically. Once Laur saw it, she could not look away. Together she and Hoku walked toward it and stood staring down. When Laur felt Quilla at her side, she reached over silently and took Quilla's hand.

The pouch had been slit, exposing the tiny nipples. Transparent tubes extended from the gut, connecting the submerged kasir with a large, patchwork machine near the vat. Fluid moved steadily through each tube, from and toward the machine. A crudely stitched incision stretched from the kasir's throat to her crotch; around it the pale gray fur had been shaved away. The kasir's eyelids flickered, then opened to reveal the violet eyes. If she saw the humans bending above her, she gave no sign.

172

"Why?" Quilla said. Her voice was unnaturally even, like her mother's when her mother was angry or disturbed. Or frightened.

"They need a womb," Hoku said and gestured. Laur glanced up to see more rows of jars. For a moment she did not understand what she saw, then realized that the jars held kasirene pups and embryos, from a tiny gray form the size of a fingernail to a pup well away from weaning. Palen's pup. Some of the forms had been slit, some flayed, some turned inside out. The lower jars held monsters. Furred, semi-human forms. Kasirene with two arms rather than four. A pouched human fetus, and others so mixed and mangled that she could not tell which characteristics of each species they possessed.

"Not gene manipulation," Hoku said calmly. "They haven't the equipment for that. But grafting, graft-rejection techniques, embryonic transference—all that they can do. Stick something into an embryo and stir it around and see what comes out." The doctor's voice broke suddenly, and she turned away.

"But the humans," Laur said.

Hoku shrugged. "I don't know. Not from us. They haven't the equipment to mess with genes, but they could mess with gametes. I guess. I don't want to know."

Quilla put her hand in the tank and touched the kasir's neck. The body moved gently in response to the pressure, but the eyes did not shift.

"She's alive," Quilla said.

"Only technically."

Quilla's hand closed around the tubes, and she wrenched them out. The kasir shivered, closed her eyes and was completely still.

"Give me the stunner," Quilla said.

Hoku shook her head. "No, Quil." The doctor looked tired, in pain, sickened, and resolute. "These deaths are enough. I keep the stunner."

Quilla and Hoku stared at each other while Laur watched them, then Quilla made a helpless gesture with her hands and turned away.

"They'll be back soon," she muttered.

"Good," Hoku said. She blew out the lamp.

Laur crouched on the floor and squeezed her eyes shut. Bright lights appeared under her lids, and she watched them, unthinking, until Hart's and Gren's return.

It seemed, to Laur, anticlimactic. The sound of the door overhead opening, treading on the floor, whispering, cursing when Hart discovered the shelves out of place. Obviously not a simple burglary, he said 'in response to some muttered comment of Gren's. They came cautiously into the darkness, Gren first, while the women crouched behind the table. When Hart, too, reached the floor, Hoku rose calmly, stunner in hand. Gren reached for something to fling at her and she hit him with the low beam. Hart watched Gren slump to the floor, then grinned at Hoku and said, "Caught me."

But his smile disappeared when Quilla and Laur stepped into the light, and he had not said a word since, not during the wait while Quilla fetched Jason and Mish, not during the quiet return to Tor Kennerin through the dark meadows, not during the restrained, painful conference in the closed living room of the Tor. Laur watched his expressionless face, each moment seeing less and less of the child she had loved and scolded, mothered and punished. It seemed to her that she attended a wake, that someone beloved had died, and she was deprived even of a body over which to mourn.

The next night, Jason and Quilla returned to Hart's home, buried the dead kasir and the pups, and destroyed the laboratory. Someone packed Hart's personal belongings, and Gren's, and brought them to the Tor. And the next morning, in the false dawn, Hetch and Jes checked the shuttle while Tham and Bakar tied Gren in a cargo hold for transport as far away from Aerie as possible. Merkit silently touched Quilla's hand and moved into the shuttle. And Hart, cold, silent Hart, mounted the ramp, destined for the university planet that his brother and sister could not attend, aimed for a future which Quilla had wanted desperately, and which he desired not at all. He stopped at the top of the ramp, Jason's hand firmly around his arm, and turned to look at the hills of Aerie, at the kaedos just visible in the pale light, at the indistinct bulk of the Tor swathed in morning mists. Then he bent his head and gave Laur such a look of frigid hatred that she gripped Quilla's arm, gasped an unintelligible plea, and crumpled. The last thing she saw was Hart's contemptuous turn of the shoulder as he followed his father into the waiting ship.

MEYA

WE HAD ALWAYS PLAYED GAMES, FROM THE very beginning. Simple games at first, the sort of things young children play: Hoops and Graces, Pitchball, Quia Tiger, and the nameless games children invent to flesh out their worlds. Later the worlds became more complicated, lots of running about and climbing things and shouting lines. Playing parts from our fantasies. But as we grew older the life-games were no longer enough. How long can you get a thrill from being an Imperium Commander, or Zeonea the MasterRat? By the time we were fifteen or sixteen, the urge to play parts had faded; we were growing adult masks of our own then, and they were strange and uncomfortable, and much too unwieldy to need other masks on top of them. But while the masks tended to cut us off from each other, all those years of games made strong ties between us. We grew apart as we tried to grow together. An uneasy time.

We? Oh, that would be about ten or twelve of us, depending on who was feuding with whom. Me, and Drel tor-Kanata, Pixie Hirem the lawyer's granddaughter, Kridee, Haley, Mertika the brewer's daughter, Wim, Teloret, Dane and Josha, Cumbe, Kabit who was Palen's pouch-sister, Puti from the Cault, some others. We were the first real generation of Aerites, we thought. Those of us who were human were all born on Aerie, and the kasirene were the first to be totally integrated into our lives. Well, it seemed total integration to us; we'd all been through school together, spent our spare time together, got roped into chores together. The fact that the kasirene had their own village seemed insignificant. In any event, we were all in mid- to late adolescence and bored that sumer, bored and lazy and out of games, energy, and ideas. ...itting around being uncomfortable with our new bodies and changing minds. And terrified that if we didn't look busy, the adults would think up work for us to do.

Tabor started it, really. He saw us sitting around the stream one day, busy staring at our feet and getting grumpy with each other, and he told us about a game they had played on NewHome during his childhood. Something to do with a ball and a stick, a playing field, two goals, and a lot of running around. It sounded perfect, so we chased the younger children out of the schoolyard and tried it, while Tabor stumped around the edge of the field, waving his cane and shouting directions. The twins clung to the flapping tails of his shirt like two small 'bots hitched to a loader. One person threw the ball at another person, who tried to hit it with the stick. If the hitter connected, the stick was dropped and a lot of running took place, and other people tried to steal the goals while some of us tried to catch the ball and others to catch the runner. Within an hour it was apparent that the game would never do. The kasirene whapped the ball so hard that it sailed over the kaedos and disappeared, which was not good because we were short on balls. But the kasirene couldn't run worth straw. They could bound, of course, and covered impossible distances that way, but they were no good at short-distance evasion running, while we were. So the game would either be the kasirene whapping the ball into the woods and then a great hunt until we found it, or we would whap the ball mightily, while the kasirene calmly caught each and every one before it came anywhere near the ground, and scooped up our runners with a great show of casual boredom. By the end of the afternoon we were exhausted and shouting at each other. Tabor apologized and limped away, trailing his children behind him.

He must have talked about it some, because Medi Lount came up with the next idea. We were hanging around the deserted marketplace, making a racket and up to no good, and she came out of her studio and demanded that we either go away or do something useful. We explained. Medi is something of a historian. She says that most of the good statues of ancient times concerned sports, and she'd done some research on the matter. She told us about a game from Terra, my parents' birthworld. Half of the players were runners who carried a ball around, and the other half were blockers; it sounded like an adult version of Pitchball. We tried it right there in the market place.

Think about it. The humans ranged from about one hundred fifty to two hundred centimeters, and about fifty to seventy kilograms (except for Wim, who was the fattest of us all). The smallest kasirene, though, weighed just under ninety kilograms and stood two hundred fifty centimeters tall. If the humans were running the ball, it was like smacking into a stone wall made of many arms and gray fur. If the kasirene ran the ball, each one lumbered down the field decked with five or six humans, each of us hanging on for dear life and not slowing the kasir down at all. And if we played with mixed teams, we had two games going instead of one, a human game and a kasirene game. It was a washout, but it looked so good that it took us two days to figure it out. Medi shrugged and went back to her clay.

Ved suggested a game having to do with ducking balls into pouches—fishing-type pouches, not kasirene-type pouches. The kasirene just stood below the hanging straw pouches and dropped the ball in, time after time. If we had the ball, though, the kasirene did a lousy job trying to catch us, but if once they got the ball, the game might as well have ended right there, for all the chance we had of getting the ball back.

It began to seem as though the only thing happening that summer was a gradually increasing rift between the humans and kasirene. Look at everything we had that was dissimilar, now that we were moving into adulthood and through our awakening sexuality. The physical differences we had always known about—their strength, our fleetness. Now an entirely new area of difference was thrust upon us, and we all viewed it with increasing distrust.

That summer sex was the most important thing in the world—after games, of course. We humans had two sexes, one of which bore and nursed children, the other of which didn't. The kasirene had two sexes also, one of which had wombs, and there the similarities ended. Kasirene pups are born as fetuses, and climb into the pouch to continue growth. It doesn't matter whose pouch, either; the males can nurture just as well as the females, and very often a kasir pup is passed from one adult to another as a pledge of love or friendship, for convenience, or sometimes merely at whim. We were beginning to understand how different that was from the human method, and they to understand om their own vantage point. And our elders didn't help. No kasir in our group had either birthed or nurtured yet, although they were well past the age when such things were possible and even desired of them. Their elders claimed it was our evil influence, while every time one of us lost a virginity, our parents blamed it on the kasirene. Oh, there was plenty of sex going around that summer, and much comparing of notes and evaluation of technique. ("You can't do it standing up," Dane said with authority. Yes, you can, I thought, but I didn't tell him that.) Still, the areas of technique and the like rarely overlapped. The rift grew; we knew it, we didn't like it, but we couldn't think of anything to do about it. Save, perhaps, give up.

And we were none of us willing to do that. It was our last year of school. Adult life began the next summer, and giving in to it early meant giving up our leisure and our companionship. We tried to stretch childhood out as long as we possibly could. It took some planning, and was thirsty work. So Mertika relieved her father's storeroom of a keg of beer, and we took it down beyond the stream one afternoon, well away from both human and kasirene villages. We stretched out on the grass, opened the keg, and discussed sports.

What resulted was just the sort of game to have been invented by a bunch of drunken adolescents on a hot summer's day, but I suppose that all sports are identical in that way. Eventually we called it "Caraem," the kasiri word for pouch, but that summer it was just "the game," and we invented it as we went along.

The schoolyard was a rectangle, about six by thirty meters, with a kaedo at the center of either end. Drel procured a couple of kasir fishing pouches and cut the bottoms out, and we hung one in each tree. The kasirene liked hitting balls with sticks, so we had one ball and one stick in the game, and to even things out Pixie Hirem invented long, curving scoops made of wood. You hooked the ball from the air with the top end, and it whizzed along the inside of the curve and came shooting out the other. If you flicked the scoop in the middle of this, the ball arched high and wide over the field. We humans liked running, provided, of course, that there was a minimum of running into walls of kasirene, but there had to be room for kasiri bounding, too. And we all liked the idea of theft—it resonated pleasantly of SwampRats.

It's impossible to explain the game this way, from the

bits and parcels that we pulled together during the next three weeks. Listen, here's what a game was like, late that summer, when we had it all figured out.

It's hot and a little humid, with a small breeze blowing in from the ocean and over the brow of the hill. We have an audience today; kasirene and humans gathered around the edges of the schoolyard, and children perched on the roof of the school or atop the fences. Wim sees all the people and gets nervous, but Dane, who's on the other team and has been trying to get into my pants all summer, saunters over and polishes his own ego at poor Wim's expense. I ignore him. We come out into the field, elaborately casual, in our uniforms. Green or purple—I always play purple, and my uniform is a bright purple shirt that Mim has sewn for me. The kasirene uniforms are lengths of cloth wrapped in a complicated manner around their shoulders. The people make a great cheering noise and we try not to look pleased. There are eight of us on each team: two human catchers and two runners; two kasirene blockers and two whappers. We humans try to look cool and dangerous, and only look nervous. The kasirene try to look fierce, and succeed in looking comical. Tabor referees the game; he lets our fans admire us for a while, then blows the starting whistle. Green's up, since we won the last game. Their whapper, Kabit, stands dead center in the field facing the green pouch, and we all spread out and watch her carefully. Tabor whistles to begin. Kabit tosses the ball in the air with her lower arms. She holds the stick with her upper arms, and as the ball comes down she whaps it directly toward the green basket; it's so smooth it looks like one even movement. Mertika nets the ball with her scoop and sends it to me, and I tuck it under my arm and run like hell down the length of the field toward the purple pouch. Around me, green blockers collide with purple blockers, a green runner tries a flying tackle which is thwarted, and my teammate Wim is standing right under our pouch, howling that I should get the ball to him. Teloret bounds past me and grabs the ball, lofts it, and whaps it to Wim, and fat Wim springs into the air and dunks the ball through the pouch. Score! Except that green Kabit has rushed under our pouch, grabs the ball, and pushes it through the pouch and out, negating our score.

"Foul!" Teloret yells. Tabor disagrees. While we argue the point, green Kridee sneaks down the field and steals our Talisman and parades down the field. Triple score for green, and the green supporters shout gleefully while purple supporters curse and groan.

Second play, purple up. Drel whaps the ball, Kridee catches it and begins his run down the field. Teloret paces him, yelling insults, and I rush in front of him and steal the ball. It's not hard; his hands are always slippery with sweat. I whip around and head back toward our own pouch, and three green kasirene descend on me, coming from all directions. I evade madly, get turned around, turn back, and the world seems full of green uniforms.

"Puti!" I yelled. Puti bounds up to me, tucks me under her arm, and we fly toward the pouch. She flings me upward, I dunk the ball, land, grab the ball, dunk it again, and Tabor blows the end-play while green players shriek foul.

"Illegal for a kasir to carry the ball!" Kridee yells.

"She wasn't carrying the ball!" I yelled back.

"Was so!"

"Was not! I was carrying the ball and she was carrying me!"

Chaos and screaming. It's a play that Puti and I worked out on the sly, and Tabor seems to be buying our reasoning. Green supporters howl insults and threats, which Tabor ignores. Double score for purple. Third play.

Green up, and they make a botch of it. Kabit drops the ball a few moments into the play, and although green makes a single score, the foul is called, and as penalty Tabor decrees that they must return our Talisman. This is of benefit to us, for there are no points in stealing back your own Talisman. Green players and supporters argue fiercely, but our Talisman is carried gently back to our end of the field. Very gently—it's forfeit the game if a Talisman is treated roughly. After all, Quilla only has two children, and she watches out for both of them. Jared is back at our pouch now, and cheerfully thumbs his nose at Decca, who sits by the green pouch and makes a rude noise at him. The score is purple, four; green, six. And we're determined to win. Fourth play, purple up.

Wim has worked out an interesting defense. As our Sedai whaps the ball and green Dane begins his run down the field, we fan into a semicircle pointing toward our own pouch and run like hell, kasirene in the middle and humans to the sides. Dane sees the kasirene coming and begins evasive running, and our line whips around him to cut him off. I rush him from the left and Pixie rushes him from the right, and when he spins to run back, Puti leaps right over him and appears as if by magic directly in front of him. Dane leaps to one side, Puti scoops the ball from him and whaps it far down the field, toward the green pouch, where the rest of our team is waiting for it. There is thorough confusion in the green team. They rush down the field toward Wim. Wim scoops the ball and flings it down the baseline to Pixie, who fronts it to me, I fake it to Taloret and we both run, each of us pursued by green players. Taloret reverses direction, and I pass the ball to Mertika, who dunks the ball through our pouch and yodels with glee. The green players realize that while they were busy trying to figure out where the ball was, Drel has stolen their Talisman and popped her into his pouch. Decca giggles and waves, and the cried of foul are deafening. Eventually they can only cite Teloret for running with the ball, and she's taken out of the play, which cripples us, but not too badly. The score: green, six; purple, twelve. It's time for a recess.

Quilla claims that the favorite sport of all Aerites is argument. When it comes to the game, the kasirene repudiate their usual gravity and argue just as fiercely, and the recess is spent howling and waving arms in the air and pointing at the playing field and cursing. We all take a drink of water. Quilla rebuttons Decca's shirt. Tabor decides that enough volume of noise has been reached, and blows the whistle for the fifth play. Everyone quiets now and is intent and serious. Dane passes me on the field and pats my ass, and I determine to land him a good one during the next play. Green up.

They very neatly whap and catch their own ball, and do a flying wedge offensive. With our Teloret on the sidelines, it's extremely effective, and they manage to steal Decca back, too. No points, but a lot of glory. Green, eight; purple, twelve.

Sixth play. Teloret is back in the game. Purple up. Kabit steals the ball from Pixie, who is easily confused, but green botches when Josha climbs the green kaedo and dunks the ball from there. Everyone cries foul, including some of the green supporters, and Josha is sidelined. Green, ten; purple, twelve. We're beginning to feel nervous.

Seventh play, green up. I confer briefly with Sedai. Drel whaps, Dane catches and runs, and Sedai grabs Dane and rushes him toward our pouch. Dane, his dignity much offended, kicks and howls and drops the ball. Wim recovers it and dunks once, I grab it and dunk twice, Pixie takes it, evades green Malin, tosses downfield to Teloret, Teloret whaps it right into our pouch, I recover it and dunk it a fourth time, and Tabor whistles furiously. Dane and Sedai are both sidelined, but now the score is: green, ten; purple, twenty.

Final play, purple up. We position ourselves around the entire perimeter of the field. Wim steals the ball from Josha and tosses it to me, and we round-robin the ball around the field, while the green players rush about in the center trying to catch us. Every once in a while we get the ball to Mertika, who dunks it and starts it around the field again, until the end whistle is blown. The green team is furious, green supporters are homicidal, Dane tells me that he wouldn't court me if I were the last woman on Aerie, and I'm so pleased I kiss him.

Serves them right. Last game they beat us twenty-four to six.

Both teams retire from the field and go pollute the stream with sweat and dirt and strategies and accusations of cheating. Puti opens the beer. Then Kabit and Puti go off to snuggle in the bushes, Wim follows me around with damp eyes, Dane puts his hand in Pixie's shirt, which she likes, and we're all friends again and as drunk as Mertika's father's beer can get us. But I go home alone.

Silly? Yes, I suppose so. But it filled the time, gave us something to do, gave Haven something to shout about. It kept Hoku busy dispensing bandages and dire predictions, and Mim busy sewing up the holes in my shirts. Kasirene used to be fairly rare in Haven, but the next summer Ped Kohl opened a beer hall, and every summer thereafter it was bursting with kasirene and humans, pounding on tables and arguing the excellence of their teams. So it changed that, too.

And it kept me from feeling too lonely. Quilla was home, of course. Tabor. The twins. But Jason had been gone for seven months, helping Hetch expand our spaceways. Mish was dealing with bureaucracies on Althing Green. And Jes was gone. He came and went as the ships permitted, appearing with presents for everyone and tall tales of grabs and tau space and exotic ports on distant worlds; going again and leaving a vacuum behind him. I thought I'd grown used to it. But he'd come home in late spring that year, with three weeks to spend and nothing to do at home. We walked alone to Cault Tereth, and we talked of many things and saw many wonders and did much of interest. Things changed.

Then he went away, and I had to get used to his absence all over again. I filled my days and my mind with bats and balls and scoops and running down the field, and they helped, they undoubtedly helped.

But nothing helped at night.

Part Five

1233

New Time

MISSING
AERIE

"For in spite of language, in spite of intelligence and intuition and sympathy, one can never really communicate anything to anybody. The essential substance of every thought and feeling remains incommunicable, locked up in the impenetrable strongroom of the individual soul and body. Our life is a sentence of perpetual solitary confinement."

—Aldous Huxley

WITHIN THE MEMORIES OF FALLING JASON
thought he could hear the voice of the universe, saying:
Think of your planet, Kennerin. Think of your plantations, your shipping company, your children, your people,
your growth. Think of your pride. I can end it as easily
as this. In less than a flash of a nod of a moment. Now.

It seemed too quick a thing to have changed his life.
The event was out of porportion to the change, as though
gnats, in the passing millisecond, had built a wall separat-
ing city from city, or world from world. He remembered
standing on the hatch shelf, holding a bill of lading, while
Captain Hetch's voice from the hold echoed Jason's
shouted items of inventory. The moment was intensely
clear in his memory: the murky overhang of the domed
port, the acridity of the air, shimmers of heat, boredom.
He remembered remembering Aerie, listing the ports and
stops between his home and this distant, grubby world.
Hetch appeared in the hold and said something tired and
grumpy. Jason turned and put his hand on the railing, letting the sheaf of papers flap closed. The railing fell. He
fell. The hatch shelf fell. In a flash of a nod of a moment.

There were spaces of darkness and spaces of light.
They seemed to flicker by him, glimpses of reality that
comprised months, then days, then seconds as time slowed
within him, leaving him stranded *lento* in a *prestissimo*
world. He woke in a hospital near the port. Tests. Pain.
His body clasped in a coffin of webbing, then in the coffin
of his own unresponsive skin. Bare and antiseptic rooms.
He slept, and woke on Solon, the medical planet. They
slid him into the Physical Reconstruction Unit and knitted
new joints for him, which froze two days later. They

grafted and implanted and maneuvered and changed. They filled him full of drugs, then, to his relief, took the drugs away again. Time changed again.

During those slow months in the hospital, Jason considered Aerie. He blocked the smell of the ward, the scurrying of android attendants and the tug of life supports in his guts, and built his world in his mind.

Aerie, as the ship spins from the grab. A world of blue ocean clasped by huge white poles, swathed in clouds, motionless against a backdrop of stars. Two fat moons, slightly absurd in their perfect roundness. Islands solidify around the equator as the ship swings into close orbit. Silently, Jason shapes their names with his lips, tasting the syllables. To'an Elt. To'an Ako. To'an Eriant sprawled at the edge of the Antarctic mass. To'an ba Eiret. To'an Betes. And To'an Cault, home. The shuttle slides over the brown plains and green mountains of Betes, over the green-blue-white of the strait, over To'an Cault's massive, sea-ridged shore. White-topped cliffs festooned with small, succulent gray plants and cascades of blue-green vines, alive with the flights of birds. The ridge crest slopes inland to the small valley of the port, up to the Tor and the ramshackle, comforting house, down to the barn and fields, flat to Haven, and beyond crops and orchards to distant woods. Kaedos thick-leaved against the sky, the delicate, beautiful lace of halaeas, magenta fourbirds above fields of airflowers, the clean, sweet smells of home. Jason stands at the shuttle hatch, unable to break the ecstasy of the moment, until an orderly speaks or his guts twinge, and he opens his eyes to the machines and monitors that keep him alive. Pain and thickness, then the ship moves again from the grab, and Aerie appears gemlike in a velvet sky.

But he was unconscious when they brought the shuttle in to To'an Cault, in accordance with the doctor's program. He woke to his bedroom in Tor Kennerin, and he stared at the wooden walls, the dark ceiling, and the shafts of afternoon sunlight that crossed the room. A smell of antiseptics and medication overpowered the scent of airflowers and the sea. The support systems buzzed and hummed quietly to themselves. For a moment he did not understand where he was.

"Jason?"

He shaped his mind away from the slow, medicated time of his private universe, turned his head, interpreted

187

his vision. The young doctor stood by the bed, looking strangely vulnerable without the protection of his hospital whites. He smiled, a lightning shift of face, and Jason prodded himself toward speech.

"Home?"

"Yes. Your wife thought it would be best."

Jason thought about that.

"You can't fix me?"

"Not completely, no. We talked about that. But you can get around, you know. You won't have to spend all your time lying in bed. Your wife was surprised that we had done as well as this."

"Her name is Mish."

The doctor smiled again.

Jason looked away. After a pause, he said, "Ozchan. I want to look out the window."

The doctor moved the bed. Jason stared through the delicate tracery of the bare halaea. The foliage of the *Zimania* in the distant fields was rust-colored with autumn. Closer, the brown fields lay tilled and waiting for winter.

Jason looked at his body. His legs made long, thin ridges under the sheet, and his arms seemed yellow under the darkness. His stomach ached where his flesh met the tubes of the life-support systems.

"Look," Ozchan said. "I knew you wanted to see the landing, so I made a tape." He held a small cylinder, silver against his chocolate skin. "I shot it from the port beside you. It's what you would have seen."

Jason raised his one good arm and knocked the cylinder from Ozchan's hand. "It's not enough," he said, "never enough. You can't change this, can you? I'm home because you can't change this."

Ozchan said nothing.

"Bring me some wine," Jason said. The door opened and closed again. He rubbed his cheek slowly against the fresh linen of his bed and sank into slow time. He wanted Mish.

When Quilla came, and Meya, and Mim, he closed his eyes, feigning sleep. They buzzed about his room like dancing flies and left him alone again.

Quilla came back that evening, pushing a complicated chair. It balanced on three large wheels in the rear and two small ones in front, and a series of trays clung to its sides. It clattered and banged, and Jason focussed on it while he pushed himself toward quickness.

"What is it?" he said to Quilla's silence.

"A chair for you. Look, it has a motor here, and the controls are along the right armrest, so you can run it by yourself. The equipment goes on the trays, and we've put in the best shock absorbers we could make." Her words came faster and faster, seeming to blur together. Jason waited for silence.

"Don't want it," he said.

"Nonsense. The carpenter's working on the stairs to make a ramp for you. It should be ready in a day or two, and in the meantime you can practice on it up here."

"No."

"Are you planning to spend the rest of your life in that bed?" Her tone was one of simple curiosity. Jason turned his head away from her. She buzzed a while longer, then left. Through the halaea branches he could see the barn glowing dimly, and two crescent moons rode the sky. He wept softly, not bothering to wipe away the tears. Ozchan came into the room, fussed about for a moment, and turned him off for the night.

Where's Mish?

On Althing Green, appearing before the Council, trying to secure our full license from the Transportation Board. There're a lot of petty legalisms she must get through. It will take some time before she's done. Then she'll come home.

Things will be better then.

How long will it be?

There is no way of telling. In real time, a few weeks, another month. Maybe two months, three at the most. In your own time, who knows how long? Be patient. She will come.

Has she come before?

Oh yes. She came three times to the hospital and sat by my bed, telling me silly stories and gossip that she made up. We talked quite a lot. We thought I was going to recover. We talked about the accident. The ship needed to be repaired. Hetch was very angry about the accident. He wants to sue the repair docks. I would like to sue them, too, but it would take three or four years to reach the Council.

Jes is fine. He's in sub-four now. Hetch has let him

command his own ship. Yes, I know. He's doing very well.

Where's Mish?

Coming soon. Be patient.

My stomach hurts. A jolt of electric surcease to the brain. A jab of chemical relief in the arm. Slowing down time, until Mish gets home.

Things will be better then.

Where's Mish?

Meya and the twins brought him breakfast in the morning and stayed with him until he had finished. They bounced around the room, shattering the stillness, throwing open the widow to let in the clear light of morning and the scent of dew. Meya's thick, swinging black hair reminded him of Mish, and it snaked around her face as she tossed her head, laughing at one of Jared's terrible jokes. Such pretty people, these three. Decca sat by his bed and stared at the blinking monitors.

"What are they?" she asked.

Jason explained slowly, feeling the words forming far back in his throat and coming through his mouth like large, uncomfortable bubbles. Decca listened solemnly, and put her hand on his shoulder.

"It hurts," she said quietly.

"Of course it hurts," Jared said. "Don't be such a lizard."

"I am not!"

Meya calmed them and poured hot tea into Jason's cup. Jared buttered a muffin for him. They seemed like swift, tiny birds, invading his room, singing an alien song. Even in stillness they flickered. Meya talked about that season's games, illustrating with broad sweeps of her arms.

He felt tired when they left, drained and saddened. In the fields the kasirene called to each other, and downstairs Mim scolded the cooks.

Ozchan and Quilla came in together. Ozchan made small adjustments on the monitors while Quilla stood at the foot of his bed, looking at him. He stared at the wall.

"Jes is coming home in two months," she said. "Mish says she'll be here a few days after that." She paused. "Ved Hirem wants to see you, but he says he can't climb the stairs. His arthritis."

When he still didn't speak, she made an exasperated

190

noise and left the room. Ozchan tried to talk him into sitting in the chair. Jason ignored him, and eventually the doctor went away.

His body felt dull, unresponsive. Dead. He twitched the fingers on his bad arm, but could do no more than that. His legs were flaccid; he couldn't feel them at all, although sometimes they sent him fraudulent messages which he always believed, then felt shamed for believing. They had grafted over the worst of the burns, but he knew the skin on his left side looked ugly, serrated, and lumpy. It felt unpleasant to his fingertips.

Mim brought him lunch and complained about household matters. He ignored her.

How would Mish ever want something like him? This collection of scars and uselessness. Ugly. The shadows in the room changed. He refused dinner and asked Ozchan to turn him off early. At least in sleep there were no scars. Yet.

The next morning Tabor came in and played on his flute. Jes had come to the hospital and played his own flute, substituting comfortable music for uncomfortable words. Jason told Tabor to go away.

In the afternoon, Hoku came.

"What are you doing here?" Quilla said.

Ozchan touched a *Zimania* leaf and smiled at her. "Just walking. Since I'm going to be here a while, I thought I'd explore a bit."

Quilla let the bough drop into place and moved toward the next bush. Ozchan trailed after her. She pushed a branch aside, reached toward the trunk, and checked the sap collectors which clung to the scaly bark.

"I left your father with Hoku," Ozchan said. "She was rather fierce with him."

"She's a fierce woman," Quilla said without looking up.

"She was lecturing him about self-pity. She was rather rough."

"He'll survive." She moved through the bushes to a neighboring row. "Hoku's been snapping at us for over seventeen years. I think we'd feel neglected if she stopped."

"Perhaps," Ozchan said doubtfully. "But your father is my patient, and I'd be happier if this was clear to everyone."

Quilla straightened and looked at him as he came

through the bushes toward her. Young man, perhaps twenty-six standard, thereabouts. First job. Dark, gleaming skin, dark, gleaming eyes. A self-assured cast of face, a cocky stance. Why did he look so vulnerable, then? There was no resemblance at all, but he reminded her of Jes.

"Hoku's not taking over," she said. "You're the specialist in this, and she knows that. But when it comes to the state of Jason's mind, she's the expert, not you. Can you live with that?"

"I suppose I'll have to. If she can get him out of bed and moving around, I guess it will be worth it."

Quilla grinned and delved into a bush. "She bit you, right?"

Ozchan laughed.

The leaves gave off a sweet, musty scent as she moved through them, and they left streaks of green and orange dust on her hands and clothing. Sunlight trailed through the bushes, creating a warm, dappled shade, and a small lizard skittered from the ground, sped up the trunk of a plant, and chattered noisily at her. The sap buckets were filling slowly and steadily.

"What are these called?" Ozchan said.

"*Zimania rubiflora.*" The bush before her held an almost-empty bucket. She frowned and ran her fingers over the bark of its trunk, then turned some leaves over. Patches of scale clung to their undersides.

"What do they do? Besides grow, I mean?"

She took white tape from her pocket and tagged the plant. "The sap is processed and used to make electronic parts. The fruit's inedible, but it makes good fertilizer."

"Electronic parts? From sap?"

"Sure. That small monitor you've got Jason hooked to —the pulse/respiration/blood pressure thing—uses parts made from the sap. The trade name is Z-line. They make it over on Shipwright."

"I didn't know that."

Quilla looked at him, surprised.

He shrugged. "I'm a doctor, not an electrician. They make them, I use them."

"And if it breaks down?"

"Send it off to be fixed. That's what repair techs are for, right?"

"Not here," Quilla said. She dusted her hands. "We're a colony world, Dr. M'Kale. A world of generalists. Not

192

enough people and too many jobs to be done, so everyone knows more than one field. I doctor plants and sometimes people when Hoku needs me, fix machinery, repair electrical problems, service the generator, farm, weave, but not too well—other stuff. It's necessary." She glanced upward. The sun was an area of brightness near the horizon. "It's about dinner time. Coming?"

They walked together through the meadow. Tilled fields stretched in curving rows toward the distant woods. Kasirene workers had gathered under the kaedos, talking and pulling food from their pouches. Quilla spotted Palen and waved, and the kasir waved back. A pup rushed over, grabbed Quilla around the knees, and chattered in kasiri. Quilla listened seriously, replied, and sent the young one bounding toward the trees again.

"Were you born here?" Ozchan said.

"No, on Terra. But my brothers and sister were. And you? Where're you from?"

"Planet called Hogarth's Landing, in North Wing. I left when I was sixteen to go to school, and haven't been back."

"Why not?"

"Too busy, I guess. And it's not exactly a pleasure planet, Hogarth's. It's a dome world. Bad atmosphere, cold, cramped. Mining world. I didn't like it while I was growing up, and I don't like it now. Not like this place at all. This is very idyllic."

Quilla smiled but said nothing. Overhead, a shuttle crossed the sky toward the port.

"That'll be Hetch," Quilla said. "Just in time for a meal, as always." She lengthened her stride. Meya rushed out of the Tor and down the hill, the twins trailing after her. Mim shouted furiously.

"It's a big event when a shuttle comes in, isn't it?"

"Yes. We're quite bucolic here," Quilla said. He looked at her as though suspecting sarcasm. She bit the inside of her cheek, repressing a smile.

The kitchen smelled of bread and stew. Quilla and Ozchan washed at the sink, then took the plates that Mim handed to them and carried them into the dining room. A cook came down the stairs, holding Jason's dinner tray. Most of the food was untouched.

Quilla talked for a moment with the carpenter and came into the dining room. "The ramp's almost finished,"

193

she said. "Perhaps tomorrow he'll have dinner down here with us."

"I wouldn't count on it."

Meya rushed in through the front door and grabbed Quilla's arm. Quilla laughed and turned around, then saw Meya's face.

"What is it, Meya? What's wrong?"

"Hetch came," Meya said, panting, "and he's got Hart with him."

The twins came into the room, looking frightened.

"I want to eat upstairs," Decca said.

"You certainly will not," Quilla said sternly. "There's nothing to fuss about."

"But Hart killed Laur," Jared whispered.

"He did not. He's your uncle, and your brother, Meya. He's not going to hurt you. You're all going to be polite to him, understand?"

"But—"

"Understand?"

Meya and the twins nodded unhappily. Quilla sent Decca to fetch Tabor, and Jared to wash his face.

"Is Hoku still here?" she said to Meya.

"Yes. She's going to stay to dinner."

"Can you find her and tell her I want to talk with her? I'll be in the living room."

Meya left the room, still looking troubled.

Ozchan looked baffled. "Something wrong?"

Quilla shook her head. "Shit," she muttered. "You'd better come along while I talk with Hoku. It'll affect Jason, and I guess you'll have to know sooner or later. But this is confidential, okay? You're not to speak about this to anyone—just me, or Hoku, or my father. Understand?"

Ozchan nodded, suddenly professional, and followed her into the living room. Hoku marched in a moment later, dropped her case on a chair, sat, and glowered at Quilla.

"Meya's terrified. What's going on?"

Quilla closed and locked the door. "Hart's back. Meya saw him come in with Hetch."

"She was only ten when he left. She could be mistaken."

"Hoku," Quilla said.

The doctor grimaced. "I suppose. Only Kennerins look like Kennerins. Why'd he come?"

"Jason?"

"Possibly. He could have heard." Hoku stared at the empty fireplace. "He'll want to see his father."

"Can we keep him away?"

"That's a dumb idea," Hoku said. "Better not to, I'd guess. Might shake Jason up, though. You, M'Kale. How strong is he?"

"It depends," Ozchan said. "Do you mean emotional stress—that sort of thing? If I'm there, if it's controlled, he can take just about anything. Question of medication. But why all the fuss? Hart's his son, right? It's natural that a parent should want to see a son who's been gone for a while. You make it sound as though Hart's some kind of monster."

Quilla and Hoku looked at him in silence.

The table was crowded with people. Quilla and Tabor with their two children seated between them, Meya on Quilla's other side, Captain Hetch looking fat and unhappy, Doctor Hoku, then Hart Kennerin and a friend he had brought with him from Kroeber, a man named Tev Drake. Ozchan sat beside Tabor, watching the faces and emotions that filled the room.

Hart was charming. He kissed Quilla and laughed when Meya and the twins shied away from him. He admired the growth of the young ones, who stared at him with solemn fascination. He shook Ozchan's hand and paid sly compliments to Hoku, and did not seem to notice when the doctor glared at him. He introduced Drake, who smiled at everyone but particularly at Quilla. She treated him with cold courtesy and turned her attention to Captain Hetch. Ozchan saw Hetch spread his hands to her, palms upward, while Hart's back was turned. Drake noticed and frowned. Mim came in bearing a pitcher of beer and the cooks followed carrying the steaming pot of stew.

"I'm from NewHome," the housekeeper muttered in response to Hart's flatteries. "We don't forget."

Quilla looked startled, and Hart laughed.

"I spilled a cup of juice on her the first day she came to us," he explained to Ozchan. "She's not forgiven me since." He turned to Quilla and smiled engagingly. "Just juice, Quil. Nothing else."

Quilla stared at him, then turned to fill Decca's plate. Ozchan wondered what it was that everyone seemed intent on not forgiving nor forgetting, but the conversation around the table gave him no clue. Hart talked about the trip from Kroeber and of Kroeber itself, told wicked stories about the faculty and his fellow students, casually mentioned an award, his advanced courses of studies, offers of teaching positions waiting for him when he finished his education. Ozchan caught Quilla's glance and raised an eyebrow, and she nodded curtly. Hart was telling the truth. Ozchan warmed to him as the young man sat in the frosty welcome of his family, trying to lighten and brighten the leaden atmosphere.

Meya spilled her cup of juice and looked on the edge of tears. Ozchan was surprised. He hadn't noticed her very much before: a pretty, cheerful adolescent, self-assured and intelligent. Not the type of girl to spill her drink at table, let alone cry over it. He looked at her more closely now. She was more than pretty, and her hands shook as Mim helped her mop things up. Quilla squeezed Meya's hands. The twins looked like identical studies in seriousness. Quilla let them all leave the room.

Tabor sighed and pushed his empty plate aside. His hands fell to his lap, and he fingered his flute.

Hart, still smiling, stood and stretched.

"I'd like to see my father now," he said, "if Dr. M'Kale thinks it would be all right."

Hoku pressed her lips together. Ozchan glanced at Quilla's expressionless face.

"I'd like to tell him that you're here first," he said tentatively. "He's not in good condition for sudden surprises, and . . . "

"Take him up," Quilla said flatly. "Jason will be disturbed one way or another. You might as well get it over with now."

Hart seemed about to speak, then closed his lips and turned toward the door.

"Hart!" his sister called. He paused with a hand on the doorframe and looked at her over his shoulder.

"If you upset him, you'll leave Aerie tonight and not come back."

Hart's smile was tinged with venom. He gestured to Ozchan and moved up the stairs. Baffled, Ozchan followed him.

Quilla rapped softly on the door, then pushed it open and slipped inside. Ozchan sat shirtless on the bed, a print-tape in his hands. He dropped the tape and pulled his shirt on quickly. She looked away from his dark chest,

196

closed the door, and leaned on it, her hands behind her back.

"What did my brother say to Jason?"

"Why do you want to know?"

She moved her shoulders against the wood of the door. "I don't believe Hart when he says he came here just to visit. There's a reason that he's not telling me, and I think it has to do with Jason. I need to find out."

"I don't understand all the fuss," Ozchan said. He touched the front seam of his shirt, then put his hands in his lap. "Hart seems like a perfectly charming person."

"You're new here. Can't you simply accept that I have to know what's going on?"

"No. I consider all conversations with my patient, to which I am a party or observer, to be confidential. Until I know enough to make a different judgment, I'll treat them as such." He sighed. "I'm a doctor, Quia Kennerin, not a spy."

"I could get Hoku up here to browbeat you," she said.

Ozchan smiled. "Your doctor is frightening, but I think she'd understand my position."

Quilla walked to the window and pulled the curtain aside. The lights of Haven winked at her solemnly. She wondered how to make him understand without letting him know too much.

"This was Tabor's room," she said, "back when the refugees came from NewHome, before we built the other wing of the house."

He left the bed and stood beside her. He smelled of leather and ozone.

"Tabor is your husband?"

"Was my father upset when Hart came in?"

Ozchan laughed and touched her shoulder. "Why don't you ask Jason yourself?"

"He won't talk to me." She moved a step away, and Ozchan put his hands on the windowsill.

"He was tense," the doctor said. "He saw Hart coming in from the pad, so he wasn't surprised. But he was tense."

"Did Hart ask you to leave the room?"

"Is Tabor your husband?"

This time Quilla laughed. "No. He'd like to be, though. He's other things. Did Hart ask you to leave the room?"

"Can we haggle sitting down? It's more comfortable."

Quilla shook her head. He remained standing beside her.

"What other things?" he asked.

Quilla looked at him expectantly.

He grimaced. "Yes, Hart asked me to leave. I told him I had to stay to monitor some sedatives. He said he'd do it for me, but I said no."

Quilla tucked her hands in her armpits and considered. "Did you have to use sedatives?"

"Tabor's the twins' father, isn't he?"

"Yes."

"I wish you'd tell me what's going on," he said, dropping his bantering tone. "Jason's having a rough time of it, and it's very hard for me to decide on the proper course of treatment if I can't find out what's going to affect him, and how." He sat at the edge of the bed, his hands between his knees. "And I don't mean about you and Tabor, either. He either was or is your lover, he's the twins' father, he lives here, but I don't know if he lives with you. So what? But I have to know about Hart."

She crossed her arms over her breasts and looked out the window.

"I could ask around," he said.

"It wouldn't do you any good. There are only three people on this planet who know what happened, and none of us is likely to tell you."

"Damn it, I'm your father's doctor. I'm trained to take confidences. Do you think I'm some sort of gossip? I don't even know anyone on Aerie to gossip with. Hoku said Hart left when Meya was ten. That was, what, seven years ago? He would have been around seventeen. What could a seventeen-year-old boy do? Get someone pregnant? From what I've seen, that wouldn't bother anyone much."

"Dr. M'Kale. I run this planet. Jason runs shipping, Mish runs interface with Althing Green, and I run Aerie. It's the way things are. I know you must be frustrated not knowing every little thing about everything, but you're going to have to get used to it. There were some problems seven years ago; that's well known. Hart left abruptly, and that's also well known. He hasn't been back until today. Because of that, and of what happened seven years ago, and my father's condition, Hart's likely to upset Jason very much. I don't want that to happen." She moved away from the window. "Jason may be your patient, but I'm the chief on this planet, and in this house. Until my father recovers, I'll stay the chief. You'd best keep that in mind."

"Is that a threat to fire me?" he said stiffly.

She shook her head. "No. Just an effort to warn you."

"Warn me about what?"

"About taking what's given to you, and leaving it at that."

She went out of the room before he had a chance to reply. The hallway was dark and quiet, and she stood still for a moment, thinking.

"Quilla?"

Tev Drake stepped out of his room. He wore a long, soft robe of fur, and in his hand he held a decanter.

"I was just about to have a nightcap," he said. "Will you join me?"

She shook her head.

"It's brandy from Charlemagne," he said and waved the bottle, as though to entice her. She wondered if he had listened at the door of Ozchan's room.

"Okay," she said. "But bring it downstairs. The living room's very comfortable." She turned before he could reply, and after a moment she heard him close his door and follow her down the hall.

A friend from Kroeber, Hart had called him. Yet he seemed a good deal older than Hart, far too old to be a student, and if he were a professor, Hart would have mentioned it. She turned on the lamps in the living room and rummaged through the cupboard for two glasses. The cupboard was fronted with polished metal; she watched Drake's reflection as he came into the room, his robe billowing around his legs. Tall? Not really, he simply gave the impression of being tall. Self-assured. Long-fingered, pale-eyed. Dark blond hair arranged in many careless curls around his pale, narrow face. An impression of careless wealth, and something more, a connection which flickered uneasily in her mind, but could not be pinned down. Sensuality? Hardness?

Drake sat on the couch before the fireplace and put the brandy on the table in front of him. Quilla set the glasses beside the decanter and sat in an easy chair. Drake poured the brandy, and when he gave her a glass his fingers rested on hers for a moment. They felt cool, hard, and powdered. She pulled her hand back and sipped at the liquor.

"It's very good," she said.

Drake smiled, thin lips taut against his teeth. "I made up my mind quite a while back that it's no use having anything that's not the best. Why bother, otherwise?"

"The best tends to be the most expensive."

"That's not a worry of mine." His fingers curved almost completely around the glass. Large ring with a pale stone. Something in the stone seemed to move.

"No?"

"I spend most of my time looking for good things, and when I find them, I take them."

"Is that how you met Hart? By looking for the good things?"

Drake gestured. "Almost. I met your brother in a tape store. He had the last copy of a tape I wanted, and he argued me out of it so successfully that I bought him a drink. I'm not used to arguing for the things I want, and I'm not used to losing. Your brother was a refreshing novelty."

"You must have many friends," Quilla murmured.

"Friendship is not essential." He smiled again. "Your brother is my friend, I think that's sufficient. When he said he wanted to come home for a visit, I paid our ways. I enjoy doing things for my friends."

Quilla smiled politely. Hart had stopped writing to them for money about three years ago, and they had assumed that he'd been granted a scholarship or had found work. He wouldn't say. Was this another thing that Drake did for his friends?

"Two fares from Kroeber comes to quite a lot," Quilla said.

"Nothing, really. I was curious about Hart's family. He told me that his older sister was intelligent, but he didn't tell me that she was also beautiful."

Quilla gave him a long, cold look. "I'm not fond of sarcasm," she said.

Drake looked bewildered and spread his hands. Mim came into the room. She looked at them and drew her eyebrows together.

"Turn the lights off when you're finished," she said.

"Of course," Drake said.

Mim gave him a look of suspicious disapproval and went out, closing the door behind her.

"Your servants are eccentric," he said.

"Mim's not a servant," Quilla said. "Hart's visit was unexpected."

"I thought we'd talked enough of your brother," Drake said. He leaned toward her, cradling the brandy glass in his palms. "I'd much rather talk about you."

200

"I wouldn't," Quilla said and smiled politely. "Are you a student, too?"

Drake sat back and laughed. Small music. "Oh, no, just bored. I've been taking a few courses, dabbling—just to pass the time, really."

"And you came here for the same reason?"

"My dear, you needn't be so prickly. I came because Hart wanted to come, and to satisfy my curiosity. Hart is an interesting and complex man. I thought it would be fascinating to see what made him what he is, and how, and why. Origins are a hobby of mine."

"I sincerely hope you find some, then," she said. She put her glass down and stood.

"I think you ought to make an effort not to dislike me," Drake said, also rising. "There is more between us than merely your brother."

Quilla pulled the door open halfway and stopped. Drake stood silently, watching her.

"Tev Drake," she said. "Of Albion-Drake. You own the company that buys our *Zimania* sap."

Drake smiled, showing teeth. "You begin to understand," he said. "Good night, my dear."

Quilla gritted her teeth and went into the hallway. She heard the tinkle of glass on glass as Drake poured himself another brandy, and she went up the stairs. No use being angry. It's probably what he wanted. All these off-worlders arrive and, the next thing you know, it's the Courts of Althing Green, sniping and suggestions and spying and playing at word games. She glanced out the stair-well window. Both moons had set, and The Spiral hung low in the sky. Well past tien'al, and she had to be up at dawn. The house was dark and quiet, and the wooden boards creaked comfortingly under her feet. She walked past Jason's room into the new wing and opened the door of the children's bedroom. There were three forms in the bed—she came closer. Meya lay between the twins, all of them curled around each other in a complication of arms and legs. Quilla frowned and straightened the covers. Jared said something grumpy in his sleep and put his face against Meya's shoulder.

Tabor, too, was asleep, sprawled diagonally across the bed. Quilla stripped and dropped her clothes in a pile on the floor, then slid between the covers and prodded him gently. He moved over and put his arms around her.

"Why so late?" he murmured.

"It's all right. Go to sleep We'll talk about it in the morning."

He made a noise of agreement and fell asleep again. She put her arm around his waist and her head against his neck. After staring into the darkness for a while, she slept.

"Jason? Father? Are you awake?"

Moonlight coming through the window lay in a square around Jason's head; his face was turned from the light and he breathed deeply and evenly. Hart touched his shoulder, then his cheek. Jason did not respond.

A small lamp sat on the table by the bed. Hart lit it and, in its wavering glow, studied the monitors and their controls. He turned a knob fractionally, then again. Jason muttered sleepily.

"Jason. Wake up."

Jason opened his eyes. They looked black in the dim light, until he turned his head toward the lamp; then they gleamed intensely blue.

"Dawn?" he said.

"No. Past midnight. I wanted to talk with you." Hart sat at the edge of the bed and took Jason's limp hand. "It's hard talking when there are other people around."

"Hard talking," Jason said. His face came more fully awake, and he watched Hart without expression.

"Is it the pain? Or the drugs?"

"Both." Jason pushed himself up on his good arm, and Hart rearranged the pillows so that he lay comfortably in them, half-sitting. "Why'd you come back?" Jason said.

"I heard about you. Wanted to see you again."

"Before it was too late?"

Hart shrugged, then smiled quickly. "I guess I'm not too welcome here."

Jason looked down. "Long time back. You never came. Only wrote for money. Like you didn't want to be around us. Didn't want us around."

"For a while I didn't—for about two or three years. I was angry. I thought you all hated me. I think some people still do."

"Not hatred," Jason said. He wet his lips. Hart handed him a glass of water and Jason sipped it cautiously. Hart put the glass by the bed.

"Shock," Jason said. "So malicious. Thoughtless. Killing people. And the other things. Not one of us, it seemed. Changeling."

"Maybe I was." Hart put his hands in his lap and looked out of the window. "I'd been robbed, you know. Everything; my home, my family. My world. All of it taken over by strangers, and you all seemed to love it. You all helped rob yourselves, and me too. I didn't understand any of you. Then I got involved with Gren. I didn't want to, at first, then later I wanted to very much. It made me different from the rest of you, knowing something the rest of you didn't. Learning things. Doing things. It gave me back that sense of being special, of belonging, that I'd lost. And I guess I thought that you all owed it to me, that anything I did was only fair, considering what had been done to me." He paused. "I'm not trying to make excuses, Jason. I don't believe that anymore, but I did then. And when you caught me, when you sent me away, it was like being robbed all over again, only more so. The first time, I still had the semblance of my world and my family. The second time, I didn't have anything at all."

"Hart—"

"I didn't come back at first because I was still angry, and later because I was ashamed. But I had to come back this time. To see you. To try to make things up to you, to the rest of the family."

"To the kasirene?"

"Possibly. Indirectly." Hart took Jason's hand again and looked at his father's face.

"I graduate next year," he said. "Biomedicine, chemistry. I'll get my certificate for surgeon five. I'm good, Jason. Best in my class. I've been doing outside work for the past three years for some of the firms near the medicine campus. I've developed some things on my own."

Jason looked at him quietly.

"I can give you your body back," Hart said, "a whole, new, functioning body."

"They tried that. It didn't work."

Hart gestured scornfully. "Plumbers. Patchwork experts. Of course it didn't work, they were doing the whole thing backward. But I can do it right, I can make it work."

"How?"

"It's complicated, and I don't think you'd understand. Technical stuff, which wouldn't really mean a thing to you. But it's something I developed myself, and it works. Can I do that for you, Jason? Will you let me try to help?"

"What do you want to do?"

203

"I told you, it's complicated. But I promise that it will work."

"I want to know."

"Can't you trust me?"

"No. Bottles and racks and dead kasirene. I haven't seen you for seven years, Hart. Don't know what you are now. Don't know if you've changed."

"That's going to haunt me for the rest of my life, isn't it?" Hart demanded. He stood from the bed angrily. "You're never going to let me forget that, and you're never going to forgive me, either. I should have known."

Jason raised his hand imploringly. "Hart . . . "

Hart twisted the knob on the monitor back to its previous setting. Jason's hand wavered, then fell to the coverlet. Hart waited until his father's breathing was deep and even again, then rearranged the pillows and tucked blankets into place. The square of light from the window had moved, leaving Jason's face in darkness. Hart blew out the lamp and walked into the hallway. He closed the door quietly and pursed his lips in a silent whistle as he strolled back to his room.

"Where are you going?" Ozchan said.

Meya jumped nervously and spun around.

"Hey, I didn't mean to frighten you."

"It's okay," she said and laughed. "I didn't hear you coming. I'm going down to play Caraem."

"Caraem?"

"It's a game. People get worked up over it."

"People usually get worked up over games." He leaned against the wall by the front door and put his hands in his pockets. "I used to play some during school, ball games and things like that."

"Yes?" Meya bent to her bootlace again. "This isn't something you'd have known before. We invented it here."

"Sounds interesting."

She looked very young and very lovely, all legs and smile and golden-colored skin. Mongol eyes, like her mother's. He wondered whether he could keep her at the Tor a while longer, whether she'd be willing to spend an hour or so just talking. Whether or not she'd be bored around him. She wasn't at all like the women he had known before: the intense, self-assured women in college; the slighters and drifters in the town. Nor did he feel tense with her, that combination of fear and yearning which

204

haunted his dealings with women. Provincial charm, he told himself wryly, and didn't believe it. He didn't know how to talk to her, what to say, what to talk about. She smiled at him, reaching for her jacket, then stiffened. He heard steps on the stairs, and two voices. Hart and his friend Drake. Meya's smile disappeared.

"Listen," she said quickly, "if you're interested, come on down with me and watch us practice. Can you leave Jason for a while? Just an hour or two? It's interesting, really. I've got to go now."

"Sure, Jason'll be all right. I'll get my jacket."

"No! Don't bother, you can use one of Quilla's. Here." She plucked a jacket from the rack on the wall and tossed it to him, then opened the door. "Come on, we're going to be late."

Hart and Drake reached the foot of the stairs. Drake saw Meya and started to say something, but she grabbed Ozchan's hand and pulled him out the door.

"That's nice," he said, laughing. He pulled the jacket on and lengthened his pace to catch up with her. "I can't remember the last time a woman ran away with me."

"Just hurry," she said. She was almost running down the track toward the village. Around them airflowers popped and wilted, and the air, although still warm, held a hint of winter. Ozchan caught up with her at the base of the hill and grabbed her hand.

"What's the rush?"

"I told you, I'm late."

"You didn't start to get late until your brother came down the stairs."

Meya glanced back up the path. Ozchan looked, too. No one there.

"I just wanted to get away from the house," she said. "I guess I'm not really late. There's no set time, anyway, just whenever we get there."

Then why the panic, he wanted to say, but didn't. Her hand felt warm and good in his.

"Then take some time and tell me about this place," he said. "I've never been to the village before. What's its name? What are all those kites for? And the windmills? Where does Hoku live? Is there a school here? How many people are there in town? What's the gray wood on the buildings? What are those crazy-looking animals over there?"

Meya laughed and pulled her hand away from his. "Do

you practice asking questions? Here, we go this way." She gestured down the street. He walked beside her, watching the village and watching her, too. "It's called Haven. We built it after the refugees came from NewHome. Do you know about that? Jason had to go rescue them, their world was about to go poof and their government was crazy, so Jason and Hetch went over there and rescued about two hundred fifty of them and brought them here. I wasn't alive then, I wasn't born until the spring after they came. Anyway, those animals are called drays. They've got six legs because everything on Aerie's got six limbs—except us and the fish, of course. Hetch arranged for them, some scientists came and took samples from some shaggies and mixed them up and made the drays. They're pretty stupid, but good for dragging things around."

"No trucks? No air cars? Just drays and feet?"

"Sure. Why would we need anything else? Oh, Hoku's got a skimmer, for emergencies, but she can't drive it. So either I drive it for her, or Quilla does, or someone in the village. Those kites generate electricity, Jason invented them. The windmills do the same thing. It's much better than burning things or trying to save the money for a power plant, isn't it?"

"They're certainly pretty. But what do you do when the wind dies down?"

"The ocean's just a few kilometers away, so there's usually a wind. But we store the power, too, of course. The gray wood's from kaedo trees. Most all of the wood is, around here. What else did you ask about?"

"I've forgotten," he said and smiled. To his relief, she smiled back. "You must answer a lot of questions. You do it well."

"No, I just like to talk, is all. Here's the school, and that's the playing field, and there's my team, in the purple. You'd best sit over on the steps, it's the safest place."

He sat on the steps and watched with growing amazement. The kasirene players surprised him; generally humans and sentient aliens didn't seem to mix that well, but the game had obviously been engineered with both species in mind. A few spectators had gathered to watch the practice and to watch him, and he felt uncomfortably on display. Then the twins sat beside him, and he relaxed.

"Meya's the best player on the team," Jared said, while Decca nodded agreement.

"Is she?"

"Of course she is. Any flaker can see that."

"Well, I haven't seen this game before, so I really can't tell."

"You haven't?" Decca looked at him with pity.

"They have different games where I come from," he said. "I think this game—and Haven, and the Tor, and everyone here—is very interesting."

Jared made a noise of disbelief. "It's just old Haven, and everyone. When I grow up, I'm going to be a spacer like my Uncle Jes, and I'll go all over the place and see everything."

"You like Jes?"

"Sure," Decca said. "He brings us stuff from far away, and tells us stories. And he plays his flute, like Tabor does."

"What about your other uncle? Hart? Does he tell stories and bring you things?"

"Oh, no," Jared said.

"He's awful," Decca said.

"But why? He seems like a very nice man to me."

The twins looked frightened. They glanced at each other, then moved closer to Ozchan, flanking him.

"You mustn't ever be alone with him," Jared said urgently. "He's a nasty, terrible person."

"Does he hurt you?"

Decca shook her head. "He never even talks to us."

"Then why are you scared of him?"

"I'm not scared of anyone," Decca said indignantly.

"Then why do you think he's a terrible man?"

"He just is. You'd better stay away from him."

"I certainly won't. He seems very nice to me, and you haven't told me why he isn't, so how do I know he is?"

Decca looked at her brother. "Maybe you'd better tell him," she said solemnly.

Jared looked uncertain.

"Go on," she said, reaching in front of Ozchan to poke her brother's chest, "before he gets into trouble."

"All right." Jared glanced around, then bent close to Ozchan's ear. "Before Hart left here, he did something really terrible. So terrible that people won't even talk about it. But Laur found out about it, and when Hart found out that she found out, he killed her."

Ozchan frowned. "I don't understand. Who's Laur?"

"Laur took care of everybody before," Decca said.

"She came here with Mish and Jason, and she took care of the house and everyone. But then Hart killed her. He just looked at her, and she fell down dead."

"What are you people whispering about?" Meya said. The twins jumped away, then laughed and threw their arms around her.

"Let me go. I need a drink of water, and I'm all dirty."

Decca scampered toward the jugs piled under a tree. Meya sat beside Ozchan and brushed hair from her face. She was bright with exercise, and her face glowed.

"What do you think of it?"

"The game? I think it's the craziest thing I've ever seen."

She looked at him quickly, then laughed. "Correct," she said. "Wait until you see a real game; it's even crazier."

She reached for the jug that Decca held out to her and took a long drink. Ozchan watched her throat move as she swallowed, and wondered if he could ask her about the twins' incredible story, then decided he wouldn't. There were too many other things he wanted to talk with her about. Children's scare-tales could wait.

When she handed him the jug, he tipped his head back, closed his eyes, and put his lips where her lips had been.

"You think he won't do it?"

Hart leaned against the tree trunk and made a negligent gesture with his hand. The legs of his pants were bunched about his knees and his bare feet dangled in the water of the small, quick-moving stream. Drake stood a few feet away, careful not to lean back and dirty the pale gray cloth of his suit.

"Jason will give in," Hart said. "It's only been four days, after all. But I can give him what he wants, and he knows it. Be patient, Drake."

"I'm patient with accomplishments, Kennerin. With progress. You haven't accomplished a thing."

"He's beginning to trust me. I think that's accomplishment enough." He bent forward to watch a small fish dart by his toes, then slid his hand into the water. After a moment, the fish moved cautiously between his fingers. He caressed the fish's round belly, then flicked its tail and it sped down the stream. Hart laughed and shook his hand. Drops of water flashed in the sunlight.

"I can't wait forever, you know," Drake said. "I've got things to do."

"They can wait a while longer." Hart wiped his feet dry on the grass and slipped into his sandals. Drake followed him down the bank of the stream.

"I used to have a hideout down here when I was a kid," Hart said. He poked through the rushes. "Had it completely provisioned, too. Cakes and water and fruit—anything I could filch from the kitchen. I'd decide that everyone hated me, and I'd come down here. Tell myself I'd never go back, but by the time night came I'd get hungry for dinner and sneak back home. Or Quilla would come and sit by a tree and sing songs, just like she was all alone, but she knew I was here. I could never figure out how." Hart smiled. "It must have been around here somewhere. Things change so fast."

Drake snorted and moved away from the stream. Hart splashed through the water, then thrust his hands into the river willows and held a rusty jug to the sunlight.

"Drake!" he shouted. "Here, catch!"

Drake flinched and held his hands out, and the jug smacked against his palms and fell into the stream. Hart grabbed it as it floated by and crossed to Drake.

"It must have been over there," he said, turning the jug over in his hands. "I must have lifted this from the kitchen, it looks like the kind of thing Laur used to keep milk in." He frowned suddenly and tossed the jug into the underbrush.

"Come on," he said. They moved away from the stream.

"I can't spend all month here," Drake said. "If your thing doesn't work out, I have to get back to Kroeber and start the treatments. And you know what happens in that case."

" 'I can't' is beginning to be repetitive, Drake. My treatment works. You ought to know that."

"I know it works on lab animals. I know it works in theory. But I don't know how it works in practice."

"Then let me practice on you."

"Oh, no. You're not doing a thing to me until I know it's safe."

"Better I use my father as a lab animal than you, is that it?"

"Listen, Kennerin"—Drake stopped under a tree and put his hands on his hips—"don't forget who you are and who I am."

"You're a sick old man who's at least sixty years older than he looks, and most of you is spare parts. I'm the person who can give you an entirely new body, one that won't need replacement parts every two years. You're a transplant addict, Drake. You have to be. But I can give you a heart that doesn't wear out, Drake. You can buy a lot of things in this universe, but you can't buy that. Except from me."

Hart grinned at Drake's silence and strode out of the woods. He stopped and waved a hand at Haven.

"Look at that," he demanded. "When I left, there were two dirty streets, some shops, an open-air market, and maybe four hundred people. See that building over there? Meeting hall, and theater, and auditorium. That's the hospital at the far end of town, over behind that stand of trees. When I was a kid, school was a one-room shack. Now it's that four-story monster. Paved streets. Water pipes. Main sewage system. We had patchwork things back then, one methane converter per household. Now they've got an entire plant to do that. And the kassies moving in, voting, running shops, just like any other bunch of lazy natives. Upwards of two thousand humans on To'an Cault, and most of them right here." He paused and glowered at the town. "Smothering the whole planet," he muttered. He turned away from Haven.

"Hart, listen. There's a shuttle coming in three days from now. Let's just get your father on it and get going. You can run his machines, by the time he wakes up we'll be back on Kroeber and halfway through his treatment. That makes sense, doesn't it?"

Hart spun around.

"He's my father, Drake!" he shouted. "And he makes up his own mind, in his own good time. Understand?"

"You're crazy," Drake said. "I offer you a fat living for the rest of your life, and you're willing to chance it on an old man's dim mind."

"You can't buy a new heart, Drake," Hart said. "Just remember that."

210

"Maybe I can get one from the same place you seem to have bought yours," Drake said.

Hart grinned mirthlessly and strode back toward the Tor.

"Jason!"

"Surprise," Ozchan said, grinning. Jason, sitting in the six-legged chair, grinned too. Quilla came around the desk and pushed a chair out of his way.

"I thought you didn't want to use it," she said.

"Changed my mind," Jason said. Ozchan pushed him up to the desk. "The room was driving me crazy."

Quilla smiled. "It's good to see you downstairs. Do you want to go outside? I've smoothed the path around the house, and it's lovely weather out—"

"No, not yet. Later." Jason looked around the room. "Feeling useless. Maybe I can help with the books?"

"Sure. I was just doing them. Hold on, I'll get some tea, all right?"

Jason nodded. Quilla went out of the room, and after a moment Ozchan followed. Jason could hear their voices in the hall, low murmurs. Talking about him. To be expected. The pain in his stomach swelled, and he grimaced. Either pain or dimness, and today he preferred clarity of mind, even if he had to pay for it.

The room still looked as it had when Mish ran the finances of the plantation and the planet. Shelves piled with books and reels, sheets of figures scattered around the desk. The window curtains pulled open to let in the late afternoon sunlight. A softboard on the wall, bristling with pins and notes. He closed his eyes and felt the wave of longing moving in him again. It's all right. She'll be home soon. It's just that some things bring her so close.

Quilla came in, carrying a tray of tea-things. She kicked the door closed behind her.

"Ozchan's off for an hour or so," she said. "I think he's gone soft on Meya."

"Sensible man," Jason said. He pushed the pain away and watched Quilla pour the tea. "Think he'll marry her?"

"Isn't that a little premature? He's only been here about fifteen days."

"Perhaps. How about you?"

"Don't start that again, Jason. I'll get married when I want to, and I don't want to."

"You might as well be married," Jason said. "Tabor lives here all the time, doesn't he?"

Quilla put her cup down slowly. "Yes. But we can't talk to each other, Jason. We don't have anything to talk about. He's sweet, he works hard, he loves the children. We never argue. But we never do anything else, either. Can you imagine being married to someone you can't talk with?"

"No," he said, thinking of Mish. "But you live together. Sleep, eat, work, raise the kids together."

"Then why bother with the ceremony? It wouldn't change things, and if things did change, then being married would just complicate matters. Why is it so important to you?"

"I don't know." He touched the hot cup with his fingertips. "I guess I like things stable, Quil. I like knowing what things are, and how they relate to each other. Marriage makes things stable, you know it's not going to disappear when you're not looking."

"Neither am I, Jase."

"I'd like to be sure of that."

She shook her head and reached for the papers. "Why don't I just give you a general rundown now, all right? We can get into the details later, but some things have changed in the past year. Our price at Shipwright, for example, is up twenty percent, but shipping's up twelve. Jes tells me that sub-five's wide open now, if we can get the ships in there to service them. And we will, when Mish gets the license. Anyway, we needed twenty kilos of source last winter, and . . . "

He tried to listen, but the pain rose and fell within him, and figures had always bored him, anyway. He wanted to be outside, hauling buckets of sap from the orchards, tossing hay in the barn, shouting in the meeting hall with Ved Hirem. Working. Active. He couldn't touch the land, and its loss pained him with an almost physical intensity. But to go to the fields now, like this—unable to run, to stride, to bend, to stretch—was unbearable. Hell. He closed his eyes, unable to fight the feeling of loss. Mish. Aerie. Mish.

"Jason, what's wrong?" Quilla knelt by his chair, her expression anxious. She touched his shoulder.

"Too tired, I guess," he whispered. "Not as strong as I thought I was."

"Do you want to go back to bed?"

He almost nodded, then remembered the room, the bed he and Mish had shared, the view through the bare halaea limbs, the smell of antiseptics overriding the distant scent of Mish's perfumes.

"No. Living room. By the window."

She pushed him out of the room. The walls of the hall moved by unevenly, then a sharp turn into the living room. Chairs and couches, rugs and curtains. The fireplace. The low tables. The cupboard. He turned his face away from his reflection. Quilla pushed his chair to the window.

"The yellow knob," he said. "Two clicks."

The analgesics slid into his system, and he felt his mind slowing again. Helpless. Useless. How could he spend a life this way, tied to chair or bed, living in a world of pain or a world of fog? No change.

"Quilla?"

She put her head close to his. "What is it?"

"Find out," he whispered. "Find out what Hart wants to do."

"About what? Jason? What do you mean?"

Her voice slid away. He turned his face toward the light and welcomed the deadening fog.

Ozchan was upstairs, taking care of her father. He had tired himself out during the day, and Ozchan said that it would probably take a couple of hours to get him back in balance. Meya thought about that, kicking her feet against the porch step. Ozchan taking care of things. She thought about his long, competent fingers. Wondered what they would feel like on her skin, and shivered. From far away, knowing worlds of which she'd never heard, languages she couldn't begin to speak. Making people well. Making people laugh. He'd tried to play Caraem that afternoon, and had made a fool of himself. Startled by the kasirene every time he looked around. Laughing at himself, and inviting the rest of the team to laugh with him. But he was quick, too, and seemed to see the entire field with one glance, always knowing where everyone was. If he stayed long enough, perhaps he'd play with the team next season.

She hoped he'd stay long enough.

The twins were asleep already. Quilla and Tabor were in Haven with friends. Mim was reading in her room. Tev Drake was down at the port, making expensive off-planet calls. Meya had made very sure that he wasn't around before sitting on the porch alone, waiting for Ozchan to finish. Hart frightened her, in a distant, uncomfortable way. but Drake seemed to take pleasure in terrorizing her. That evening, before dinner, he had waited outside the washroom until she was finished, and she'd had to squeeze by him to escape. Yesterday he'd put his hand on her crotch, and when she tried to push him away, he'd laughed and hurt her. The night before she'd locked her door for the first time in her life. He'd stood outside rattling the knob quietly and whispering to her until she threatened to wake up the family. When she was sure he'd gone, she'd slid into bed with the twins again. They wanted to know why she did that so often now, and she didn't know what to tell them. She wished, fiercely, that he and Hart would leave immediately, or that he'd fall off something or under something and kill himself. Anything to keep him out of her life.

"Damn!"

She gasped and leaped away from the steps, far back on the porch.

"Who is that?"

"Me," she said, "Who are you?"

"Hart." Her brother limped onto the porch, holding to the railing. "I hit my shin against something." He sat and began removing his boot.

"Serves you right, sneaking around at night."

"I wasn't sneaking around." He pulled the boot off and inspected his shin. "Shit."

"What is it?"

"I think I've broken the skin. I can't see."

She reached inside and unhooked the hall lamp, then lit it and placed it beside Hart. She stood well away from him and leaned down cautiously to look.

"You didn't break anything," she said, "just a bunk, is all."

"Well, it's my bunk, not yours, and it hurts like hell."

"Put some cold water on it."

"Wonderful. And how am I supposed to get to the cold water?"

214

"Oh, just wait here." She went to the kitchen and filled a bowl with water, then brought it out to him.

"You didn't bring a towel," he said.

"Too bad. Use your socks."

Hart frowned at her, then stuck his tongue out. She laughed quickly, surprised.

"Not that way," she said. "Can't you do anything right?"

She came around the lamp and knelt beside him. His skin looked a bit scraped, but nothing other than that. She wrung the sock in the water and laid it across the shin.

"Now just hold it there for a while, and it'll feel better."

"Thanks." He touched her hand, and she jumped back from him. He looked at her quietly in the lamplight. His face looked like Jes'.

"Why are you afraid of me?" he said.

"I'm not."

"Yes, you are. Every time I come into a room, you look like you're about to faint."

"I do not!"

"Oh, come on. Everyone on this planet treats me like some kind of monster, and no one will even tell me why."

"You ought to know why well enough."

"What's that supposed to mean?" he said angrily.

She tensed her thighs, ready to leap away from him, and licked her lips.

"You killed Laur," she said.

Hart just stared at her.

"You did. Just before you left, you looked at her and she fell down dead."

He closed his eyes. It didn't look as though he were faking it, and Meya frowned, puzzled.

"I loved Laur," he said finally, quietly. "I think I loved her more than anyone else. She had a shock. She was an old woman, and her heart gave out. She was almost eighty, Meya. They didn't even tell me that she was dead, not until I'd been gone almost a year. I just thought she'd fainted in the heat. I was mad at her, and Jason was in a hurry, or I'd have gone to her. But they wouldn't let me. And they didn't let me know." He looked up at her. "I didn't kill her, Meya. I couldn't hurt someone I loved that much."

She stared at him. He pulled himself upright and picked up his boot.

215

"I suppose no one's ever going to believe me," he said bitterly.

"I believe you," she whispered. But he was already in the house, and she didn't know if he had heard.

Hart opened his father's door quietly and stepped inside. It was almost v'al; both moons were down, and the darkness in the room was thick and quiet. He felt for the table by the door and put the lamp down, then lit it.

"Hello, Hart."

Quilla sitting in a chair beside Jason's bed. Ozchan near the window, leaning against the wall with his arms crossed. Jason sitting up in the bed, his eyes alert but his lips pale with pain. Hart took an involuntary step toward the door before forcing himself to remain still.

"Come on in," Quilla said. "There's a chair left."

He pulled the chair away from the wall and sat, putting his hands in his pockets. Quilla and Ozchan looked at each other quickly, then looked at him again. He kept silent.

"I told Quilla you had some plan," Jason said finally. "We want to know what it is."

"I don't think it's any business of hers," Hart said. "It's strictly between you and me."

"Not if it's medical," Ozchan said. "I'm your father's physician."

"My father's keeper, you mean." Hart heard the anger in his voice and calmed himself carefully. They'd have had to know one way or another, soon enough. Too bad they'd found out this early, but there was no help for it. He leaned back in the cushioned chair. "My father's keeper," he said again. "He needs a keeper now, without one he'd die. No offense, Doctor, but it's the truth, and you know it."

"You said you could give me a new body," Jason said.

"No. I said I could give you your body back again. Not a new one. They're working on that at Kroeber, and they'll be successful, eventually. But they have to do it with clones, a transfer technique. It would take fifteen to seventeen years to grow a clone for you. It's too long, and you don't have the facilities here to do it."

Ozchan shook his head. "They can force clones faster than that."

"Not for a transfer, they can't. The donor body has to

216

be identical to the original, or the transfer doesn't take. When you force a clone, too many things change. It won't work properly. Perhaps someday they'll keep clone banks, fresh and waiting for need, but not yet. Transfer isn't what I had in mind."

"Perhaps you'd best tell us exactly what you do plan," Quilla said.

He looked at her. Cold, distant, hating him. "You wouldn't understand it," he said. "And even if you did, even if I could prove to you that the technique was completely safe and guaranteed to work, you still wouldn't let me do it. Be honest, Quil."

Was that a flicker of discomfort on her face? She moved her shoulders slightly.

"We're talking about Jason," she said, "our father. I wouldn't let you do anything to hurt him, no. But if you could help, if you convinced me that you could help him . . . " She shrugged.

"I'll be back," Hart said, rising and leaving the room quickly. Quilla said something indistinct behind him. He walked down the dark hallway to his room, locked the door behind him, and opened his clothes bag. He dumped the clothing on the floor and detached the lining, pulled it out, and reached inside.

Papers and reels, layered carefully along the bottom of the bag. A cushioned box, which he held under his arm. He gathered the papers together and took them to his father's room, where he handed them across the bed to Ozchan.

"What are those?" Jason said.

"Basically, the background, theories, and results of the technique."

"Tell me about it."

"I can't. Not in detail. I'd have to talk in symbols. But I've discovered how to reprogram your DNA to rebuild your body. Not grafting, not transplants, nothing like that. A more elegant process, and infinitely simpler. I inject a chemical into your bloodstream, and once it's been distributed to all parts of your body, I inject a potentiator. And your body starts to rebuild itself. It's that simple."

Ozchan put down the papers. "I can't make heads or tails of this. For all I know, this could be a chemical formular for turning water into wine."

217

"Come now, *Doctor*. Surely you remember medical school chemistry better than that."

"I'm not a stink-mixer, Quia Kennerin," Ozchan said angrily.

"No, and that's the trouble with all of you." Hart rose and paced around the room. "You're all diddlers. Learn how to plug this into that, put in this drug, take away the other. What do you really know? Do any of you bother to find out why things work, what makes them what they are? Why some people heal and others don't, and what that healing actually is? No, you come up with magical names for it, as if mere noises could explain it. Witch doctors, all of you. Remove part A and substitute part B. Chop it up, and if that doesn't work, chop it up some more. And if you're still up a tree, take the patient—never the person, you understand, never the man or woman, just the *patient*—and stick it in some magical machine. Twist some knobs. Say secret words. Put on your feathers and beads and shake your rattles around the hospital. And you've done everything modern medicine can be expected to do. If the patient doesn't recover, if the patient dies, it's never your fault, is it? You've done your very best, after all. And never, not for one single moment, have you understood what the fuck you've done."

Hart leaned across Jason's bed, staring at Ozchan.

"Go back to your textbooks, Doctor. Find a text on ontogeny. If it's a good one, you'll find the chemical explanation of growth. Don't expect it to be too thorough; it's for physicians, after all. Not stink-mixers. But what I've isolated is the key mixture, the fertilizer for growth. And I've adapted it for use on the postnatal."

He turned to look at his father. "It's not pleasant, Jason. It won't hurt, but you'll be out of it, you won't know what's going on. Your flesh and bones will grow very flexible, very soft. You'll be kept alive by machine, but that's true now. You'll start redeveloping from the spine, just as a fetus would. The genes know the pattern, know the stopping points, the limits. Once you've achieved full new growth, I can stop it at any physical body age that you want. Would you like to be eighteen again, Jason? Twenty-five? Thirty-two? I can do it, and when you awaken, you'll be completely whole. Weak, of course; all those new muscles will need toughening. You'll have to learn to walk again. It will be slow and somewhat painful

218

for a while. But within a year you'll be whole, and well, and strong. A week for preparation, maybe six for restructuring. The rest in physical therapy. That's what I'm offering. It's that simple, Jason. And it's your choice."

"But how do we know it works?" Quilla demanded.

"It works," Hart said. He went back to his chair and sat. "At the back of those papers is a description of previous experiments. The tapes are time-light studies of those same experiments. It works."

Ozchan glanced through the endpapers, then turned to Jason.

"I don't recommend it, Jason. It's new, it's unknown. These experiments may not prove anything at all. I don't like the entire idea."

"Go away," Jason said wearily. "You're arguing over me as though I were dead, or close to it. Get out, all of you. I want to think."

"Father . . . " Quilla said.

"Get out! And don't touch the monitors, Ozchan. I can reach them myself. Out!"

Quilla walked out angrily, and Ozchan followed. Hart paused at the door, then turned, but Jason's brusque gesture sent him, too, on his way. Quilla and Ozchan had already left the hallway. Hart stopped and leaned against the wall, sucking air into his lungs greedily. He hadn't realized how tense he'd been.

He tapped on Drake's door, in search of brandy.

"Who is it?" Drake whispered suspiciously.

"Hart. Let me in. I need something to drink."

There was a noise of bolts and chains, and of something being dragged. Then the door opened.

"Why all the fortifications, Drake? This isn't Shipwright, you know. No thieves or vandals. Do you have any brandy left? I think I've finally made some progress tonight, we may not have to wait much longer." Hart picked the decanter from the table and poured a large shot into a glass. "Better," he said, and turned around.

Drake leaned against the wall, staring at him. He held his gray robe clenched tight. As Hart watched, Drake let the robe fall open. An ugly scarlet rash spread over Drake's chest and into his groin.

"It's starting," Drake whispered. "First the rash, then the skin rejects, then the organs stop. The glands, Hart. I'm falling apart."

Hart walked to him and prodded at the rash with his finger, then took a sip of the brandy.

"You've got a month at least, Drake. There's plenty of time."

"Plenty of time for what?" Drake shouted.

Hart hushed him and listened carefully. The house remained quiet.

"Plenty of time before anything serious starts. I'll give you some ointments for the rash. Patience, Drake. God rewards patience."

"With what?"

Hart smiled and opened the door. "Eternal life," he said pleasantly, and raised the glass of brandy in a toast.

Jason dreamed that he ran in the meadows south of Haven, ran through the tall, thick grasses of the central plain. Dreamed that he swung through the ledges of the barn, rope clenched in his hand; he could feel small pieces of hay tickling his back under the pleasant roughness of his shirt. He opened his hand and fell, turning and twisting, through barn and sky and sea, flying effortlessly; spread his arms to catch the wind and swooped down the length of his island, touched the southern mountains and scooped snow from their glaciered tops. Banked west over forest and shore, over a chain of pale beaches and a froth of tides. Danced on the grim northern cliffs, welcoming the blowing winter and launched himself over the clean northern sea. Clouds and the shadows of clouds, mist and coolness on his taut skin, and a whisper of singing around him increasing to the shrieks of storm. He rode the rain, tumbled into the churning ocean and climbed again, up beyond the clouds, into a sphere of thin air and clarity, and south again, to warm Haven. Mish spilled from a cloudbank, laughing, grabbed his hand and tumbled him with her into the warmth of the meadow. Spread her hair around them, smiling, and slid onto him, around him; put her hands on his shoulders and he put his hands on her hips, feeling them moving, a triangle of sensation from palm to cock to palm again. Her eyes. Her breasts. Her knees. He arched beneath her, shouting, and the cries of joy became sounds of agony, the pulsing of his cock became spiders in his belly. He woke shaking, damp, into a world of pain.

He reached blindly for the knobs on the monitor, feeling for the right one. Turned it one click, two. Three. The pain slid into fog. He dropped his hand to his crotch and held his genitals.

Yes, he thought before the programmed sleep took him, yes.

For three days the Tor bustled. Jason took the first injection and they waited for it to permeate his body, while pieces of equipment were brought from the hospital in Haven and set up in Jason's room. A softbed, which Hart fiddled with until it pleased him. A respirator. Hookups to the monitors and cleansors already present. Thermostatic controls. The room began to look like the bridge of a starship. Ozchan watched the change with suspicion and unease, but Jason had been firm in his decision, and Hart did seem to be cautious and thorough in his work.

The evening of the third day, Hart ran some tests and decreed that Jason was ready for the second injection. They moved Jason into the softbed. He looked small and quiet amid the humming machinery.

"If this doesn't work," Quilla said under her breath, but Jason heard her and put his hand on hers.

"If this doesn't work, it won't be any worse than before," he said.

"But it might kill you!"

"How long would I have lived otherwise?" he said softly. "Frozen and drugged—I might as well have been dead."

"You were never a gambler," she said.

"Perhaps I've changed." Jason smiled and nodded to Hart, who slid the needle into his arm. Within a moment, he had slipped into unconsciousness. Hart hooked up the equipment, double- and then triple-checked it, and allowed the bed to fill with liquid. Jason floated silently, attached by an umbilicus of plastic to an electronic womb. Quilla stared at it, then shivered and moved next to Tabor. He put his arms around her.

"Did you have to do it that way?" she whispered.

Hart looked at the transparent vat, expressionless, and shrugged.

Winter moved in, perpetual clouds and a constant rain. Ozchan had spent his childhood on a dome-world, where the climate never varied from one month to the next; had

221

spent his school years in a place where winter brought clear days and days of snow, a place with emphatic seasons. The unchanging rain depressed him; Meya's news that it would rain almost without letup until spring made him wonder if his sanity would survive. But the Kennerins moved smoothly into their winter routines, as busy now as they had been during the autumn, although at different tasks. Quilla and Tabor spent most of their days in the barn, mending equipment and talking with Aerites and kasirene about next spring's planting. Mim and the cooks took the kitchen apart and put it back together again, scrubbing every millimeter of the room and its furnishings. Each morning the twins, complaining bitterly, slogged down the muddy hill to the school in Haven, and each evening slogged back up, filling the house with the smell of damp clothing, and with shouts. Hart spent most of his time in Jason's room. Drake, succumbing perhaps to boredom, was less and less in evidence as the days passed.

Meya worked around the house, mending things, making things. Ozchan followed her, begging for something to do. She made clothing, set new panes into a broken window at the back of the house, repaired a pipe near the hot tub. Let him hold tools or pound nails, and they talked to the sound of rain and wood. Told each other stories about their families, their friends. The lives they led, the lives they hoped to lead. Moved closer, until one evening they moved into each other's arms and didn't part until morning. He woke to the curve of her body against his, remembered, looked at her with surprise, with apprehension. She smiled and pulled him close to her again. Into her again. Things became easier.

Yet a tension remained, apart from himself or Meya, centered in the room by the halaea branches upstairs, in the transparent vat with its slowly changing occupant. The feeling lay stretched and taut in the hours of their lives, never relaxing and never snapping. Ozchan would find it in the expressions of Quilla's face as she gazed into the vat, in the sound of Tabor's flute, the shouting of Mim in the kitchen, and he would stand silent, testing it, before moving toward Meya again. It seemed that time had stopped.

"I'm dying! I'm falling apart! Look at me!"
"Indeed, you are. Fascinating."

"Damn it, I'm not a lab animal. I'm not one of your goddamned experiments. You've got to help me, Hart. Look, look at my arms. At my mouth—look at that. You've got to do something for me!"

"Stop shouting, Drake. You've got plenty of time left."

"I don't want time—I want you to help me."

"Be patient. Jason's progressing well. He should be finished with the vat in another four weeks or so. Then you go in."

"I won't last four weeks, I'll be dead by then."

"No you won't. You'll be pretty vile, true, but not dead. If it comes to that, I can keep you alive on the machines in Hoku's hospital until the vat is ready for you. Calm down, Drake, there's nothing to worry about."

"You're trying to kill me, aren't you? I'll remember this, Kennerin. I'm not going to forget what you're doing to me. If you think you'll ever see a fremark from me after this—"

"Drake. Shut up. You're not going to die. I'm not trying to kill you. What do you expect me to do, anyway? I can't do grafts and transplants on you. They don't have the facilities here, and there are no donor banks, either. Just wait, be calm, be patient. In four weeks I'll give you the body of an eighteen-year-old, and when you run through that one, I'll give you another. Four weeks is a small price to pay for that."

"In four weeeks I'll be dead."

"Only if you really want to be. Here, have some more brandy and shut up for a while, will you? I want to finish this tape."

"I won't forget this, Kennerin."

"No, I don't imagine that you will."

Meya put down the saw and pushed hair from her face. Rain beat monotonously against the windows, a hollow, infinitely lonely sound. The house creaked in the wind, the chimneys sighed. Quilla and Tabor were in the barn, the twins were at school, and Mim had gone to Haven to visit friends. Ozchan left in the morning to spend the day at the hospital with Hoku; Meya thought about his tall brown body beside Hoku's tiny, wrinkled one, then of his body beside her own. He had left small marks on her shoulders last night. She put her fingers on them gently and felt suddenly flushed, remembering the

223

tastes and textures of his body. She stripped off the leather apron and hung it on the wall, then washed her hands and went into the kitchen.

Sweet rolls, still hot from the morning's baking. Cool milk. She sat at the kitchen table and ate slowly, wondering how to spend the rest of the afternoon; something to fill the time until Ozchan's return, something to fill her mind. To the barn? No, she didn't feel like listening to important talk about vegetables and grains. Into Haven? Hoku and Ozchan would be busy, would not welcome an unexpected visit. She could visit Puti and play with her new pups, could see who was at Kohl's. But the prospect of dressing in water clothes and slogging through the mud did not appeal to her, and she suspected that, once in Haven, she would head straight for the hospital. Making herself obvious.

She finished the rolls, washed and dried cup and plate, and stood at the kitchen door, staring at the gleaming floors.

She could go upstairs and visit Jason. The twins wouldn't do it, they found the sight disquieting; their grandfather floating, almost shapeless, in a crystal coffin. Quilla, too, tried not to enter the room, and when she did so, looked at the vat with something approaching horror. But Meya found it no more upsetting than the sight of her energetic father lying broken in a bed, or pushed around the house in that silly chair. At least now he had the dignity of mystery, and she found his room to be a place of promise rather than a place of fear.

She would take her newest tape upstairs and read to him. After all, Mim visited him each evening to gossip about the events of the day, and Tabor often spent hours in Jason's room, playing his flute. Tabor claimed that unborn children could hear music, and didn't see why this shouldn't be true of Jason, too. Hart treated this idea with contempt, but Meya didn't see why. Besides, Hart would be down at the landing pad now, picking something up that the morning's shuttle had brought. No likelihood of his finding her reading to her unborn father and make her nervous with voiced and unvoiced sarcasm.

Jason's room was quiet save for the hum of the machines, and dark save for the lights of the dials and the

224

phosphorescence of the liquid in the vat. She lit the lamp beside the vat and sat in the easy chair.

"Hi, Jason. I thought you might be bored, so I brought something to read to you. It's something Ozchan loaned me, a novel about some space explorers who go off the edge of the universe. I'm already on the fourth chapter. Ready?"

Eventually the sound of her own voice lulled her to sleep, and she woke, startled. Some noise. She looked quickly into the vat, but Jason remained peacefully suspended, and the dials of the machines seemed correctly set. Noise again, something in the hallway.

"Who's in there?" a voice whispered.

Drake. Her stomach felt cold. No one in the house. She hadn't seen Hart's friend in more than a week, but remembered his prying, his grabbing, his insistence. She turned out the lamp, then moved as quickly and quietly as she could to the far side of the machines and crouched between them and the wall.

"Anyone in there?"

The door opened, admitting a shaft of light from the hallway. Sounds of scuffled walking, and the lamp was lit again. Door closing, lock locking. She held her breath and looked around for something to use as a weapon. Save for the reel of tape, there was nothing.

"Good," Drake said. "All alone now. Very good. Stealing my life, you know that, old man? That's my vat you're using. Yes. I paid for all that research. I funded all those experiments. That vat is mine. And now I'm dying, and your son, your sucking, vicious son, won't let me use it. Makes me wait until you're done. Why should I wait, old man? Tell me that. I'm Tev Drake. I am very, very rich. You, you're just backwash, just colony. I could wipe you out and never notice. Why should I wait for you? You don't need it, you can wait. You weren't dying. Not much. That's my vat, and I'm going to use it. Yes indeed. Now."

Meya poked her head around the edge of the monitor and saw Drake at the vat, his hands reaching for the controls. Red hands, black hands, strips of flesh and strips of skin slack and flapping, something wet. A fingernail hung attached by one thread of flesh. The hand-thing touched the controls.

"Stop that!" she screamed.

225

Drake spun around, and she screamed again when she saw his face. She jumped away from the monitor and held the tape reel in her hand as though it were a weapon. Drake laughed.

"Stupid girl. Going to stop me with screams and a novel. You've had lots of practice screaming, haven't you? I hear you, at night, rolling around in that bed of yours. Having fun, aren't you? Put that down. Get out and I won't hurt you."

"You stay away from my father."

"Melodrama!" Drake's face appeared to smile. "Think of something new today, little girl. Amuse me."

He edged around the vat toward her. She retreated, backed into the pile of equipment left over from Jason's life before the vat. Things clattered as they fell, and Drake jumped.

"Doesn't matter," he said. "No one at home but you and me. Make noise, girl. Scream some more. It pleases me."

Meya felt behind her. Beakers. Bedpan. Linen. Something cool and round and heavy—the side pole for the bed. She tightened her grip on it.

"Get out of this room," she said. "Get out and I won't tell anyone you were here."

"Such a generous offer. Come out of there. Now. I haven't time to play games with you."

"Get out of this room!"

Drake paused. "What would you like, little girl? A planet of your own? A little ship to scoot around the world with? Or just a fortune? I can give them to you, anything you want. Think of that. You could go anywhere you wanted to. You could be so rich you could buy this planet, and everyone on it. Isn't that nice? Come on, tell me what you want, and I'll give it to you, and you can go away." He edged closer.

"I want you to leave my father alone."

"Oh, not fair. Then what would I get? Something for something, girl. Name a price."

"No price. Get out."

Drake cursed and leaped at her. She swung the pole. Drake ducked and threw the discarded tape reel at her. It hit her forehead and she fell. Things went very black and very red. Drake kicked her side, and she couldn't react. Something made a large booming noise in her ears,

226

and she struggled to hear through it. When she opened her eyes she couldn't see, then things swam into a very liquid focus. Drake was no longer above her. Someone was talking, almost singsong; she couldn't understand the words. She pushed herself up on her elbow, fighting nausea.

Drake was by the control panels, his hideous hands busy with something. She groped for the pole, grabbed it, and pushed herself upright. Drake didn't turn around. He talked, talked, the skin of his hands fluttered. The fingernail fell. She staggered around the vat behind him, raised the pole, and brought it down on the back of his head. Again. He fell. Again. He continued falling. Again. Again.

Something oozed from his head. She dropped to her knees beside the vat and vomited.

"Meya!"

Hands grabbed her shoulders and pushed her up. She raised her head to look at Hart's face.

"Drake," she said. "To kill Jason. Did something to the machines."

Hart dropped her. She lay with her cheek against the floor and heard him cursing, doing something to the machines, cursing again. He hauled her up again.

"How long? Since he touched the machines, how long?"

She shook her head, bewildered.

He propped her against the wall and returned to the controls. His hands danced amid the dials and knobs, and he turned his head, controls to vat to controls to vat. She turned her head slowly and looked into the vat. Jason looked the same, and she closed her eyes.

Eventually Hart left the controls and squatted beside her.

"It looks all right," he said, frowning. "I can't see any changes. I think it's all right. Try to remember how long it was."

"Don't know. I was asleep, and Drake came in and talked. Wanted to use the vat. I tried to stop him. He hit my head and I fell down. He did something to the controls. I hit him, and I fell down again." Her throat felt nauseous again. "Is he—"

"He's dead. Stupid bastard, there were only two weeks to go." Hart took her chin in his fingers and tilted her

227

head. "You're a mess, and we've got to do something about your forehead. It's a good cut there."

"What about . . . about him?"

"Drake?" Hart rocked back and frowned. "Get rid of him somehow, then clean up the mess. Shit. He's an important man, he'll be missed. They'll come looking for him."

She put her hands to her face and tried to clear her mind. "What if they find him? What will they do to me?"

"I don't know. It was self-defense, defense of Jason. But he was rich, Meya. I don't think they'll buy self-defense. They wouldn't kill you for it, but they might demand stasis."

"Hart!"

"Hush. I was just thinking aloud. Of course they won't find him. We'll get rid of him somehow, make up some story. Can you stand up?"

She pushed herself up against the wall and swayed. Hart muttered and went to the supply cabinet, came back with a hypo and an ampule.

"It's a stimulant," he said. "Should clear your mind, get you going for a while. It won't hurt you."

She looked at him and held out her arm. He cradled her elbow in his hand and paused, staring at her eyes.

"You trust me?" he said.

She looked into his cold blue eyes and nodded.

It was still early afternoon. That confused her; it should have been much later. Days later. They wrapped Drake's body in a sheet and then in plastic, carried it down the stairs and through Mim's sparkling kitchen, into the rain. Down the hill, away from the Tor, from the barn, and from Haven. She left Hart with the body and the shovel, and went back to the Tor. The stimulant layered an illusory clarity over her nausea. She cleaned the room, swabbing up blood and vomit and what she knew, distantly, to be Drake's brains. The scrubbing made her feel no cleaner, but the work comforted her body, the rhythms. Hart came back and helped, then guided her to the hot tub. They stripped and washed, then slid into the water. Steam rose from her hands. Rain beat against the wooden roof of the tubhouse. Sweat stung her eyes. Hart hauled her from the tub and back to the Tor, put her in bed, gave her an injection. She touched his hand and the room disappeared.

228

When she woke, Ozchan lay beside her, and it was night. She moved away from him on the bed and lay awake, staring at the darkness. The next morning she pleaded fatigue and remained in bed, battered by Ozchan's concern and Mim's home remedies. Hart told people, casually, that Drake had decided to leave and had taken yesterday's shuttle. The story was not questioned.

In the afternoon, when the house seemed quiet, she rose and dressed. Hart was not in his room, and she hesitated, then reluctantly went down the hall toward Jason's room. It looked clean and tranquil, no different from before. Hart looked up from the vat and came to her, guided her to a chair, sat beside her.

"You look terrible," he said.

"Feel it. I can't stay here, Hart. Can't sleep, can't eat. Can't talk to anyone. I keep seeing his face . . . feeling the pole hitting his head."

"Think about something else."

"I can't," she said angrily. "I can't turn everything off the way you can. Give me something, make it go away."

Hart shook his head. "Then everyone would want to know why you were out all the time. Meya, you've got to fight it yourself. Be strong."

She stared at her hands. "Maybe it would be easier if we told people."

"For God's sake, Meya! We have enough problems without that."

"Then what am I supposed to do?"

Hart made a gesture of exasperation and stood. Meya looked at Jason.

"I'll go away for a while," she said. "That won't be strange. I'll go spend a week with Puti, or Teloret. In the village."

"With kassies," Hart said scornfully.

"Yes." She stood. "With friends."

He came in front of her and put his hands on her shoulders.

"You'll be all right there? You're sure?"

She nodded and put her head on his shoulder, and after a moment Hart stroked her hair gently.

By evening she was gone.

"I don't understand," Ozchan said bitterly. "Things were going so well for us, and suddenly she just disappears. Heads off to visit friends, gone for a week. What in hell goes on here, anyway?"

Tabor shrugged. "I don't know. I've been thinking about it for seventeen years, and I can't figure it out. They're like that, all of them. Jason says that they're all solitary people; Hoku says they're just dense. They see everyone through layers of themselves."

"Everyone does that." Ozchan stretched his feet toward the fire. "You seem to put up with it well enough," he said.

"Being Quilla's bedmate? It has its rewards."

"That's cynical enough."

"Nothing cynical about it. I'd rather be around her than otherwise. I'd rather be around the children. It's not a bad life."

"Wonderful. What about love?"

Tabor smiled. "You think it's not there? We live in different worlds, she and I. We speak different languages, and sometimes translation's difficult. She loves me, but she can't talk about it. I think she's afraid of it. She loves the children. I love her. Not everything has to be a grand passion."

"Is that what I have to look forward to? A life of translation?"

"I don't think so. Meya's different. She's more intense, in outward ways. More open. I think she's just very disturbed about something, and she's taken time out to clear her head. But if she's in love with you, I'd imagine there will be lots of grand passion. Enough for the entire family."

"Clear her head about what? Me?"

"Possibly." Tabor looked worried and glanced around the barn. The firepot by their feet cast a small light; beyond that, the barn was dark and quiet. Save, of course, for the perpetual sound of rain. "I think it's more than just you, though—something having to do with Hart."

"What?"

"I don't know. I wish I did. The entire thing makes me feel prickly."

"Prickly. That's a good word." Ozchan leaned forward. "What did Hart do, Tabor? Seven years ago, what did he do to make everyone hate him this way?"

"Something. There was a crazy old man, Hart lived with him. An old biologist, or was before he came to

230

Aerie. They were up to something pretty grim, from the sound of it, but no one will talk about it. I think Hoku knows, and Quilla, Jason, Mish. I think some of the kasirene may know, but I'm not sure. Anyway, one day, all of a sudden, Hart and Gren—that was the old man— were gone, and no one said a word about anything."

"And the old woman? Laur?"

"Bad heart. She doted on Hart, you'd have thought he was her own child. Whatever it was that he did, it must have been quite a shock to her, and then he seemed to blame her for it. Her heart gave out."

"That doesn't sound like his fault."

"Not directly, no. He's very good at making things not seem his fault."

"He's trying to help Jason," Ozchan said.

Tabor shook his head. "It was Jason's choice, and we had to go along with it. But I don't trust Hart. I wouldn't trust him if he were frozen in stasis. Whatever is bothering Meya, I'm willing to bet it has something to do with Hart. I can't prove it, but I'm sure."

"Tenuous grounds, Tabor."

"Perhaps. But the only ones I've got."

Ozchan sighed and stared into the firepot again. Outside, the rain continued to fall.

The man in the vat was beautiful, the body firm and clean of line, like an artist's conception of the perfect man. Skin dark and glowing, face serene, unlined. His chest rose and fell easily as the respirator hummed. The level of the fluid in the vat dropped slowly, and Quilla reached for Tabor's hand.

The room was silent. Mim stood at the foot of the vat, her clenched hands making a small bump under the fabric of her apron. Ozchan beside her, face intent, and Hoku beside him. Hart, moving from vat to controls and back, face set. Tabor. They had sent for Meya. The kasirene said she had gone to a village farther down the island. They sent a messenger, but she had not arrived in time. The children were in Haven, staying with friends. Mish and Jes were not due for another three weeks.

The vat was empty. Hart and Ozchan lifted away the sides and put them on the floor, then Hart carefully suctioned liquid from Jason's nose and mouth and unhooked the respirator. Jason breathed alone, and the sound mingled with the breathing in the room. Quilla's shoulders relaxed. Jason's legs twitched.

"It will take a while," Hart said quietly. "He'll have to get used to his body, regain control of it. Reestablish things. Don't expect him to jump up and start running around."

"The body seems to be fine," Hoku said. "What about the mind?"

"Untouched," Hart said. "Give him time."

He bent over his father and touched Jason's cheek with his fingertips.

"Jason," he said, "wake up."

Jason's body moved gently, sleepily.

Quilla dropped Tabor's hand and leaned over her father. "Jason," she said quietly, "time to wake up. Come on, it's morning. Jason."

The eyelids fluttered and opened, and Jason's deep blue eyes stared at her face. Past her face. It's all right, she told herself. He's coming out of it. Needs time.

"Jason," she said again, and touched his cheek.

Jason's eyes stared past her. And there was nothing behind them at all.

Hart pushed her aside roughly and grabbed for the electroencephalograph. He pasted the electrodes to Jason's head, his fingers almost trembling, turned, flicked the power switch.

The screen lit. The graph read absolutely flat.

Quilla stared, her mind a total blank. Hart slowly put his forehead against the machine.

"That's how long," he whispered. "Sweet Mother! That's how long."

Quilla grabbed him and threw him aside, screaming that he'd killed her father. He stared at her stupidly, the words made no sense, and she shouted them again and hit him. Tabor grabbed her, and she tried to hit Tabor.

"Not true," Hart said. "I didn't. Not true."

"Bullshit!" Hoku said angrily. "That thing isn't Jason. What are you trying to hide, Hart? First Laur dead, now Jason. I'll bet Gren's dead, too. Am I next? Or Quilla? How about your mother, Hart, are you planning to kill her, too?"

"I didn't kill—"

232

"He's not there!" Quilla screamed. "There's nothing in there! *You killed him!*"

"I didn't! Drake—" And the words froze within him. Drake. Meya, the only one who believed him. Who trusted him.

"That's right, blame it on someone who isn't here," Tabor said. "That's your usual excuse, isn't it?"

If he told them about Drake, he'd have to tell them about Meya. He stared at their contorted faces, the hatred, the anger. Tell them, tell them and Drake gets all the blame. Tell them and escape. And they'll know about Meya, and they'll never be able to hide that knowledge. And Meya will go into stasis. Meya will die for seventy years and never be allowed back home. Tell them and go free.

"No!" he shouted, turned, ran from the room. One second, two—he reached the head of the stairs and they rushed after him, still shouting. He almost fell down the stairs, recovered, ran from the house. Mud sucked at his shoes. He slid down the hillside, running blindly toward the port, toward the fortnightly shuttle. The world was full of screams.

It became dream-like. Shuttle in the rain, drawing its hatch closed. Leaping for the rim, scrambling up, diving inside just as the hatch snapped shut. Leaning against bulkhead, wet, panting, crying, while the crew stared at him in bewilderment.

"What the suckin' hell is this?" the shuttle's captain said.

"Leaving with you," Hart said. "I'll pay."

"Strap him down," the captain said. "Fuck, we're off schedule already."

The engines howled. Someone pushed Hart into a seat and cinched the webbing around him, someone yelled about clearing the pad, something like a soft cushion pushed him into the seat.

Meya had put her head against his shoulder, had given him her arm. Trusted him. Of all of them, only Meya. Black villain to the rest, but he could protect her, at least. Make some payment for her faith.

The same crew that he'd spoken to two weeks before. Same shuttle that serviced Aerie the day of Drake's death. It would be easy to find their stored passenger lists, to add the name of Tev Drake to it, start-port Aerie, stop-port . . . where? Someplace, there would be no trouble picking someplace.

A life for a life.

When they reached the ship, the captain took him aside.

"Money, no luggage, dripping wet. Looks like someone was chasing you."

Hart remained silent.

"No business of mine," the captain said. She pushed her cap back on her head. "Where're you headed?"

"What's your last stop-port?"

"Gregory system. South Wing."

"Fine," Hart said, "that'll do fine."

They gave him a cabin, and one of the crew members sold him some clothes. He put the clothes in the locker, threw his own down the chute, and climbed into the bunk. For a long time he lay stiffly, staring at the smooth, curved bulkhead walls. For a long time after that he wept.

QUILLA

"IT'S NOT TRUE," MEYA KEPT SAYING. "You've got to listen to me. It's not true."

But we were too upset, too busy, too murderous to listen to her. She'd arrived just a few hours after Hart's escape, and had to put the story together from our shouts and threats. Eventually she rushed into the storeroom, came out with the rifle that Jason had kept locked away, and blew a hole in the living room ceiling. That shut everybody up long enough to let her start talking, and after that we had to listen.

Much as some of us didn't want to. How horribly eager we were to think the absolute worst, and think it truth and justice.

She shouted until we'd heard her story. She showed us the place they'd hidden Drake's things: his clothes, his pretties, his brandy bottle. She took us to Drake's grave and went away while Tabor, Ozchan, and I dug up the man's rotting body. Ozchan performed an on-the-spot autopsy, and we buried him again.

When we came back to the Tor, wet and muddy, Meya sat beside Jason, holding his hand. The scar on her forehead, the scar we'd thought had come from falling in the workroom, seemed terrible and bright. We stood at the door of the room, looking at her, and she raised her head and stared at us calmly.

"Perhaps you'd better call the Federation," she said calmly. "But first you'd better call Hart. And apologize."

The first was unthinkable. The second shamed us, but we tried, anyway. We couldn't find him. He wasn't at Kroeber, had never returned. The shuttle captain said only that Hart had gone to the end of the line, a main grab from which ships spilled out to a number of systems, and we could not trace him from there. We did discover one thing, however: Tev Drake was listed as a passenger on the shuttle, leaving Aerie on the date of his own death —destination, Kaipha's Beard. Hart had taken that same shuttle two weeks later. Meya had the grace not to say anything. I felt like a pile of lizard shit.

The problem of Jason remained. He lay in the bed, breathing, heart beating, the perfect semblance of a perfect man. And totally mindless. Hoku and Ozchan had checked him over and over. Ozchan had sent to Solon for their library on brain death and spent weeks scratching through the tapes for anything likely to help us. The results were frustrating. Had a recording been made prior to the accident, Jason could have been flown to Solon and reprogrammed. Had the brain tracks been cleared but not killed, Jason would be alive—not Jason, nothing more than a full-grown baby, but alive and capable of learning. But Hart had very carefully ensured that Jason's brain would not be affected by the treatment, had not wanted to do anything that might disturb his father's mind.

Meya tended to our father, washing him, changing his position, rolling him over, reading to him, speaking to him as though he would hear her and understand, would open his eyes and smile at her. Ozchan said it was nothing to worry about, that Meya was not sliding into a world of fantasy. After watching her closely for a while, I believed him. When, in frustration, Hoku suggested that Jason's body be stopped, Meya protested with such fury that the subject was dropped. Besides, if it was to be anyone's decision, it would have to be that of Mish.

She hadn't been told, by Jason's express wish. He wanted her to return to find him whole and growing, in the process of recovering completely. Wanted to give her the gift of his new body. So she hadn't been told, either of the treatment or of the accident. Luckily, communications between Aerie and Althing Green were expensive, and the messages that went between us scarce. It was no problem to smooth the matter over, to give an appearance of normality. "No change in Jason," I would transmit; she would not know in what ways it was true. And she was in the last few weeks of the license hearings, hearings which could very well determine all our futures. If she left before they were completed, we would not be granted further hearings for

236

another five years standard, at the least. Or so we told ourselves, assured ourselves, and kept our doubts quiet.

Ozchan could have left. There was no longer anything he could do for Jason, yet he stayed. Meya announced that she was pregnant, and Hoku confirmed this. Three days later she married Ozchan; she said Jason wanted it that way.

Well, why not? Tabor and I talked about it that night, about Meya and Jason and Ozchan, Hoku's practice, Haven's growth, Aerie-Kennerin's expansion, the twins and their schooling, household matters. Books he had read or I remembered. Music. Farming. Philosophy. The talk didn't seem strange to me, breaking all my years of effective silence around him. We made love. I listened for the sound of his flute as I worked, listened for the tapping of his cane in the house. Thought one night of what life would be like if he were no longer with me, if he, not Jason, lay mindless in that bed. The images frightened me, filled me with pity for my mother and what she would find on her return, terror for myself.

We didn't speak of marriage. It seemed beside the point. What bound us together was far stronger than any ceremony could create, far more important than words spoken or certificates bandied about. Jason had talked about the certainty of things, and I finally knew what he had meant.

Hoku and Ozchan set up practice together. No one in Haven trusted him, at first. Hoku said it was to be expected; he said that she'd so terrified everyone that only her opinion was considered valid, only her treatments effective. She agreed.

And Jes arrived. He listened to our stories, then turned silently and climbed the stairs to Jason's room. Meya touched her belly and followed him. Ozchan rose, but I shook my head and went myself. I had seen the cold, hard look that Jes had sent Meya's husband when he saw them standing together.

Jes stood by Jason's bed, his fists clenched, staring at his father. I stopped by the open door, ready to grab my brother if the need arose. Meya watched him calmly, sadly.

"Jason?"

Jason looked on the verge of waking, skin warm and dark, hands folded at his sides. Face serene. As usual, as usual. His eyelids never moved.

"Jason?"

237

Meya reached across the bed toward her brother.

"Jessie, please . . . "

"How could you?" he shouted. "You, Meya, of all people! How . . . " He stopped and turned abruptly from her, hiding his face. She came to him and put her hand on his arm.

"Jes . . ."

He spun around, his fist clenched, but when his hand reached her cheek his fingers were open and he touched her slowly, gently. She kissed his palm. Then he pushed her back and ran from the room.

I caught Meya, steadying her.

"Are you all right? Are you hurt?"

"I'm sorry," she whispered. We held each other for a moment, then went downstairs.

Before we could tell Jes about Drake, about Meya, he went down to the communications shack at the pad and put through an urgent message to Mish and told her all about it. I suppose they must have commed back and forth for over an hour; the bill came to seven hundred fremarks. Jes came back from the pad with a certified, double-validated message from Mish. It was very short and quite to the point. It said, "Stop him."

Legally, she had the right. Morally, she had the right. Jes confronted us in the living room and put the message on the table, looking at us as though we were a community of strangers. I suppose we were.

"You're worshipping a corpse up there," he said flatly. "Jason's dead and you know it. Jason died when that murderer touched the controls, when our brother killed him, and you know that, too."

"Jes, listen to me," Tabor said.

Jes ignored him. "What do you think you're doing up there?" he shouted. "Preserving him, so that when Mish comes home it will be even worse? She's been bracing herself for Jason's death ever since he came back to Aerie. She knew he'd want to die at home, she knew that he would die, even if he didn't understand that. Do you think it would be any easier for her, coming home to a shape of Jason's that's whole and young and breathing, and none of Jason inside at all? What are you, a family of ghouls?"

"It's my fault," Meya said quietly. "They wanted to do it before, and I wouldn't let them."

"Then you can do it now," Jes said and left the room.

I think he was being a coward. If any one of us could

238

do it, he could, and should, have. But we said nothing, and Meya rose and went upstairs. After an hour she came down again. We heard her putting on her water clothes in the hall, and the sound of the door opening and closing behind her. Ozchan rose, but Tabor shook his head and went himself, followed Meya through Haven to the kasirene village, and saw her safely to Teloret's door. Left her there, where she had gone before for comfort and help.

She'd used a hypo full of digitalis, one of the drugs Ozchan kept stocked in his room, for emergencies.

Two days later Mish came home.

Part Six

1233-1234
New Time

ALMOST
SPRING

"Single-mindedness is all very well in cows or baboons; in an animal claiming to belong to the same species as Shakespeare, it is simply disgraceful."

—Aldous Huxley

MISH DESCENDED ON AERIE LIKE A BOLT OF alien lightning, and her family stood aside, watching, as she roared up the hill from the landing field and into the house. Meya held out her arms, but Mish pushed her aside and glared around the room.

"Where is he?" she demanded.

Quilla dropped Tabor's hand and stepped forward. "In Haven," she said. "The undertaker—"

"Bring him back. This is his home, and he belongs here." She turned to stare past Meya at Ozchan. "You're M'Kale. I'll talk to you later. Where's Mim?"

"Here, Quia Mish."

"We'll need food, wine, beer, bread, meat. Quilla, you send out invitations for the wake. Tonight."

Phlegmatic Mim stared down at Mish, her arms crossed and her expression grim. "Quia Jason wouldn't want a fuss," she said.

"You were in his confidence, I suppose?"

"Mim's right," Tabor said quietly. "He liked things to be peaceful."

"So we'll have a peaceful wake. Get going. I want all the stuff up from the storerooms. And get this place clean, it's a mess."

Quilla caught Meya's eye and formed the word "Hoku" with her lips. Meya nodded and moved toward the door.

"Where're you going?" Mish said.

"Into Haven to tell Klein to bring Jason back," Meya said calmly.

Mish stared at her, then nodded and left the room. Quilla followed her, and stopped when she saw Mish staring at the ramp on the stairway.

242

"What's this?"

"The ramp for Jason's chair. So that he could move up and down stairs."

"What chair?"

"One that I made for him, with wheels and a place for his monitors. He didn't use it very often."

"Jason in a chair?" For the first time she sounded uncertain. The twins appeared at the top of the stairs and looked down at her solemnly, their hands clasped tightly together. Mish gasped and turned quickly, almost running into Tabor.

"Go take care of your children." she shouted, and pushed past him. Mim came out of the room, gave Quilla a flat, hard look, and went into the kitchen.

"Quia Kennerin . . . " Ozchan said.

"Get out," Mish said. Ozchan came out of the room and closed the door behind him. Quilla sat at the foot of the stairs beside Tabor, and the children came and sat in her lap. Ozchan put his hands in his pockets and shook his head.

"Can't you give her something to calm her down?" Quilla said.

"I doubt if she'd let me. Is Hoku coming?"

"Meya went to get her." Quilla pressed her cheek against Decca's hair.

"She's got her thinking turned off," Decca whispered. "Just faces and words, but no thinking."

Jared slid onto Tabor's lap and stared at the living room door. "She's inside like Hetch's 'bots," he said.

"Don't talk about her like that," Tabor said.

Jared shrugged. "She is," he said.

Quilla put her arms around Decca and closed her eyes. The rain had slackened, and she heard the whoosh of the skimmer as it came up the hill and stopped before the door. Hoku came in, holding her bag and her side. She leaned against the doorframe, looking at them, and tilted her chin questioningly. Quilla nodded toward the living room door. Hoku opened the door and went inside. Meya came in and pushed damp hair from her face.

"She was expecting it," Meya said, almost angrily. "She had her bag packed and everything. She'd even told Klein to bring . . . to get . . ."

Ozchan tried to hold her, but she pushed him away and went upstairs. Jes came in from the kitchen and looked at them.

"The guilty parties," he said.

Ozchan put his hands on his hips and glared at Jes, who stared back. Quilla looked from one to the other, and groped for Tabor's hand.

Hoku closed the door behind her and leaned on it, watching Mish pace back and forth. Mish stopped pacing and put her fists on her hips.

"Well?"

"Well," Hoku echoed gently. She moved toward a chair. "Welcome home."

"Welcome! This place is a mess, people keep grabbing at me, Mim talks back to me, Meya's impossible, it's complete chaos, and Jason's . . ."

Hoku let the silence settle, then said, "Dead, Mish."

Mish's hands plucked at the sides of her tunic. Hoku put her bag down on a table but remained standing.

"Jes said that Hart tried to do something to him. Tried to change him."

"That's true."

"And it didn't work."

"That's not true. It worked beautifully."

"Then why did my husband die?" Mish shouted.

Hoku frowned thoughtfully. "There was an accident. The controls were turned off for a moment, his brain lacked the oxygen it needed. But it would have worked, Mish."

"It was no accident. Jes said—"

"Jes wasn't here."

"—that some friend of Hart's—"

"Jes wasn't here."

"Jes didn't believe it. Jes said you were all hiding something."

Hoku sat carefully, her back stiff against the back of the chair, and put her hands in her lap.

"Hart brought a man named Tev Drake with him. Drake was a transplant addict, an old man although he didn't look like it. Hart told Drake that after Jason had been through the treatment, Drake could take it. Drake started to fall apart and didn't want to wait. He tried to disrupt the treatment, and Meya stopped him."

"Then what? They told him it was a no-no and sent him away?"

"Jes didn't tell you?"

"Jes said that Drake had left. Said that he didn't believe

it. Said that he checked the records, and Drake was signed onto a shuttle that left the day Quilla said he left. Well, I believe it. And I'll tell you why."

Mish clenched her hands at her sides and leaned over Hoku. "They let him go because he owns Albion-Drake, and if they'd stopped him, we'd have lost our processors. They sold my husband for their planet—that's what they did. They killed Jason."

"Drake didn't own Albion-Drake."

"He owns fifty-two percent of it, and that's enough."

Hoku thought curses at the Kennerins. Why hadn't they told Jes the truth? For fear of harming Meya? More likely Jes had heard the outline of the story and rushed off to com Mish, and the rest had been so angry at this that they'd refused to tell him the rest of the story. Probably refused to talk with him at all. Hotheaded Kennerins.

"Mish, do you really think your family would . . ."

"What else am I to think? I sent Jason home so that he could, could die with some dignity, with some peace. And they turned him into a circus, they played games with him. They killed him, all of them."

"It was Jason's decision."

"It was not! He was in no condition to make decisions like that. And when that man did whatever it was that he did, they didn't have the sense to stop him. They just let him go."

"Shut up!" Hoku yelled. Mish looked at her, surprised. "You want to know why Jes thinks all of that? It's because he didn't listen any more than you are now. Do you want to know what really happened, or would you rather go on hating everyone? Maybe you're enjoying all of this too much to give it up. Maybe you like thinking you've raised murderers."

"How can you say that?"

"With my mouth. It's very easy. You make words with your tongue and lips and throat, and you just let them out."

"Don't play with me."

"Who's playing with whom? Do you think you're thinking at all? Or just making a lot of noisy garbage?"

"Jason's dead!" Mish spun around to face the window and put her head against the glass. Hoku watched her for a moment, feeling for her mind.

"Meya found Drake in Jason's room. She tried to stop him and he hit her, and while she was out he did something to the controls. She pulled herself together, picked up a bedrail, and bashed his head in. By then it was too late. Hart found her, reset the machines, and together they buried Drake and hid his stuff. They were afraid that if anyone found out Meya would be tried and put in stasis. They didn't realize how extensive the damage was. Meya went to stay with the kasirene, and while she was gone the treatments ended and they tried to wake Jason up. When the rest realized what had happened, that Jason was mindless, they turned on Hart and accused him of killing Jason." Hoku paused. "I was there. I accused him just like the rest of them. We wouldn't listen to him, and he ran off—caught the shuttle before we could catch him. Then Meya came back and made us listen. We dug up Drake. He's planted west of here, just into the woods. But by then it was too late to find Hart and apologize."

"That's a very nice story," Mish said slowly. "But Meya hasn't the guts to kill anyone, and Drake's name is on that passenger list."

"Hart was on that same shuttle two weeks later. We think Hart changed the lists."

"Why?"

"To protect Meya."

Mish looked at Hoku scornfully. "You can make up a better fairytale than that," she said.

"You want us to go dig Drake up again?"

"And what would that prove? That you've got a corpse in the woods? So what?"

Hoku reached for her bag. "You do believe me, you know. Somewhere in that mess, you believe me."

"Mind-reader," Mish said bitterly.

"Yes," Hoku said. "And shall I tell you something else? There's something floating around in there that you don't want to think about, that shames you. You're hiding it with a lot of hate and noise and shit, but it's not going away. Want to know what it is?"

"Tell me," Mish said sarcastically. "The date of my birth? Statistics? My favorite dish? Tabor?"

Hoku shook her head. "He could have waited," she said gently. "He could have waited for me. He left without even saying good-bye."

Mish started crying. She stood, her arms at her sides, eyes open, her body shaking with great, silent, tearing sobs. Hoku guided her to the couch and sat beside her.

246

Mish turned blindly, and Hoku cradled her, rocking and murmuring softly into Mish's graying hair.

That afternoon Klein, the undertaker, brought Jason's body to the Tor and placed it in a coffin in the living room. He'd done a good job, Quilla thought. Putting gray in the hair, age lines on the face. Jason looked his age again. The people of Haven came quietly to the door, bearing gifts of food and sorrow, and sat about the room, staring at the wooden box on its ungainly, rough-hewn trestles. Tabor sat in a corner. Occasionally he'd place the flute to his lips, then put it on his lap again without having played it. The kasirene came, Palen and her children, Teloret, Puti, old Altemet supported by his equally aged friends. Cooks and field workers and laborers, shoulder to shoulder with the human builders and farmers and carpenters. Ved Hirem sat beside the coffin and refused to move. The lawyer dozed gently, his head resting on the coffin's side, then woke with a start, stared around the room with bleary eyes, and gazed sadly at the coffin until his eyelids descended and he slept again. Simit, now the headmaster of Haven's two schools, brought his pupils and one by one they passed the coffin, pausing to stare at Jason's quiet face and folded hands, at the old quilt from his bed which covered him, at his long, brown fingers. Quilla watched them filter through the room and realized, for the first time, that Jason was a hero to these people, had taken them in when their world no longer wanted them, had guided them, advised them, given them homes and land, crops to plant and a future to anticipate with eagerness rather than with dread. Most of the adults remembered Jason in the cold, bleak winter of Great Barrier, rushing the fences with them, leading them across the snowfields to Hetch's waiting shuttles. Remembered him carrying children and old people and the sick, remembered him waiting until the very last shuttle before leaving. Jason Kennerin, savior and friend.

Yet Quilla remembered him, through her guilt, as the parent in whose love she had spent her childhood, as the father who, when she was older and needed him more, disappeared for far too long, far too often, into his other concerns. As the man she rarely saw, and whose life rarely touched her own, save for the occasional flash of wisdom, of compassion, coming always too late. Possibly he had given up the one family in order to help the other, larger,

247

one, perhaps he had done the right and proper thing. Yet a small, ingrained resentment persisted, and she would pause beside him as she moved from room to room, lean in to touch his fingers or his eyelids, trying to read an answer from his still forehead and calm lips. People came and went, spoke quiet words, and she moved through the house, accepting condolences and gifts, giving thanks in her mother's name, and coming back to the coffin to touch her dead father again, and again to wonder.

Jes and Ozchan stood facing each other over the dining room table. Quilla stopped at the door and watched them. They didn't notice her.

"If not for you, *Doctor*, my father would be alive," Jes said with quiet viciousness.

"Perhaps you'd better learn the truth before you go making accusations."

"I don't think you're capable of telling the truth," Jes said. "I don't think you want to."

"Big spaceship captain," Ozchan mocked. "So used to emergency flash decisions. Knows exactly what's going on all the time. Knows best."

"What are you trying to hide from me?"

"Nothing. Every time we try to talk to you, you listen to three words and go off shouting and fucking things up."

"Listen, off-worlder," Jes said, reaching across the table toward Ozchan's throat.

"That's enough," Quilla said. They turned quickly toward her. "Do you want everyone in Haven to hear you?"

"Maybe everyone in Haven should," Jes said.

Quilla closed the door behind her. "Remember a pair of green pants and a shirt, Jes, for the tenth Beginning-Day? Remember the teasing you used to get about Taine?"

"So what?"

"Remember?"

"Sure I remember. Meya did those things. But what the hell difference does it make?"

"Go get yourself a drink and catch your temper, and talk to Meya."

"Quilla . . . " Ozchan said urgently.

She waved him away. "Go on," she said to her brother. "And listen to her. She'll tell you."

"She's married to this snake," Jes said.

"Makes no difference. If you won't listen to the rest of

us, at least listen to her. You don't have to believe it, but at least listen."

Jes looked from Quilla's face to Ozchan's, and back to her.

"All right," he said finally. "Where is she?"

"At the tubhouse. Bring her back with you when you're done."

Jes went out.

"He'll kill her," Ozchan said, and moved toward the door. Quilla blocked him.

"No he won't."

"Let me out, I want to be there. She'll need help."

"No she won't. Go take care of Mish."

"And if he does hurt her?"

"Then it's my fault, isn't it? Go watch my mother. She needs you more than Meya does."

Ozchan made a gesture both frustrated and angry, and went into the living room. Mish sat at the head of the coffin, her eyes open and dry; except for the small rise and fall of her breasts as she breathed, she could have been a statue, or a corpse. Ozchan casually put his fingers to her neck, as though feeling for her pulse, and looked into the coffin. Quilla turned away.

Mim put a large scarf over her face and refused to take it off. She looked ghostly and startled quite a few of the Aerites who came to the kitchen door with their gifts of cakes and ale. Quilla stood beside her for a time, looking into the crowded living room. Light poured from the open hall door through the scarf and illuminated Mim's face. She was weeping, standing stiffly, shoulders proudly back; an invisible sorrow betrayed by a shaft of light. Mim had stumbled toward Hetch's shuttle, her arms full of holocubes which fell scattered on the snow; family, friends, lovers left dead or missing in Great Barrier's winter camps. Jason had stuffed the cubes in his pockets and half-carried her across the snow. To Mim, also, Jason was a hero.

The next morning they buried Jason in the small cemetery on the hill east of Haven. The grave site overlooked the town, Tor Kennerin, and beyond it, southward, to the barn and the rolling fields of crops and *Zimania* orchards. Kayman Olet, the town's only preacher, said a few words which were blown away on the rising wind, they bowed their heads, some wept, dirt covered the coffin, and it was over. Jes stood holding Meya's arm, and he looked at Quilla with mute apology. She nodded, but noticed that Jes kept his back turned to Ozchan, and when, on the way home, Ozchan took Meya's hand, Jes moved away from them quickly.

Mish stopped in the yard in front of the house and looked south. The gray clouds stretched unbroken out of sight, but no rain fell.

"It's almost spring," Mish said.

Quilla put her arm around her mother, and together they went inside the house.

Quilla pulled her hair back from her face and glanced wearily out at the rain. Mish's spring had not yet presented itself; for all the weather showed, it could still be Eiret Tapan, with spring three months away. According to the kasirene calendar, it was now Tov Pel ke'Biant, and the skies should have been warm and clearing. That they weren't was one more misery to add to Quilla's accumulating list.

She had spent the past two weeks with Mish in the office, going over Aerie-Kennerin's accounts, unearthing papers, while Mish worked her way through them with fierce determination. Now that they had full licensing, were there enough profits to add a fifth ship to the line? Why the need for source, didn't they have enough already? The com charges were far too high; they should consider adding a comsystem of their own, something between Aerie, the ships, and possibly Althing Green. And what about Albion-Drake? With Drake gone, perhaps they could buy into it. Good to have all ends of the sap line in their control. Quilla had argued and exampled and searched and traced accounts until her head seemed filled with numbers, and today, finally, it looked as though the job was over. Mish had announced that she was satisfied with Quilla's management of the planet, and decreed that Quilla remain in charge while she herself returned to the spaceways—to help Hetch, she said. There was too much to do, and Jes, although slated for eventual control, needed more experience. Quilla thought Jes had most of the experience he needed, that Mish's desire to return to space was simply a desire to be away from the place where Jason had died, but she kept silent. Jes accepted his mother's dictum quietly, and spent most of his time with Meya in the kasirene village. Quilla envied them, and wished that she, too, were down in the village, gathered around a fire with the kasirene and exchanging elaborate lies.

Hetch had arrived that morning and, after eating, had gone into the rain to visit Jason's grave. Now he returned and Quilla heard him in the hallway, stamping his boots on the mat and fumbling with his heavy water clothes. She called to him and he came into the office, looking far thinner than before, but still round, still bald. His face looked older. He kissed her cheek and sighed as he lowered himself into a chair.

"Mish isn't down yet? Good. Last time I was late she gave me hell."

"You're safe this time. The tea's still hot, you want some?"

"Do you have to ask?"

She handed him a cup, and he wrapped his pudgy fingers around it and looked at her through the steam.

"I'm sorry about your father," he said. She gestured wearily. "I've known him and worked with him for, what, twenty-seven, twenty-eight years now. He was a good man." He paused. "I feel as though it were my fault."

"It wasn't, Hetch." Quilla picked up her own cup and blew at the hot tea. "The commission's investigation pinned the refitters on that one. There's no way it could have been your fault, and no way you could have prevented it."

Hetch nodded unhappily and sipped at his tea.

Quilla gathered the last stack of papers and reels together and layered them into a box, clearing the desk for Mish's conference with Hetch.

"Mish'll probably have some lunch sent in here," she said. "I don't think she'll want to lose any time."

"I know she won't," Hetch said. He seemed to shift gears in his mind, and his face relaxed. "I've worked with some tough people before, but she takes it. She's got a mind like a computer and the energy to match. I think that if she wasn't as damned good at the job as she is, I'd resent it."

"Umm," Quilla said. She sealed the box and carried it to a storage shelf.

"She's quite an operator, that Mish," Hetch continued. "One hell of an operator."

"I know. She used to be my mother."

Hetch looked at her, surprised, then rose and crossed

251

the room to her. He put his hand on her cheek and looked up at her sternly.

"You know your mother's been through a rough time," he said. "Be more charitable, Quilla."

"Charitable, hell. I haven't seen my children in two weeks, I'm beginning to forget what Tabor looks like, and I'm tired." She smiled quickly. "So tired I'm about to fall over my tongue. I didn't mean it, Hetch. Forget it."

He patted her cheek and Quilla smiled again, reflecting that of all the people on Aerie, only Hetch could get away with this avuncular treatment, and only Hetch would try. Then Mish swooped into the room and Mim followed, carrying lunch for two on a large tray. Quilla slipped out of the room.

First, she decided, beer and a long, hot soak in the wooden tub. Then lunch, then a nap, then the children would be home. She felt as though they had been away for months; the longing for them surprised her with its intensity. She took a beer from the kitchen, a rain cape from the hall, and crossed the damp ground toward the tubhouse.

She piled her clothes in a locker and climbed the steps to the tub, then saw that it was already in use. Ozchan lounged in it, his hands loosely clasped around the edges of the tub, and his body half-floating. Beyond his steaming figure, water dripped over the edge of the roof, obscuring the stand of kaedos. He saw her and edged over, and after a small hesitation she dropped into place beside him, wincing at the heat of the water.

"It's only fifty centigrade," Ozchan said. "Nowhere near the boiling point."

She slid down until her chin hit the surface of the water, and closed her eyes. Ozchan shifted beside her, creating small eddies of heat against her skin. She stretched her legs carefully until they rested on the bench at the far side of the tub, and felt her muscles relaxing.

"So what have you been up to these past two weeks?" she said.

"This and that. Setting up schedules with Hoku, learning the practice. I think Ved Hirem's really got arthritis."

"No one else does. Think that, I mean. When he wants to, he can out-sprint anyone in Haven."

"But the symptoms—"

"Are all in his head."

"That's what Hoku says." Ozchan stretched his arms

252

along the sides of the tub. One hand rested in Quilla's hair. She ignored it.

"What else? How's Meya?"

"I've barely seen her," he said with dissatisfaction.

"She's recovering, Ozchan. It was harder on her than on us."

"I know. But she's my wife, damn it. We've been married barely a month, she's carrying my child. I think I have a right to know what she's up to."

"Do you? That's what's wrong with marriage, you know. Sign a sheet of paper and immediately you think you own someone."

"I don't think I own her," he said stiffly.

"Then stop worrying about it."

"But how do I know what she's up to? Where she's going, and who she's going with? What she's doing and who she's doing it with?"

"Oh-ho," said Quilla.

"Stop that. She wasn't a virgin, you know."

"I'd have been surprised if she was. Were you?"

'That's beside the point. If she had someone here before, she could be having someone here now."

"So?"

"So, that's unfaithful!"

"What's faith?" Quilla said easily. "Quit scowling and listen to me. Where do you make boundaries on love? Are you being unfaithful if you fuck someone else, or if you love someone else? Or if you stop loving one to love another, instead of loving both? What about that, if there are two, which one are you being unfaithful to? Do you think a piece of paper freezes people, locks them in, turns them into things that they aren't? Meya married you because she loved you, and needed you, and she still does. But I don't believe she mortgaged her soul to you, and I don't believe she expects you to mortgage yours to her." Quilla closed her eyes and rested her head against his hand. "She needs to be away now. She's had to kill one person and let go of another. Don't ride her, Ozchan. She'll be back."

"Do you really believe all of that?" he said.

She nodded.

"Have you ever been? Unfaithful to Tabor?"

"Tabor and I didn't live together until the twins were seven years old."

"That's no answer."

253

"You asked a dumb question. If you mean, have I slept with anyone other than Tabor, the answer is yes. If you mean would I do it again, the answer's still yes. And if you mean, would Tabor do the same thing, has he done the same thing, you'll get the same answer."

He moved his hand so that her head turned toward his.

"Would you fuck with me? Now? Here?"

"Perhaps," she said, not moving. Ozchan put his other hand between her legs.

"But I won't," she said. "Because you'd be fucking not because you want to, but because you want to hurt Meya. And of all the reasons for making love, that's the stupidest one of all."

He moved away as though she had hit him. She drew her knees up under her chin and looked at him, her head tilted. She couldn't help smiling, and after a moment of frozen-faced anger, he smiled back.

"All right," he said. "One for your team. I'm a jealous man, I suppose. And I'm upset that she's spending so much time with Jes, when it's obvious that Jes hates me."

"He seems to, doesn't he? What did you do to him?"

"Do to him? Nothing. I cared for his father. I married his sister. I live in his house. I don't know what the hell he's got against me. I haven't poisoned his dinner, but he acts as though I have."

Quilla frowned. "It's odd. I thought he'd get over it after the first week, that he was shaken by Jason's death and that was that. I haven't seen much of what's gone on recently, but I really can't believe that Jes hates you that much. Jes has never hated anyone."

"That's a big statement. Besides, you're his sister."

"I'm Hart's sister, too," Quilla said sharply.

Ozchan nodded. "I'm afraid he'll make her hate me the way he does."

"Give Meya credit for having a stronger mind than that. If you're that worried, why don't you ask her?"

"I've tried to. I can't. She gets to bed late and goes to sleep immediately, and by the time I'm awake the next morning she's gone. The rest of the day she's always with Jes, and I can't very well ask her in front of him, can I?"

"I suppose not. Tell you what, I'll try to talk to Jes, okay? This isn't an offer to spy, but we've had enough dissension around here lately. I'll see what I can do."

Ozchan nodded and glanced at the clouds.

"What time is it?" he said.

"Jev'al," she said immediately.

"Lord, I'm going to be late, and Hoku will have my ass." He clambered from the tub and dried off. Quilla watched him until he looked embarrassed. She looked away.

"Listen, if you can help me with Jes . . . "

"Sure."

Ozchan clambered down the steps and into the rain. Quilla remembered her beer, but when she reached for it, it was warm. She made a face and climbed from the tub, dried, dressed, and went through the rain toward the Tor.

Word got out to Haven that Quilla was free again, and throughout the next day she was besieged by people come with complaints, suggestions, reports, requests. Mish and Hetch were still locked in the office, so Quilla dealt with the people in the living room. They sat patiently along the edges of the room, waiting their turns, and she could no longer imagine Jason's coffin in the room. Most of the requests she turned aside easily; see Hoku, take this to Judge Hirem, talk this over with Kayman Olet. Others took some time, some thought, some scurrying around for records and documents. In mid-evening Tabor came to the door and stood watching her for a time, and when the last stragglers had left, he brought her some dinner and sat beside her as she ate.

"You need a secretary," he said, handing her a glass of wine.

"No, I need two of me. Why won't these people take things to the right places first, instead of bringing them all to me? I'm not judge and arbitrator and marriage counselor and confessor and land manager all in one."

"To them you are."

"Lady of the castle?" she said, and he smiled.

"Sure—Quia Tor Kennerin."

"No, thanks." She pushed her plate aside and stretched. "The children have eaten?"

"And bathed, and gone to bed. Did you know that Jared's writing a book?"

"I barely know what day it is. I saw them yesterday afternoon, and again this morning, and that's been it. I don't like this, Tabor."

"I don't either, but it'll be over soon. They've been

saving things up since Jason got here. They'll be done soon."

"Hah! Argument is the Aerie national sport, remember?"

Tabor laughed and laid wood carefully in the fireplace, then put his cane on the floor and sat on the rug, warming his hands. Quilla brought the wine and glasses with her to the hearth and sat on the rug beside him. The wood crackled and hissed as translucent flames slid around the dark gray kaedo wood.

"Remember the first winter you spent in the Cault," Tabor said, "after I made all sorts of promises about how good it would be?"

"During the blizzard, the time the barn fell in?"

"And we spent a month with the drays quartered downstairs, and burned all the chairs to keep warm."

Quilla laughed. "Some wonderful vacation. Some great time." She touched his ear. "I've missed you, Tabor. That's what I hate most about this sort of day, these past two weeks. I don't think we've talked once since Mish got here."

"Having just discovered talking, it would be a pity to lose it again this soon."

She nodded, then frowned. Tabor put his fingertips on her cheek. "Why the grimness, Quil?"

"Talking. Have you been around Jes much lately?"

"Not really. He's been keeping to himself."

"I know. Squiring Meya around, and scowling at Ozchan. I tried to talk with him last night, and it was like talking with the avenging angel. I can't figure out what in hell is wrong with him."

"Jason?"

"That's part of it, sure, but not the whole thing." She turned around and put her head on Tabor's lap. "Something must have happened during his last trip out, something he won't tell me about. It's changed him."

"Does he have to tell you about it, Quil? It's his business, not ours."

"Except that he's been rude and unpleasant, and he hates Ozchan, and none of us can figure out why." She frowned. "At the funeral, did you see how he looked at Taine? If I didn't know him better, I'd have been frightened. He looked . . . savage. Of course, he hasn't been close to her since her marriage, but why that look? It's not like Jessie to hate people, Tabor. You know that."

"People change."

"Not that much. Not that quickly."

Tabor looked down at her and shook his head. "I think if there's anything we should have learned this winter, it's that people change faster than we expect, that perhaps people are never what they seem to be."

"So we're to accept Jes' nastiness and leave it at that?"

"If necessary."

"And if it hurts Meya? Or disrupts her marriage?"

"Why this sudden concern with marriage?"

"Not marriage per se. I'm more concerned about Meya and Ozchan. And us. And Jes." She paused. "There's something going on, Tabor. Do you think you could . . . well . . . "

"Talk with him? Pry out all his guilty secrets? Put him to the question?"

"Lady above, you don't have to be so grim about it."

Tabor chuckled. "I'll talk with him. I don't promise to interrogate him, but I'll talk, if he wants to talk with me."

"I suppose that's as much as I can ask of you."

"On that subject, yes."

"And on other subjects?" She grinned. "For example, the subject of tonight."

"I see. I take it, Quia, you wish to retire."

"Right. I would like to seek the solitude and tranquility of my own room, and fuck until daybreak."

"That's a serious request. I'll have to take it under consideration."

She moved her head on his lap. "Big deal, Quia Negotiator. I think you already have."

Tabor sighed melodramatically and followed her upstairs.

Jes sat by the window in Ped Kohl's beer hall and scowled at the rain. It was marketday, and, despite the wetness, the market across the street was filled with people. The vendors had rigged white awnings over their stands, under which Jes could see piles of fruits and vegetables, stacks of jugs, sides of meat hanging in neat, red rows and dripping blood onto the wet pavement. A fishmonger's cart moved through the crowd, laden with shining forms and drawn by an unhappy dray. The dray stopped before a vegetable bin and mooed disconsolately, and the kasir came out of his stand, shouting and flapping his four arms angrily.

Jes signaled for another beer and slumped lower in his chair. Meya was at the dressmaker's, being fitted for something expandable. She had announced that for the next eight months she intended to pamper herself. Jes couldn't see why she was so happy at the prospect of a bloated belly and a brat, why she was so serenely confident that of all the things she'd done wrong since winter's beginning, this and her marriage were the two things she had done right. Merry domesticity. The damned family was full of it. Except for Mish, of course. And Hart. And himself. Three out of five miserable, and although he understood his own lack of reason, the feelings remained.

Meya's friend Mertika brought him his beer and wanted to talk, but he put her off. She shrugged and went away, waggling her ass as she retreated. Attractive enough. Were this any other world, any other port, he would have smiled, touched, followed her upstairs or out back or wherever, spent a pleasant half hour, and never seen her again. But this was Aerie, Haven, and Meya's friend. He frowned into his beer. Either bangs or merry domesticity, and neither one satisfied him.

Shouting arose in the market. The dray had shied, overturning the fish cart. The fishmonger shouted at the kasir greengrocer, while children gathered and gleefully tossed fish about. Some of them landed back in the cart. The monger turned from the greengrocer and began yelling at the children. Jes watched, almost smiling, then saw Taine standing near the vegetable bin. She carried a baby in her arms, and a small child clung to the edge of her raincape. Jes pushed his seat into the shadows and watched her, expressionless.

She was, if possible, even more beautiful than before. Maternity had smoothed the angles of her face, had softened the rigidity of her back and brought a glow to her face quite different from the icy gleams of her youth. Yet her mouth was tight at the corners, and her fingers, he knew, were ragged at the tips from biting. She had put those fingers on his chest the last time he was on Aerie. Meeting him alone on one of Haven's quiet, night-time streets; accidentally, she had said. It had been a long time. She had missed him.

"You have a family now," he told her. "Isn't that what you wanted?"

She smiled. "It's what I thought I wanted."

He smiled back, cautiously, reaching for friendship.

"And perhaps you've decided you want something different?" he said casually.

"Not *different*. More, maybe, but not different." She put her hand on his chest. "I've missed you, Jes. Truly. I think about you. Think about being with you."

His chest felt tight. The darkness seemed to close around them. Separate them from the rest of the world, from reality. He clenched his hands, fighting the urge to hold her.

"Jes?" She moved closer to him. "I want you."

He pulled back abruptly. "You're Kayman Olet's wife," he said harshly. "Do you have that kind of marriage?"

"Does it matter?"

"My God, of course it matters! It—it wouldn't be honest, Taine. It wouldn't be right."

"You are a romantic," she said mockingly. "I thought you'd have outgrown that, left it between the legs of some spaceport whore somewhere."

"Is that what you're trying to be yourself?" he demanded. "Which one was I to be, fifteen? Number thirty? How many since you married, every male on Aerie?"

She hit him hard on his jaw, cried out, then cradled her hand against her breast. "You bastard," she said with quiet venom. "You shitty, immaculate bastard. You're so goddamned pure you can't be bothered to see other people at all, can you?"

"Pure!"

"I just hope that someday you grow up enough to see shades of things, that you learn that some things can't be only right or only wrong because they're stuck somewhere in the middle. And I hope to God that, when you do, it'll hurt so much you'll die of it!"

She had run from him, awkwardly, holding her injured hand, leaving him furious, baffled, jaw and cock aching equally. He had not seen her from then until the day of Jason's funeral, when she stood beside her husband, eyes downcast, the perfect preacher's wife. Look at me now, he had wanted to shout at her. Look at all the gray places, Taine. Look, I'm hurting, just like you wanted me to. But she had avoided glancing at him, had tendered her condolences to his mother, his sisters, and left him entirely alone.

He clenched the stein and sat unmoving until Taine

and her children left the marketplace and disappeared down Schoolhouse Road. Then he pushed back his chair, dropped a fistful of change on the table, and left the beer hall.

Meya stood surrounded by meters of cloth, wearing only her shirt. She turned quickly when Jes entered and waved at the material.

"Five more minutes," she said.

He went back outside and leaned against the porch railing. Soon Meya joined him. She pulled her raincape closed and touched his arm.

"Want to go home?" she said.

"I don't care. Let's get out of Haven."

At the Tor end of Schoolhouse Road, though, he turned east toward the landing pad. Meya followed silently. He heard her footsteps in the mud and paused until she was beside him, then took her hand and tucked it into his pocket.

The pad was deserted, save for the covered form of Hetch's shuttle, parked to the side of the enlarged pad. The com hut was locked. Jes produced a magkey and opened the door, and they went inside. Cold, damp air filled the hut, bearing the scent of metals and the musty odor of wet clothing. Jes closed the door and lit a lamp, and Meya looked down at the committer.

"So many places to talk to," she said, putting her finger on the unlit directory. "So many places I've never seen."

"It's no loss. The universe is full of ugly, uninteresting places and ugly, uninteresting people. You're better off here."

"You only see the ports, Jes."

"True. I only see the ports." He opened his raincape. "Are you warm enough?"

"I'm fine," she said, but she left her cape closed. Jes looked out the window at the shuttle.

"Hoku asked me if I wanted to know its sex," she said. Jes looked at her. She smiled and put her hand on her stomach. "I told her I'd rather not."

"Why doesn't Ozchan take care of you? Why do you have to see Hoku?"

"Because he's my husband. It's not good doctoring to take care of your own family."

"Nice excuse." He turned to the window again.

Meya put her hand on his arm.

260

"Jessie. Come on. There's been enough trouble. We don't need more of it."

"I'm not making trouble," he said angrily. "Have they gotten to you, too?"

"Who?"

"The rest of them. Quilla tried to grill me two days ago, and last night Tabor did the same thing. Why can't they all just leave me alone?"

"Because you've been acting different. Oddly. They care about you."

"And you?"

"You know that already."

He made a gesture of disbelief, shaking her hand from his arm. She stood behind him and put her arms around his waist, tucking her hands into his front pockets.

"Don't bite me, Jes.'"

He felt her head resting against his shoulder blades. He put his hands in his pockets on top of hers.

"This was such a magical place," he said quietly, "when I was a kid. Such adventures waited here—so many things to do, so much excitement. I think I knew from the beginning where I wanted to go, what I wanted to do with my time. Who I wanted to be. And I tried hard enough, and I did it."

"Yes."

"You know what's really there? Long, boring runs that are all alike, that begin to blend together because there's no difference between them. Ports and bars and whorehouses that could be anywhere. Same people, same smells, same conversations. When something gets exciting, it means that something's wrong. And that's not enjoyment, it's fear."

"Then why do it?"

He closed his eyes. "It's quiet there, Meya. Dark and silent and clean. Infinite possibilities. Look at the screens and you know that anything can exist, anything can happen. All that darkness and silence is potential, growing, changing. Space is alive, Meya. More alive than anything I've ever known." He paused, and she moved her head gently. Listening. "It's easy to feel like God there. Cut off from everyone, riding the entire universe. Riding *with* the entire universe. Being God because everything is godlike. I can't explain it very well. It makes my head feel clean."

"Do we bother that? Is the change too great?"

"No." He opened his eyes and looked out at the gray

261

rain, the covered shuttle, the dark hills stretching out of sight in the mist. "There's a change, yes. Different. Not on all planets, just here. Just Aerie. There's no love in space, Meya. There's bigness, and density, and void, and, well, transcendence. Satori. It makes your blood hot and your heart beat faster and your lungs grab for air, it makes your skin tingle. But then the watch is over, and there's something missing. Like making love with ghosts. Like making love with whores in the ports. Nothing there. All by yourself again. Feeling used."

He felt her shiver, and turned around. She stepped toward him and he wrapped his cape around her, closing her in with him.

"The love was here, at home," he said. "Jason, Mish, Quilla, the twins. You. I'd come home and eat the love, stuff it in, grab for it. Greedy. And after a while there would be something missing here, too. I'd miss the quiet. I'd miss the ecstasy. Home would bounce me into space again, and after a few runs space would bounce me back home. I thought it would be that way forever, and then you changed that, too."

"Jessie . . . "

"I know. All right. I won't talk about it. But it's what I expected when I came home this time, and instead I found nothing at all. Quilla busy with Tabor. Mish gone. You and that off-worlder. And everyone worshipping a breathing corpse."

"Hush." She put her fingers on his lips. "Don't. If we were wrong, it was wrong on the side of hope. I couldn't help thinking that I'd walk in there one morning and he'd sit up and ask for breakfast. That Hoku or Ozchan would discover something that would make him whole again. We were foolish, Jes, but it was a love-foolishness. It was so hard to lose him again."

"So you used up all your love on a corpse, and there was none left for me."

"Don't be stupid." She pulled away from him and crossed to the committer. Jes stared at her belly.

"Why?" he said. "You did it deliberately. Why?"

"I needed Ozchan. I needed a baby. There was so much life ending, I needed something to start. And I love him, Jes."

"But not me."

"Don't. Not again."

He ignored the pleading in her voice. "Well, go love

262

him, then. Fill yourself up with brats, until there's nothing left of you but babies."

She lifted her head and stared at him.

"Do you think," she said deliberately, "that if I didn't love you, I'd be here listening? I'd have spent all this time with you? Hearing you hating people? I kept hoping that you'd get over it, but you don't, you just get further away. If there's no love left for you anymore, maybe it's because you don't feel any of it yourself."

"That's not true!" he cried, but she had opened the door and disappeared into the rain. He froze, staring at the door, and counted methodically. When he reached five hundred, he walked out of the com hut and locked the door behind him.

The cloud cover had lifted at dusk, just in time to reveal a flaming sunset which colored the bottoms of the retreating clouds and turned the distant woods into silhouettes of bare kaedo trees. The family gathered on the front porch to watch, and Jes stood off to one side, watching them. Meya stood apart from Ozchan, and turned suddenly to go inside. Ozchan, watching her go, saw Jes and looked at him coldly. Jes ignored him. In a moment Meya came back with Mish. Mish put her hands on the railing and stared westward. The sun flashed and vanished, and colors leached quickly from the sky.

"Jason should have seen that," Mish said softly. Meya touched her shoulder, and Mish looked at her youngest daughter and smiled quickly, uncomfortably. Mish moved away, then turned back and patted Meya's arm, and went inside again. Quilla and Tabor turned to go.

"I missed it," Hetch said, coming onto the porch.

"It'll happen again," Ozchan said, and took Meya inside. Hetch came over to stand beside Jes.

"Spring?" Hetch said, nodding toward the clearing sky. A few stars appeared to the east.

"Almost. Might have a few more drizzles first. Nothing much."

"Then we can start planning to leave. Mish said she wanted to go as soon as winter ended."

Jes nodded and walked down the porch steps.

"No dinner?" Hetch said, surprised.

"I had a late lunch in Haven," Jes said. Hetch accepted the lie and went inside.

Jes walked around the side of the house and looked in

the dining room window. Mim passed through the room carrying table linen, and the twins followed her, carrying plates and cups. They put the crockery down on a sideboard and helped Mim lay the cloth. Mish came in, said something, and went out toward the kitchen. Quilla and Tabor moved from the kitchen to the table, carrying pots of food. When Meya and Ozchan entered, talking with Hetch, Jes moved away from the window and down the hill. Happy family, he thought. Ozchan hadn't looked very happy.

The barn was dim and quiet, and smelled of hay and drays. Jes walked between the stalls, listening to the cattle settle in. The lofts above were lined with bales of hay or boxes of goods; rows of curing pots for the *Zimania* sap took up one end of the large building. A corner was filled with equipment and machines. He wondered if the twins played in the barn, as he and Quilla and Hart had played, wondered if there was room left for playing anymore. He grabbed a rope and tugged at it experimentally, then swung up it to a lower loft, then higher. The farther up he moved, the more the barn seemed familiar, until, at the highest loft, he sat with his feet dangling over the drop and closed his eyes, and could feel no change at all.

Jes and Quilla and Hart. He lay back along the loft's wooden floor and thought of what it must have been like the day Hart unplugged Jason and found out he had died. Younger brother. Had he come home with thoughts of redemption? Of trying to make whole that which he had broken? If it had been anyone other than Hart, if it had been Ozchan, they would have listened before striking, would have tried to understand. The benefit of the doubt.

It could be argued that it was Hart's own fault, that what he had done seven years before dictated the reaction he had found in that hushed, violent room. It would be a silly argument, though. How had he felt, when his father lay there and breathed and didn't waken? Or when his family chased him to the shuttle? What did he feel like now? Jes thought of confusion, possible hatred, a terrible loss, but the emotions didn't tie in, didn't solidify. Of one thing Jes was certain; Hart had thought of Meya. One thing there in common. At least.

I should find Hart, he thought as he sat up. Tell him to come home. Try to trace him. Look for him. He swung down a rope, down another, and reached the barn floor. The drays mooed inquisitively as he left the barn.

The Spiral sat high in the night, out again for the first time since autumn. Jes walked up the hill. The dining room window was dark now; upstairs all the windows were dark, save that of the room Meya shared with Ozchan. Jes stared at it, then turned away from the house.

The tubhouse, too, was dark. Jes took his clothes off and piled them in a locker, showered quickly, and climbed into the tub. He put his flute on the ledge beside him and soaked, trying to shut out the voices in his mind. They pestered him—Meya's voice, Quilla's, Tabor's, saying uncomfortable things to him. He reached for the flute and blew a few notes, then wiped his mouth on a towel and tried again. The music came more clearly now, rising through the tendrils of steam from the water. He concentrated on the melody, trying for an absolute purity of tone. The tone muddied and he stopped and dried the flute with the towel, but did not leave the tub.

"Tabor? Mind if I join you?"

Jes moved the flute from his lips and turned slowly. Indistinct form on the steps, but he recognized the voice.

"Sure, Ozchan," he said with sarcastic pleasantry. "Come right on in."

A lightstick flared briefly and went out, leaving an afterimage of Ozchan's dark body against the dark night.

"I didn't know you played the flute," Ozchan said.

"Tabor taught me, years ago."

"It's a pity he didn't teach you manners, too."

"Did you take Beginning Sarcasm in medical school, Doctor, or did you pick it up on your own?"

"I'm getting a bit tired of this," Ozchan said. He moved onto the platform around the tub and stood at the far side, facing Jes. Jes squinted to see him through the steam. He put his flute down carefully under the ledge. "Just why are you mad at me? Because I took care of your father? I did the best any doctor could be expected to do. Ask Hoku. I didn't kill him, and you ought to have enough sense to know that."

"You all killed him," Jes said, "just by allowing him to make that decision. I don't really know how you acted around him before. You could very easily have made life so miserable for him that he had to decide that way. But I don't blame you for that, not in particular. Meya tells me that it really was Jason's choice. That people were as kind as they could be. No, Doctor, I don't blame you for my father's death."

"I'm sincerely grateful," Ozchan said. "Then what in hell is your complaint?"

"Why should I have a specific complaint? Maybe I just don't like you, generally. I don't like the shape of your mouth."

"That's shit. You came bullying in and started throwing hatred around as though you had a surplus. Maybe you do. Maybe every male Kennerin in the universe is a bastard, and there's no help for it. But I just wish that you'd leave me and my life the hell alone."

"Including Meya?"

"Especially Meya. What kind of hold do you have over her, anyway? What are you trying to do to her? She hasn't said more than ten words to me since you got here. Listen, I don't mind if you hate me; you can hate whoever you want. But don't start fucking up my wife's head, understand?"

Jes pulled himself out of the water. "My sister, Doctor. Long before she was your wife."

"What the hell difference does that make? You don't own her."

"Any more than you do."

They crouched at either side of the tub, staring through the steam.

"I don't want to own Meya," Ozchan said. "All I want to do is live my life with her in peace. I don't think that's an unreasonable request. Things are hard enough here without that kind of trouble."

"What kind of trouble?"

"You want to know, Kennerin? I think you got here and for some insane reason decided to hate me. I think you've been working on Meya ever since. I think Meya had someone here before I came, and you're trying to send her back to him. For all I know, you've succeeded."

Jes put his feet in the hot tub and laughed. Ozchan cursed and ran around the side of the tub toward him, and Jes slid into the tub and away.

"Someone before you got here, Doctor? Oh, yes, indeed. And try to send her back to him? Positively. You're very astute, Ozchan. Was that your last course in medical school—Advanced Perception?"

"Can't you understand, Jes? I came to your world. I didn't know where the hell it was, or who was on it, and

I liked it here. I liked your family, I liked Haven, I liked your people. And I fell in love with your sister. I think she loves me, too. She was willing to put other people behind her, she wouldn't have married me otherwise. Why in hell did you have to come and fuck it up?"

"Maybe the spurned party feels strongly about all of this. Have you thought of that? Maybe this other person has some interest in the matter. Maybe, Doctor, you're not all alone on paradise."

"She made the choice by herself!"

"I don't think she did. I think the other party never had a say in the matter at all."

"All right." Ozchan stood back from the tub's rim and put his hands down. "Tell me who this other party is, we'll work it out. We'll talk to him. But let's stop this . . . this sabotage."

Jes came out of the tub again. "You really want to know?"

"Yes. Who is he?"

"Me," Jes said.

"Shit. I should have known you wouldn't be serious." Ozchan turned as if to go, and Jes came around the side of the tub and grabbed his arm.

"You listen to me, Doctor, because I'm being damned serious. You want to know about your wife? Two years ago I came home for leave, and we walked south, she and I. I was miserable, I'd discovered things about myself and what I was doing that disturbed me. I needed room, and she made room for me. So we walked for two weeks, and we talked, and we saw things, and we even managed to laugh after a while. We see things the same way, she and I. We know the same things, we share history. We feel alike. And one night it started to rain. It does that down in the Cault. Summer rains—we weren't expecting them. We made a small shelter and crawled into it, and when it got cold we piled all our bedding together and crawled in. And we did feel alike, Doctor. We felt almost identical." Jes shook Ozchan sharply. "Think about that, Doctor. Think of what it's like to make love to someone who's so much like you that it seems you're in her mind and she's in yours. Think of what it's like to make a joke by nodding your head at something. No words at all, just sharing, Doctor. Going to sleep and feeling that you're having the same dream. Knowing all the movements, first time. And it was her first time. Two weeks, and we really were alone in paradise." Jes flung Ozchan's arm to the side. "That's what you came in and screwed up, Doctor. Do you want to try to compete with that?"

"You bastard," Ozchan said and swung at him. The blow caught Jes by surprise and knocked him into the water, and before he could surface Ozchan had leaped in beside him and was pummeling his head. Jes caught Ozchan's arms and pushed him away, then grabbed him around the waist and pushed him underwater. Ozchan flipped around and bit his shoulder, and Jes backed away, cursing. The doctor surfaced and came at him again. Their bodies slid together and apart as they grappled; hot water rushed against Jes, adding to the heat of the fight. His body tingled and his heart beat fiercely. Ozchan's skin slid smoothly against his own. He reached dizzily to block the other's weak blow, slipped, grabbed, and slumped onto the tub's inner bench, with Ozchan sprawled on his lap. They froze, staring at each other, their faces inches apart, arms and legs tangled together. The heat in Jes' body centered between his legs. Ozchan's body was half-turned, one leg under Jes' knees. He felt Ozchan's erection graze his thigh.

Ozchan put his hand on Jes' forehead.

"I cut you," he said, and Jes felt the words on his lips. He turned his head slowly. Ozchan moved his hand back until it tangled in Jes' hair, and pulled him down. Their lips met.

"Jes?"

"I didn't mean to do that."

They had floated apart in the tub. Ozchan turned, feeling the edge of the bench against his hip.

"Did I hurt you?"

"No." Jes made a small, amused noise. "Only some of my ego."

The smaller moon was up, casting a dim light into the tubhouse. Jes lay with his head against the ledge, eyes closed. Ozchan watched him.

"Have you always——" he said.

"What?"

"With men?"

Jes shrugged. "I haven't always with anyone. In space it makes no difference. Small crew, long runs. Whoever's handy."

"Sounds cold."

"It isn't." Jes opened his eyes and looked at Ozchan. "You're my first knocker, though. That way."

"Knocker?"

"Civilian. Non-spacer."

"Does it make a difference?"

"Yes." Jes paused. "This is Aerie. Home. Everything here makes a difference."

"You're not my first spacer," Ozchan said.

"Tell me."

Ozchan was silent. Jes touched his foot.

"Come on. Tell."

"Hogarth's is a Third Reformation world," Ozchan said. "You know what that is?"

"I've seen a couple. Fundamentalist, aren't they? Religious group."

"With a vengeance. Good word for them. Vengeance. Rigid and small-minded. Fanatics. It seemed, when I was a kid, that everything I did was against either God's laws or Hogarth's customs. No games, games are sinful. No singing, singing's sinful. The only books in the house were religious tracts and one battered first-aid text. I knew them all by heart. The port was way out of town, off limits."

"They always are, on those worlds."

"Be grateful for it. I took to hanging around there, watching the ships, talking to spacers. Dreaming about running away. One day a spacer picked me up, fed me dinner, took me to his room. I stayed the night."

"Poor backwash innocent, corrupted by the vile spacer," Jes said. Ozchan looked at him, but Jes didn't smile.

"No. I was sixteen. I knew what he wanted. I wouldn't have gone if I hadn't wanted it, too." Ozchan shrugged. "It felt better than anything I'd ever done on Hogarth's. I left before daybreak and went home, but my parents heard me coming in. I wouldn't tell them where I'd been or what I'd been doing, so they hauled me off to the prayer house and locked me up for five days. Shouting and praying over me, exorcising demons. Beating me to beat the devils. They said if I told them where I'd been that night, it would be a sign that the devil had released my soul."

"This?" Jes leaned over and ran his fingertip along Ozchan's side. The scar was almost invisible; Ozchan was surprised that Jes had noticed it.

"Yes. A year before they'd caught two kids committing

abominations. They didn't say which ones, but it was a boy and girl, so I guess they were fucking. They beat the devils out of them, too, then tied them to the altar in the prayer house and prayed over them, until they starved to death. I could guess what they'd do to me, and to the spacer, if they caught him. But I was more worried about myself, so I kept quiet and they kept beating me. The fifth night I got free; they didn't have me tied down, just locked in. I broke the lock and ran for the port. Found the spacer. He hid me in the infirmary, wrapped in bandages until I looked like a white sausage. When he left three days later, he took me with him."

"And you became a spacer?"

"No. I was in bad shape. They took me to Solon and left me there, and when I recovered some people took an interest in me. I was bright, so they got me into the school on a Strays and Needful scholarship."

"And you lived happily ever after."

"Don't be sarcastic, Jes. When you grow up twisted, it takes a long time to untwist again. I'd only had one woman before Meya, and it wasn't a good experience. I get along fine with women until they take their clothes off; and it's downhill from there."

"And you're using my sister to untwist, is that it?"

"We've already done our fight, Jes. Let's not do it again. Let me finish."

Jes leaned back slowly, keeping his eyes on Ozchan. The doctor nodded a quick thanks and took a deep breath.

"When they asked me to come here with your father, it scared me. I put on a pretty good front, sure, but I was frightened anyway. I hadn't left Solon since getting there. For all I knew, I'd be coming to another Third Reformation planet, or worse. There's almost nothing about Aerie in the main references. But I talked with Mish on the com-lines and met Hetch a couple of times. They didn't seem to be monsters, and I couldn't spend the rest of my life on Solon. So I did a Restructuring and took the job."

"How extensive?"

"Not very. Nothing new added, nothing taken away. Loosening a few structures. Making things a bit more open. It helped. I liked it here, I liked the people. Quilla told me about The Law, that you can't, what, hurt or injure . . ."

"No person shall harm or defraud, or cause to be harmed or defrauded, any other person."

"That. And that's it, isn't it? It made so damned much sense. Almost everything here makes sense."

"We're not Utopia, Doctor."

"I know that. I was here with Jason, remember? Anyway, I started spending time with Meya, and it felt good. So I spent more time with her, and it felt better. And the night she came to my room, it felt so good that it wasn't until the next morning that I realized what I'd done, how much I'd changed. I fell in love with her. I'm still in love with her."

Jes looked at him silently.

"All right," Ozchan said angrily, "I don't give a damn if you don't believe me."

He started to climb out of the tub. Jes caught his ankle and he balanced precariously.

"Come back in," Jes said. "We're not finished yet. I believe you." He released the ankle. Ozchan stepped back into the tub and looked at him.

"But it's a pretty odd way of loving someone," Jes said, "going crazy every time the person you love needs to be away for a while."

"I'm jealous. I was afraid that she was seeing someone else, and whoever he was, he'd, well, be better than I am." Ozchan looked down at the water. "Were you?"

"Not this time. She wouldn't."

Ozchan looked up, but now Jes was staring at the water.

"She said it was over—that part of it. Said that now she had you, and the baby. That she needed someone all the time, not just two or three times a year. That she didn't want to spend her life hiding the most important parts. If it weren't for you, I knew she wouldn't have changed. Wouldn't have done that. I think I was wrong. She said she loved you, too, but I didn't pay too much attention to that."

"Going crazy every time the person you love needs to be away for a while," Ozchan quoted back at him.

"I didn't say I was sane. I knew it was crazy, and I did it anyway."

"Crazier than I am?"

"I think we're even on that. But I'm one up on you when it comes to abominations," Jes said.

"I don't pay much attention to that anymore. When

271

fucking lizards and eating white bread on the Sabbath are both abominations, the idea gets shabby pretty fast."

Ozchan climbed out of the tub. After a moment Jes followed. They dried and dressed in silence, and Jes knelt to search for his flute. When he stood again, Ozchan put a hand on his chest.

"Peace?"

Jes looked at him, and covered Ozchan's hand with his own.

MISH

MEYA CAME TO ME IN THE STUDY, INTER-rupting my conversation with Hetch, but before I could reprimand her she put her hand on my shoulder.

"Come," she said solemnly, and I came with her.

The first sunset of the spring. The first time the clouds had broken since winter, and the sky lit with brief glory, pink, red, violet, dark blue, turquoise, pale gray. The end of the rains. I put my hands on the rail and felt the colors moving through me, felt myself part of the sky, the budding trees, the land waiting for plow and seed. A vast and peaceful glory. The sun fell below the horizon, and the colors faded from the sky, leaving their ghosts settled comfortably within me.

"Jason should have seen that," I said, and realized that Jason had. It was Jason's peace, Jason's heart beating in the sunset, that I had felt. Jason's gift.

Meya put her hand on my shoulder, and I smiled quickly at her, and had turned away before I understood her expression. A little wistful, somewhat lost. A yearning. She looked like an orphan, and it struck me that in many ways she was. Always Jason's child, never mine. And that was no one's fault but my own.

I didn't have the words for that, didn't even have it clearly in my mind, but I turned and patted her arm, and hoped that she would understand the promise.

I was halfway to the stairs before I realized that I didn't have to go there, that I had things to do that evening. Not talking with Hetch, not the manic activity that had sustained me since my return. Tables to set. Dinner to help with. A meal to eat, people to talk with. People to learn all over again. The thought frightened me, then

I felt Jason's gift again, still warm, still comforting. I went into the dining room, into the kitchen, into life again.

Jes didn't come in to dinner. Not surprising; he'd been cold and sharp all winter, an angry, distant man. Immediately after dinner Ozchan left the house. Meya bit her lip and continued clearing the table, and instead of going into the living room, I stayed to help her. We still didn't have the right words for each other, but working together seemed to help. Tabor's music floated into the room, and the voices of the twins at play. Hetch in the midst of some tall story. For a moment I listened for Jason's voice, for Laur scolding the children; for a moment the world seemed turned on itself, confused.

"Mish?" Meya said.

I shook my head. She came around the table and put her arms around me. Tall daughter, warm daughter. I put my head on her shoulder and she put her head on my head, and we stood like that, swaying slightly. Then I pulled away. She immediately dropped her arms and began to step back, but I leaned forward and kissed her.

"Come on," I said. "There're still the pots to scrub."

"Tabor and Ozchan did them yesterday," she said, smiling at my smile. "We can just wipe them off and put them away, Mim will never notice."

And that's what we did, giggling like conspiratorial children.

It seemed a night for reconciliations. When Jes and Ozchan finally came in, long after the children and Mim had gone to bed, we heard their steps and voices raised in the hallway, and we hushed. Meya looked at the door apprehensively.

"You've got your head in your ass," Jes said angrily.

"And you've got yours in a vacuum," Ozchan retorted.

The front door slapped shut. Meya put her hand on her stomach.

"Prove it, medicine man," Jes said.

Ozchan marched into the room, closely followed by my son. They both ignored us.

"Here," Jes said, and grabbed the West Wing Directory. Ozchan took it from him and paged through it rapidly.

"Second section," Jes said, "under H, in case you've forgotten."

Ozchan glared at him and turned to another section of the book.

"There!" he said triumphantly. "Forty-two two, forty-four five, seventeen."

"Let me see that." Jes took the book away and looked at the page. "Shit."

Ozchan assumed a look of superiority and stuck out his hand, palm up. Jes swore and dug three fremarks from his pocket. Ozchan calmly took two of them.

"Never bet," he said, "with the most retentive mind on Aerie. Never tangle with a man with a permastick brain."

"Right. What's Meya's due date?"

Ozchan looked at him, frowned, and Jes laughed and hit his shoulder lightly.

"Big retentive mind," he said cheerfully. "Permastick nonsense. You want a drink?"

He nodded, still frowning. "Meya, what's the due date?"

"Fen Tov Biant Bols," she said.

"That's the reason. I can't remember those damned kasiri names," Ozchan muttered, then laughed. Meya looked from husband to brother in bafflement.

Jes had a bandage on his shoulder and a piece of plaster on his forehead. Ozchan's arm was bruised, and he walked favoring his right leg. That, I decided, was the reason for the sudden camaraderie. They'd tried to kill each other, and the experience had done them good. Children, I thought, then remembered that Jes was twenty-seven that year, and Ozchan twenty-six.

And Quilla thirty-two. Tabor near forty, the twins eleven, and I fifty-five. How things had changed while I was gone. And I'd been gone for far too long a time.

Instead of leaving with Hetch, as I had planned, I told Jes that he was now the Kennerin head of Aerie-Kennerin Shipping, and sent him off into space. He did an odd thing before he left—he kissed Meya, then Ozchan, and the kisses seemed identical to me.

And he promised to look for Hart.

We received reports throughout that summer, while Meya's stomach grew and I learned my family over again. Jes followed the trail to the Gregory/Acanthus Main Grab, and lost it there. The grab served as a nexus for lines to twenty-five different planets and four sub-grabs; it would take time to find out where Hart had gone, and Jes could only fit the search in among his other duties. It became a process of elimination, and each month his report to us contained more names to cross off the list.

Someone out there had remembered the botany of Terra. We crossed off Philodendron, Acacia, Ceropegia, Lilium, and Rhus the first month, Euphorbia, Dracenea, and Opuntia the second, only Jasmine and Tillandsia the third. During Biant Meir, the fourth month of Jes' absence, we crossed off Augustine and Holt's World, and Quilla claimed relief at the end of the flora.

At the end of Biant Meir, Hoku died.

Ozchan came home one afternoon and told us that we were needed in Haven, at Hoku's house, not at the hospital. She had refused to be moved, and lay in her small living room staring out the window at the marketplace. It was a market day, but the stalls were closed, the area silent. People gathered before her house, but she had us chase them away. She didn't intend to die in the middle of a circus, she said.

She didn't seem ill to me, until I said something and she looked beyond me, over my right shoulder. She couldn't see.

Her hands, always slim and strong, lay bent on her lap. Lined. Spotted. They, more than anything else, reminded me that Hoku was an old woman. Older than Laur when Laur had died. Dying of being old.

She formally gave her practice to Ozchan, and said he'd be sure to screw it up, but it was his anyway, and God help the people of Haven. And she told him that love shared was better than love separated. He looked both uncomfortable and surprised. I suppose he'd never gotten used to Hoku's soul-peering. Perhaps none of us ever had.

She told Quilla that she approved.

"Of what?" I said.

"That's her business, not yours," Hoku said peevishly.

She said something quietly to Meya which I didn't hear, but which caused Meya to look at Ozchan, startled, then walk to him and hold his hand tightly.

She told Tabor that if you've wanted something long enough and you still don't have it, you're a fool to keep wanting it. He thanked her gravely.

All she said to me was, "Tell Hart I was wrong. Tell Hart that I apologize."

Then she told the twins to hold her hands, that she had something important to teach them. They stood on either side of her, unsmiling, and she closed her eyes and died.

They put her hands down slowly, before we realized what had happened, and turned to Quilla.

"That was very good," Decca said.

Then we did the things that had to be done and went away.

I asked Jared what it was that Hoku had taught them.

"Emptying quietly," he said. I didn't understand.

Two weeks after Hoku's death, three men came to the Tor and sat in the living room, their hands folded in their laps, asking me questions about Drake. We had known that this had to happen, that Drake could not disappear silently, without leaving bubbles of questions in his wake. I kept my hands thrust into the pockets of my skirt, and smiled, and told them somewhat lies.

"I wasn't here when Drake and my son came," I said to them evenly. "I had business to attend to on Althing Green. You understand."

They nodded, short motions of head accompanied by cold glances.

"My daughters told me that he left a few weeks before my . . . my husband's death." I took my hands out of my pockets and twisted my fingers together. "I'm afraid I didn't worry about Quia Drake much. It was an upsetting time. For all of us."

"Perhaps," one of them said, "we could talk to your daughters. Since they were here, they might be able to help us."

I rose to call Quilla, but Meya came into the room and leaned against the mantel, her hand resting on her swollen belly.

"I was here," she said. "I'm Meya M'Kale Kennerin."

The men looked at her. One averted his eyes and spent the remainder of the session staring at the fireplace. Embarrassed, I realized suddenly, by my daughter's pregnancy. The absurdity of it calmed my nervousness, and I smiled.

"Yes, of course I remember when he left," Meya said calmly. "I didn't see him go, but one morning he'd left. Taken a shuttle out." She paused and looked at them. "We were quite happy to see him go. Drake was a very unpleasant man."

"Did he mention where he was going? To you? To your brother, perhaps?"

Meya shrugged. "He certainly didn't say anything to me about it. His conversations concerned other intentions."

I put my hands back in my pockets. They felt sud-

277

denly clammy, and I wanted to tell Meya to be quiet, not to take such chances; felt a twinge of my old dislike of her, and firmly put it away.

"It took you quite a while to worry about him," I said. To my relief, they looked away from my daughter to me. "Nine months, is it? Ten, since he's been here?"

"He often takes extended trips," the embarrassed one said. "But generally he checks in, if only to collect his profits."

"Profits," I said.

"Tev Drake is the major shareholder of Albion-Drake. Surely you know that."

I looked at Meya, surprised.

"I think he mentioned that to Quilla," she said. "It didn't seem very important."

"It *is* very important," the embarrassed one said reprovingly to the fireplace. The other two nodded firmly. "Drake's absence is a very serious problem for the company."

"How serious?"

"Serious enough."

Meya shrugged again and stood away from the mantel. "You might check the passenger lists of *Rhani-ka's Falcon*," she said. "That was the only ship in port the day he left; he was probably on it."

"What about your port records?"

"We're too small to keep entry records," I said. "We depend on the passenger lists. I think that would be your best try now. You can use the com shack at the port to reach the *Falcon*." I stood. "Now, if you'll excuse us, we have work to do."

They stood, their eyes still unfriendly. Meya went to the door.

"I hope you find him," I lied politely.

"So do we, Quia Kennerin."

"If you do," Meya said, "would you give him a message from me?"

"Quia?"

"Tell him that if he ever comes back to this planet, I'll have him shot." She left the room.

The men looked at each other without expression, and went down the hill. I never saw them again, but a month later we had word that Tev Drake could not be found, and was presumed dead in the Gregory/Acanthus sector. Meya greeted the news with relief.

But I thought about Albion-Drake with increasing frequency. We had the plantation, we had the shipping line. If we could acquire the processing factory our profits would double, and we'd be paying nothing to outside concerns. The thought excited me, and I felt alive and enthusiastic for the first time since Jason's accident. I talked it over with Quilla and Jes, and began laying plans. It would take time, effort, and money, but it would be worth it.

Jes came home the day before Meya had her baby. It was an easy enough labor, an easy enough delivery. She lay in her room, amid husband, midwife, brother, sister, mother, people bustling in and out doing things, holding her, talking. Music. It seemed a madhouse, but between contractions she smiled, requested things. When the contractions came, it seemed that everybody in the room breathed with her.

The baby was born at sunset, a chubby, dark-skinned boy with the intense, colorless eyes of infancy. Meya put him to her breast, refused to name him, and fell asleep.

Jason. Mish. Quilla. Jes. Hart. Meya. Decca. Jared.

Tabor. Ozchan. Laur. Mim.

Hoku. Hetch. Tham. Merkit. Bakar.

Palen. Altemet. Drel. Teloret. Cumbe. Kabit.

Ved. Taine. Mertika. Medi. Ped. Wim. Dane. Haley. The hundreds of names in Haven, on To'an Cault, on Aerie.

She called him Jason Hart M'Kale Kennerin.

What could we do but approve?

Part Seven

1235

New Time

SPIDER

"Things are seldom what they seem,
Skim milk masquerades as cream."
—Sir W. S. Gilbert

THICK STONE WALLS MUTED THE ROAR OF
Saltena. The cries of streetvendors, like the heat and
Saltena's strong, shaded light, entered only dimly through
the recessed window, and even these traces disappeared as
Hart drew the shutters closed. The cool obscurity of the
room increased. He returned to the desk and sat, placing
his hands palms down on the wood. They bracketed the
neat pile of papers and tapes.

Across the desk, the man and woman glanced from the
pile to Hart's face and back again. They held hands, the
man's fingers dancing nervously over the woman's. Hart set
his hands down sharply on the pile, and they jerked back.

"I can't help you," Hart said calmly. "I don't know what
made you think I could."

"But you examined our daughter," the man protested.
'You tested her, we were told that you could—"

"You helped our friend," the woman said.

"Different," Hart said. The woman folded her hands on
her lap and stared at him. *"In utero,"* he said. "Detection
and correction well before birth. But your daughter is seven
years old. Perhaps an exo-surgeon could help her, but I
certainly can't."

"Then why did you keep her here?" the man said angrily. "Why didn't you tell us first thing, instead of getting
our hopes up?"

Hart shuffled the papers, glancing over them. "I was curious. And perhaps what I learned from her will help me
to help others." He did not bother to disguise the cynicism
in his voice. He stood. "Take your daughter and go home.
And next time, come to me before the birth. Possibly I
can help you then."

"But that's illegal," the woman whispered.

"So is this."

Hart ushered them to the door. A child sat on the tiled floor of the courtyard, solemnly watching the fountain. She turned as her parents entered. Dark hair, pale skin, eyes as blue as Hart's own. Her parents thought her eyes deformed. All aristocratic girl children had green eyes; her blue ones cast doubt on her paternity and were a source of embarrassment. Hart smiled quickly at her over her parents' shoulders, and she stared at him without expression. She, too, thought herself deformed.

She took her father's hand. Hart watched as the family passed through the opened gate and into the baking street. They disappeared beyond a twist of buildings. The houses shouldered against each other, presenting high, white faces to the dust and cobblestones. Narrow windows, set well above the street, appeared black against the sun-washed walls, and the decorative ironwork over them and over the door filigreed an even darker blackness across the openings.

A scrawny, black-eyed child bearing a tray of iced fruit jellies edged close and whined his supplication. Hart pushed him away and closed the ironwork gates, then the wooden doors. He pushed his straight black hair from his face as he walked through the corridor to the courtyard and climbed the open stairs to his bedroom. Melthone, his manservant, argued with the cook, their voices falling and rising unrhythmically; even more distantly the washer complained over his steaming tubs. Hart walked into the bedroom and closed the door.

"Hart?"

The woman sat up, bracing herself on her elbows. Bars of light from the shuttered window slipped over her nakedness.

"What took you so long?" she said. "I began to think you'd left."

"Business."

Her skin was pale, smooth, aristocratic, and flushed slightly under his gaze. Dark hair tumbled over her shoulders, framing her slim face and narrow green eyes.

"Hart?"

She elongated the "a" and purred the "r." Hart thought of the feel of her skin, the whiteness of her legs against his own dark hips. His body tightened.

"Is anything wrong?" she said.

"No."

"Come to bed, then." She leaned back against the pillows.

"No." He crossed to the windows and opened the shutters.

"Close it!" she cried, scooting across the bed away from the sunlit rectangle.

"Your husband's out of town. Relax."

"Please. It makes me nervous."

The house across the street faced them, its own windows dark and secret.

"I like it this way. Come here, Tara. Let me see you in sunlight."

She knelt on the bed, more puzzled than angry.

"You've completely lost your mind. Close that window before we're both in trouble."

"Afraid of novelty?" he said mockingly. He crossed the room swiftly and with one hand grabbed her arms, pulling them above her until she gasped. "Amazing how many virginities a well-raised Saltena wife has, isn't it?" He spoke with clinical detachment while his finges probed her body. "Here, and here, and here." His hand looked almost black against her skin. "Modest married lady, naked in the room of an out-worlder. And you like it, don't you? Like this, and this. Oh, yes, and this, Tara, this best of all."

He released her and returned to the window, wiping his fingers on a handcloth.

"You're a hypocritical and frivolous woman, from a society of hypocritical and frivolous people. You're predictable, lady. The predictable bores me."

She swung her legs over the edge of the bed and reached for her skirt.

"Be careful, Hart," she said angrily. "Consider our positions. I don't think you can afford to insult me."

Hart smiled. "A woman caught in adultery is stoned, lady. Consider our positions."

She paused, surrounded by billowing material, and stared at him. "That makes you safe?"

"I'm a citizen of the Federation and of my home planet. You can't touch me. You'd have to extradite me, lady, provided you could claw your way from under a pile of rocks."

She laced her bodice. Her anger seemed to have melted. "It's not that simple . . . " she began.

"I'm not interested."

"Very well." She scooped her cloak from the clothes stool. "I'll give you some gratuitous advice, anyway, outworlder. Because you amuse me. You only see the surfaces of this planet. Surfaces are deceptive."

"Madam, I am forever thankful. Now get out."

She threw a crystal goblet at him. Hart moved, and the goblet flew past him through the window to shatter in the street below. Someone yelled furiously. Tara clattered down the stairs and through the courtyard to the servants' entrance. Hart waited until he saw her hooded figure pass quickly along the street below, then closed the shutters and fastidiously straightened the bed. The pillows smelled of her perfume. He stripped the cases and carried them downstairs to the washer. The old man looked at him with quick suspicion as he bent over his tubs again.

Hart lay in a hammock in the shaded courtyard and closed his eyes. He thought about children with blue eyes.

The city of Saltena, the planet Gregory 4, provided Hart Kennerin with profit and pleasure in equal measure, and in abundance. The white spires of the cathedrals soared above his plots and assignations, the tolling of bells accompanied his casual, continual ruttings and orchestrated the deft manipulations of his hands. The strong light of Gregory's primary, the cream-colored haze of Saltena's sea mists, the perennial dance of rainbows in the moist heavens combined to create an atmosphere of sultry, sensuous luxury through which Saltena's citizens moved slowly and warily, burdened by their laws and by their fears. And Hart, in counterpoint, swaggered through the city, golden-skinned Mongol with deep blue eyes, shaping its airs and expectations to the movement of his will.

The laws of the planet forbade birth control; Hart provided his clients with subtle devices, clandestine snippings of fallopian tube or vas deferens, sub-rosa abortions. The laws of the planet proscribed genetic manipulation; Hart provided his clients with green-eyed daughters and golden-eyed sons, trimmed the hereditary deficiency here, removed the unsightly gene there, poking and prying in fertilized ova, disturbing the laws of Gregory, and the laws of God.

To the rest of the Federation, Gregory 4 was a joke, an orbiting asylum for lunatics who forbade what the remainder of the Federation accepted as unquestioningly as it accepted air, or coils, or fremarks, or food. But to Hart, Gregory 4 was a treasure house, and he slipped and sipped and skipped through its unhappy aristocrats and unhappy laws, accumulating riches as he went.

Tonight, as always, Jem Stonesh dressed in black. The crowds parted for him as he crossed the party toward Hart; he bowed, smiled, paused to exchange a brief pleasantry, his dark robes highlighted by the gleaming cloth and sparkling jewels around him. Heads bent respectfully, polite laughter followed his words. But this was a sophisticated crowd; there were no demonstrations toward his badge of office. No one kissed his ring.

"Menet Kennerin."

Hart, glass in hand, sketched a bow. "Your Eminence."

Stonesh peered up at him and smiled easily, creasing the rounded fullness of his cheeks.

"I don't believe I've had the pleasure of meeting you before, Menet, although I'm told that you've lived here a year now."

"We haven't moved in the same circles, Your Eminence." Hart returned the smile. Two abortions, a gene pruning, and an affair had paved his way to this gathering, and he wondered how many of the graceful, black-haired aristocrats suffered agonies at seeing him converse with the short, fat archbishop of Saltena. His smile broadened.

"I trust that this will not be the case in the future," the archbishop said. "You come from Kroeber?"

"Yes. I'm told that Your Eminence also schooled there."

"Years ago, Menet Kennerin. Well before all of this." His gestures included the elegant room, its occupants, and the gaudy red ring on his finger. "The school has undoubtedly changed considerably in the interim."

"Perhaps."

"Come. I'll exercise the prerogative of an old man and drag you away to some privacy, and you may tell me of

Kroeber. It seems, as I grow older, that I live even my own youth vicariously."

Hart laughed and followed Stonesh from the room. People loitered in the hallway; they paused to watch Hart and the archbishop pass, and once Hart thought he heard someone gasp.

Stonesh ushered him through a doorway into a small library. Rows of tapes lined the walls, and hand-scanners littered the many delicately wrought tables. Along one wall stood a closed, glass-fronted case; Hart crossed to it and read the titles while the archbishop pressed a call button by the windows.

"Brandy, Menet?"

"With pleasure. Is this your collection? It's excellent, and extensive."

"Thank you. It's mine only in that the archbishopric keeps it, and adds to it on occasion. The Descartes is my contribution."

The door opened and a servant pushed a cart into the room. Stonesh dismissed him and poured the brandy himself.

"I think you'll agree that it's far more peaceful in here. Besides"—the archbishop smiled—"I believe I've generated a sufficiency of coronaries among your clients already. Am I correct, Menet?"

Hart rolled the snifter between his palms. His stomach felt cold and tight. "And if you are, Your Eminence?"

"Then I am a very observant man, am I not? Do sit down, the brandy is as excellent as the collection, though not as old."

Hart sat, uneasy behind his calm expression. The archbishop settled into an easy chair and stretched his legs.

"To be truthful, Menet Kennerin, I am not an observant man, not in that sense, although my colleagues are. I'm simply a fat old cleric, more weary than wary, a little short of breath and increasingly short of time."

Hart expressed polite disagreement, and the archbishop nodded.

"As one ages," he continued, "one's world becomes increasingly interior. Yet one cannot spend all one's time locked in one's own skull. Stagnation sets in quickly. I am constantly in search of information, Menet Kennerin. I am endlessly, and of necessity, curious. Talk to me."

"Of Kroeber, Your Eminence?"

287

Stonesh laughed, delighted. "I did school there, almost forty years ago. And you?"

"I left eighteeen months ago, standard."

"With diplomas, I expect."

Hart shrugged, continuing the gesture to raise the snifter to his lips. The archbishop contrived to look like a deceptively lazy cat, and Hart's tension increased.

"Oh, come, Menet. I can easily ask for a scan, but it would be far more civilized this way."

"Biomedicine, chemistry, surgeon five, biotheory, atomic biology. Doctorates."

The archbishop raised his eyebrows. "All of them?"

Hart nodded. "Surely you know all this."

Stonesh waved his comment aside. "I'm pleased. I'd hate to believe that our brave citizens and worthy parishioners are placing their lives in the hands of a charlatan. I take it that most of your degrees are through examination?"

"How else?"

"Fraud." Stonesh smiled. "Calm yourself, Menet. I am presuming that you are a honorable man."

Hart raised the snifter and watched the archbishop through curves of glass and brandy. Certain that Stonesh had manipulated him from the moment he stepped into the room, he wondered suddenly if the archbishop had even arranged Hart's invitation to the reception. The thought did not please him.

"How old are you?" Stonesh said.

"Twenty-five standard years."

"You see. It's hard to believe that a man your age could have accumulated that impressive list of doctorates. Have you practiced medicine before?" Stonesh demanded. "Been admitted before the Examiner's Board? Interned?"

Hart stood quickly and brandy climbed the sides of the snifter. "Are you going to arrest me? If that's what you're leading to, do it now and get it over with, but stop playing with me!"

The archbishop sighed and folded his hands on his lap. He looked at Hart mildly.

"I very much doubt whether you'll renew that offer once you learn more of our Holy Office. Do sit again."

"I won't be interrogated!"

"You have no choice. Sit!"

Hart sat.

Stonesh rubbed his temples with his fingers, then re-filled the snifters.

"I am not a pious man," the archbishop said. "I am, if anything, a political creature. These robes, this ring, are as much a symbol of politics as they are of religion. And if God does exist, I doubt whether He keeps that strict an eye on the denizens of Gregory Four. Do I shock you, Menet Kennerin?"

"Do you want to?"

"I want to make a point, and an important one. Were I the religious leader I am supposed to be, I would turn you over to the Holy Office with no compunction whatsoever. But I'm not that man, nor do I wish to be." The archbishop gestured toward the door. "Silks and jewels, wines and music. Frosting, Menet. Deceptive frosting. The theocracy of Gregory Four is one of the most repressive in the system, and whenever you repress a basic human need, or one of those insistent, uncomfortable human desires, people find ways around the repression, and vice flourishes. How many of our pious, law-abiding aristocrats are clients of yours? No, don't answer. I'm making a point, in an old man's garrulous, roundabout way. It's useless to spend time ferreting out each and every panderer or prostitute, abortionist or gene changer. As a politician my only interest is in assuring myself that these scum are, at least, competent. So I've no interest in putting you out of business, Menet Kennerin. The opposite in fact. You're as necessary an evil as am I. Unless"—the archbishop raised an admonitory finger—"unless there are deaths. Or you breathe a word to anyone of this conversation, or of others we may happen to have. If you do, Menet, or should one of your clients die through your actions, I think you'll have a personal and extensive knowledge of our Holy Office."

The archbishop smiled, stood, patted his dark robes into place. "Well past my bedtime, I'm afraid, and surely you want to rejoin the party."

"I don't understand you," Hart said, rising slowly. "Not your words, they're clear enough. But I don't understand why."

Stonesh smiled again and put his hand on the door.

"My nephew is the Regent, Menet Kennerin. Good night."

Hart stepped into the corridor and bowed, puzzled, as

289

the archbishop of Saltena closed the door between them.

Lights dimmed in the theater, and the voices of the audience hushed. Hart, resplendent, sat alone in his box. The glow from the program shaded blue on his golden skin. Old stuff, tonight: Targon, Kawamitsu's Fourth Elegy, Jannesdatter. Saltena was not a city to welcome innovation.

"Turn off the gram," a muffled voice said.

Hart resisted the urge to look behind him and fingered the gram to darkness. An abortion, perhaps, or a snip job. They often came to him this way, hidden in cloak and darkness, bringing their petty terrors and petty wants. And their purses. But it had been a long time since the last client, and Hart waited, relaxed, with patient curiosity.

Cloth rustled as someone sat in the other chair, well back from the reflected lights of the stage. The orchestra was tuning diligently below the bow of the projectors, and the director had not yet appeared.

"I've been asked to speak to you about your connection with the archbishop."

"Hello, Tara."

"How did you know?"

"The pitch of your voice, my dear. It's unmistakable, inimitable, and unpleasant. What do you want?"

She sighed. "I do wish you'd stop trying to infuriate me, Hart. You're so clumsy at it."

Hart crossed his arms and remained silent. Behind him, cloth rustled as Tara moved in her chair.

"You talked with the archbishop last month, at the reception."

"That's right. And since then my practice has disappeared. Do you think the two are connected, dear?"

"Please, Hart. Of course they are."

"And now you're confused. There have been no arrests, no mysterious disappearances, no accidents. So what, you wonder, went on?"

"Yes."

"Is the archbishop connected with the Holy Office?"

"Not directly. But he *is* the archbishop."

"There have been no incidents?"

"No."

"And last week your friend Lady Tomin died of a septic abortion."

Tara was silent.

"Go away, Tara. And tell your friends that I'm still in business. And still safe."

"On your word alone, Hart? We're not that naïve. You'll have to do better than that."

Hart paused. The orchestra's director appeared, and a flutter of applause covered Hart's silence.

"I propose a trade," he said at last. "Information for information."

She made a quick, suspicious noise.

"Tell me about the Regent."

"The Regent! What is there to know about the Regent?"

"He doesn't make public appearances. I'm curious."

"The Regent is God's appointed representative on Gregory," Tara said, as though reciting from memory. "The Regent is God's agent until such time as He Himself comes to us. The Regent is to be revered and obeyed, for by our reverence and obedience to him, we revere and obey God."

"And?" Hart prompted.

"It's said he's crazy," she whispered, "Locked up. That he looks like a shoat. That he has no mind. Rumors."

"Perhaps he doesn't exist."

"Impossible," Tara said firmly. "We'd have heard."

Hart nodded, remembering the extensive gossip network of the nobility, and how profitable it had been for him.

"Well?" Tara said.

"Well, what?"

She sighed again. "What did the archbishop say?"

"His Eminence and I discussed the merits of higher education," Hart said, smiling into darkness.

"That's a lie."

"I'm afraid not."

"I don't trust you."

"You'll have to, won't you, my dear? Give my regards to the Lord your husband, if you'd be so kind."

Her clothing rustled as she rose. Hart glanced back and saw a clenched white fist visible against the dark fabric of her cloak.

The curtains parted and closed behind her. Hart steepled his fingers, leaned back, and prepared to enjoy the concert.

They returned, as they had to, to the shuttered sanctuary of his treatment rooms and the quiet fastness of his laboratory. Silken robes and silken bodies, and if the poor also sought services like his, he did not know of it, nor did he care. Hart specialized in the pain-filled solutions to pain, and his clients paid handsomely for the suffering he prescribed.

He saw the archbishop on occasion, at receptions or other functions of the Court of the Regent of God. The old man would smile, pause, exchange a bland word or two, and go his way again. Hart ceased to worry about the meaning of their conversation and looked on the archbishop with the same reverent contempt as did the rest of the court.

The summons came one hot afternoon some months after their initial conversation, while Hart lay in his darkened bedroom, idly stroking the soft body of a client's son. The boy, fresh into adulthood, stirred languorously, murmuring with his mouth pressed to Hart's shoulder. Hart caressed his spine delicately, and the boy shivered.

The knock on the door startled them both. The boy dove completely under the covers, while Hart snatched at his robe.

"I'm not to be disturbed," he shouted. "Go away."

"Please, master, there's one to see you."

"I gave you instructions, Melthone. I'm busy, go away."

"Master, please. It's the archbishop."

Hart paused. The boy stuck his head out of the covers, terror-stricken.

"Where is he?"

"Outside, master. In his carriage."

"Tell him I'll be right down."

The servant's footsteps moved down the stairs. Hart threw off his robe and began hurriedly to dress.

"You'll be all right," he assured the boy. "I'll go down. You can see the street from this window. Get dressed, and when his carriage leaves go downstairs. Melthone will show you out the back."

"But the Quisitors, the Office——"

"Hush." Hart cupped the boy's chin in his palm and kissed his mouth. "You'll be fine, I promise. But wait until his carriage is gone, understand? Good."

He slipped from the room and ran downstairs, his fingers busy with his overshirt. The archbishop's carriage, like its owner, was squat and round, and Stonesh's face looked pale against the seat's black fabric.

"Your Eminence, forgive my tardiness. I was napping."

"Indeed."

The archbishop pushed open the carriage door and gestured Hart to enter.

"Then I won't feel guilty for taking you from something important," he said easily. "Come ride with me, Menet Kennerin. There's something I wish to show you."

The carriage started with a jolt.

"Anything Your Eminence wishes to show me is sure to be of interest."

The archbishop smiled. "I should hope so, Menet Kennerin. I'm taking you to meet my nephew."

"Frankly, Your Eminence, I don't think I can do anything for him."

"Perhaps. Perhaps not."

Hart glanced at the archbishop, then looked down the broad slope of the lawn. The Regent sat on the grass in a puddle of shadows, staring with fascination at a small, bright bird which perched on his fingertip. The bird spread its wings and danced along his hand, and the Regent gurgled happily. Filth streaked his face, black hair matted about his cheeks and nape, and his gaudy robes were spotted with food stains and grease.

"Has he been this way always?"

"Since infancy."

"And, despite that, he's the Regent?"

The archbishop spread his hands. "It's a hereditary post, Menet Kennerin. My nephew was the old Regent's only son."

A hot breeze passed over the garden and tweaked at the Regent's oily beard. The bird fluttered nervously.

"He's been seen by physicians?"

"Only as necessary to preserve his life."

"But something could have been done, surely, during his childhood, or before birth. This was not necessary."

"It's man's place to preserve what God has given, not to change it. That is God's law, and the law of Gregory."

"Yet God gave us the ability to better ourselves."

"As a test, Menet Kennerin. There are trials of commission and trials of omission, and often our goals are best encompassed through inaction."

The archbishop stood. Hart rose, and together they walked down the slope, keeping to the shade of the ancient trees.

"Therefore," Hart said, "even were there something I could do for your nephew, there is nothing I would be allowed to do."

"True."

The Regent stroked the bird's back gently. A brawny servant leaned against a tree trunk, thick arms folded over his chest.

"I am told that while on Kroeber you did work on a transfer technique." The archbishop raised the cowl of his robe against the light, and put his hands in his sleeves. He moved through the sunlight like an oval of darkness, from which glowed the pale oval of his face.

"Your informants are thorough."

"Thank you. Was the technique successful?"

Hart frowned. "Generally."

"Only generally, Menet Kennerin?"

"There were some failures, due to mistyping. The donor body has to match within eight nines, or the transfer is unsuccessful."

"Ah. A clone would then be the preferred donor?"

"Yes." Hart looked at the Regent. "But transfer doesn't improve on the basic material, Your Eminence."

"No? You'll have to forgive my ignorance, Menet." The archbishop smiled. "It is, of course, dangerous to speculate on the mechanics of evil, but a shepherd must have some knowledge of wolves. I would have thought that healthy tissues replacing diseased tissues would have a beneficial effect."

"Only marginally. The mind is more than a simple physical accumulation of tissues and blood. A transferred lunatic is a lunatic still, Your Eminence."

The archbishop stopped. The Regent, a few meters away, lost interest in the bird. He shook it away. The bird floundered, its clipped wings flailing at the air, and dug its claws into the Regent's finger. The Regent bellowed and closed his hand around the bird, then opened his fingers cautiously. The bird lay crushed in his palm. The Regent prodded it, then began plucking its feathers.

"My nephew is God's innocent," the archbishop murmured. "In twenty-one years he has never sinned."

"Not once, Your Eminence?"

"Animals are amoral creatures, Menet Kennerin. They lack free will, and that which cannot choose to sin cannot sin." The archbishop moved away, and Hart followed. "I should be pleased at my nephew's state of grace. But God's great innocent is not Gregory's great leader."

"Yet it is a hereditary post, Your Eminence."

"It is indeed."

"He has been Regent since——?"

"For the past year, since my brother died."

The Regent raised the dead bird to his mouth and nibbled. The servant looked on impassively.

"My nephew, for obvious reasons, is without issue."

Hart remained silent. Stonesh turned down an avenue. Trees hid the sunlit lawn, but the Regent's babbling followed them.

"The succession is cloudy, Menet Kennerin. There have been some unexpected deaths and an inconvenient birth. It would be useful if my nephew had a son."

"A marriage, Your Eminence?"

"The Regent is sterile."

Hart stopped. The archbishop took a few more steps, then turned to face him. Minuscule yellow flowers in the grass hemmed his robe.

"Are you asking me——?"

"I am asking you nothing, my friend. We are simply conversing."

Hart gestured impatiently. "Our conversation leads to dangerous grounds, Your Eminence."

"Danger is a relative thing."

"Relative to you, perhaps. Quite real to me."

The archbishop took his hands from his sleeves and clasped them loosely before him. "You have been in real danger since you entered Gregory."

"Then perhaps it grows increasingly distinct. Your Eminence doesn't feel it?"

"I am the archbishop of Saltena, Menet Kennerin, and you are an abortionist, an out-worlder, and a dark man. I recommend that you keep this in mind."

"And justice, Your Eminence?"

"Sarcasm is unnecessary. Justice and mercy belong outside these walls. They have no meaning here. For you, perhaps, they have no meaning anywhere on this planet."

Hart unclenched his fists slowly, staring at the archbishop's placid, friendly expression.

"I could leave."

"You could try."

"I could do as you wish—"

"As *I* wish, Menet?"

"Whatever. I then become dispensable, do I not? I then become a liability."

"Perhaps. Yet I am an honorable man, or as honorable as circumstances permit."

"Is that my bond?"

"Yes."

Hart gestured impatiently. "Why me? The Regent is twenty-one, why wasn't this arranged earlier? Surely you've had other biophysicians on planet before I arrived."

"Perhaps they were incompetent. They tend to be, Menet. Perhaps I did not trust them."

"And you trust me, Your Eminence?"

"Yes. But come, there is something further of interest here."

Hart followed the archbishop down the avenue, clenching and loosening his hands. It was hot under the trees and heavy with the scent of flowers.

The avenue opened into a formal topiary garden. The archbishop paused beside a dense bush clipped to the shape of a saint; the grafted yellow leaves of the halo glowed sullenly in the heat and light. When Hart reached him the old man continued down the path. They walked side by side between rows of vegetable martyrs.

"While on Kroeber, you experimented with sperm-base cloning."

"Is there anything Your Eminence does not know?"

"As you remarked earlier, Menet, my informants are thorough. Were your experiments successful?"

"Surely you know as well as I."

Stonesh pulled his cowl back. "They were conducted privately, Menet Kennerin. You seem to thrive on the clandestine."

"As Your Eminence thrives on the obscure?"

The archbishop nodded, pleased.

"They failed," Hart said. "I was young, I lacked the proper equipment, the proper knowledge. I haven't felt the need to try them again."

They reached a hedge wall, pierced by a single, buffered opening. Stonesh paused and tucked his hands in his sleeves. He rocked back on his heels and looked up at Hart, squinting against the light.

"You tried twice. Once with the sperm of a failed biologist who was first your mentor, then your follower. The second time you used your own sperm, and an improved exo-uterus. It seemed that you had succeeded. During the eighth month, the uterus aborted of itself. When you returned from classes the old man told you of the abortion and said he had disposed of the fetus. You beat him severely, and not for the first time. The next day he was gone."

Hart stared, wordless. The archbishop moved away from the hedge opening and Hart stepped through.

The green walls formed a small antechamber from which the twisted, geometric arms of a maze reached back toward the palace. A serving woman sat in the small enclosure, her traditional blue skirts spread around her on the grass. She looked heavy and almost asleep. A small boy tumbled at her feet, playing with a ragged doll. Golden brown thighs and buttocks flashed in the light, and stocky arms tossed the doll from side to side. Thick black hair shifted as he moved his head.

"How can I be sure?" Hart murmured.

"How can you doubt it?"

The child turned, saw Hart, and gazed at him with eyes of Hart's own blue, set between the epicanthic lids common to all Kennerins. Hart felt suddenly cold in the sultry air.

"I could make a child," he murmured. "From any base, to look like this. From anyone."

"Perhaps," the archbishop said. "The old man's name is Gren. He is slightly smaller than you, although his stoop shrinks him. A scar on the right cheek, like a thick crescent. Scars on his back. He went from Kroeber to Aloquin, and thence to Farseer. He said the child was his nephew. He was easy to trace, Menet Kennerin. An old man, obviously insane. Suspicious of everyone, yet far too confused to assume even the most rudimentary disguise. We bought your son from him, Menet, a standard month ago."

"You bought . . ."

"For two cases of alcohol, Menet. It was easily done."

The child lost interest in the strangers and turned to his doll again. He sat the doll on his lap and kissed it solemnly.

"Tomorrow you dine with my nephew and myself," the archbishop said quietly. "My nephew is fascinated by medical apparatus, and you will bring some for his amusement. The day following the Regent will marry. Soon thereafter you will be granted a private audience with the Regent Consort. Nine months later we will have a birth. And you, Menet Kennerin, will have your son."

Stonesh gestured. The serving woman rose, scooped the child and doll into her arms, and disappeared into the twisting arms of the maze. Hart stared after them. The child's laughter, high and light, filled the green-walled square.

The carriage started unevenly and bumped over the cobbled roadbed. Hart held his case as the high gate of the palace curved overhead, then dropped behind. Immediately the quality of the road deteriorated. The engine whined as the coachman urged the carriage into a lower gear. Darkness had long since fallen, yet Saltena's air remained hot and viscous. As the carriage moved deeper into the city, the stench of garbage and sweat replaced the palace's heavy miasma of flowers.

Tonight the child had dined with them, dressed in miniature court finery and seated at the table across from the Regent of God. Its clear voice mingled with the Regent's meaningless babble; it used fork and spoon while the Regent shoveled food with filthy, regal fingers. When, at the meal's end, a woman came to take the child away, Hart rose and stood between them. The woman glanced at the archbishop, who nodded an assent, and Hart knelt before the boy.

"What's your name?" he said.

"Spider."

"That's an odd name."

"Gren called me Spider because I climb things."

"I see. Do you like your name?"

"Yes. Don't you?" Spider looked at Hart solemnly, and in his child's blue eyes Hart saw himself and his father before him.

"Yes. I like your name. Spider. Did Gren ever kiss you good night?"

"No."

"May I?"

"If you want." Spider slid from his chair into Hart's

298

arms. Carefully, as though touching crystal, Hart put his arms around the boy, drew him close, and kissed his cheek. His skin was sweet and smooth. Hart moved his head away slowly.

"My turn," Spider said. His kiss was quick and dry.

"Bedtime," the woman said firmly.

Immediately, obediently, the child skipped from Hart's arms and crossed the room. As Spider passed through the door, Hart raised his head and met the archbishop's eyes. The Regent burped, and a serving man came in with Hart's small case.

The carriage stopped and a footman opened the door. Hart climbed out and stood before the gate of the house, watching the carriage move out of sight along the narrow street.

Melthone scurried across the courtyard, still in his day clothes.

"Master . . . "

"Later," Hart said. He threw his cloak over a bench in the courtyard.

Melthone patted the air with his hands. "Master, there is one to see you."

Hart stopped. "Who?"

"The lady Tara, master. She insisted. I could not turn her away."

"Where is she?"

"In the sitting room, master. She's been here since nightfall."

"Tell her I'm not yet home."

"I'm sorry, master, she heard the carriage."

"Then tell her I'm bathing—tell her anything. If you can't get rid of her, she'll have to wait." Hart pushed the servant toward the closed door of the sitting room. When he had reluctantly shut the door behind him, Hart hurried across the courtyard and into the kitchen, then through the pantry to the door of the wine cellar. He unlocked the door, locked it again behind him, and descended the dark stairs. The wall felt cool and damp under his fingers. He unlocked a second door at the foot of the stairs and entered his laboratory.

It hummed gently, a cushion of almost inaudible sound which absorbed the rhythms and harmonies of Hart at work. Cells passed through sensors and scanners, were discarded or preserved, weighed on scales of the increasingly minute. Dead tissues and defective cells were scrapped, cell membranes and plasma membranes inspected; ectoplasm, endoplasm, and chondriosome considered, vacuole and plastid reviewed. Nuclear membranes stepped forward for evaluation, unfit centrioles and centrosomes fled the ranks, nuclear sap and chromatin reticulae suffered scrutiny, nucleoli split like oranges and laid bare their secrets. Hart rubbed his shoulders and bent forward again. Helices danced under the gentle probings of his equipment, ribonucleic acid and dioxyribonucleic acid and miscellaneous mischievous proteins paraded themselves. Hart read through the stuff of creation, picking, choosing, accepting, refusing, lost in a world of the sub-microscopic. Gross physical deformities were eliminated, closely followed by the seeds of deformities; roughnesses fell away, discontinuities took flight, until only one infinitesimal blemish remained in the chain, the awkward twist of a twisted mind. Hart paused, fingertips lightly balanced on the controls of his machines, then stood and stretched thoroughly. His thighs ached. A nudge of this, a push of that, would define the fractious blip in the smooth strand, place it reformed and tractable in the ranks of its fellows. Hart peered at it closely, shaking his hands alternately to loosen the fingers. A second's work to reshape, refine, change. Still he hesitated, then pushed the workplate into suspension. He sterilized a swab and carefully removed a few million cells from his own throat, then swallowed a wide-awake and set to work. He hummed as he ran the cells through the selection process, smiled as he snipped and excised, sang as he deleted the twisted gene from the Regent's son-to-be and made a microscopic substitution. The future Regent of God on Gregory would have his father's pale, smooth skin, tilted golden eyes, narrow chin and narrow shoulders, and Hart Kennerin's mind.

A few simple procedures served to nudge the cell on the road toward birth. Hart observed its progress until he was satisfied, then shunted it into a keeper and stood. The light in the laboratory dimmed and disappeared, until only the red glow of the keeper broke the darkness. Hart kissed his fingertips to it wearily and went upstairs.

Pale dawn light flushed the courtyard. The fountain murmured against a backdrop of early city noises. Melthone lay uncomfortably asleep beside the sitting room

300

door, his legs splayed awkwardly across the tiles. Hart stepped over him and opened the door. Tara had gone, leaving the scent of her perfume and a note propped against an empty crystal decanter. Hart yawned as he opened the folded paper.

"Your diligence," Tara had written, "would be commendable or possibly amusing, were it not also exasperating. I trust that I'll see the results nine months hence. I'm sure you've done a beautiful job for whomever, considering the time you've spent on it. I also trust that you had an equally lovely evening with the archbishop and his family. How cozy you've become with our little aristocracy, Menet Kennerin. Don't let it go to your head."

Hart looked beyond the open door to the sunlit courtyard and remembered the feel of sturdy limbs and smooth, golden skin. He hadn't realized how much he had suddenly to lose.

The wedding took place with such quiet that it caught the aristocracy by surprise. They reacted with a mixture of curiosity and anger, insulted that their usually comprehensive gossip system had not provided so much as a hint of the marriage. The bride, the younger daughter of a country family, made her first appearance at court the day after the ceremony. A plain, shy girl of no more than twenty years, she stood beside the archbishop, lost in the finery of her clothing and the weight of her new crown. Hart observed her with clinical curiosity, wondering whether she had been told of the child she would bear; whether she possessed sufficient sense, or sufficient terror, to be trustworthy in her silence; whether, having fulfilled her role, she would disappear quietly into death. Her ultimate fate was of secondary interest to him, though. He observed her wide hips and heavy breasts, the strong muscles of her back, and approved.

Tara emerged from the throng around the dais and sat beside him on the bench. Her jewelry tinkled as she settled herself comfortably, and the maroon velvet of her gown gleamed in the light. She frowned toward the dais and tugged gently at her lower lip. Hart had seen her make that unconscious gesture before, framed by the tumbled blankets of his bed.

"What do you think of her?" Tara said, still looking at the Regent Consort.

"Nothing."

She made a small noise of disbelief. "She's still a virgin, after the wedding night."

Hart laughed. "You know all about her hymen, and didn't know about her wedding. How provoking that must be."

"The palace laundry was not advised of the marriage, although I suppose that your friend the archbishop told you all about it, and well in advance."

"Of course," Hart said seriously. "The archbishop and I always discuss these matters of state. He listens to everything I say, and always takes my advice."

Tara looked at him, then returned her attention to the dais. The consort looked regal, bovine, and tired.

"She's my cousin," Tara said, and smiled at Hart's surprise. "We're all cousins here, you know. One way or another."

"The eyes," Hart said. "Coloring."

Tara shrugged. "Four hundred years of inbreeding. It's a wonder we're not *all* insane. Speaking of breeding, did you make the baby?"

"What baby?"

"Don't be coy. I've spent a month of nights with you, I know when you're up to something. Whose is it?"

"Come now, lady mouth. You know I don't betray confidences."

Tara flushed and Hart smiled widely. "Don't tell me you're ashamed of your one talent, Tara." He ran his fingers over her lips and probed quickly. "It's the only thing about our relationship that I miss. You're very good at that, you know."

"Stop it," she whispered, pushing his hand away. "Someone may see you."

Hart leaned closer. "You've a lovely mouth, Tara. Especially in the dark."

"Then whose baby was more important than my mouth?"

"You are a tenacious bitch." Hart sat back. "No hints. Besides, it didn't take." He spoke with casual cynicism, but the corners of his mouth were tight. Tara glanced at him, delighted.

"I'm *so* pleased," she said. "Poor Hart, no baby, no money. You should charge for labor, not for results." She stood, smiled at him, and moved across the room. Hart stared after her. The consort and the archbishop retired, but the party would go on until dawn. Hart went to find his cloak. The dancers and the music seemed mechanical, the lights garish, the room closed and hot. He stood at the door, waiting for his carriage and wondering whether he could find a bedmate for the night.

The carriage arrived. Hart stepped inside, then drew back sharply when a hand touched his arm.

"Relax, Menet," the archbishop said. "I merely wish to speak with you privately. Tell the coachman to drive toward the waterfront."

"The docks, Your Eminence?"

"It's a long and private route."

Hart leaned from the window and shouted directions. The carriage jolted into gear and moved down the broad avenue. Stonesh was silent, and Hart sank back against the seat, staring at the few lights they passed.

"Well," said the archbishop finally, "what do you think of Saltena's new consort?"

"A cow. A baby machine. I suppose that's why she was chosen."

"Hardly flattering to the lady, Menet, but generally truthful. I want that baby machine operating as soon as possible."

"It's possible now. Bring her to my house, and . . . "

"Impossible. You've no idea how dangerous that would be. I'll arrange to have you visit her quarters . . . "

"Then it can't be done." Hart leaned forward. The archbishop was invisible in the darkness, save for an occasional vermilion gleam from his ring. "To implant her I'll have to fix the zygote in a syringe, put her in a see-through, and guide the syringe in visually through the wall of the abdomen and into the uterus. I'll need a stasis-field, sterilizers, the see-through, wraps, pulser—more equipment than you could fit in a travel cart. It's impossible to smuggle all of that into the palace, Your Eminence. If it's to be done at all, it's to be done at my house."

"You're sure?"

Hart didn't answer. The archbishop sighed. "The timing of her cycle is perfect. Rumors are beginning to circulate. The doctors tell me that my nephew is as close to ready as he'll ever be."

"To fucking, Your Eminence?" Hart tried to imagine the Regent in intercourse.

"At least to making the attempt. She will be so inebriated that she won't be able to tell the difference. Then while she sleeps, you implant her. Tonight." The archbishop paused. "I suppose we could drug her."

"No. I want as few chemicals in her system as possible." Hart put his fingers on the archbishop's neck. The old man flinched slightly, but did not push Hart's hand away. "There's a blood vessel here, Your Eminence, under my fingers. A slight pressure on it causes unconsciousness. A great deal of pressure causes death."

"Yes?"

Hart drew back. "After your nephew has finished with her, after she falls asleep, I'll make sure she stays unconscious. We'll transport her to my house, implant her, and return her."

The carriage stopped. Water hissed against pilings, gleaming in the starlight. Ships creaked at anchor. Hart opened the window and looked about in silence, then raised his face to the coachman.

"The palace."

In the dim light from the stars, the archbishop nodded.

"Tonight?" the consort whispered. Hart listened to the terror in her voice. He stood quietly behind the screen where the archbishop had placed him. A chair banged as it fell on the dressing room floor, and the consort giggled nervously.

"Come now, hurry up." A deep, female voice. "Here, take it off. You can't keep the Regent waiting."

"Is he in there? Is he there already?"

"Of course not, goose. You have to be ready first. Give me your glass."

"Give it back!" Clank of glass on glass. Splash of liquid. Rustle of cloth.

"There."

"Please. I'm not ready yet, I haven't prayed yet, please, just five more minutes, please, I won't bother you, just another minute. . . ."

Her voice receded into the bedroom. Hart leaned against the wall. His stomach felt uneasy. The other woman returned, called a few parting admonitions and encouragements into the bedroom, and closed the door. Fabric rustled again, closet doors banged open and shut, and she left the room. Hart listened to the muffled noises from the bedroom and wondered whether the consort wept or prayed.

Soon the outer door opened. The Regent's babble, tinged with eagerness, filled the room. A physicianly voice murmured. Hart resisted the urge to peek. The inner door opened. A moment later the consort began to scream. Hart thought about a sunlit lawn and a crushed bird. He held his hands over his ears and thought about his son. The screams stopped.

The Regent, snoring, was carried from the room. Jem Stonesh peered around the screen and beckoned, and Hart followed him into the bedroom. The consort lay slack, her white gown bunched about her hips, covered with vomit. Hart touched her wrists, lifted her eyelids, and pressed his hand against her neck. He pulled her gown into position, wrapped the coverlet around her, and picked her up. She was surprisingly light.

Melthone had the night off. The house was dark and silent as Hart stopped in the courtyard and shifted the woman in his arms. Stonesh bolted the door and padded after him.

"Wait in there," Hart said, tilting his chin toward the sitting room door.

"I want to observe."

"I don't perform before an audience."

"Menet Kennerin . . ."

"Your Eminence! This is a surgical procedure, not a political one." He stared at the archbishop. "Wait in there."

Stonesh turned and crossed the courtyard. When he was gone, Hart slung the consort over his shoulder and went into the laboratory.

He cleaned her first, carefully sponging the vomit from her body. She looked tiny under the harsh lights, breasts and hips narrowed by shadows. He adjusted the lighting. Fresh scratches lined her thighs and bled as he cleansed them. She was still a virgin.

He administered a sobor and attached the electrodes of the pulser; the rhythm of her breathing changed as the electronic anesthesia slid through her brain. He moved her under the see-through and set to work.

Three hours later, when he was sure the implant had taken, he detached the electrodes and washed the paste from her skull. She turned her head, murmured, helpless in her sleep. He touched her breasts, remembering her screams; she seemed the ultimate victim, sacrificed first to the Regent's clumsy insanities, then to the cold objectivity of Hart's needles and lights. He rested his right hand on her abdomen, noting that the tiny puncture had disappeared. The laboratory hummed gently around him.

"You've given me a child," she said.

Hart jerked, and his left hand went to her neck. She grasped his wrist and held him, not fighting. Her eyes were calm and he relaxed his hand, letting it rest lightly on her throat.

"Were you told?" he said.

"No."

"You're dreaming this."

"No." She moved her head to look around the laboratory, and Hart felt the muscles shifting in her neck. "I am to give the Regent a son. I'm not stupid. He cannot give me a child, so you did."

She moved her hips under Hart's hand, and he shook his head.

"You're still a virgin."

She looked at him. "Change that."

Hart stared at her, then shook his head again.

"The Regent cannot break me, so you must. Or none of this will work." Her body tensed under his hand, as if in anticipation of pain. Victim. Hart struggled to keep his body calm. "Take me," she said.

"You're being used," he said.

"Take me."

"You're condoning it."

"Take me.

He gestured helplessly, caught in her mysterious calm, and loosened his clothing. She stiffened momentarily, moved against him, turned her head away in silence, touched his back. When her body had relaxed around his, he caressed her neck and pressed.

The archbishop was asleep in a chair before the dark fireplace. He woke with a start, rubbed his eyes, and followed Hart to the waiting carriage. Hart held the bundled consort in his arms, and his hand, under the coverlet, caressed her smooth shoulder.

He turned over uneasily, his fingers tangled in the blankets, and his mouth shaped words of negation. He dreamed that he walked through the cemetery on Aerie, near his home, past the frozen, accusing fingers of his family to his father's grave. As he approached, the grave

leaped to flames. He ran toward the stream, but dead
Laur barred his path. He turned, and his family filed
slowly through the fire, untouched, not looking at him. He
approached the grave again and the heat drove him back.

He sat crying in the hayloft, small, miserable. His sister
held him and whispered comfort, but when he looked at
her face she became his mother, became the archbishop,
became the Regent. The Regent opened Hart's fist to reveal a dead bird. The bird became a spider. The spider
became his son. He took the child's hand and walked
along Saltena's waterfront, trying to tell him something so
important that it fled both mind and mouth before he could
shape it. The child laughed at him. The archbishop,
drowning in a cask of Malmsey, spoke of the soul. The
consort stood naked, stomach bulging. Her belly moved,
and Hart saw the outline of a goat under her taut white
skin. She looked at him with calm green eyes, and when
he reached for her she dissolved to fog, leaving the goat
mewling at his feet. Spider leaped into the cask of Malmsey, hiding in the archbishop's black robes. The Regent
bellowed, animal noise, dense with oxen or the fury of the
axe. Hart groaned, captured in the manacles of sheets,
and no light dawned.

The musicians in the gallery sawed and thumped and
blew and pounded, the director waved his arms freneti-
cally, the open mouths of the chorus strained toward the
vaulted ceiling, but the results of their disparate energies
drowned in the noise of the crowded ballroom. Courtiers
on the dais hovered about the smaller throne, hiding the
rounded figure of the consort. A buffet supper filled long
tables; servants wriggled through the multitudes, carrying
goblets of bright wine. A scent of flowers blew in the open
windows and was lost in a labyrinth of perfumes. Beyond
the palace walls, the city glowed with festivities. Saltena
celebrated the consort's pregnancy with exuberance and
alcohol, and if any harbored doubts or complaints, they
went unvoiced.

Hart lounged near the dais, watching the consort appear
and disappear behind the throng of well-wishers and physicians. She laughed and chattered, an eager country child
delighted with the attention she received. Hart watched
her with cynical curiosity, convinced that under her
pleased, pale face lay not bone and muscle, but a laby-

rinth whose complexity he could not gauge. The consort turned her head, her glance brushed by him but did not stop, and he pressed his shoulder against the wall, suddenly uncomfortable.

The archbishop ended a conversation and came down the dais steps. His pale face was almost pink tonight. Hart left his corner and slipped through the crowd, almost losing sight of the small cleric. Stonesh paused to exchange pleasantries with a lord and lady, and Hart waited, impatient, until the couple moved on.

"Your Eminence."

"Menet Kennerin, I trust you are enjoying our celebration as much as we—"

"I need to talk with you."

"But this is an occasion for joy, Menet. Not for conversation." The archbishop's voice was pleasant, but his glance chilled.

"We had a bargain."

"Perhaps we can discuss this at a later date." Stonesh smiled pleasantly and nodded over Hart's shoulder. "Lord Herm, you're looking well. I trust your health has improved."

Hart refused to be dismissed. He stood doggedly at the archbishop's side until the rheumatic old lord had moved away, then touched Stonesh's shoulder.

"I've given you your child," Hart whispered fiercely, still smiling. "Now give me mine."

Stonesh gestured abruptly and led the way from the ballroom into a dark garden. The air was cool and fresh. Hart breathed deeply, his hands thrust under his belt. His fingers felt clammy.

"You make yourself a nuisance. A dangerous nuisance," Stonesh said. All pleasantry had fled his voice.

"I want my son."

"You'll have your son when we have ours, not before. Those were the terms of our agreement."

"But I've not seen him in two months, nor had word of him. Must I wait another seven?"

"Parental distress, Menet Kennerin? Paternal concern? For almost three years you had no son at all, and now you find seven months burdensome."

"Your Eminence. Please. At least let me see him now and then. At least that."

Stonesh tucked his hands in his sleeves and looked at Hart. A smile formed slowly at the corners of his mouth.

"Well and truly hooked, my cynical out-worlder. Gullet and fins, backbone and belly."

"I trust you're sufficiently pleased."

"I am." The archbishop paused. "You may see your son each Fastday, from sext to vespers. Will that satisfy you?"

"It will have to, won't it?"

"Indeed. And no further public demonstrations, Menet. You endanger all of us. Including your son."

"You would kill a child?"

The archbishop shrugged. "I am a political man." He turned to go.

"Your Eminence. One thing further."

"Yes?"

"The consort. Are her physicians considering the rejection effect?"

"I beg your pardon?"

"Rejection effect. It sometimes affects clone-impregnated women when none of the genetic material is theirs. It's rare, but I routinely check my patients for it monthly until birth. It's preventable, if caught in time."

"It affects only clone births?"

"Yes."

"This is fine news." The archbishop frowned. "And how, pray tell, am I to have the physicians check for complications of an illegal procedure?"

"I'm sure Your Eminence will manage," Hart said, bowing. "Your Eminence always does."

Three days later, when Hart appeared to visit his son, Spider held forth a scrap of paper and refused to speak until his father had read the message.

"You have managed to ensure your continued usefulness. Next week bring the necessary." The note was unsigned.

Hart smiled and tucked the paper into his pocket. Within a few minutes he and his son were tumbling happily down the Regent's lawn, their laughter mingling with the cries of birds.

Summer's heat increased. The wealthy fled the city to country estates or seashore mansions, and the poor crept through deserted alleys, clinging to the scanty shade of trees and walls. This year the archbishop remained in Saltena. Hart, on his way to tend the consort, saw him often; Stonesh, seated in stifling garden, or dim, windowless room, would raise his head from a book and nod distantly, and

Hart bowed sketchily as he went his way, black case slapping against his thigh. The consort accepted his ministrations and tests in silence, flaccid with heat; Hart began to doubt his own memory, unsure that the consort was not, after all, the bovine baby machine of his first analysis. Occasionally he saw the Regent about the grounds. God's agent moved slowly and with increasing confusion, and once Hart noticed the Regent's face swollen with bruises. He wondered whether the servants beat their master, and whether anyone cared. The Regent bellowed fretfully about the stifling rooms, and his wife's belly swelled before her. During her seventh month, she had Hart bolt the doors of her room and commanded that he make love to her. He closed his eyes and imagined her bound, broken, weeping, bathed in the harsh lights of his laboratory, unconscious beneath his hands. She reached orgasm and thrust him from her, turning away in silence. Hart smoothed his clothing quickly and left. Tara, lovely in the robes of a Lady of the Chamber, sat in the anteroom, a piece of needlework on her lap. She raised her head and smiled as he passed, and his back felt cold. He took anger and his throbbing sex home with him and buggered Melthone until daylight. The stench of the city reached through the flowers of the palace gardens, and it seemed that summer would never end.

Then, with unexpected grace, Saltena moved into autumn. Sea mists dissipated on cool winds into crystalline mornings, translucent afternoons, evenings brilliant with a feast of stars. Late-blooming trees along the avenues opened in clusters of green and magenta flowers, under which the returning citizens strolled easily in the gentling heat. The urchins selling ices and fruits took on the faces of choirboys, and the bells of the cathedrals floated on the cool air.

On the last Fastday of autumn, Hart arrived at the palace garden to find Spider talking solemnly with the consort. Hart paused in the shadow of trees as Spider held out his ragged doll and discoursed, waving the doll to emphasize his words. The consort leaned over the bulk of her middle, staring at Spider's mobile face. Hart clenched his fists and walked to them over the freshly mown grass.

"Menet Kennerin," the consort said.

Spider dropped his doll and leaped into Hart's arms.

Hart kissed his son and bowed awkwardly. "Your Highness."

"Your son is delightful. Are all children this charming?"

"I've no idea, madam." He turned away.

"Menet! I did not dismiss you!"

He turned back. In her green robes and huge belly, she looked like an outraged frog. Hart grinned.

"Madam, I'm not yours to dismiss. I've come to see my son, not to serve you."

"I am the Regent Consort."

Hart nodded at her middle. "Indeed, you are."

She shifted uncomfortably. Her fingers twisted together on her lap. "You dislike me," she said.

Hart was silent.

"You object to my speaking with your son?"

"Yes."

"Why?"

"I prefer people with only one face, madam."

She laughed abruptly and spread her hand over her middle. Her fingers were straight and tense. "I'm doing my best," she said.

Spider reached for his doll. Hart placed the child on the grass.

"I'm afraid," the consort whispered. Hart made an expression of polite inquiry. "I think I'm going to die. My mother did, when my brother was born. He died too. I don't want . . . I'm afraid." She wet her lips and looked at Hart. "On other planets they have ways of making it easier, don't they? They have ways to make sure a woman doesn't die. My friends said so, when we could talk. I know it's illegal, but there are ways, aren't there?"

"I don't believe this face, either," Hart said.

She sat back in her chair and drummed her fingertips on her belly. "I was told you'd be difficult," she said conversationally.

"I try to fulfill expectations." He reached for Spider.

"Not yet," she said. "I take it that your child is the payment for mine. Perhaps your son's life will be payment for my life."

Hart stopped in the act of taking Spider's hand and looked at her without expression.

"My mother bled to death. Presumably this is also in store for me. Or perhaps a fever will set in, from which I won't recover. These things are easily arranged, given opportunity. I don't intend to die."

Hart shrugged. "This is a common worry, madam, with

311

women about to have their first child. Your fears are groundless, and . . . "

"Don't be a fool, Menet. I'm not. You must have suspected this from the beginning, but I've only just had my fears confirmed. And my child is due within the week." She pushed herself from the chair and stood before him. "You come under my uncle's protection, yet I am told that I can trust you. You can't trust him. You and your son can be killed as easily as I, and are as much a liability alive. Help me and I'll guarantee that you both leave the planet safely."

"Save and preserve me from the hands of women," Hart said angrily.

"The hands of women may all there is to save and preserve you," she replied. "Help me. If you don't, I won't harm you. I won't need to."

"If I help you, and am caught, I guarantee our deaths."

"When I am delivered safely, you will be on your way off planet."

"How?"

"Trust me."

"I'd sooner trust the startides."

She shook her head. "You are an out-worlder, Menet. You can't begin to understand the complexities of the succession, the seats of power, the factions and alliances here. In many things you would be wise not to trust me. In this, you must."

Spider tugged at Hart's arm. Hart lifted his son to his hip.

"You will see me tomorrow evening for my examination," the consort said. "Tell me your decision then." She turned and moved up the slope of lawn, walking with a flat-footed sway. Hart looked at the windows of the palace. Jem Stonesh stood framed in glass, looking down at the broad sweep of lawn. Hart could not see his expression.

"Have you ever been outside, in the city?" he said abruptly. Spider shook his head. "Do you want to go?"

"Yes!"

Hart glanced once more at the archbishop, then carried his son toward the gate. No one stopped them.

Mummers and fancifers performed along the shaded boulevards, shaking their rattles at the passersby. Piles of chilled fruits and ices lined the curbs, and Spider was soon

312

covered with the residue of sticky sweets. In the early evening they went to the dock to see the lightships string their gaudy lanterns and sail into the ocean decked in man-made stars. The wind smelled of salt and fish. Spider put his head on his father's shoulder and mumbled sleepily. The crowds at the dock drifted away, amid the noise of flutes and conversation. The cathedral bell rang vespers.

"He looks much like you."

Hart turned slowly. The cloaked figure beside him pushed its cowl back, and Tara smiled.

"He also looks heavy. You'd probably appreciate a carriage."

He followed her, his mind blank and dull. Her carriage waited, doors open. She took Spider on her lap as Hart entered the carriage and closed the door. The engine started smoothly and the docks faded into the night.

"Did you ever look this innocent?" she said, brushing the dark hair from Spider's forehead. He shifted in her arms and pressed his face against her breast.

"I suppose so. Once. Give him to me."

She opened her arms. Hart lifted Spider onto his lap and held him closely. The night air was mild, and the city's streets teemed with people. Lights glowed from windows and opened doors, and the magicians along the main boulevard stood in puddles of light, surrounded by the curious. Music drifted into the carriage amid the scent of flowering trees.

When the carriage halted at the palace gate, Tara turned to him and smiled.

"You'll have to give him to me now. I'll take him inside."

Hart tightened his arms around his son.

"It's all right, he won't be harmed. Come now, you lose all your charm where this child is involved. Let's not sit here until dawn. He'll be fine, I promise."

"On what authority?"

Tara's smile widened. "I have important friends."

Hart opened his arms. Spider protested sleepily as Tara lifted him from the carriage and handed him to a figure just within the gates. The doll slid from Spider's arms. Tara bent to it, then tucked it under the child's belt and waited while the figure disappeared into the palace. She spoke a few quiet words to the coachman, then leaned in the window and placed her finger on Hart's lips.

"Things are *never* what they seem," she said, and walked quickly through the palace gate. The carriage started. Hart leaned his head against the cushioned rest, too tired even to speculate.

"Yes," Hart said. The consort's arm waited for the jab of his needle. When he didn't move, she turned her face toward him.

"Good. Finish the test."

"There is no test. I take your blood home and flush it down the sink." He snapped the hypogun into his case. "It convinced people that I was necessary alive."

She smiled and stood from the bed. "You're not as much a fool as I thought," she said as she crossed to the doors and opened them. Tara entered and closed the doors quietly. Hart looked at her blankly, and the consort nodded.

"Good," Tara said briskly. "We'll deliver here, tonight. You can induce labor. Can you shorten it? What equipment will you need? Can you bring it here now?"

Hart sat on the bed and crossed his arms. "How do I get off the planet? When? I want Spider here. I want to know all the details first."

The consort put her hands on the small of her back. "There will be a carriage at the garden gate and a skipsloop at the port. You'll be taken to Anselm and you'll stay with some friends. There's no extradition treaty between Anselm and Gregory, so you should be safe. After that, it will be up to you."

"I want Spider here. Now."

"We'll bring him while you're bringing your equipment."

"I have it." Hart tapped his case.

By the time Tara returned with Spider in her arms, the consort was stripped to her shift and lying in the large bed. Tara set Spider on a couch in the corner. Hart kissed his son's forehead and pressed the hypogun against the child's buttocks. Spider's eyes blinked, then his arms relaxed around his father's neck. He turned on his side and slept. Hart covered him with a blanket and returned to the bed.

He didn't like inducing labor. He didn't like rushing it. He didn't like Tara as his only assistant. He didn't like the bolted, unguarded doors. The rhythms of labor beat through the consort's body and she strained in the bed, her lips taut and white. Tara stripped to her own shift and worked quickly to Hart's orders. Over the consort's paced breathing, Hart heard the occasional animal sounds of the Regent. Spider thrashed in his sleep.

Within two hours the waters broke. Tara stripped sheets from the bed and put new ones in their place. The consort sipped water from a crystal glass. The Regent bellowed.

Five hours after labor began, Tara braced the consort's feet as she supported herself on hands and knees, and Hart eased the baby from her body. The infant gasped and lay quietly in Hart's hands, then opened its eyes. They were clear, deep blue, set in an alabaster face.

"Is he all right?" the consort said.

"He's fine," Hart said. He knotted the umbilical cord and cut it. Tara took the child and cleaned it while Hart dealt with the placenta. The consort fell asleep.

"He has your eyes," Tara said. Hart stood beside her and looked at the infant.

"The eyes will change," Hart said. "He has my mind."

Tara glanced at him and shook her head, then put the baby on the bed. The consort's arm circled it protectively, and she slept on. Hart and Tara cleaned the room.

"My carriage," Hart said.

"The garden gate. Right down the corridor, then outside along the maze and left at the pool. You'll see the gate. Tell the coachman 'Anselm.' I've arranged to have your things sent after you."

Hart nodded and lifted Spider from the couch while Tara slipped into her dress. He froze at the sound of commotion in the hallway. Someone battered at the locked doors.

"Madam! Awaken! Grievous news! Madam! Let me in!"

The archbishop. Tara shook the consort and flipped the blankets over the infant, then pulled a screen between Hart and the room. The archbishop pounded with increased vigor. Spider woke, and Hart put his hand over the child's mouth. Spider nodded and pushed Hart's hand aside. Tara opened the door.

"Hush," she said. "She's had an uneasy night."

Hart peered through a crack in the screen and saw Stonesh and the physicians shoulder into the room. The archbishop stood by the bed and took the consort's hand.

"What is it?" she said sleepily.

"Madam, terrible news. I am sorry, your condition, but it was necessary. Please do not grieve yourself too harshly." The archbishop paused. "The Regent, your husband, is dead."

The consort clutched the bedclothes to her neck. "How?"

"Madam, he fell. You must not grieve yourself, madam. Consider the child."

She sat, still holding the covers to her neck. "Poor, bereft Saltena," she said slowly. "First the Regent dies, then his young wife follows shortly, in childbed, of grief. Such a blow. Save that I am well, and my child is well, as you can see." She pulled aside the blankets and held the baby to her breast.

Archbishop and physicians crowded around the bed. Tara shooed them back and began explaining about the sudden labor, how lucky they were that Menet Kennerin, respected off-world physician, had been there to help, no time to summon the doctors. Stonesh turned toward her, and she stared at him triumphantly as she spoke. His lips tightened. Hart watched in increasing bafflement from behind the screen, as though watching actors on a stage. When Tara finished speaking he stepped into the room, on cue, with Spider in his arms.

"I'm pleased to have been of service," he said, and wondered who had written the line.

Servants and courtiers crowded through the doorway to see the calm, smiling consort and her newborn son. Witnesses, Hart thought. They'll never touch her now.

Perhaps.

Stonesh impatiently ordered people from the room, and in the confusion Tara touched Hart's arm.

"Go now," she said.

He turned, then turned back. The consort smiled serenely, the archbishop gentured in his robes, the physicians craned their necks and stretched inquisitive hands toward the mother and child. Servants watched goggle-eyed. Tableau. The play was over. Hart looked at Tara's upturned face. Things, he thought, are never what they seem.

"How did the Regent die?" he said.

"He fell, Menet." She smiled swiftly. "With some assistance from his friends."

316

Hart stared at her. She touched his arm, and he left the room and walked quickly down the corridor. Dawn paled the sky. The shrubbery of the maze seemed two-dimensional, and the cries of morning birds echoed with hollowness. As he reached the garden gate, the bells of the city began to ring.

HART

SHE SENT THE CLOTHING, THE JEWELS, THE tapes, everything save my medical instruments, all jumbled together in a shipping trunk marked HOUSEWARES and addressed to Hart Kennerin, care of Ortega, Great House, Benetan, Anselm. She even included clothing for Spider.

But no note, no message. I didn't expect one. Do characters in a play live apart from the stage? Is there life after the final curtain? Gregory 4 seemed as closed to me as a theater when the play is done—to have pried behind the scene, tried to peek through the heavy curtain, would have been unmannerly. And I had no desire to view the empty stage.

The stage of Anselm, too, seemed deserted. Our hosts never appeared, and I suspected the entire house to be populated only with masterless servants. They tended to our needs, fed us, cleaned the rooms, and left us otherwise alone. It suited. The silence and solitude cushioned my mind, gave me the space in which to assess the past two years. Space in which to breathe. Space in which to watch the small, growing alien who was my son.

Spider. Solitary child, yet without the coldness of solitude; warm child, without the suffocation of heat. I could not remember myself at Spider's age, yet it seemed to me that I had been different. Old Gren had forced a self-sufficiency on my son which I had lacked; Spider lived in a world of constant change, which he accepted as part of the structure of the universe. My son would not, did not, presume ownership of the world in which he lived. As I had done. I do not think he looked particularly like me, save insofar as he looked unmistakably like a Kennerin. But Spider was four, and I twenty-six, that year. Life had carved me, and barely set its blade to him as yet.

He did the things which, I presume, children of his age liked to do. He talked and ate, he broke things and made things. He gave and demanded attention; he praised the things he liked and howled at the things he didn't. He showed an interest in my books, and when I began teaching him to read he learned quickly. I supposed him to be bright, but had no basis for comparison. I supposed him to be beautiful, and I think he was.

I had not conceived of how much it was possible to love someone. It astounded me, this strange emotion that I felt while watching him playing in the garden, watching him sleeping in the bed beside my own. Had Mish or Jason felt this love for me? Had I known it existed a year back, I would have said no, without hesitation, without doubt. Now I no longer knew, was no longer sure. It seemed so much a thing entirely of my child and myself, of such particularity, that I could not expand it, could not imagine its existence apart from us. Yet it remained such a basic emotion—as all-encompassing as hatred, anger, or desire—that I could not comfortably believe it to be true only of myself. I prodded it, poked it, tried to catch it sleeping, attempted to dissect it, and eventually learned to leave it be.

Much as my son filled my life, though, I was forced to consider the rest of the world. Our invisible hosts seemed willing to provide infinite hospitality, but I could not stay on Anselm. There was nothing for me to do, as I discovered after certain discreet inquiries. Anselm was well provided with biophysicians, who worked legally and openly. There were some hints of clandestine work, but I discovered that I had lost my taste for it. Eventually, I was sure, the absent Ortegas would tire of supporting us, and I did not wish to deplete my capital on the simple necessities of life. We would have to leave Anselm, and the prospect pleased me.

Anselm and Gregory 4 had no extradition treaty, that much was true. But there are ways of removing a person which have no connection with laws, treaties, governments. I wished to take no chances—not with myself, especially not with my son. I chose a day to visit the port's transport office when, according to the Benetan news service, there would be no Gregorian ships on planet. Indeed, the port was almost deserted that morning, and the man behind the transport desk seemed peeved that I had disturbed his half-slumber. He pushed the logs across the counter to me, and I flipped through them, paging through lists of ships, fares, and destinations. They seemed alike to me.

Spider asked for a glass of water. The man leaned over his counter and looked at my son.

"Sure," he said, and brought the water in a small cup. Spider thanked him.

"What's your name?" the man said, hunkering down to Spider's level. I smiled, pleased at a stranger's seeming acknowledgment of my son's worth.

"Spider."

"Spider, and what else? Only one name?"

"Spider Kennerin." Spider handed the cup back gravely.

"That's a good-sounding name." The man looked at me, and straightened up. "Seems familiar, somehow."

I smiled casually and reached for Spider's hand.

"It's not an uncommon name," I said.

"Here it is." He went back around the counter and poked through a binder. "Seem to remember someone looking: I should have it here somewhere. Fellow named Kennerin. Heath? Harl? Something like that."

"Don't know him," I said. I closed the directory. "I think I'll have to think about this," I said. "I'll be back."

He was still flipping through the binder. "Wait, here it is. Some guy logged in, looking for a Hart Kennerin. About a year ago."

I shook my head and walked toward the door.

"Sorry," I said.

"Fellow name of Jes. Can't make out the last name."

I stopped, then came back slowly.

"A year ago?"

"Year and three months, standard. Take a look."

The log page showed a Jes Kennerin, Captain, logged in on port call, stayed three days, left again. Business: looking for a brother. Looking for me.

Spider tugged at my hand and said that he wanted to

look out the window. I let him go and turned to directory again.

Anselm to Gregory/Acanthus Main Grab. Two berths open on the *Scathe* from Main Grab to Althing Green. Two berths from Althing Green to West Wing Terminus on the ship *Pollux*. And the freighter *Absalom* to Haven Port, To'an Cault, Aerie. The trip would take three weeks.

I booked passage and the next day sold all my jewels, save one, in the markets of Benetan. The one I left as a guest-gift for my hosts, and four days later Spider and I went home.

Why?

I didn't know, not then, as I bought tickets, sold jewels, packed. Meya's remembered whisper, perhaps, on the darkened porch of Tor Kennerin.

"I believe you."

Did she? At first I thought that she didn't. Later I was less sure. Was I going home to answer a question?

Spider filled my heart, my mind, my sight. Why? Because he was Spider, certainly—and also because he was mine. I could not conceive of not loving him, of ceasing to love him; could not believe anyone capable of not loving my son. Had I, too, been loved that much? Had Mish bent over my bed at midnight, fixing covers, watching me? Would she remember? Was there any love remaining for Hart, Spider's father, Jason's son?

Oh, I had left them in fury, betrayed again, robbed again, and come to a different planet. Cocky. Aggressive. Superior. Hart, maker and changer, above and beyond. And I had been led as a puppy is led, entangled like a clumsy arachnid in a larger creature's web—entangled myself, blind and stupid. I had learned bitter, unexpected truths, on a world where truth seemed merely another layer of the game.

I had thought them evil. Mish, Quilla, Hoku, Ozchan. Thought them cruel and witless, and understood, finally, that they were no more evil than I—less. Oh, certainly less. I didn't know them, now. Not the people I had wanted them to be, and equally not the people I had thought them to be. And how could I know myself until I knew them?

The scent of airflowers on an autumn night.

Why go home? I didn't know. Perhaps I'll never know. But in that moment in Benetan's transport shed, hearing my brother's name, I knew I was going home as surely as I knew I breathed. The reasons didn't seem to matter.

The closer we came to Aerie, however, the less sure I was of my decision. Save for the fact that Jes had looked for me, I knew nothing of what had happened to my family, had little idea what to expect from them. Chaos and hatred, perhaps. Quilla's stretched and screaming face. Or cool, unwelcome welcome—oh, those dreary conversations, those nights of empty boredom. Petty people and their petty wants, petty voices, petty vices. Hoku's wrinkled grimness, Mim's frozen contempt. I wondered whether Spider would understand if we were refused entrance, if our family turned us away. What would my mother say to me?

I almost stopped the journey there, but I remembered Meya, and the uncertainty returned. Perhaps, I thought, we don't change; we simply unlayer ourselves, or find ourselves looking more deeply into others. Moving beyond the surfaces. I held tickets in my hand that would take me to a home I did not know, people I did not know any more than I knew myself. Mish, Quilla, Meya, Jes. Tabor, Ozchan. I could not let myself stop without some clear knowledge of what was waiting for me in the house on the Tor above Haven. And I could only learn this by going home.

Yet when we arrived, I held back at the ship's hatch, still within the shadows, looking over the port. It had changed in the past two and a half years. More buildings. The old com hut replaced with something shiny and bristling with equipment. The road to Haven paved. But kaedos still lined the distant hills, and the scent of the sea and airflowers mingled with the acrid smells of the port. I took Spider's hand in mine and stepped out of the shuttle.

The transport office, where we picked up our luggage, was almost empty. The woman behind the counter barely looked at me as she rented me a dray.

"Just leave it at Kohl's, center of town, can't miss it. Put it in the stable, there'll be no one there now to do it for you."

"Why?" I said, but she had turned back to her invoices and didn't hear me. Spider helped me lug the bags to the port's stable, and a spacer helped us load the dray.

"Might have to wait a while to get a room in Haven," he said, seaming the pouches on the dray's broad back. "Town's pretty much closed."

My chest tightened. "Why?"

"Big celebration of some sort. Everyone's up the hill."

I ran quickly through my mental calendar of Aerie's holidays, but nothing fit.

"Know what they're celebrating?"

"Someone said they bought a mining farm. Big event hereabouts." The man shrugged. "Some birthday, too."

"Birthday?"

"Yeah. Smallest one, looks a bit like your kid. He's two years old today. I guess they just decided to celebrate everything at once."

I must have looked baffled. He grinned and picked up his own bags.

"Whole flock of them up that hill. This one, the kid, I think he belongs to the youngest—Meya, Mara, something like that. Meya, that's it." He started to leave the stable.

"Wait," I said. "Is there some place to stay here? At the port? If there's no one in Haven——"

"Kohl always leaves his door open," the spacer said. "All we've got here's the stable, and I don't think it'd be too comfortable."

I looked around the stable uncertainly. Celebration. The entire population. My family. I'd had no idea, no image, of what a homecoming would be like, but this bothered me. Appearing like a ghost at the feast. Spider looked at me, came over, and took my hand.

"Listen," the spacer said, "go take your kid to the party. They won't mind. You want to make yourself popular, just grab a beer, stick it in the air, and say, 'Here's to Jason Hart, many more,' and drink."

I looked at him.

"That's the kid's name," he said, as though explaining something to a moron. Then he slung his bags over his shoulder and went up the road toward Haven.

I stood holding my son's hand and the dray's harness. A couple of fourbirds flapped by overhead, and the sun touched the tops of the kaedos. Evening, and night coming fast.

"I'm tired," Spider said.

I put him on the dray, amid the bumps and hummocks of our luggage, and started up the road toward home.